I0614541

"Down on your knee--a kneeling confession! or you are condemned beyond hope of grace" said Katrine.   Page 392.
Frontispiece.   *Darnley.*

DARNLEY

A Romance of the Times of Henry VIII and Cardinal Wolsey

By G. P. R. JAMES

Author of "Richelieu," "Mary of
Burgundy," "Ticonderoga," etc.

"I do not think a braver gentleman,
More daring or more bold, is now alive
To grace this latter age with noble deeds."
SHAKESPEARE.

WITH FOUR PAGE ILLUSTRATIONS
BY J. WATSON DAVIS

A. L. Burt Company, ❧ ❧ ❧
❧ ❧ ❧ Publishers, New York

DARNLEY.

CHAPTER I.

> In this King Arthur's reign,
> A lusty knight was pricking o'er the plain.
> DRYDEN.

ON the morning of the twenty-fourth day of March, 1520, a traveller was seen riding in the small rugged cross road which, traversing the eastern part of Kent, formed the immediate communication between Wye and Canterbury. The horseman and his beast, who journeyed onward together towards Canterbury, were apparently well calculated to encounter what the profane vulgar call the ups and downs of life; for never a stouter cavalier mounted horse, and never a stouter horse was mounted by cavalier.

The rider was a man of about five or six and twenty—perhaps not so old; he was a tall fair man, with the old Saxon blood shining out in his deep blue eye, and in his full short upper lip, from which the light brown mustache turned off in a sweep, exposing its fine arching line.

His apparel was not such as his bearing seemed to warrant: though good, it was not costly, and though not faded, it certainly was not new. Nor was the fashion of it entirely English: the gray cloth doublet slashed with black, as well as the falling ruff round his neck, were decidedly Flemish; while his wide boots of un-tanned leather, pushed down to the ankle, evinced that he did not consider his journey likely to prove long, or at least very fatiguing.

1

He did not appear to have furnished himself with more than the complement of offensive arms, usually worn by every one above the rank of a simple yeoman; namely, the long straight double-edged sword, which, thrust through a broad buff belt, hung perpendicularly down his thigh, with the hilt shaped in form of a cross, without any further guard for the hand; while in the girdle appeared a small dagger, which served also as a knife: added to these, was a dag or pistol, which, though small, considering the dimensions of the arms then used, would have caused any horse-pistol of the present day to blush at its own insignificance.

In point of defensive armor he carried none, except a steel cap, which hung at his saddle-bow, while its place on his head was supplied by a Genoa bonnet of black velvet, round which his rich chestnut hair curled in thick profusion.

It was a shrewd March morning, and the part of the road, at which the traveller had now arrived, opened out upon a wide wild common, whereon the keen northwest blast had full room to exercise itself unrestrained. The road which the traveller had hitherto pursued proceeded still along the side of the hill, but branching off to the left was seen another rugged gravelly path, winding over the common.

At the spot where these two separated, the horseman stopped, as if uncertain of his further route, and looking for some one to direct him on his way.

The traveller paused, undetermined on which of the two roads to turn his horse, when suddenly a loud scream met his ear, and instantly setting spurs to his horse, he galloped towards the quarter from whence the sound seemed to proceed. Without waiting to pursue the windings of the little path, in a moment he had cleared the upland, towards the spot where he had beheld the pines, and instead of finding that the country beyond, as one might imagine from the view below, fell into another deep valley on that side, he perceived that the common continued to extend for some way over an uninterrupted flat, terminated by some wide plantations at a great distance.

In advance, sheltered by a high bank, and the group of pines above-mentioned, appeared a solitary cottage formed of wood and mud. As the traveller rode towards it the scream was reiterated, and now, guided by his ear, he proceeded direct towards a little garden, which had been borrowed from the common, and enclosed with a mud wall. The door of this enclosure stood open, and at once admitted the stranger into the interior, where he beheld an old woman, of the poorest class, striving, with weak hands, to stay a stout rosy youth, of mean countenance, but good apparel, from repeating a buffet he had bestowed upon the third person of the group, a venerable old man, who seemed little calculated to resist his violence. Angry words were evidently still passing on both parts, and before the traveller could hear to what they referred, the youth passed the woman, and struck the old man a second blow, which levelled him with the ground.

In a moment the traveller was off his horse, and by the young man's side. "How now, Sir Villain!" cried he, "art thou mad, to strike thy father?"

"He's no father of mine," replied the sturdy youth, turning away his head with a sort of dogged feeling of shame. "He's no father of mine—I'm better come."

"Better come, misbegotten knave!" cried the traveller; "then thy father might blush to own thee. Strike an old man like that! Get thee gone, quick, lest I flay thee!"

"Get thee gone, thyself!" answered the other. "Who art thou, with thy get thee gones? I am here in right of Sir Payan Wileton, to turn these old vermin out; so get thee gone along with them!" and he ran his cye over the stranger's simple garb with a sneer of sturdy defiance.

The traveller gazed at him for a moment, as if in astonishment at his daring; then, with a motion as quick as light, laid one hand upon the yeoman's collar, the other upon the thick band of his kersey slop breeches, raised him from the ground, and giving him one swing back, to allow his arms their full sweep, he pitched him at once over the low wall of the garden into the heath bushes beyond.

Without affording a look to his prostrate adversary, the stranger proceeded to assist the old man in rising, and, amidst the blessings of the good dame, conveyed him into the cottage. He then returned to the little garden, lest his horse should commit any ravages upon the scanty provision of the old couple, and while tying him to the gate-post, his eye naturally turned to the bushes into which he had thrown his opponent.

The young man had just risen on his feet, and, in unutterable rage, was stamping furiously on the ground, without, however, daring to re-enter the precincts from which he had been so unceremoniously expelled. The stranger contented himself with observing that he was not much hurt; and after letting his eye dwell for a moment on the cognizance of a serpent twined round a crane, which was embroidered on the yeoman's coat, he again entered the cottage, while the other proceeded slowly over the common, every now and then turning round to shake his clenched fist towards the garden, in the last struggles of impotent passion.

"Well, good father, how fares it with thee?" demanded the traveller, approaching the old man. "I fear that young villain has hurt thee."

"Nay, sir, nay," replied the other. "Not so; in faith he did not strike hard: an old man's limbs are soon overthrown. Ah! well I remember the day when I would have whacked a score of them. But I'm broken now.— Kate, give his worship the settle. If our boy had seen him lift his hand against his father, 'faith, he'd have broken his pate. Though your worship soon convinced him—God's blessing upon your head for it."

The stranger silently sat himself down in the settle, which the old woman placed for him with a thousand thanks and gratulations, and suffered them to proceed undisturbed with all the garrulity of age, while his own thoughts seemed, from some unapparent cause, to have wandered far upon a different track. He awoke with a sigh. "But tell me," said he to the old man, "what was the cause of all this?"

"Why, Heaven bless your worship," replied the cottager, who had been talking all the time, "I have just been telling you."

"Nay, but I mean, why you came to live here?" said the traveller; "for this is but a poor place!" and he glanced his eye over the interior of the cottage, which was wretched enough. "I think you said that you had been in better circumstances?" continued the traveller.

"I did not say so, your worship," replied the old man, "but it was easy to guess; yet, for twelve long years, have I known little but misery. I was then gate-porter to my good Lord Fitzbernard, at Chilham Castle, here hard by—your worship knows it, doubtless? Oh! 'twas a fair place in those days, for my lord kept great state, and never a day but what we had the tilt-yard full of gallants, who would bear away the ring from the best in the land. My old lord could handle a lance well, too, though he waxed aged; but 'twas my young Lord Osborne that was the darling of all our hearts. Poor youth! he was not then fourteen, yet so strong, he'd break a lance, and bide a buffet, with the best. He's over the seas now, alas! and they say obliged to win his food at the sword's point."

"Nay, how so?" asked the traveller. "If he were heir of Chilham Castle, how is it he fares so hardly, this Lord Osborne?"

"We called him still Lord Osborne," answered the old woman, "for I was his nurse when he was young, your worship, and his christened name was Osborne. But his title was Lord Darnley, by those who called him properly. God bless him forever! Now, Richard, tell his honor how all the misfortunes happened."

" 'Twill but tire his honor," said the old man. " In his young day he must have heard how Empson and Dudley, the two blackest traitors that ever England had, went through all the country, picking holes in every honest man's coat, and sequestrating their estates, as 'twas then called. Lord bless thee, Kate! his worship knows it all."

" I have heard something of the matter, but I would fain understand it more particularly," said the stranger. " I have learned that the sequestrated estates have been restored, and the fines remitted, since this young king was upon the throne."

" Ay, truly, sir, the main part of them," answered the old man; " but there were some men, who, being in the court's displeasure, were not likely to have justice done them. Such a one was my good lord and master, who, they say, had been heard to declare, that he held Perkin Warbeck's title as good as King Harry the Seventh's. So when they proved the penal statutes against him, as they called it, instead of calling for a fine, which every peasant on his land would have brought his mite to pay, they took the whole estate, and left him a beggar in old age. But that was not the worst, for doubtless the whole would have been given back again when the good young king did justice on Empson and Dudley; but as this sequestration was a malice, and not an avarice like the rest, instead of transferring the estate to the king's own hand, they gave to one Sir Payan Wileton, who, if ever a gallows was made higher than Haman's, would well grace it. This man has many a friend at the court, gained, they say, by foul means; and though much stir. was made some eight years agone, by the Lord Stafford and the good Duke of Buckingham, to have the old lord's estates given back again, Sir Payan was strong enough in abettors to outstand them all, and then——but I hear horse's feet. 'Tis surely Sir Payan sent to hound me out even from here."

As he spoke, the loud neighing of the stranger's horse announced the approach of some of his four-footed fraternity, and opening the cottage-door, the old man looked forth to ascertain if his apprehensions were just.

The cloud, however, was cleared off his brow in a moment, by the appearance of the person who rode into the garden.

" Joy, good wife! joy!" cried the old man, " it is Sir Cesar! It is Sir Cesar! We are safe enough now!"

" Sir Cesar!" cried the traveller, " that is a strange name!" and he turned to the cottage-door to examine the person that approached.

Cantering through the garden, on a milk-white palfrey, adorned with black leather trapping, appeared a little old man, dressed in singular but elegant habiliments. His doublet was of black velvet, his hose of crimson stuff, and his boots of buff. His cloak was black, like his coat, but lined with rich miniver fur, of which also was his bonnet. He wore no arms, except a small dagger, the steel hilt of which glittered in his girdle; and to turn and guide his palfrey, he made use of neither spur nor rein, but seemed more to direct than urge him, with a peeled osier stick, with which he every now and then touched the animal on either ear.

His person was as singular as his dress. Extremely diminutive in stature, his limbs appeared well formed, and even graceful. He was not a dwarf, but still considerably below the middle size; and though not mis-shapen in body, his face had that degree of prominence, and his eye that keen vivacious sparkle, generally discovered in the deformed. In complexion, he was swarthy to excess, while his long black hair, slightly mingled with gray, escaped from under his bonnet, and fell upon his shoulders.

In this manner he approached the cottage, his look at first rapidly running over the figures of the two cottagers and their guest; but then turning to their faces, his eye might be seen scanning every feature, and seeming to extract their meaning in an instant.

At the cottage door, the palfrey stopped of itself, and slipping down out of the saddle with extraordinary activity, the old gentleman stood before the traveller and his hosts with that sort of sharp sudden motion that startles, although expected. The old man and his wife received their new guest with reverence, almost approaching to awe; but before noticing them farther than by signing them each with the cross, he turned directly towards the traveller, and doffing his cap of miniver, he made him a profound bow, while his long hair, parted from the crown, fell over his face and almost concealed ·it: " Sir Osborne Maurice," said he " well met."

The traveller bowed in some surprise to find himself recognized by the singular person who addressed him. " Truly, sir," he answered, " you have rightly fallen upon the name I bear, and seem to know me well, though in truth I can boast no such knowledge in regard to you. To my remembrance this is the first time we have met."

" Within the last thousand years," replied the old man, " we have met more than a thousand times; but I remember you well before that, when you commanded a Roman cohort in the first Punic war."

" He's mad! " thought the traveller, " profoundly insane! " and he turned an inquiring glance to the old cottager and his wife; but far from showing any surprise, they stood regarding their strange visitor with looks of deep awe and respect; however, the traveller at length replied, " Memory, with me, is a more treacherous guardian of the past: but may I crave the name of so ancient an acquaintance? "

" In Britain," answered the old man, " they call me

Sir Cesar; in Spain, Don Cesario; and in Padua, simply Cesario il dotto."

"What!" cried Sir Osborne, "the famous—"

"Ay, ay!" interrupted the old man; "famous, if it may so be called. But no more of that. Fame is but like a billow on a sandy shore, that when the tide is in, it seems a mighty thing, and when 'tis out, 'tis nothing. If I have learned naught beside, I have learned to despise fame."

"That your learning must have taught you far more, needs nor further proof than your knowledge of a stranger that you never saw—at least with human eyes," said Sir Osborne, "and in truth, this, your knowledge, makes me a believer in that art, which, hitherto, I had held as emptiness."

"Cast from you no ore till you have tried it seven times in the fire," replied Sir Cesar; "hold nothing as emptiness that you have not essayed. But hark; bend down thine ear, and thou shalt hear more anon!"

The young traveller bowed his head, till his ear was on a level with the mouth of the diminutive speaker, who seemed to whisper not more than one word, but that was of such a nature as to make Sir Osborne start back, and fix his eyes upon him with a look of inquiring astonishment, that brought a smile upon the old man's lip. "There is no magic here," said Sir Cesar. "You shall hear more hereafter. But hush! come into the cottage—for hunger, that vile earthly want, calls upon me for its due: herein, alas! we are all akin unto the hog—come."

They accordingly entered the lowly dwelling, and sat down to a small oaken table placed in the midst; Sir Cesar, as if accustomed to command there, seating the traveller as his guest, and demanding of the old couple a supply of those things he deemed necessary. "Set down the salt in the middle, Richard Heartley—now bring the bread—take the bacon from the pot, dame, and if there be a pompion yet not mouldy, put it down to roast in the ashes. Whet Sir Osborne's dagger, Richard. Is it all done?—then sit with us, for herein are men all alike. Now tell me, Richard Heartley, while we eat, what has happened to thee this morning, for I learn thou hast been in jeopardy."

Thus speaking, he carved the bacon with his dagger, and distributed to every one their portion, while Sir Osborne Maurice looked on not a little interested in the scene, one of the most curious parts of which was the profound taciturnity that had succeeded to garrulity in the two old cottagers, and the promptitude and attention with which they executed all their guest's commands.

The old gentleman's question seemed to untie Richard Heartley's lips, and he explained that though he had built his house and enclosed his garden on common land, which, as he took it, " was free to every one, yet within the last year Sir Payan Wileton had demanded for it a rent of two pounds per annum, which was far beyond his means to pay, as Sir Payan well knew; but he did it only in malice," the old man said, " because he was the last of the good old lord's servants who was left upon the ground, and he, Sir Payan, was afraid, that even if he were to die there, his bones would keep possession for his old master; so he wished to drive him away altogether."

" Go forth on no account!" interrupted Sir Cesar. " Without he take thee by force and lead thee to the bound, and put thee off, go not beyond the limits of the lordship of Chilham Castle; neither pay him any rent, but live house free and land free, as I have commanded you."

" In truth," answered the old man, " he has not essayed to put me off; but he sent his bailiff this morning to demand the rent, and to drive me out of the cottage, and to pull off the thatch, though our Richard, who has returned from the army beyond the seas, is up at the manor to do him man service for the sum."

"Hold!" cried Sir Cesar; "let thy son do him man service if he will, but do thou him no man service, and own to him no lordship. Sir Payan Wileton has but his day—that will soon be over, and all shall be avenged—own him no lordship, I say!"

"Nay, nay, sir, I warrant you," replied the old man, "'twas even that that provoked Peter Wilson, the young bailiff, to strike me, because I said Sir Payan was not my lord, and I was not his tenant, and that if he stood on right, I had as much a right to the soil as he."

"Strike thee! Strike thee! Did he strike thee?" cried Sir Cesar, his small black eyes glowing like red-hot coals, and twinkling like stars on a frosty night. "Sure he did not dare to strike thee?"

"He felled him, Sir Cesar," cried the old woman, whose tongue could refrain no longer; "he felled him to the ground. He, a child I have had upon my knee, felled old Richard Heartley with a heavy blow!"

"My curse upon him!" cried the old knight, while anger and indignation gave to his features an expression almost sublime; "my curse upon him! May he wither heart and limb like a blasted oak! like it, may he be dry and sapless, when all is sunshine and summer, without a green leaf to cover the nakedness of his misery; without flower or fruit may he pass away, and fire consume the rottenness of his core!"

"Oh! your worship, curse him not so deeply; we know how heavy your curses fall, and he has had some payment already," said the old cottager: "this honorable gentleman heard my housewife cry, and came riding up. So when he saw the clumsy coward strike a feeble old man like me, he takes me him up by the jerkin and the slops, and casts him as clean over the wall on the heath as I have seen Hob Johnson cast a truss out of a hay-cart."

"Sir Osborne, you did well," said the old knight;
"you acted like your race. But yet I could have wished
that this had not happened; 'twould have been better that
your coming had not been known to your enemies before
your friends, which, I fear me, will now be the case. He,
with whom you have to do, is one from whose keen eye
naught passes without question. The fly may as well find
its way through the spider's web, without wakening the
crafty artist of the snare, as one on whom that man has
fixed his eye, may stir a step without his knowing it.
But there is one who sees more deeply than even he
does."

"Yourself, of course," replied Sir Osborne; "and indeed I cannot doubt that it is so; for I sit here in mute
astonishment to find that all I held most secret is as much
known to you as to myself."

"Oh, this is all simplicity," replied the old man; "these
are no wonders, though I may teach you some hereafter.
At present, I will tell you the future, against which you
must guard, for your fortune is a-making."

"But if our fate be fixed," said Sir Osborne "so that
even mortal eyes can see it in the stars, prudence and
caution, wisdom and action, are in vain; for how can
we avoid what is certainly to be?"

"Not so, young man," replied Sir Cesar: "some things
are certain, some are doubtful; some fixed by fate, some
left to human will; and those that see such things as
are certain, may learn to guide their course through
things that are not so. Thus, even in life, my young
friend," he continued, speaking more placidly, for at first
Sir Osborne's observation seemed to have nettled him,—
"thus, even in life, each ordinary mortal sees before him
but one thing sure, which is death. If he cannot avoid;
yet, how wholesome is the sight to guide us in existence!
So in man's destiny, certain points are fixed; some of
mighty magnitude, some that seem but trivial, and the
rest are determined by his own conduct. Yet there are

none so clearly marked that they may not be influenced
by man's own will, so that when the stars are favorable,
he may carry his good fortune to the highest pitch by
wisely seizing opportunity; and when they threaten evil
or danger, he may fortify himself against the misfortunes
that must occur, by philosophy; and guard against the
peril that menaces, by prudence. Thus, what study is
nobler, or greater, or more beneficial, than that which
lays open to the eye the book of fate?"

The impressive tone and manner of the old man,
joined even with the singularity of his appearance, and
a certain indescribable, almost unearthly fire, that burned
in his eye, went greatly in the minds of his hearers to
supply any deficiency in the chain of his reasoning.

Sir Osborne Maurice mused. If it be asked whether
he believed implicitly in that art which many persons
were then said to possess, of reading in the stars the
future fate of individuals or nations, it may be answered,
No. But if it be demanded whether he rejected it absolutely, equally, No.

In the meanwhile Sir Cesar proceeded: "I speak thus
as preface to what I have to tell you; not that I suppose
you will be dismayed when you hear that immediate
danger menaces you, because I know you are incapable of
fear; but it is because I would have you wisely guard
against what I foretell. Know then, I have learned that
you are likely to be in peril to-morrow, towards noon;
therefore, hold yourself upon your guard. Divulge not
your proceeding to any one. Keep a watchful eye, and
a shrewd ear. Mark well your company; and see that
your sword be loose in the sheath."

" Certainly, good Sir Cesar, will I follow your counsel,"
replied Sir Osborne. " But, might I not crave that you
would afford me further information, and by showing me
what sort of danger threatens me, give me the means of
avoiding it altogether."

" What you ask I cannot comply with," answered the

old man. "Think not that the book of the stars is like
a child's horn-book, where every word is clearly spelled.
Vague and undefined are the signs that we gain. Certain
it is that some danger threatens you; but of what nature
who can say? Know that, at the same time as yourself,
were born sixty other persons, to whom the planets bore
an equal ascendancy; and at the same hour to-morrow
each will undergo some particular peril. Be you on your
guard against yours."

"Most assuredly I will, and with many thanks," replied Sir Osborne. "But I would fain know of what
reason you take an interest in my fate more than in any
of the other sixty persons you have mentioned."

"How know you that I do so?" demanded Sir Cesar
dryly. "Perchance had I met any one of them in this
cottage, I might have done them the same good turn.
However, 'tis not so. I own I do take interest in your
fate, more than that of any mortal being. Look not surprised, young man, for I have cause: nay more—you
shall know more. Mark me! our fates are united forever in this world, and I will serve you, though I see,
darkling through the obscurity of time, that the moment
which crowns all your wishes and endeavors is the last
that I shall draw breath of life. Yet your enemy is my
enemy, your friends are my friends, and I will serve you,
though I die!"

He rose and grasped Sir Osborne's hand, and fixed his
dark eye upon his face. "'Tis hard to part with existence
—the warm ties of life—the soft smiling realities of a
world we know—and to begin it all again in forms we
cannot guess. Yet, if my will could alter the law of fate,
I would not delay your happiness an hour; though I
know, I feel, that this thrilling blood must then chill—
that this quick heart must stop—that the golden light and
the glorious world must fade away—and that my soul
must be parted from its fond companion of earth forever and ever. Yet it shall be so. It is said. Reply not!

Speak not! Follow me! Hush! Hush!" and proceeding to the door of the cottage he mounted his palfrey, which stood ready, and motioned Sir Osborne to do the same.

The young knight did so in silence, and rode along with him to the garden-gate, followed by the old cottagers. There, Richard Heartley, as if accustomed so to do, held out his hand; Sir Cesar counted into it nine nobles of gold, and proceeded on the road in silence.

CHAPTER II.

Illusive dreams in mystic forms expressed.

BLACKMORE.

" AND now to you and yours," said Sir Cesar, after he had proceeded some way with the young knight. " Whither do you go ? "

" My first care," replied Sir Osborne, " must be to seek my father, at whose wish I have now returned to England. To you, who know far more of me and mine than I ever dreamed that mortal ear had heard, I need not say where my father dwells." As he spoke, Sir Osborne drew up his horse, following the example of his companion, whose palfrey had stopped at a point where the road, separating into two branches, gave the traveller the option of proceeding either towards Canterbury or Dover, as his business or pleasure might impel. At the same time the young knight fixed his eye upon the other's face, as if to ascertain what was passing in his mind, seeking, probably, thence to learn how far the old man's knowledge really extended in respect to himself and his concerns.

" It is a long journey," said Sir Cesar, thoughtfully, " and 'twill take you near three weeks to travel thither and back. Much may be lost or won in three weeks. You must not go. Hie on to Dover and thence to London ; wait there till I give you further news, and be sure that my news shall be of some avail."

" It cannot be," answered Sir Osborne Maurice. " Before I take any step whatever I must see my father ; and though I doubt not that your advice be good, and your knowledge more than natural, I cannot quit my road, or wait in any place till I have done the journey to which duty and affection call me."

"Your own will, then, be your guide, though it be a bad one," answered Sir Cesar. "But mark, I tell you, if you pursue the road you are on, you will meet with danger, and will lose opportunity. My words are not wont to fall idly."

"Whatever danger may occur," replied Sir Osborne, "my road lies towards London, and it shall not be easy to impede me on my way."

"Ho, ho! so headstrong!" cried the old knight; "i' God's name, then, on! My palfrey goes too slow for your young blood. Put spurs to your steed, sir, and get quick into the perils, from which you will need my hand to help you out. Spur, spur, Sir Knight; and good · speed attend you."

"By your leave, then," replied Sir Osborne, taking the old man at his word, and giving his horse the spur; "Sir Cesar, I thank you for your kindness; we shall meet again, when I hope to thank you better—till then farewell!"

"Farewell, farewell!" muttered the old knight; "just the same as ever! If I remember right he was killed in the first Punic war, for not taking the advice of Valerus the soothsayer; and though now his soul has passed through fifty different bodies, he is just as headstrong as ever;" and with these sage reflections Sir Cesar pursued his way.

Leaving him, however, to his own meditations, we must now, for some time, follow the track of Sir Osborne Maurice, whose horse bore him quickly along that same little tortuous road, in the midst of which we encountered him in the beginning. Within a mile of the spot where he had left the astrologer, Sir Osborne drew in his bridle, and standing in the stirrup, looked round him on both sides over the high bank of earth, which in that place flanked the road on either hand.

After gazing round for a moment, and marking every trifling object with an attention which was far more than the scenery merited, from any apparent worth or picturesque beauty, he turned his horse into a small bridle-path, and riding on for about a mile, came in front of a mansion, which, even in that day, bore many a mark of venerable antiquity.

A small eminence, at about five hundred yards' distance from it, gave him a full view of the building, as it rose upon another slight elevation, somewhat higher than that on which he stood. Above the branches, which were scarcely green with the first downy promise of the spring, was seen rising high the dark, octagon keep of Chilham Castle. It was a building of the old irregular Norman construction, and the architect, who probably had forgot that a staircase was requisite till he had completed the tower, had remedied the defect by throwing out from the east side a sort of square buttress, which contained the means of ascending to the various stories of which it was composed. On the west side of the keep appeared a long mass of buildings of a still more ancient date, surrounded by strong stone walls overgrown with ivy, forming a broken, but picturesque line of architecture, stretching just above the tops of the trees, and considerably lower than the tower, while a small detached turret was seen here and there, completing the castellated appearance of the whole.

Sir Osborne paused, and gazed at it for five or ten minutes in silence, while a variety of very opposite expressions took possession of his countenance.

The moment after he had again entered upon the road to Canterbury, a sudden change took place in the pace of his horse, and perceiving that he had cast a shoe, the young knight was forced, although the sun was now getting far west, to slacken his pace. Proceeding but slowly, it was nearly dark when he reached the little village of Northbourne, where, riding up to the smithy, he called loudly for the farrier. No farrier, however, made his appearance; all was silent, and as black as his trade, and the only answer which Sir Osborne could procure, was at length elicited from one of a score of boys, who, with open eyes and gaping mouths, stood round listening unmoved for a quarter of an hour, while the knight adjured the blacksmith to come forth and show himself.

"Can I have my horse shod here or not, little varlet?" cried he at length to one of the most incorrigible starers.

"Ye moy, if ye loyke," answered the boy, with that air of impenetrable stupidity which an English peasant boy can sometimes get up when he is half frightened and half sullen.

"He means, ye moy, if ye can," answered another urchin, with somewhat of a more intellectual face, "for Jenkin Thumpum is up at the hostel shoeing the merchant's beast, and Dame Winny, his wife, is gone to hold the lantern. He! he! he!"

"But how far is it to the inn, my good boy?" demanded Sir Osborne.

"Oh, it's for half an hour up the road, ye see," replied the boy.

"But you are sure the blacksmith is there?" demanded Sir Osborne.

"Oy, oy!" replied the boy, "as sure as eggs are bacon, if he's not coming back again. So if ye go straight up along, you'll meet Jenkin coming, and Dame Winny holding the lantern. Ha! ha! ha!" It was quite dark when Sir Osborne Maurice arrived at the gate of the hostel, or inn, which consisted of a long row of low buildings, running by the side of the road, with a straw-yard at the nearer end; into this the traveller guided his horse by the light of a horn lantern, which was held by no other hand than Dame Winny herself, while her husband, Master Thumpum, pared the hoof of a stout gelding which stood tied to the stable-door.

As soon as the good lady heard the sound of a horse's feet entering the court, she raised her melodious voice to notify to the servants of the house a traveller's arrival.

"Tim Chamberlain! Tim Chamberlain!" cried she, "here's a master on horseback."

The chamberlain, for by such sonorous title did he designate himself, came forth at the summons, presenting not only the appearance of an ostler, but of a bad ostler too; and after assisting the knight to dismount, he took from the saddle the leathern bags, which commonly accompanied a traveller on a journey in those days, and running his hand over the exterior, with the utmost nonchalance, endeavored to ascertain whether the contents were such as might be acceptable to any of his good friends on the road.

Sir Osborne's first care was of his horse, which he ordered to be shod, for the purpose of proceeding immediately, but finding its foot somewhat tender, he at length determined upon passing the night at the inn, rather than injure an animal on which his further journey greatly depended; and leaving the chamberlain to examine his bags more at his leisure, he entered the kitchen, which was then the common room of reception.

Night had by this time rendered the air chilly, and the sight of a large blazing fire, which greeted his eye as he pushed open the door, promised him at least that sort of reception for which he was most anxious, as he did not propose to himself any great communion with those who might be within. The apartment was not very inviting in any other particular than the cheerful blazing of the large logs of wood with which the hearth was strewed, for the floor was of battened mud, and the various utensils which hung round did not do great credit to the hostess' housewifery.

In those days, the close of evening was generally the signal for every traveller to betake himself to the nearest place of repose; and with his circle round the fire, and his own peculiar chair placed in the most approved corner of the vast chimney, mine host of the inn seldom expected the arrival of any new guest after dark. It was then, if his company were somewhat of his own degree, that he would tell his best story, or crack his best joke; and sometimes even, after many an overflowing flagon had gone round at the acknowledged expense of his guests, he himself, too, would club his tankard of toast and ale, for which, it is probable, he found sufficient means to make himself kindly reparation in some other manner.

In such course flowed by the moments at the inn, when Sir Osborne Maurice, pushing open the door of the kitchen, interrupted the landlord in the midst of an excellent good ghost story, and made the whole of the rest of the party turn their heads suddenly round, and fix their eyes upon the tall, graceful figure of the young knight, as if he had been the actual apparition under discussion.

The assembly at the kitchen fire consisted only of six persons. Mine host, as above stated, in his large arm-chair, was first in bulk and dignity. Next to this dignitary sat a Portugal captain, who occupied a seat between mine host and hostess. His neck was rather of the longest, and at the end of it was perched a mighty small head, whose front was ornamented with a large nose, two little dark twinkling eyes, under a pair of heavy black brows, and a mouth of quite sufficient size to serve a moderate-minded pair. His dress was more tolerable than his face, consisting of a dark brown doublet, slashed with light green with trunks and hose to correspond; while in his belt appeared a goodly assortment of implements for cutting and maiming, too numerous to be recited; and between his legs, as he sat and rocked himself on his chair, he held his long sword, with the point of which he ever and anon raked ashes round a couple of eggs that were roasting on the hearth.

Smiling on this jewel of a captain, sat our landlady in

the next chair, a great deal too pretty to mind the affairs of her house, and a great deal too fine to be very good.

On the right hand of the hostess stood the cook, skewering up a fine breast of house lamb, destined for the supper of a stout old English clothier, Jekin Groby by name, who, placed in the other seat of honor opposite mine host, leaned himself back in a delicious state of drowsiness between sleeping and waking. The sixth person was the turnspit dog, who, freed from his task, sat on his rump facing his master, on whose countenance he gazed with most sagacious eyes, seeming much more attentive to the tale than any one else but the cook.

As I have said, Sir Osborne threw open the door somewhat suddenly, startling all within. The landlord became motionless; the landlady screamed; the cook ran the skewer into her hand; the turnspit dog barked; Jekin Groby knocked his head against the chimney; and the Portuguese ran one of the eggs through the body with the point of his sword.

It has been said that a good countenance is a letter of recommendation, and to the taste of mine hostess it was the best that could be given. Thus, after she had finished her screams she got up with her very best curtsey, drew a settle to the fire next to herself, bade the turnspit hold his tongue, and ordered Tim Chamberlain, who followed hard upon Sir Osborne's footsteps, to prepare for his worship the tapestry chamber.

"I seem to have scared you all," said Sir Osborne, somewhat astonished at the confusion which his entrance had caused. "What is the matter?"

"Nay, marry, sir, 'twas nothing," replied the landlady, with a sweet simper, "but a foolish ghost that my husband spoke of."

"The foolish ghost has broken my head, I know," said Jekin Groby, rubbing his poll, which had come in contact with the chimney.

"Nay, then, the ghost was rude, as well as foolish," remarked Sir Osborne, taking his seat.

"Ha! ha! well said, young gentleman," cried the honest clothier. "Nay, now, I warrant thou hast a merry heart."

"Thou would'st be out," answered Sir Osborne. "My heart's a sad one," and he added a sigh, that showed there was some truth in what he said, though he said it lightly.

"They say, that thin doublets cover alway gay heart," said the Portuguese captain. "Now, senhor! your doublets was not very thick, good youths."

"Good youth!" said Sir Osborne, turning towards the speaker, whom he had not before remarked, and glancing his eye over his person—"good youth! what mean you by that, sir?" But as his eye fell upon the face of the Portingal, his cheek suddenly reddened very high, and the glance of the other sunk as if quelled by some powerful recollection. "Oh! ho!" continued the knight, "a word with you, sir," and rising, he pushed away the settle, and walked towards the end of the room.

"Pray don't fight, gentlemen!" cried the hostess, catching hold of the skirt of Sir Osborne's doublet. "Pray don't fight! I never could bear to see blood spilled. John Alesop! husband! you are a constable; don't let them fight!"

"Leave me, dame; you mistake me. We are not going to fight," said Sir Osborne, leading her back to the fire; "I merely want to speak one word to this fellow. Come here, sir!"

The Portugal captain had by this time risen up to his full height, but as he marched doggedly after the young knight, there was a swinging stoop in his long neck that greatly derogated from the dignity of his demeanor. Sir Osborne spoke to him for some time in a low voice, to which he replied nothing but "Dios! It's nothing to I! Vary well! Not a word!"

"Remember, then," said the knight, somewhat louder.

" If I find you use your tongue more than your prudence,
I will slit your ears ! "

" Pan de Dios ! you are the only man that dare to
say me so," muttered the captain, following towards the
fire, at which the knight now resumed his seat, and where
mine host was expatiating to Jekin Groby, the hostess, the
cook, and the turnspit-dog, upon the propriety of every
constable letting gentlemen settle their differences their
own way. " For," said he, " what is the law made for ?
Why, to punish the offender. Now, if there is no offence
committed, there is no offender, then would the law be
of no use ; therefore, to make the law useful, one ought to
let the offence be committed without intermeddling, which
would be rendering the law of no avail."

" Very true," said his wife.

" Why, there's something in it," said Jekin Groby,
" for when I was at court, the king himself ordered two
gentlemen to fight. Lord a mercy, it seemed to me cruel
strange ! "

" Nay, when wert thou at court, Master Jekin ? " demanded the landlord.

" Why, have I ate lamb and drank ale at thy house
twice every year," demanded the indignant clothier,
" and know'st thou not, John Alesop, that I am clothier,
otherwise cloth-merchant, to his most gracious grace
King Henry ? And that twice he has admitted me into
his dignified presence ? And once that I stayed six weeks
at the palace of Westminister ? Oh, it is a prince of a
king ! Lord, a' mercy, you never saw his like ! "

" Nay, nay, I heard not of it," replied the landlord.
" But come, Master Jekin, as these gentlemen don't
seemed inclined to fight, tell us all about the court, and
who you saw there, while the lamb is roasting."

The honest clothier was willing enough to tell his
story, and including even the knight, every one seemed
inclined to hear him, except indeed the Portugal captain,
who was anxious to recommence his flirtation with

Master Alesop's dame. But she, having by chance heard a word or two about slitting of ears, turned up her nose at her foreign inamorato, and prepared herself to look at Sir Osborne Maurice, and to listen to Jekin Groby.

"Oh, it is a prodigious place, the court!" said the clothier, "a very prodigious place indeed. But to my mind, the finest thing about it is the king himself. Never was such a king; so fine a man, or so noble in his apparel! I have seen him wear as many as three fresh suits a day."

While the good clothier proceeded, the Portuguese had more than once fidgeted on his seat, as if with some willingness to evade the apartment, and at length had risen and was quietly proceeding towards the door, when the eye of Sir Osborne Maurice fixed upon him, with a sort of stern authority in its glance, which he seemed well to understand, for without more ado he returned to his settle, and showed as if he had merely risen to stretch the unwieldy length of his legs, by a turn upon the floor.

In the meantime, Jekin Groby went on.

"It is a forward age and a bad, I wot, and the next will be a worse, seeing that all our young gallants are so full of strange fantasies—that is not to say all, for there is the young Earl of Darby, God bless his noble heart! he is an honest one and a merry, and right English to the core. One day he meets me in the ante-chamber, where I had always leave to stand to see all the world go in and out, and he says to me, 'Honest Jekin Groby,' says he, 'dost thou stand here in the ante-room, waiting for my lord cardinal's place if he should chance to die?' 'Nay, my good lord,' I was bold to answer, 'I know that here I am out of place, yet my lord cardinal's would not suit me.' So then he laughed; 'Why not?' says he, 'for certainly thou art of the cloth.'—But hark! they are crying in the court."

The honest clothier was right, for sundry sounds began to make themselves heard in the court-yard, an-

nouncing the arrival of no inconsiderable party, who, if
one might judge by the vociferation of the servants, were
people that made some noise in the world.

Up started mine host, as well as his rotundity would
let him, up started mine hostess, and out rushed the cook;
while, at the same moment, a bustling lacquey, with riding whip in hand, pushed into the kitchen, exclaiming,
"What's this! what's this! but one tapestried room, and
that engaged? Nonsense! it must be had, and shall be
had, for my young lady and her woman!"

"A torch! a torch!" cried a voice without. "This
way, lady. The rain is coming on very hard; we shall be
much better here."

All eyes turned towards the door with that anxious
curiosity which every small body of human beings feels,
when another person is about to be added to the little
world of the moment. But fastidious, indeed, must have
been the state that could have found anything unpleas-
ing in the form that entered. It was that of a sweet,
fair girl, in the spring of womanhood; every feature was
delicate and feminine, every limb was small and graceful,
yet with that rounded fulness, which is indispensable to
perfect beauty. Her color was not high, but it was fine;
and when she found herself before so many strangers, it
grew deeper and deeper, till it might have made the
rose look pale.

By this time the hostess had advanced, and a venerable
old man in a clerical robe had followed into the room,
while mine host himself rolled forward to see what best
could be done for the accommodation of the large party
that seemed willing to honor his inn with their presence.

"I heard something about the best chamber being engaged," said the young lady, in a voice that sweetly cor-
responded with her person, at the same time turning half
towards the hostess, half towards the clergyman; "I
beg that I may disturb no one, any chamber will do for

me and my woman, if you think we cannot reach the Manor to-night."

"Ay! but if we can have the best chamber, I don't see why not, lady," said the lady's-maid, who by this time had followed.

Sir Osborne Maurice advanced. "If it is to me," said he, "that the best chamber has been assigned, I shall feel myself honored in resigning it to a lady, but infinitely more, if my memory serves me right, and that lady be Lady Constance de Grey."

"Good heaven, Master Osborne Maurice!" said the lady, coloring again with evidently no very unpleasant feelings; "I thought you were in Flanders. When did——"

But she had no time to finish her phrase, for the old clergyman cast himself upon Sir Osborne's neck, and wept like a child. "My dear Osborne," cried he, "how? when? where?—But I am a fool—how like you have grown to your dear lady mother.—Pardon me, my lord—I mean, sir—I don't know what I'm talking of.—But you know you were my first pupil, and like my child—and I never thought to see you again before my old eyes were covered with the dust. Alack! alack! what a fine man thou art grown. 'Tis just five years, come May, since you came to take leave of me at the house of this my honored lady's father: and, mind you, how you taught her to shoot with the bow, and how pleased my good lord her father was to see you."

"I have not forgot one circumstance of the kind hospitality I then received," said Sir Osborne, "and never shall, so long as I have memory of anything."

"Ay, but she has lost the archery," said the old clergyman. "She has lost it entirely."

"But I have not lost the bow, Master Osborne," said the lady, with a smile: "I have it still, and shall some day relearn to draw it."

There was a strange difference between the manner of

the clergyman and that of the lady, when addressing the young knight. Lady Constance evidently saw him with pleasure, but she seemed to feel, or to suppose, that there existed between them a difference of rank, which made some reserve on her part necessary; while, on the contrary, the old man gave way to unlimited joy at meeting with his former pupil, though qualified by an air of respect and deference, which mingled strangely with the expressions of fondness that he poured forth.

By this time, the host and hostess having removed from the fire, and the Portugal captain having quietly slipped away in the bustle, no one remained near it but Jekin Groby, and he not being very terrific of aspect, Lady Constance placed herself in one of the vacant seats, till such time as her chamber should be prepared. Sir Osborne wrung the old tutor's hand affectionately and whispered, while he followed to the side of Lady Constance, "I have a world to say to you, and much upon which to consult you."

"Good, good!" replied the old man, in the same subdued tone, "when the lady has retired."

Having seated themselves round the fire, the conversation was soon renewed, especially between the tutor and Sir Osborne, Lady Constance sometimes joining in, with her sweet musical voice, and her gentle engaging manner, and sometimes falling into deep reveries, which seemed not of the happiest nature, if one might judge by the grave, and even sad cast, that her countenance took, as she fixed her eyes upon the embers, and appeared to study deeply the various forms they offered to her view.

In the meantime, the clergyman gradually engaged Sir Osborne to detail some of the adventures which he had met with during the five years that he had served in the imperial army, then combating in Flanders; and there he spoke of "moving accidents by flood and field, of hair-breadth 'scapes in the imminent deadly breach," and of much that he had seen, mingled with some small portions of what he himself had done; and yet when he told any of his own deeds that had met with great success, he took care to attribute all to high good fortune, and a happy chance. It was thus, he said, that, by a most lucky coincidence, he happened to take two standards of the enemy, before the eyes of the late Emperor Maximilian, who, as a recompense, honored him with knighthood from his own sword.

"Indeed!" exclaimed Lady Constance, waking from her reverie, "then I do congratulate you most sincerely. The road to fortune and to fame is now open to you, Sir Osborne, and, I feel sure—I know that you will reach the goal."

"A thousand thanks, lady, for your good augury," replied the knight; "nor do I lack hope, though there are so many competitors in the field of fame, that the difficulty of winning renown is increased. In the army of Flanders, there is many an aspirant, with whom it is hard to contend."

"True," replied Lady Constance; "but even that makes the contention more honorable. Oh! we have heard of that army, and its feats of arms, even here. We cannot be supposed to have received the names of all who have done high deeds; but, they say, that the young Lord Darnley, the son of the unhappy Earl Fitzbernard, is realizing the tales of the knights of old. You must have met him, Sir Osborne Maurice. Do you know him?"

"I cannot say that I know him well," replied the knight, "though we have served long in the same army. He has gained some renown, it is true, but there are many men at arms as good as he."

"I know not well why," said Lady Constance after a pause, "but I have always been much interested in that young gentleman's history. The unexpected, and seemingly undeserved train of misfortunes that fell upon his house, and the accounts that all men give of his gallantry and daring, his courtesy and accomplishments, have made him quite one of my heroes of romance."

Whether it be true that very high praises of another will frequently excite some small degree of envy, even in the most amiable minds, matters not; but Sir Osborne did not seem very easy in his chair, while Lady Constance recited the high qualities of his companion in arms. " I have heard," replied he at length, " that the fame which Lord Darnley has acquired, either justly or unjustly, has even reached the ears of our sovereign lord the king, and has worked much in favor of those claims, which his family make to their forfeited estates. It is well known that his grace is the flower of this world's chivalry; and as the young lord is somewhat skilful in the tournois, and at the barriers, the king has, I hear, expressed a wish to see him, which, if he should come over, may turn favorable to his cause."

" God grant it may ! " said Lady Constance, " although I have never seen the young gentleman, and though the person who now holds his estates is cousin to my deceased father——"

" Good God! is it possible," exclaimed Sir Osborne, " that my lord your father is dead? But I might have divined it from seeing you here alone."

Lady Constance sighed. " I am indeed alone in all the world," said she. " My father has been dead these three years. My Lord Cardinal Wolsey claims me as ward of the crown, and as I am now in my one-and-twentieth year, he calls me to a place I hate—the court. Knowing no one there, loved of no one there, I shall feel like an inexperienced being in a sad strange world. But when the time comes that I may command my own actions, if they will ever let me do so, I will return to my father's halls, and live amongst my own tenantry. But to change a painful subject; my good father," she continued, turning to the clergyman, " were it not well to send a messenger to Sir Payan Wileton, to let him know that we shall not arrive at his house to-night, though we will take our forenoon meal with him to-morrow."

The old clergyman seemed somewhat embarrassed. "I know not what to do," said he. "'Twould be better not to go at all,—yet what can be done? You promised to go as you went to London, and one ought always to keep one's promise. So what can the lady do?" and he turned abruptly to Sir Osborne, not so much as if he asked his advice, as if he made him an apology.

"Why, the lady had certainly better keep her word," answered Sir Osborne, with a smile; "but you know, my good old friend, that I cannot judge of the circumstances."

"Ay, true; I forgot," answered the other. "She must go, I am afraid, though she knows what the man is, and dislikes him as much as any one——"

At this moment the chamberlain entered, with Lady Constance's woman, announcing that the tapestry chamber was now warmed and lighted; and the young lady left them, with many apologies to Sir Osborne, for depriving him of his apartment.

"I warrant you, madam," said Tim Chamberlain, "his worship will be well lodged; for 'tis but the next room to that he had, and 'tis all as good, bating the tapestry."

"I am a soldier, lady," said Sir Osborne, "and not much accustomed to tapestry to my chamber, without it be the blue hangings of the sky, spangled with the starry broidery of heaven; but, in truth, I wish they had given me but a tramper's garret, that I might at least have had some merit in giving up the room."

As the honest clothier, Jekin Groby, who was little heedful of ceremony, still sat by the fire, though apparently in a doze, the conversation of Sir Osborne Maurice with his old tutor could not be so private as they could have wished, especially as the cook and the chamberlain were bustling about laying forth a table for supper, and two or three lacqueys who had accompanied the litter of Lady Constance, were running in and out, endeavoring to make as much noise as possible about nothing. However, they found an opportunity to appoint a place of meeting in London, to which both were journeying, and it was agreed that the first arrived should there wait for the other. Many questions concerning the state of England did Sir Osborne ask of the old man, for whom he seemed to entertain both reverence and love; and deeply did he ponder all the answers he received. Often also did the tutor look anxiously in the face of the young knight, and often did Sir Osborne return it with the same kind of hesitating glance, as if there were some subject on which they both wished to speak, yet doubted whether to begin.

At length Sir Osborne spoke out, more to the clergyman's thoughts than his words. "We will talk of all that hereafter in London," said he; "'twere too long to expose now—but tell me one thing: know you, my good father, a celebrated man called in Italy, Cesario il dotto?—Is he to be trusted?—For I met with him to-day, when he much astonished me, and much won upon my opinion; but I knew not how far I might confide in him, though he is certainly a most extraordinary man."

"Trust your life in his hands," exclaimed the tutor. "He is your father's best and dearest friend, and never has he ceased his efforts to serve him. We used much to dispute, for I am bound by my calling to hold his studies as evil, but certainly his knowledge was wonderful and his intentions were good. God forgive him if he err in his opinions! as in truth he does, holding strange fantasies of many sorts of spirits, more than the Church allows, with various things, altogether heretical and vain. But as I have said, trust him with your life, if it be necessary; for he is a true friend and a good man, although his knowledge and his art be altogether damnable and profane."

" 'Tis strange I never heard my father name him," said Sir Osborne.

" Oh! he bore another name once," replied the tutor, " which he changed when he first gave himself to those dangerous studies, that have since rendered him so famous. It is a custom among such men to abjure their name; but he had another reason, being joined in a famous conspiracy some thirty years ago."

" Why," said Sir Osborne, " he does not seem a very old man now."

" He is fully eighty," replied the clergyman, " and there is the wonder, for he seems never to change. For twenty years he was absent from England, except when he came to be present at your birth. At length everybody had forgotten him but your father, and he is now only known by the name of Sir Cesar. Yet strange as it may seem, he is received and courted by the great, he knows the secrets and affairs of every one, and possesses much influence even in the court. It is true I know his former name, but under so strict a vow to conceal it, that it can never pass my lips."

" But how came he present at my birth?" demanded Sir Osborne, whose curiosity was now highly excited.

" He came to calculate your nativity," replied the tutor, " which he did upon a scroll of parchment——"

" Fifty-six yards long by three yards broad," said Jekin Groby, waking, " which makes just one hundred and sixty-eight, yaw——Bless me, I forgot; is supper ready? Host, host! Cook, serve quick, and these gentles will take a bit of my lamb, I am sure."

" I thank you, good sir," said the knight, " but I must to bed, for I ride betimes to-morrow."

" So do I, 'faith," said the clothier, " and by your leave, Sir Knight, I'll ride with you, if you go toward to Lunnun, for my bags are well lined, and company's a blessing in these days of plunder and robbery."

" With all my heart," replied Sir Osborne, " so that

you have your horse saddled by half-past five, we will to Canterbury together."

"Well, I'll be ready, I'll be ready," said the clothier; "but sure you'll stay and taste the lamb and ale? See how it hisses and crackles! O, 'tis a rare morsel, a neck of lamb! Stay, stay."

"I thank you, 'tis not possible," replied the knight; "good-night, my excellent old friend," he continued pressing the tutor's hand, "we shall soon meet, then, at the house of your relation, Doctor Butts; till then, fare-well!"

CHAPTER III.

" You have the captives,
    Who were the opposites of this day's strife :
We do require them of you."

SHAKSPEARE.

THE chamber of Sir Osborne Maurice was next to that
of Lady Constance de Grey, and from time to time he
could hear through the partition the sweet murmuring of
her voice, as she spoke to the woman who undressed her.
Whatever were the thoughts those sounds called up, the
young soldier did not sleep, but lay pondering over his
fate, his brain troubled by a host of busy meditations,
that would not let him rest. It was not that he either
was in love with Lady Constance, or fancied himself
in love with her. though he neither wanted ardor or
feeling, nor quickness of imagination; and yet he thought
over all she said with strange sensations of pleasure, and
tried to draw the graceful outline of her figure upon the
blank darkness of the night. And then again he called
up the fortnight that he spent some five years before, at
the mansion of her father when he had gone thither to
bid farewell to his old tutor; and he remembered every
little incident as though 'twere yesterday. Still all the
while, he never dreamed of love. He gave way to those
thoughts as to a pleasant vision, which filled up sweetly
the moments till sleep should fall upon his eyelids; and
yet he found that the more he thought in such a train, the
less likely was he to slumber. At length the idea of the
Portugal captain crossed his mind, and he strove to
fix at what moment it was that that worthy ·had quitted

the kitchen of the inn, by recalling the last time he positively had been there. He tried, however, in vain, and in the midst of the endeavor he fell asleep.

The sun had fully risen by the time Sir Osborne woke, and finding himself later than he had intended, he dressed himself hurriedly and ran down to the court, where he met the honest clothier, already prepared to set out. His own horse, thanks to the care of Jekin Groby, had been accoutered also; and as nothing remained for him to do but to pay his reckoning and depart, all was soon ready, and the travellers on the road.

"Ah! ha! Sir Knight," said the clothier, with good-humored familiarity, as Sir Osborne sprung into the saddle, "what would they say in camp, if it were known that Jekin Groby, the Kentish clothier, was in the field before you. Ha! ha! ha! that's good. And you talked, too, of being off by cock-crow. Lord 'a mercy! poor old Chanticleer has almost thrown his own neck with crowing, and you never heeded his piping."

"I have been very lazy," said the knight, "and know not, in truth, how it has happened. But tell me, honest Master Groby, did you remark last night at what hour it was that the vagabond Portuguese took his departure?"

"Why, 'twas just when my young lady, Mistress Constance, came in," said the clothier. "He slipped away, just as I've seen a piece of cloth slip off a shelf, fold by fold, so quietly that no one heard it, till, flump! it was all gone together. But bless us," he continued, "how comical! our horses are both of a color. Never did I see such a match, only mine has got a white foot, which is a pity——bought him in Yorkshire when I went down after the cloth. The cheats, however, painted me his white foot, and 'twas not till I'd had him a week that I saw his foot begin to change color. Vast cheats in Yorkshire. Steal a man's teeth out of his head if he sleeps with his mouth open."

"It is a good horse though," said Sir Osborne; "rather

heavy in the shoulder. But it is a good strong horse, and would bear a man at arms well, I doubt not."

Jekin Groby was somewhat of a judge in horseflesh, notwithstanding his having been gulled by the Yorkshire jockeys: and what was more, he piqued himself upon his knowledge, so that he soon entered upon a strain of conversation with Sir Osborne, which could only be interesting to connoisseurs. This continued some way as they trotted along the road, which offered no appearance of anything bearing the human form divine, till they came to a spot where the way had been cut between two high banks, formed of chalky soil mingled with veins of large flints. On the summit of one of these banks was perched a man, who seemed looking out for something, as he stood motionless, gazing down the road towards them. Upon his shoulder he carried a pole, or stave, as it was called, some thirteen feet long, with a sharp iron head, such as was frequently carried by the people of the country in those days, serving both as a means of aggression and defence, and also as a sort of leaping pole wherewith they cleared the deep ditches by which the country was in many parts intersected. The man himself was apparently above the ordinary height. Whoever he was, and whatever was his occupation, no sooner did he see the travellers, than descending the bank by means of the veins of flint, which served him as steps, he ran on as hard as he could, and then turning off through a little stile, was seen proceeding rapidly across a field beyond.

"Did you remark that fellow with his long pole?" demanded Sir Osborne. "We have frightened him: look, he runs."

"He is vexed to see more than one at a time, Sir Knight," replied Jekin Groby. "Odd's fish! I am glad I had your worship with me."

"Why he can mean us no harm," said Sir Osborne. "The moment a man flies, he changes from your enemy and becomes his own. But that fellow was evidently looking out for some one; now if he know not that you are travelling here with your bags well lined, as you express it, which doubtless you are too wise a man to give notice of, to every one, he cannot be watching for us, for my plunder would not be worth his having. I rather think that he is some fellow hawking foul, by the long stave he has on his shoulder."

"It may be so," replied the cloth-merchant. "One is bound to think charitably and never to judge rashly; but i' faith, I am mistaken if he is not a vast rogue. As to their not knowing that my bags are pretty full of angels, trust them for that. No one is robbed without the consent of the chamberlain or hostler where last he lodged. The moment you are off your beast, they whip you up your cap-case or budget, as it may happen, and if they can't find out by the weight, they give it a shake, after such a sort as to make the pieces jingle. Then again, as for his pole or stave, as you term it, those fellows with their staves are so commonly known for robbery on the roads, that no honest man rides without a pistol at his saddle-bow, or something of the kind to deal with them out of reach of their pike, which sort of snapper, truly, I see your worship has got as well as myself."

"Oh, you need not fear them," said Sir Osborne, somewhat amused at the alarm of the clothier, though willing to allay it. "You are a stout man, and I am not quite a school-boy."

"Oh, I fear them? I don't fear them!" replied Jekin, affecting a virtue which he had not; for though, in truth, not very sensible to fear of a mere personal nature, yet his terror at the idea of losing his money was most pious and exemplary. "A couple of true men are worth forty of them; and besides, the fellow has run away.—So now to what I was telling your worship about the horse. He cleared the fence and the ditch on t'other side; but then there was again another low fence, not higher, nor—let

me see—not higher nor—zounds! there's Longpole again
—Lord; how he runs!—he's a-poaching, sure enough."

During the next mile's journey, the same occurrence
was repeated four or five times, till at last the appearance
of the man with the stave, whom Jekin Groby had by
this time christened Longpole, was hardly noticed either
by the knight or his companion. In the meantime the
horsemen proceeded but slowly, and at length reached a
spot where the high bank broke away, and the hedge re-
ceding, left a small open space of what appeared to be
common ground. Sir Osborne looked down it for a
moment, then suddenly reined in his horse, and pointing
with his hand, cried to Jekin Groby, who was a little in
advance, " I see two men hiding behind those trees, and
a third there in the hedge. Gallop quick; 'tis an am-
bush."

The clothier instantly spurred forward his horse, but
his passage was closed by two sturdy fellows, armed with
the sort of staves which had obtained for their companion
the name of Longpole. Animated with the same courage
in defence of his gold that inspires a hen in protection
of her chickens, Jekin Groby drew forth his dags, or
horse-pistol, and with the bridle in his teeth, aimed one
at the head of each of his antagonists. The aggressors
jumped aside, and would probably have let him pass, had
he not attempted too boldly to follow his advantage. He
pulled the triggers, the hammers fell, but no report ensued, and it was then he felt the folly of not having well
examined his arms before he left the inn.

In the meanwhile Sir Osborne Maurice was not unem-
ployed. At the same moment that Jekin had been attacked, a man forced his way through the hedge, and
opposed himself to the knight, while sundry others hastened towards them. Sir Osborne's first resource was
his pistol, which, like those of the clothier, had been
tampered with at the inn. But the knight lost not his
presence of mind, and spurred on his horse even against

the pike. The animal, long accustomed to combat where still more deadly weapons were employed, reared up, and with a bound brought the knight clear of the stave, and within reach of his adversary, on whose head Sir Osborne discharged such a blow with the butt-end of his pistol as laid him senseless on the ground.

With a glance of lightning, he saw that at least a dozen more were hurrying up, and that the only chance left was to deal suddenly with the two, who were now in a fair way to pull the clothier off his horse, and having dispatched them, to gallop on with all speed. Without loss of a moment, therefore, he drew his sword and spurred forward. One of honest Jekin's assailant's instantly faced about, and with his pike rested on his foot, steadfastly opposed the cavalier. However, he was not so dexterous in the use of his weapon, that Sir Osborne could not, by rapidly wheeling his horse, obtain a side view of the pike, when by one sweeping blow of his long sword he cleft it in twain. One moment more and the unhappy pikeman's head and shoulders would have parted company, for an arm of iron was swaying the edge of the weapon rapidly towards his neck, when suddenly a powerful man sprang up on the knight's horse behind, and pinioned his arms with a force, which, though it did not entirely disable him, saved the life of his antagonist.

Using a strong effort, Sir Osborne so far disengaged his arm as to throw back the pommel of his sword into the chest of this new adversary, who in a moment was rolling in the dust; but as he fell, another sprang up again behind the knight, and once more embarrassed his arms; other seized the horse's bridle, and others pressed upon him on every side. Still Sir Osborne resisted, but it was in vain. A cord was passed through his arms, and gradually tightened behind, in spite of his struggling, where being tied, it rendered all farther efforts useless.

Hitherto not a word had been spoken by either party. It seemed as if, by mutual understanding, the attacking and the attacked had forborne any conversation upon a subject which they knew could not be decided by words.

At length, however, when they had pulled Sir Osborne Maurice off his horse, and placed him by the side of Jekin Groby, who had now long been in the same situation, the tallest of the party, evidently no other than the agreeable gentleman that had watched them along the road with such peculiar care, and whom we shall continue to call Longpole, advanced, holding his side, which was still suffering from the pommel of Sir Osborne's sword, and, after regarding them both, he addressed himself to the knight, with much less asperity than might have been expected from the resistance he had met with.

"Thou hit'st hard!" said he; "and I doubt thou hast broken one of my ribs with thy back-heave. Howsoever, I know not which of you is which, now I've got you. Faith, they should have described me the men, not the horses; both the horses are alike."

"Is your wish to rob us or not?" said Sir Osborne; "because, in robbing us both, you are sure to rob the right. Only leave us our horses, and let us go; for to cut our throats will serve you but little.

"If I wished to rob thee, my gentleman," answered Longpole, "I'd cut thy throat too, for breaking my companion's head, who lies there in the road as if he were dead, or rather as if he were asleep, for he's snoring like the father-hog of a large family, the Portuguese vagabond! However, I'll have you both away, then those who sent to seek you will know which it is they want. Hollo! there, knock that fellow down that's fingering the bags. If one of you touch a stiver, I'll make your skins smart for it."

"I see several Portuguese," said Sir Osborne, "or I mistake. Is it not so?"

"Ay, Portuguese and Dutchers, and such like, mixed," replied Longpole. "But come, you must go along."

A light now broke upon the mind of Sir Osborne. "Listen," cried he to the Englishman, as he was preparing to lead them away; "how comes it that you Englishmen join yourselves with a beggarly race of wandering vagabonds, to revenge the quarrel of a base-born Portuguese captain upon one of your own countrymen? Give me but a moment, and you shall hear whether he did not deserve the punishment I inflicted."

Longpole seemed willing to hear, and one or two others came round, while the rest employed themselves in quieting the knight's horse, that, finding himself in hands he was unaccustomed to, began plunging and kicking most violently.

"I will be short," said the knight. "This Portuguese had agreed to furnish a cargo of fruits to the imperial army in Flanders; 'tis now two years ago, for we had a malignant fever in the camp. He got the money when they were landed, and was bringing them up under a small escort, which I commanded, when we found our junction cut off by the right wing of the enemy's army, which had wheeled. The greatest exertion was necessary to pass through a hollow way; the least noise, the least flutter of a pennon, would have betrayed us to the French outposts, who were not more than a bow-shot from us; when our Portuguese stopped in the midst, and vowed he would not go on, unless I promised to pay him double for the fruit, and not to tell anybody of what he had done. If I had ran my lance through him, as I was tempted, his companions would have made a noise, and we were lost, so I was obliged to promise. He knew he could trust the word of an English knight, so he went on quietly enough, and got his money; but then I took him out into a field, and, after a struggle, I tied him to a tree, and lashed him with my stirrup leathers till his back was flayed. He was not worth a knight's sword, or I would have swept his head off. But tell me, is it for this a party of Englishmen maltreat their countrymen?"

"You served him right, young sir," answered Longpole; "and I remember that malignant fever well, for I
was then fletcher to Sir John Pechie's band of horse
archers. But, nevertheless, you must come along, for
the Portuguese and his men only lend a hand in taking
you to Sir Payan Wileton, who tells us a very different
story, and does not make you out a knight at all."

Sir Osborne replied nothing (for it seemed that the
name of Sir Payan Wileton showed him reply was in
vain), but suffered himself to be led on in silence by
Longpole and five of his stoutest companions, while the
rest were directed to follow with Jekin Groby and the
two horses, as soon as the Portuguese, whom the knight
had stunned, should be in a fit state to be removed.

For some way Sir Osborne was conducted along the
high-road without any attempt at concealment on the
part of those who guarded him, and even at a short distance from the spot where the affray had happened, they
stopped to speak with a carter, who was slowly driving
his team on to the village. " Ah! Dick," said he addressing Longpole; " what hast been at?"

" Why, faith," answered the other, " I don't well know.
It's a job of his worship's. You know he has queer
ways with him; and when he tells one to do a thing, one
knows well enough what the beginning is, but what the
end of it is to be no one knows but himself. He says
that this gentleman is the man that excited the miners
on his Cornish lands to riot and insurrection, and a deal
more, so that he will have him taken. He don't look it,
does he? If it had been to-morrow, I'd not have gone
upon the thing, for to-day my sworn service is out."

" Ay! ay!" said the other, " 'tis hard to know Sir
Payan. Howsomdever, he has got all the land round
about, one way or t'other, and everything must yield
to him; for no one ever withstood him but what some
mischance fell upon him. Mind you how when young
Davors went to law with him, and gained his cause, about

seven acres field, he was drowned in the pond when out
hawking not a year after. Do not cross him, man! Do
not cross him! For either God's blessing or the devil's
is upon him, and you'll come to harm some way if you
do."

"I'll not cross him, but I'll leave him," said Longpole;
"for I like neither what I see or hear of him, and less
what I do for him. So, fare thee well, boy."

Sir Osborne Maurice had fallen into a profound reverie, from which he did not awake during the whole of
the way. The astrologer's prediction of approaching
evil, and a thousand other circumstances, of still more
painful presage, came thronging upon his mind, and took
away from him all wish or power, either to question his
conductors, or to devise any plan for escape, had escape
been possible.

The way was long, and the path which Longpole and
his companions followed, led through a variety of green
fields and lanes, silent and solitary, which gave the young
knight full time to muse over his situation.

The manner in which he had been made a prisoner, so
different from the open fair course of any legal proceeding; the persons who had seized him bearing no appearance of officers of the law; the doubt that the chief of
them had himself expressed as to the veracity of the
charge, and the presence of a set of smuggling Portuguese
sailors, all showed evidently to Sir Osborne that his
detention solely originated in some deep wile of a man
famous for his daring cunning and his evil deeds. The
mysterious vagueness, too, the shadowy uncertainty of
the predicted evil, which seemed even now in its accom-
plishment, in despite of all his efforts, weighed upon his
mind; and it was not till the long heavy brick front of an
old manor-house met his view, giving notice that he was
near the place of his destination, that he could arouse his
energies to encounter what was to follow.

The large folding doors, leading into a stone hall, were

pushed open by his conductors, and Sir Osborne was brought in, and made to sit down upon a bench by the fire. One or two servants only were in the hall, and they, unlike the persons who brought him, were dressed in livery, with the cognizance of Sir Payan, a snake twisted round a crane, embroidered on the sleeve.

"His worship is in the book-room, Dick," said one of the men, " take your prisoner there."

These few words were all that passed, for an ominous sort of silence seemed to hang over the dwelling, and affected all within it. Without reply, Longpole led the young knight forward, followed by two of those who had assisted in securing him, and at the end of a long corridor, which terminated the hall, knocked at a door in a recess.

"Come in!" cried a voice within, and the moment after Sir Osborne found himself confronted with the man whose name we have often had occasion to mention, with but little praise, in the course of the preceding pages, Sir Payan Wileton. He was seated in an arm-chair, at the farther end of the small book-room, about a hundred volumes, in gay bindings of vellum and of velvet, orna- mented the shelves, and two or three others lay on a table before him, at which also was seated a clerk, busily engaged in writing.

Sir Payan himself was a man of about fifty, of a deep ashy complexion, and thin, strongly-marked features. His eyes were dark, shrewd, and bright, and sunk deep below his brows, in the midst of which was to be observed a profound wrinkle, which gave his face a continual frown. His cheek-bones were high, his hair short and grizzled, and his whole appearance had perhaps more of sternness than of cunning.

On the entrance of Sir Osborne Maurice, for a moment no one spoke, and the two knights regarded each other in silence, with an austere bitterness that might have spoken them old enemies. But while he gazed on the young knight, Sir Payan's hand, which lay on some papers before him, gradually contracted—clenched harder and harder, till at length the red blood in his thin knuckles vanished away, and they became white as a woman's by the force of the compression. But it was in vain! Sir Osborne's glance mastered his, and dashing his hand across his brow, he broke forth.

"So this is he who excited my tenants and laborers to revolt against the king in that unfortunate Cornish insurrection, and who led them on to plunder my bailiff's dwelling, and to murder my bailiff! Clerk, make out instantly the warrant for his removal to Cornwall, with copies of the depositions taken here, that he may be tried and punished for his crimes on the spot where they were committed."

"Sir Payan Wileton," said the knight, still regarding him with the same steady determined gaze, "we meet for the first time to-day, but I think you know me."

"I do, sir, I do!" replied Sir Payan, without varying from the hurried and impatient manner in which he had spoken at first; "I know you for a rebellious instigator to all kinds of mischief, and for a homicide. Speak, Richard Heartley, did the prisoner offer any resistance? Has he added any fresh crimes to those he has already perpetrated?"

"Resist!" cried Longpole; "ay, your worship, he resisted enough, and broke one of the Portuguese's heads, but not more than was natural or reasonable. The other one resisted too, yet it was easy to see that this one was of gentle blood, which was what your worship wanted, I doubt. But however, as they were both mounted on strong black horses, such as your honor described, we brought them both up."

"Umph!" said Sir Payan, biting his lip—"there were two, were there?" and he muttered something to himself. "Send me here, the captain——or Wilson, the bailiff. It must be ascertained which is which—though there can be no doubt—there can be no doubt!"

"Mark me, Sir Payan Wileton," said Sir Osborne, the moment the other paused. "Mark me, and take good heed before you too far commit yourself; we know each other, and therefore a few words will suffice. Five people in England are aware of my arrival, and equally aware of where I slept last night, and when I set out this morning. Judge, therefore, whether it will not be easy to trace me hither, and to free me from your hands."

Sir Payan Wileton had evidently been agitated by some strong feeling on first beholding the young knight, but by this time he had completely mastered it, and his face had resumed that rigid austerity of expression, with which he was wont to cover all that was passing in his mind.

"Railing, sir, and insinuations will be found of no use here," he said, calmly. "Clerk, make good speed with those warrants. Oh, here is Wilson. Now, Wilson, look at the prisoner well, and tell me if you are sure that he is the person who assaulted you yesterday, and who led the miners when they burned your father's house in Cornwall. Look at him well!"

The young man, whom it may be remembered Sir Osborne Maurice had despatched so unceremoniously over the wall of old Richard Heartley's garden, now advanced, and regarded the knight with a triumphant grin.

"Oh, ho, my brave bird! what, you're limed, are you?" he muttered, and then turning to Sir Payan; "Yes, your worship, 'tis he," he continued, "I am ready to swear that 'twas he led the men that burned Pencriton house, and that threw me over the wall, because I struck old Heartley for calling your worship an usurping traitor and——"

But at that moment Longpole laid a grasp upon his collar that almost strangled him.

"You struck my father, did you!" exclaimed he; "then pray God to make all your bones as soft as whit-leather, for if they're but as crisp as buttered toast, I'll break every one in your skin!"

"Silence!" cried Sir Payan Wileton; "silence, Heartley! if your father has been struck, I will take care he shall have satisfaction."

"With your worship's good leave I will take care of it myself," replied Longpole. "I never trust any one to give or to receive a drubbing for me. I like always to calculate my own quantity of crabstick."

"Silence!" said Sir Payan; "again I say silence! My good Richard, I assure you, you shall be satisfied. Clerk, swear Wilson to the depositions he made. Oh, here is the Portuguese. Captain, is that the man you remember having seen in Cornwall when you were last there?"

"Yes, yes, el pero! that was himself;" cried the captain; "I sawed him at the ale-house at Penzance with my own eye, when I went to fetch the cargo of coal."

"You mean of tin, captain," said Sir Payan.

"Yes, yes, of ten," replied the Portuguese. "It was just ten, I remember."

Sir Osborne's patience was exhausted.

"Vagabond! thief!" cried he, "do you remember my scourging you with the stirrup leathers in Flanders, till there was not an inch of skin upon your back?"

"Yes, yes, that was your turn," said the captain; "I scourge you now."

"Remark what he says," cried Sir Osborne, to those who stood round, "and all of you bear witness in case——"

"Prisoner, you stand committed," cried Sir Payan, in a loud voice. "Take him away! Suffer him not to speak! Richard Heartley, place him in the strong-room at the foot of the staircase, and having locked the door, keep guard over him. Captain, stay you with me; all the rest go."

The commands of Sir Payan were instantly obeyed,

and the room being cleared, he pressed his hands before
his eyes, and thought deeply for some moments.

"He is mine!" cried he at length, "he is mine! And
shall I let him out of my own hands now that I have him
—when 'twould be so easy to furnish him with a hook and
a halter wherewith to hang himself, as the good chaplain
and John Bellringer did to the heretic Hun in the Lol-
lards' Tower last year? But no, that is too fresh in the
minds of men, and too many suspicions are already busy.
So, my captain—I forgot—sit down, my good captain.
I am, as we agreed, about to give this young man into
your hands to take to Cornwall. Why do you laugh?"

"He, he! Cornwall!" cried the captain; "I do not go
in Cornwall."

"Nay, some time in your life you will probably
voyage to Cornwall, as well as to other lands," said Sir
Payan. "Now, 'tis the same to me, whether you take
him there now, or a hundred years hence; you may carry
him all over the world if you will, and drop him at the
antipodes."

"I understand, I understand," replied the Portuguese:
"you have much need to get rid of him, and you give
him to me. Well, I will take your present, if you give
me two hundred golden angels * with him"—Sir Payan
nodded assent. "But let me understand quite all well,"
continued the captain; "you want me to take him to
Cornwall. There is one Cornwall at the bottom of the
sea; do you mean that?"

"'Twere fully as good as the other," said Sir Payan;
"if the journey were short, and the conveyance sure."

"Two cannon-shot will make it a quick passage," replied the captain; "but they must be made of gold, my
good worship."

"Why of gold?" demanded Sir Payan—"oh! I catch
your meaning. But you grow exorbitant."

* Angel—an English gold coin varying in value from 6s. 8d. to
10s.—Ed.

4

"Not I," said the Portuguese; "I only ask two hundred angels more. Why, an indulgence will cost me half the pay. It's very dear drowning a man. If you like me to take him and leave him in Turkey with the Ottomites, I will do it for the two; but if I send him to Cornwall, he! he! he! you shall give me four."

"But how shall I know that it is done?" said Sir Payan, thoughtfully; "but that must be trusted to. You are not such a child as to be pitiful. Men know how to avenge themselves, and you heard his boast of having scourged you. If you be a man, then, do not forget it."

"Forget it!" cried the Portuguese, his dark brows knitting till they almost hid his eyes; "give me the order under your hand and fear not."

"What! an order to murder him!" cried Sir Payan: "Think you my brain is turned?"

"No, no! You have the wrong," said the Portuguese; "I mean an order to take him to Cornwall—it shall be very easy to drop him by the way. If I was exorbitant, as you call me, I had make you pay more, because for why? I know you would eat your hand to get rid of him: else why have you make me bring you news of him when he was in Flanders? Why you pay three spies two crowns the month to give you news every step he took? —Oh! I know it all: but it is this: I am an honest merchant and no rogue, and when I pop him in the sea, I do a little bit of my own business, and a big bit of yours, so I do not charge you so much as if it was all yours. Is not that honest?"

"Honest!" said Sir Payan, with a grim smile; "yes, very honest. But mark me, Sir Captain. I'll have some assurance of you. Thus shall it be. I'll give you a warrant to take him to Cornwall, but you shall sign me a promise to drop him overboard by the way, so that there be no peaching; for when our necks are in the same halter, each will take care not to draw the cord on his fellow, lest he be hanged himself."

"Well, well," said the Portuguese, "that's all right. No fear of me, and you will not for your own sake. But look here, Sir Payan. What have you intended to do with the other man that was taken, with him, as they tell me, who was at the inn-house, and will tell it to all the world? He's the fat clothier; give him to me too, and let my men have the clearing of his bags. You owe them something for the job, and one has had his head broke, and will die by the time he is aboard. Besides, they were never paid for bringing you up the whole cargo of strong wine, five years past, which was paid for by Dudley, the sequestrator."

"Then he should have paid for the carriage," said Sir Payan.

"But he never got it!" cried the Portuguese. "You kept all, when you heard he was in prison, good Sir Payan; and when they did take his head off, you drank the wine yourself. But, say, will you, or will you not, let my men have all that is inside that fat clothman's bags, and I will take him, so that you shall never see him again? if not, your whole business shall soon be known by everybody in the world, by his tongue."

Sir Payan thought for a moment. "It must e'en be so," said he at length. "Take him, but do not hurt him; and as to his bags, do as you like."

"Oh, hurt him, no!" answered the other. "In six months he shall be so good a sailor as any of the others, and two thousand miles away. But we must get off to-night. I will go down, get the boat close under the cliffs, and be back by about one o'clock in the morning. Have all ready against I come, the gold and the order—warrant, as you call it, and all; and lock all my men up in the big granary, with a thing of bacon, and a big cask of liquor; so shall they be all drunk before three, and asleep by four, and sober again by the while I am back, and nobody hear anything about their being here at all."

"That you must do yourself before you go," said Sir Payan. "In the meantime, I must take care that the prisoners be kept out of sight, for a lady cousin is to be here by noon, and neither she nor hers must hear of this. I myself must be away. She came not yesterday, when she should have come; and fain would I pick a quarrel with her house, for they have lands too near my own to be any others than my own. So, though I have ordered her a banquet, yet shall she be served with scanty courtesy—then, if one word of anger fall from her—there shall more follow."

"Oh! if I be here when she shall come," said the Portuguese, "I will give her some cause either to be pleased or angry."

"What wilt thou do, fellow?" demanded Sir Payan, sternly. "Beware! remember she is of my blood."

"Oh, nothing, nothing," replied the captain; "only tell her some little compliment upon her beauty. But, my good worship, can you trust all your men about these prisoners?"

"All! all!" replied Sir Payan. "There is no fear. No one of them but I could hang one way or another, and they know it. All except Heartley, and he is bound to me by an illegal oath, wrung from him by fear of seeing his father driven out this hard winter. But 'tis past noon now.—Ho! without there! Send in my clerk. What, are the horses saddled? Farewell, Sir Portuguese, till one i' the morning."

CHAPTER IV.

'Thrice had I loved thee
Before I knew thy face or name :
So in a voice, so in a shapeless flame,
Angels affect us oft, and worshipped be.'

DONNE.

THE place to which Sir Osborne Maurice was conveyed, when the servants, according to their master's
commands, removed him from the book-room, was a
large dark chamber, running along beneath the whole
extent of the principal staircase, and some way into one
of the towers beyond. The old manor-house, which, for
many reason, Sir Payan still inhabited, even after dis-
possessing Lord Fitzbernard of Chilham Castle, although
built of brick, in a more modern style than the ancient
holds of the feudal nobility, had not entirely abandoned
the castellated architecture formerly in use. Here and
there, upon the long front of the building, was fastened a
large square tower, useless as a defence, and inconvenient
as a dwelling; and at every angle appeared an imposthu-
mous watch-turret, of a redder brick than the rest, like
warts upon the face of a drunkard. The curse of small
windows also was upon the house, making it look as
sombre without, as it was dark and gloomy within, and
the thick leafless wood that swept round it on both
sides, excluded great part of that light which might otherwise have found its way into the gloomy mansion.

Darker than all the rest was the chamber to which
Sir Osborne Maurice was conveyed; the whole of that
part, which was under the staircase, receiving no light
whatever, except from the other half that, placed in one
of the square towers, possessed the privilege of an un-

glazed window, near the ceiling. The use to which Sir
Payan Wileton applied this room, was in general that
of a prison for deer-stealers and other offenders, who
came before him in his magisterial capacity, which offenders he took care should ever be as numerous as there
were persons, of the lower orders, who opposed or displeased him.

The men who conducted the young knight, shut the
door immediately upon him; and thus being left to
ruminate over his fate, with his arms still tightly pinioned
behind him, and scarcely light sufficient to distinguish
any objects which the room contained, it may well be
conceived that his meditations were not of the most
pleasant description. But, nevertheless, indignation had
roused his spirit, and he no longer felt that depression of
mind, and abandonment of hope, which, for a time, had
overpowered him. His first thoughts, therefore, were
now of escape and revenge, but for the moment no means
presented themselves of either; and though he searched
round the apartment, ascertaining the nature and extent
of his prison, which only consisted of that room and a
large closet, containing some straw, no chance whatever
of flight from thence presented itself, and he was obliged
to wait in hopes of circumstances proving his friend.

In about half an hour, the voice of Sir Payan Wileton
was heard without, giving various orders, and a moment
after the trampling of horses sounded as if passing by
the window. To Sir Osborne, accustomed for several
years to watch with warlike acuteness every motion of
a shrewd and active enemy, these sounds gave notice
that his persecutor was gone for the time, and even the
circumstance of his absence excited in the bosom of the
young knight fresh expectation of some favorable opportunity.

Hardly had Sir Payan departed, when the lock squeaked
harshly with the key, and the tall fellow, whom we have
denominated hitherto, and shall still continue to denom-

inate, Longpole, entered, and pushed the door behind him.

"The devil's gone out on horseback," said he, coming near Sir Osborne, and speaking low, "and I have just got a minute to thank your worship."

"To thank me, my friend!" said Sir Osborne somewhat doubting the man's meaning; "what for should you thank me?"

"For throwing a man over the hedge that struck my father," said Longpole, "and by that I see you are a true heart, and a gentleman—and a knight into the bargain, I am sure, in spite of all Sir Payan's tales, and his minion's false swearing; and if I were not his sworn servant, I'd let you off this minute, if I could find a way."

"But is it not much worse to aid in so black a plot as this, than to leave this vile suborner, who is not your born master, and never can be lawfully, if you be the son of old Richard Heartley. Only hear me."

"Nay, Sir Knight," said Longpole; "faith, I must not hear you, for I must mind my oath, and do as I'm bid, though it be the devil bids me. I only came to thank you before I brought the other prisoner here, and to tell you, that though I have forgotten and forgiven many hard knocks, I never forget a good turn, and that you'll find, whatever you may think now. Every dog has his day, but the dog-days don't last all the year."

After this quaint hint he waited for no reply, but quitted the room as fast as possible, and in a moment after returned, pushing in the unfortunate Jekin Groby almost drowned in his own tears.

"Here, I've brought your worship a great baby," cried Longpole, before he closed the door, "who has wasted as much salt water in five minutes as would have pickled a side of bacon."

As soon as they were alone, Sir Osborne attempted to comfort the unhappy clothier as far as he could, assuring him that he had nothing to fear, for that he was not in the least the object of the attack, which had only comprised him, on account of his being present at the time.

"But my bags! my bags!" blubbered Jekin Groby; "they've got my bags—Four hundred and twelve golden angels, and a pair of excellent shears, oh! oh! oh! I know it's along of you that I've got into the scrape. Oh, dear! oh, dear! Why the devil didn't you tell me you had made the Cornish men revolt, then I wouldn't have gone with you; I'd ha' seen you damned first. But I'll tell King Henry and Lord Darby, I will— and I'll have back my angels, I will—Lord! Lord! to think of my being committed for aiding and abetting Osborne Maurice, alias Osborne Darling, alias Jenkins, alias Thompson, alias Brown, alias Smith, to make the Cornish folks revolt—I that was never there in my life."

"Nor I either," said the knight, calmly.

"Why they all swear you were!" cried Jekin Groby, leaving off weeping, "and that you and five hundred miners burnt and sacked the towns, and I believe carried away the steeples on your back, for a matter of that, you did so much. They all swear it."

"And they all swear falsely," answered Sir Osborne, "as you may very well see, when they swear that you were there aiding and abetting me."

"Gads! that's true too," said Groby: "if they swear such big lies about me, why mayn't they do the like about you? I thought that nice young lady, and that goodly old priest, would not ha' been so fond of your worship if you had been a robber and an insurrectionist. Lord a' mercy! I beg your worship's pardon with all my heart." As Groby lost sight of the subject of his bags, his grief abated, and looking round the room, he added,

"I say, Sir Knight, is there no way of getting out of this place? What think ye o' that window?"

"If I had my hands free," said Sir Osborne, "I would try to climb up and see."

"Gads man! let's see your hands," said Groby "mine are tied too, but I've managed many a tight knot with my teeth. Turn round, your worship—more to the light, such as it is—Ah, here I have it, the leading cord—now pull—well done, millstones! It gives!" and what by dint of gnawing and pulling, in about five minutes Jekin Groby contrived to loosen the cord that fastened the knight's arms, and a very slight effort on Sir Osborne's part finished the work, and freed them completely. The knight then performed the same good office to his fellow-prisoner, and poor Jekin, overjoyed even at this partial liberation, jumped and sang with delight. "Hist! hist!" cried he at length, "if I remember, that long rascal of a fellow did not lock the door: let us see.—No, as I live, the bolt's not shot!—let us steal out,—but first I'll look through the keyhole. Out upon it, there he sits, talking to two of his fellows; ay, and there's a latch too on the outside of this cursed door, with no way to lift it?

"The window is the surest way," said the knight, "if I can but reach it. Lend me your back, good Master Groby, and I will see.—The sun shines strong through it, and yet I cannot perceive that it throws the shadow of any bar or grating."

"Welcome to my back," said the clothier; "but oh, do not leave me in this place, pray don't ye, Sir Knight."

"On my honor I will not," replied the knight, "though it is not you they care to keep. Once I were away, you might have your liberty the next hour. But still I will not leave you."

"Thank you, Sir Knight, thank you," said honest Jekin; "all I ask is, when you are up, help me up too: and if we can get out, leave me as soon as you like, for the less we are together, I take it, the better for Jekin Groby.—And now up on my back; it is a stout one."

Jekin now bent his head against the wall, making a kind of step with his two clasped hands, by means of

which Sir Osborne easily got his elbows on the deep
opening of the window, which, from the thickness of
the wall, offered a platform three feet wide, and with an
effort he swung himself up. "Clear, all clear!" cried
he, joyfully: "and now, my good Jekin, let us see how
we can get you up.—Stay, let me kneel here," and turning round, he knelt down, holding out his hands to Jekin
Groby. But it was in vain that Sir Osborne, with all
his vast strength, strove to pull up the ponderous body
of the Kentish clothier. He succeeded, indeed, in raising
him about a foot from the ground, and holding him there,
while he made a variety of kicks against the wall, and
sundry other efforts to help himself up, all equally ineffectual; but at length Sir Osborne was obliged to let
him down, and still remained gazing upon him with a
sorrowful countenance, feeling both the impossibility,
with any degree of honor, to leave him behind, and the
impracticability of getting him out.

Poor Jekin, well understanding the knight's feeling,
returned his glance with one equally melancholy; and,
after remaining for a moment in profound silence, he
made a vast effort of generosity, that again unloosed the
flood-gates of his tears, in the midst of which he blubbered forth, "Go, Sir Knight, go, and God speed you.
Heaven forbid that I should keep you here! Go!"

Sir Osborne jumped down, and shook him by the hand.
"Never!" said he, "never! But there seems still some
hope for us. That tall fellow, that we called Longpole
this morning, is more friendly to us than he seems. And
I can tell him something that will perhaps make him
serve us more completely, if he will but hear me. Let
me see whether he is now alone." And by the same
means that Jekin Groby had before used to ascertain that
the man was there, Sir Osborne discovered that the two
other servants had left him, and that he was alone. "Hist!
Richard Heartley!" said Sir Osborne, putting his mouth
to the key-hole, "hist!"

" Who calls?" cried Longpole, starting up.

" 'Tis I," said Sir Osborne, " open the door and speak to me."

" I dare not! I must not!" cried Longpole. " Have patience!" he whispered, " Have patience! I will come to you after dark."

" Yet listen to me," said Sir Osborne, but at that moment a sound of horses' feet was again heard through the open window, and, unwillingly, he was obliged to desist.

The arrival of some guest now took place, as Sir Osborne judged by the sounds which made themselves heard. The inquiries for Sir Payan, the directions for tending the horses, and the orders to have them at the gate in an hour, the marshalling to the banquet-hall, the cries of the serving men, and all the fracas that was made, in that day, in honor of a visitor.

" By heaven!" said Sir Osborne, " it is Lady Constance de Grey. I remember she purposed coming here towards noon. If we could but let her know that we are here, or good old Dr. Wilbraham, her people would soon free us. But never does it fall better. Longpole has gone from his watch, or he might tell her. However, the door is only held by this latch; let us try to force it. Place your shoulder with mine, good Groby. Now a strong effort." But in vain. The giant door stood unmoved, and Sir Osborne was obliged to resign himself to his fate.

Presently the noise of serving the repast in the chief hall died away, and the servants retiring to their own part of the house, left the rest in quiet, while not a sound stirred to communicate to the bosoms of the prisoners any sensation either of hope or expectation. After about a quarter of an hour's pause, however, a door opened, and the voice of Lady Constance was heard speaking to Dr. Wilbraham.

" Nay, my good father," she said, " do not go yourself to seek them. Though we have been treated with but little courtesy, yet we may stay a quarter of an hour longer. Perhaps the servants have not dined, and that is the reason they do not come."

"By your leave, lady, I will go," said the chaplain, "and will see that the horses be brought up; for to my poor mind we have stayed here too long already for the civility we have received. I will not be long."

"Dr. Wilbraham!" cried Sir Osborne, as the door shut—"Doctor Wilbraham!" But the good tutor turning another way, passed on without hearing the voice of his former pupil, and silence resumed her dominion over the part of the house in which they were placed. In a minute or two after, however, a heavy foot announced to the watchful ears of the young knight the approach of some other person, but he turned away towards the hall where Lady Constance had been left, and seemed to enter.

Shortly the voice of the lady made itself heard, speaking high and angrily, in a tone to which the lips of Constance de Grey seldom gave utterance.

"I do not understand what you mean, sir," said she, coming out of the hall. "Where are my servants? Where is Dr. Wilbraham?"

"That was not your way, my pretty lady," cried the voice of the Portuguese captain. "Let me kiss your loafly hand, and I will show you the way."

"Stand off, sir!" exclaimed Lady Constance. "Dare you insult me in my cousin's house?"

"This way! this way! Lady Constance de Grey," cried Sir Osborne, in a voice that shook the hall. "This way there are friends. Throw up the latch."

At that moment the unscrupulous Portuguese seems to have offered some still greater insult to the young lady, for, with a scream, she darted towards the spot to which the voice of Sir Osborne directed her, and throwing up the latch, as he called to her to do, ran in, followed close by the Portuguese. Urged by fear, Lady Constance

Sir Osborne raised his arm, and in a moment laid the Portuguese
grovelling on the ground.   Page 61.

Darnley.

flew directly to the knight, and, recognizing a friend, clung to him for protection. The captain, not observing that his hands were freed, did not scruple to pursue her, even close to the side of the prisoner, calling to her not to be afraid, that he would show her the way. But Sir Osborne raised his arm, and in a moment laid the Portuguese grovelling on the ground, with the blood gushing from his mouth and nostrils.

Lady Constance still clung to the knight, who, totally forgetting the possibility of escape, endeavored to soothe her, and calm her agitation. Not so Jekin Groby; after pausing for a moment, confounded by the whole business, he at length bethought him, that as the door was open he might as well walk out, and with this intent made a quick step or two towards it. His purpose, however, was defeated by the Portuguese who recovered from the blow, and perceiving the design of the clothier, started upon his feet, and jumping through the open door, banged it in the face of honest Jekin, at the same time making the whole house ring with his cries of "Help! help! The lady is letting out the prisoners, and they shall all get loose. Help! help!" and getting hold of the rope of the alarm, he rung such a peal as soon brought the whole household, together with the servants of the Lady Constance, round the door of the strong room.

Various were now the cries and exclamations. "What's the matter?" "Are they out?" "Which way did they go?" "Where's the lady?" "Oh, Lord!" "Oh, lauk!" "Oh, dear!" "Dear me!" "How strange!" "Who'd have thought it?" While the Portuguese, with his face all streaming with blood, explained to them that Lady Constance wished to let the prisoners out, and that he, notwithstanding their efforts, had shut them up all together, by the valor of his invincible arm, and he called his bloody muzzle to bear testimony to the truth of his asseveration.

"You lie, you vagabond thief!" cried one of the young

lady's servants. "It was you stole my riding whip, when you ran away in such a hurry from the inn last night."

"You must make a great mistake, my friend," said Dr. Wilbraham, who had come up amongst the rest; "Lady Constance de Grey has too much respect for the law to assist any prisoners to escape from the house of a magistrate. Let me in here, and we shall soon hear the truth of all this."

"And let me in!" "And let me in!" "And let me in too!" cried a dozen voices, and all prepared to rush into the room, the moment any one raised the latch, on which Longpole had his hand for the purpose.

"Devil a one of you!" cried Longpole. "Curiosity, I've heard say, was one of the great vices of the old gentlewoman of Babylon, and so certainly I shall not gratify yours. March, every one; for his worship when he went away, gave me charge of the prisoners, and I am to answer for them when he comes back. The only one that goes with me shall be his reverence, who, God bless him, taught me to read and write, and speak French, when I was little Dick Heartley, the porter's son at the old castle."

"And art thou little Dick Heartley?" exclaimed Doctor Wilbraham. "We are both changed, Dick; but open me the door, good Dick, for by that Portuguese's speech, I fancy the young lady is here also, with the prisoners, though I conceive not how."

Heartley accordingly opened the door, sufficiently to allow the clergyman to pass, and then following, he shut it, taking care to put his dagger under the latch, to prevent its obstructing his exit, in case of the servants leaving the spot during his stay.

At first the change from a bright light to comparative obscurity prevented the good tutor from distinguishing clearly the objects in the apartment to which he was admitted by Longpole; but who can express his astonishment when he beheld Sir Osborne? Forgetting Lady

Constance and every other circumstance, he clasped his hands in a sort of agony.

"Good God!" exclaimed he, "is it possible? You here! You, my lord, in the power of your bitterest enemy? Oh! Osborne, Osborne! what can be done to save you? And is it you?" cried he, raising his voice, and turning to Longpole, in a tone of bitter reproach; "and is it you, Richard Heartley, that do the work of gaoler upon your own born lord and only lawful master?"

"My born lord!" cried Heartley, springing forward; "what does your reverence mean? Who is he? They told me his name was Maurice—Osborne Maurice."

"Osborne Darnley, they should have said," replied the young knight. "Your old lord's son, Dick Heartley."

Heartley threw himself at his lord's feet. "Why did not you tell me? Why did not you tell me?" cried he. "I'd sooner have chopped my hand off. I that first taught you to draw a bow and level an arrow. I that sought you all through the camp at Terrouenne to be your servant and servitor, as in duty bound, only that you were away guarding the fort bridge on the Lambre. Cut my hand off! I'd rather have ripped myself up with my dagger."

It may be supposed that the surprise of Lady Constance and of Jekin Groby was somewhat analogous to that expressed by Longpole on finding that the person they had known only as Osborne Maurice, or at best as Sir Osborne Maurice, an adventurous soldier, whose necessitous courage had obtained for him the honor of knighthood, was in fact the young Lord Darnley, whose misfortunes and accomplishments had already furnished much employment for the busy tongue of fame. To the young lady, especially, this discovery gave a sensation of timid shame, for the interest she had so unguardedly displayed in his fate—an interest which nevertheless she might perhaps feel heightened when she found all that she had heard of Lord Darnley identified with all that she knew of Osborne Maurice.

"I, too, may ask, my lord," she said, "why you did not tell me—or rather, why you did not tell my father, who ever expressed the deepest interest in your fate, and in his lifetime might have served you?"

"Your noble father, lady," replied Lord Darnley, "was well aware who I was, even when I was a guest at his mansion, and he, as well as the rest of my friends, thought it best that I should still conceal my name while in England, in order to veil me from the machinations of a man, whose unaccountable interest at court, and unscrupulous nature, were almost certain to carry through whatever villainous attempt he undertook against me. Our lands and lordships he holds not as we did, by chivalry and tenure of possession, but only as steward of Dover Castle, an office given and recallable at pleasure. You now see how wise was the precaution, since here, in the midst of the most civilized country in Europe, I have been unlawfully seized, on the king's highway—accused of fictitious crimes, and destined to a fate that only time will show—to think that I, a man at arms, long used to camps, and without boasting, no bad soldier either, should be like an infant in the hands of this deep-plotting usurper! 'Tis enough to drive me mad!"

"No, no, my lord," said Heartley, or, as we have called him, Longpole, "don't you fear. They say that when Old Nick stirs the fire, he is sure to burn his fingers, and when he salts a birch broom he pickles a rod for his own back. But stay, let me see that there is no one at the door listening—no, there they are, at the farther end of the hall, but they can't hear. So, my lord, I'll undertake to get you out this blessed night. My oath to Sir Payan is up at twelve o'clock to-night."

"No oath can bind you to commit a crime," said the clergyman, "and that it is a crime to aid in any way in detaining your lord here, can easily be proved."

"Oh! your worship," said Heartley, "I can't reason the matter with your reverence, you'd pose me in a minute; but, nevertheless, I'll keep my oath, and I can give you a good reason for it—it would do my lord no good if I was to break it—there are twenty people round about, that would all join to stop him if I were to let him out this moment, and with my young lady's three servants to boot, we should still be beaten by the numbers. We must wait till after dark; ay, and till after the bell rings to bed at eleven, but then I will find means to free my lord."

"But may they not have thus time to commit some evil deed?" demanded Lady Constance, "and your tardy succor may come too late."

"No, no! my lady," replied Longpole, "I heard yon Portuguese, who is just riding away, tell his rascally slavish crew, as he was locking them up in the granary, that at half-past one he was to be back; and then they were to carry down the two prisoners to the ship, for which they were to have two hundred gold angels amongst them. Now we shall be far enough before half-past one."

"At all events, my lord," said Lady Constance, "it will not be long before we are at Canterbury, from whence we can send you sufficient succor, backed with authority, competent to procure your release."

"But remember, lady," said the knight, "that I am but Sir Osborne Maurice, and no one must know me as anything else if it can be avoided, for it is of the utmost consequence to my interest, that at present I should not appear before our noble, but somewhat wayward, king, as I really am. And now, let me return you a thousand and a thousand thanks for your kind interest, past and present; to which, but add one favor. When I am free give me but one little glove from this fair hand,"—and he raised it to his lips—" and I will place it on my pennon's pike, and write underneath it, gratitude; and if it falls in the listed field, or the battle plain, Darnley is dead."

5

"Nay, nay, my lord," replied Lady Constance, with a blush and smile, "too gallant by half! But you are a prisoner, and I believe promises made in prison are not held valid. Wait, therefore, till you are free, and in the meantime you shall have my prayers and best wishes, and such aid as I can send you from Canterbury, I will."

There is a witchery in the sympathy of a beautiful woman, whose influence all men must have experienced, and all women understand; and though our hero felt the most devout conviction that he was not the least in love in the world with Lady Constance de Grey, there is no knowing how far his gratitude for the interest she took in his fate, might have carried him, had she remained there much longer; and even when she left him, and he heard the horses' feet repass the window of his prison, he felt as if he were ten times more a prisoner than before.

At the same time that Lady Constance departed, our friend Longpole also left the prisoners, promising however to see them from time to time during the day, and to find means of liberating them at night. In this arrangement Jekin Groby took care to be specially included, and trusting implicitly to the promises of Dick Heartley on the score of his freedom, his only further consideration was concerning his bags.

"Don't you think, my lord," said he, after waiting a moment or two in order to see whether Lord Darnley would finish his meditative perambulations, "don't you think King Harry will make this Sir Payan, or Sir Pagan as they ought to call him, refund my angels? Eh, my lord?"

"If there be justice in the land," replied Darnley; "but mark me, good Jekin, you call me my lord. You have heard me say that it may be of the utmost detriment to my interest if I be known as Lord Darnley. Circumstances have put you in possession of my secret, but if you would pleasure me—if you would not injure me, forget from this moment that I am any other than Sir Osborne Maurice; call me by no other title, think of me under no other name."

"No, indeed, my lord," said Jekin, "I promise your lordship never to call you my lord again—I won't indeed, my lord—lord! lord! There, only see, my lord, I have called you my lord again. Well, it does come so natural to one, when one knows that you are my lord, to call you my lord—What a fool I am! But your lordship will forgive me—and so I'll go and sleep in that straw in the closet, and forget it all, for I shan't get my natural rest to-night that's clear.

So saying, Jekin nestled himself in the straw which had attracted his attention, and shutting the door to exclude all light, he was soon buried in a profound sleep, while Sir Osborne (which, according to his wish, we shall not cease to call him) continued his meditations, walking up and down, as if on guard at some dangerous post.

CHAPTER V.

'This is a devil and no monster : I will leave him; I have no long spoon.'

THE TEMPEST.

SIR PAYAN WILETON knew not what happiness is. He had drank the intoxicating bowl of pleasure, he had drained the boiling draught of revenge; pride, avarice, vanity, had all been gratified in turn; but peace he had never sought, content he had never found, and vengeful passions, like the Promethean vulture, preyed upon him for ever. Possessed of the vast estates of Chilham Castle, joined to those he also held of Elham Manor and Hyndesford, his wealth had been fully sufficient to create for him that interest amongst the powerful of the land which he could not hope to obtain by virtues or qualities. Thus powerful, rich, and full of desperate fearlessness, he was dreaded, detested, courted, and obeyed. He felt, too, that he was detested, and hating mankind the more he became the tyrant of the country round. Seeking to govern by fear instead of esteem, he made his misanthropy subservient to his pride and to his avarice; and wherever he received, or pretended an offence, there he was sure both to avenge and to enrich himself. Thus his life was a continual warfare, and in this active misanthropy he took as much delight as his heart was capable of feeling. It was to him what ardent spirits are to the drunkard, or the dice-box to the gambler.

But there was one constant thorn that goaded him, even in the midst of the success that attended his other schemes; namely, the fear that the king might deprive him of the stewardship of Dover Castle, by which alone

he held the estates of Chilham. In vain he had used all
the influence he possessed to have the grant made absolute, or to hold his land by sergeantry, as it had been
held by Lord Fitzbernard; the king was inexorable, and
imagined that he did equal justice when he refused to restore the estates to the forfeited family, or to grant
the feof thereof to Sir Payan. Indeed, it had been held
by cunning lawyers of the day, that Lord Fitzbernard
could not lawfully be dispossessed, except under an attainder, which had never been attempted against him;
and that if it could be proved that the estates had not
reverted to the crown by any default of tenure, or by extinction, Sir Payan's right would fall to the ground; and
that the only effect of the king's patent of the stewardry
of Dover, would be to alienate that office from the family
holding the estates.

Sir Payan was too wise to moot the question, and Lord
Fitzbernard, hiding his indigence in a far part of Wales,
had neither the means nor opportunity of succeeding in
a suit against him. The few friends, indeed, that the test
of misfortune had left the earl out of many acquaintances,
strongly urged the king to revoke the grant which his
father had made to a bad man, and to restore the property to a good one; but they never ventured to hint to the
choleric king that the grant itself was illegal.

However, Sir Payan had long foreseen that a time
would come when the young heir of Chilham Castle
might wrench his heritage from the hand that usurped
it, and he resolved, at all hazards, to strike where the
blow would be most effectual. Several painful indigni-
ties had induced the aged Earl of Fitzbernard to drop
a title and a name, to the splendor of which his means
no longer were proportioned; and burying himself in a
far part of Wales, he devoted his whole time to endow-
ing his son with both those elegant and warlike accomplishments, which he fondly hoped would one day prove
the means of reinstating his family in the halls of their

ancestors. " Fulbert de Douvres," he said, " the founder
of our family in England, won the lands and lordships
of Chilham at the point of his lance, and why should not
Osborne Darnley, the only descendant of Rose de Douvres, his daughter, regain his patrimony by his good
sword?"

Happily, his very poverty had removed the old earl
from any county where the influence of Sir Payan Wileton might be felt, or where his machinations could be
carried on successfully. Yet more than one attempt had
been made to carry off the young heir of Chilham Castle,
and little doubt could be entertained in regard to whose
hand had directed them. All, however, had been frus-
trated by the extraordinary foresight with which the old
earl guarded his son, seeming to have an intuitive knowledge of the time when any such attack was likely to take
place, and to be always prepared to avoid or repel it.

At length, however, the time came, when the young
Osborne Maurice (as he was now called) was to encounter alone all that his enemies could do against him;
but it seemed as if his father had now lost all fear, and
bidding him resume his real name when he joined the
army, he sent him forth unhesitatingly to win renown.
How he acquitted himself, we have in some measure seen,
and will now proceed with the circumstances that followed immediately upon his return to his native country,
after five years of arduous military service.

The bosom of Sir Payan Wileton, during his absence
from the house where he had left his prisoner, was agitated by a thousand various passions. Triumph,—malice,—pride,—fear that he might yet, by some unforeseen
circumstance, escape from his hands,—newer and vaster
projects of ambition, still as he made one step sure, seeking to place another still higher,—the feeling of a difficult enterprise accomplished,—the heart-steeling preparation for a fresh crime and mingled still withal an
unwonted thrilling of remorse, that, like sounds of music

amidst cries of riot and tumult, made discord more dis-
cordant,—all occupied the void place of thought, and
made him gallop quickly on.

Thus he proceeded for some way, but when he had
ridden on for such a space as he computed that Lady
Constance would remain at his dwelling, he turned his
horse, and prepared to return home, having by this time
striven to remove from his face all trace of any emotion,
and having also, in some degree, reduced his feelings to
their usual still, determined action.

As he returned, he checked the speed with which he
had set out, and was proceeding leisurely on the road,
when he heard the cantering of a horse coming up behind, and, turning round, perceived the somewhat curious figure of Sir Cesar the astrologer. It was one, however, well known to Sir Payan, who, (as too often is the
case) was destitute of religion, but by no means eman-
cipated from superstition, and who, while he rejected the
light of revelation, could not refrain from often yielding
to the wild gleams of a dark imagination.

In the still agitated state of his mind, too, when a sort
of feverish excitement stimulated him to seek from any
source of knowledge, what would be the future consequences of his meditated actions, he looked upon the coming of Sir Cesar as a benefit at the hands of fortune, and
prepared to take advantage of it.

Doffing low, therefore, his plumed hat as the old knight
rode up, and bowing almost to his saddle-bow, " Welcome,
worthy Sir Cesar," he said, " any news from your splendid
friend his grace of Buckingham? "

Sir Cesar touched his palfrey between the ears with his
small baton to make it slacken its pace, and then, after
regarding Sir Payan with his keen dark eyes, as was
usual with him on first encountering any one he knew,
he replied, " Welcome, fortunate Sir Payan Wileton.
Your star is in the ascendant! " and, while he spoke there
was a sort of cynical sneer on his countenance, which

seemed hardly to wish well to him that he congratulated.

"It is?" replied Sir Payan: "but condescend, good Sir Cesar, to ride to my dwelling and pass one day with me, and I will tell you more."

"What can you tell me that I do not know already?" demanded the other. "Do you think I know not how much you merited from fortune, by your deeds when Perkyn Warbeck fled from Taunton? Do you think I know not that your enemy is in your power.—I do, I do: and as I love the fortunate, I will come and stay one day at your house, though you know I tarry nowhere long."

"I know it well, and hold your sojourn the more honor," answered Sir Payan: "but let us on, good Sir Cesar, there is much information which I will seek at your hands, and I know that you never refuse to give it when it is asked for no idle purpose."

"No," replied the astrologer; "every man who seeks knowledge from me shall find it, were he worse than Satan himself; but woe be unto him if he turns it to an evil account—the deeper damnation be upon his head!"

Putting their horses into a quick pace, they now soon reached the manor-house, the owner of which showed his guest with some ceremony into the banquet-hall. "How now!" cried he, observing the repast which had been set before Lady Constance still upon the table; "why have not these things been removed? and where is Heartley?"

The answer involved a long account of what had happened during his absence, in which the story of the Portuguese having frightened Lady Constance till she fled into the strong-room, was told with a greater degree of accuracy than might have been expected, though the length of time which she remained there was rather exaggerated, and some comments upon the conduct of Heartley, otherwise Longpole, were added, calculated to take from him Sir Payan's confidence. He had prevented every one from going in, the servant said, but himself, and had remained all the time the lady was there.

"He did right," was the laconic reply of Sir Payan; " go to the granary, where are the Portuguese and their contraband goods, and bid the red-haired Dutchman who speaks English to come hither directly. The key hangs on the nail in the passage."

Sir Payan's plan was formed at once. He doubted not that the communication which had taken place between his prisoner and Lady Constance would lead to her seeking means to effect his liberation the moment she arrived at Canterbury, or at least to set on foot some investigation; for although he knew not that they had ever met before, he left sure that the young knight would make his situation known to every one who might in any way procure his release. Under this conviction, he determined to risk the event of sending down Sir Osborne by daylight, in the custody of the Portuguese, accompanied by two of his own servants, who might, in case of necessity, produce the warrant for his detention, and who would not be missed from his own household.

The servant whom he had sent to the Portuguese, however, soon returned, with a countenance in which might be seen a strong desire to laugh, contending with an habitual dread of Sir Payan. "What is the matter, villain?" cried the knight. "Where is the Dutchman?"

"Lying in the granary, please your worship," replied the man, restraining his merriment, "dead drunk, tumbled across a Portuguese's face, that makes him heave up and down by dint of snoring."

Sir Payan stamped his foot with anger and disappointment. "And the rest," demanded he; "all the rest?"

"All dead drunk, please your worship!" replied the servant; "I kicked them all, to make sure, but not one of them answered me a syllable but, umph!"

"Go!" said Sir Payan, "fetch me Heartley. Sir Cesar,

give me your advice. This is my embarrassment," and he proceeded to state to his companion the difficulty into which the news he had just heard had cast him.

This proceeding may appear at first somewhat extraordinary, but it was very often the case in regard to Sir Cesar, that people acted as Sir Payan Wileton, in letting him into their most private affairs, and even into secrets where life and death were concerned, having such perfect confidence in his foreknowledge of events, that it would have seemed to them folly to conceal them.

It was not, however, the nature of Sir Payan Wileton to confide wholly in any one, and though he informed the old knight that he apprehended the influence of Lady Constance de Grey might be exerted the moment she arrived at Canterbury to procure the release of his prisoner, or at all events that her representations might cause an immediate investigation of the affair, which would prevent his disposing of Darnley as he proposed; and though also perfectly convinced that Sir Cesar, by his superhuman knowledge, was well aware of the fate he meditated for his victim, he could not bring himself to unfold to him that part of his plan, merely saying he intended to send the turbulent youth, who, as he was well informed, came to seek no less than his ruin and his death, to some far country from whence it would be difficult to return.

Sir Cesar listened in calm, profound silence, then fixing his eyes on Sir Payan, uttered slowly, " The grave! "

Sir Payan started from his seat.

" You know too much! you know too much! " cried he. " Can you see thoughts as well as actions? "

" Yes! " replied Sir Cesar; " I see and know more than you dream of; but calm yourself, and fear not. Lady Constance will not arrive at Canterbury before seven o' the clock: you know the haste of magistrates and magistrates' men, and can well judge whether she be likely to find a man so generous as to abandon his supper and

his bed of down, for a cold ride and a cold reception. At
all events, they could not be here before two i' the morning, and ere that he will be gone. Rest satisfied, I tell
you, that they may come if they will, but before they
come he will be gone."

Sir Payan's fears were very much allayed by this assurance, for his confidence in Sir Cesar's prophecies was
great, but he felt still more secure from the examination
to which he subjected our friend Longpole, who managed to evade his questions, and to quiet his fears, with
infinite presence of mind. The lady, he said, had been
so terrified by the insolence of the Portuguese captain,
that she had run into the strong-room, not knowing
where she went, and was more like one dead than alive;
and that as for the prisoner, he thought of nothing but
thrashing the Portuguese, against whom he seemed to
have an ancient grudge.

Sir Payan was satisfied, but still his roused suspicion
was never without some effect, and to Longpole's dismay
he demanded the key, which he said he would now keep
himself. There was, however, no means of avoiding it,
and Heartley was obliged to resign into the hands of Sir
Payan the means by which he had proposed to effect his
young lord's delivery.

"Sir Cesar, I humbly crave your excuse for one moment," said the crafty knight. "Stay, Heartley, where
you are, and removing those things, arrange the board
for a second banquet—for a banquet such as I give to my
best and noblest friends. Open those cupboards of plate,
and let the vessels be placed in order."

So saying, he quitted the apartment, and proceeded to
the room in which Sir Osborne was still pacing up and
down, waiting impatiently the approach of night. The
key turned in the door, and with a firm step Sir Payan
entered, and stood before his captive. For a moment
they paused, and eyed each other as when they had first
met, and it was only by a strong effort that the young

knight stayed himself from seizing the persecutor of his race, and dashing him to pieces on the floor of the prison.

At length Sir Payan, after having glanced his eye round the chamber, spoke, and in the deep hollow tones of his voice no agitation made itself heard.

"You said this morning that we knew each other," said the knight—" Osborne Lord Darnley, we do—I have long sought you—I have found you, and you are mine own."

"Calm, cold-blooded, mean-spirited villain!" answered Darnley, "what seek you with me now? Is it not enough to have ruined a noble house?—Is it not enough to have destroyed your benefactor?—Is it not enough to have swept away the happiness of me and mine, without seeking further to injure those on whose head your detestable arts must already have exhausted themselves?"

"I have done enough for my revenge, young man," replied Sir Payan; "I have done enough for my ambition—but I have not done enough for my security."

"For your revenge!" cried Darnley: "what mean you, ruffian? My father was your friend—your benefactor. Compassionating your indigence, did he not aid to raise you with his purse and with his influence, till you could hold your head amongst your noble kindred, of whose house you are now the shame?"

"Your father insulted me with his services," answered the knight, "after your mother had insulted me with her scorn."

"Name not my mother, traitor!" exclaimed Darnley, his eyes flashing fire. "Profane not her name with your accursed lips, lest I tear you limb from limb."

Sir Payan laid his hand on his dagger with a grim smile. "We waste time, young man," said he: "to the purpose for which I came. There is yet in my redder blood some drops of that weak thing called pity. I would rather see you live than die; but if you would live, I must be lord of Chilham Castle indeed, and indeed. No stewardship of Dover and holding by tenure of good pleasure for me. Within this hour, then, sign me over for yourself and for your father all right and interest, claim and title, to the lands and lordship, which you and yours did formerly possess, and you are free as air. But if you will not——"

"What then?" demanded Darnley.

"Why, then, I will hold by a still better tenure," replied Sir Payan—"the extinction of the race of Darnley!"

"Then hold by it, if such be Heaven's will," replied the prisoner. "But beware yourself, for in your best-laid schemes you may chance to fail, and even here on earth meet with that sure damnation for which you have toiled so long. Were I willing to stain myself with crimes like yours, this hour were your last, for yon dagger were but a poor defence against a man who knows his life is lost."

Sir Payan took a step backward to the door. "Will you sign?" said he, laying his hand on the lock.

"Never!"

"Then farewell!" and he quitted the apartment.

"Oh, the villain!" cried Jekin Groby, poking his head out of the closet. "Oh, the downright immense villain! What a damaged piece that man's conscience must be! I'm all quaking with only hearing him. But don't you think, my lord—that is to say, Sir Osborne, that if you had just knocked his brains out, we might have got away?"

"Oh, no!" replied the knight. "If, as Longpole told us, we could not have escaped when aided by Lady Constance de Grey's servants, much less could we do so now. Better wait till night, which surely cannot be far distant, for it seems to me we have been here an age."

Nevertheless, hour after hour went by, and the provoking sun, which had now fully come round to that side

of the house, continued to pour his beams into the high
window, as if willing to sicken the prisoners with his un-
wished-for light. Nor did much conversation cheer the
passing of their time. Sir Osborne was silent and meditative, and Jekin Groby, growing more and more tired of
his situation, kept running in and out of the closet, now
sitting still for a moment upon the straw, now walking up
and down, not at all unlike a tame bear in his den.

Occasionally, indeed, a word or two of hope, or doubt,
or inquiry, passed between the prisoners; and Jekin, who
felt in himself an internal conviction that he was a man
of as much consequence in the world as any human being,
could not conceive how Sir Payan Wileton could have
forgot to inquire where he was, when he did not find him
in the same room with the knight. On this he wondered,
and better wondered, till his companion replied, " I told
you before, my good Jekin, Sir Payan's designs only
affect me, and possibly he may have forgotten you altogether. But it seems growing darker. I wonder
Longpole has not been here to speak to us, according to
his promise."

" I should not wonder if he were playing us a trick,
and were not to come at all," said Jekin. " Oh, dear!
What would become of us? Lord 'a mercy, I don't like
it at all! "

In about a quarter of an hour, however, their hopes
were raised and disappointed. The key once more
turned in the door, and both the knight and his companion expected to see their friend Heartley, but in his
place appeared two of the servants of Sir Payan, one of
whom brought in some provisions, while the other stood
at the door. The sight, however, of the roast beef and
jug of ale was very gratifying to the entrails of the
worthy clothier, who looked on well contented while the
man laid them down on the ground before him.

" Now, my good fellow, an we had a little salt," said
Jekin, " we could fall to."

" Fellow me no fellows," answered the servant. " Eat what you've got, my forward chap, and thank God for it."

" Ay, but would'st have me tear it with my teeth?" cried the clothier. " I'm not a wild beast, though you do keep me in a den."

" Well, I will cut you a muncheon* with my dagger," replied the serving-man. " Look to him, Will, that he do not smite me while I kneel," and so saying, he stooped and cut several slices from the meat with his side knife, which being done, he rose, and left the strong room quickly, as if almost afraid of its denizens.

" Now, sir," cried Jekin, " come and keep your spirit up with some of the best comfort in nature. Oh, to my mind, there is no consolation on earth like roast beef and ale."

But Sir Osborne had no inclination to join in the good clothier's repast. The auguries which he drew from the appearance of these two strange serving men, and the absence of Longpole, were not of a nature to increase his appetite, and he looked on silently, while Jekin, without any sacrifice to the gods, devoured great part of the beef, and made manifold libations of the ale.

" Jekin," said Sir Osborne, when the clothier had finished, " I am afraid Sir Payan Wileton has discovered that our friend Heartley is not quite cordial to his interests, and that he may take means to prevent his aiding us. Now, there is no reason that you should stay here as well as I, therefore, as soon as it is dark, I will help you up to the window as you did me. Drop down on the other side; and speed as fast as you can to any town where you are well known, there get together a body of a dozen horsemen, and scour the sea-coast from Sandwich to Hythe. Wherever you hear of a Portuguese vessel, there stop, and keep good watch, for I doubt not

* Muncheon—Something to eat—to munch on. *Ed.*

that this Sir Payan intends to send me to some far land, and perhaps sell me for a slave—kill me I do not think he dare. Your pains shall be well paid. The night is coming on, so you had better mount first, and see the ground on the other side, that you may drop fair."

"No, no, my lord—that is, Sir Osborne," said Jekin: "dang it, no! you would not go away and leave me, so I'll not go away and leave you. Lord 'a mercy! that's not fair any way."

"But by going you can serve me far more than by staying," said Sir Osborne; "so try to mount on my shoulders that you may see the ground."

It was with great difficulty, however, that the honest clothier was persuaded to make the attempt, and when he did so, it was in vain. Somewhat corpulent and shorter than the knight, even when standing upright on Sir Osborne's shoulders, he could hardly get as much of his arms over the opening as the other had done.

No resource therefore remained but to wait patiently the event, and much need of patience had they to support them. Day waned, night fell, hour after hour passed by, and yet no sound gave them notice that any friendly being existed within the mansion. The curfew-bell, the distant village clock, the barking of some watchful dogs in the hamlet, and the remote echoes of persons passing to and fro in the different halls, were all that marked the passing of time to the prisoners: and hope began gradually to wax dimmer and more dim, like the flame of a lamp whose oil is out. At length, after a weary silent pause, the clock was heard to strike again; but so faint were the sounds before they reached their ears, that Sir Osborne could hardly count them. "I counted but eleven," said he, "and yet methought the last hour that struck it was eleven too."

"Oh, 'tis twelve, 'tis twelve!" replied Groby; "I did not take heed to count, but I am sure it is twelve."

"Hush!" cried the knight, "I hear some one on the outside. Hark!"

"'Tis but a bat," said Jekin; "I heard its wings whirl past the window."

"Hush!" cried the knight again, and as he spoke, something darted through the opening and fell at his feet. Feeling over the ground with his hands, he soon discovered the object of his search, which was a small roll of parchment, "It is a letter," said he, "but what is the use of throwing me what I cannot see to read? It must be for to-morrow morning."

"Open it! open it!" cried Jekin; "methinks I see something shining through the end. It casts a light upon your hand."

Sir Osborne rapidly unrolled the scroll, when to his joy and surprise he found it covered with large luminous characters, in which, though somewhat smeared by rolling the parchment, was written legibly, "Pull up the rope gently that is cast through the window. Catch the settle that is tied to it. Make no noise. Come out, and be speedy."

"Oons!" cried Jekin, "this is magic. The fairies are our friends."

"Oh! brave Heartley," cried the knight, "I thought he would prove true. But let us lose no time. Jekin stand you under with me, and extend your arms, that the settle may not make a noise by falling."

By searching along the wall the rope was found, and by pulling it gently the knight soon began to feel a weight at the farther end. For some way it ascended silently, as if a person without held it from the wall, but then, when it had been raised about six or seven feet, it grated desperately till it entered the opening in the wall, which by courtesy we have termed window. The cord had been so adjusted as to insure its entrance; and as soon as Sir Osborne was certain that it had passed sufficiently, and hung upon the very brink, he gave it a sudden jerk,

6

and, catching it with a strong hand as it fell, secured possession of the tall settle or hall stool with scarcely any noise.

"Now, good Jekin," said he, "we are free. I will mount first, and then help you up; but, standing on this settle, and pulled by me above, you will not have much difficulty."

"Oh, no! I warrant you, your worship," replied Jekin. "And when we are once out, let every man run his own way, say I. Your worship's company may prove somewhat dangerous, and I am a peaceable man."

"Well, be it so," answered the knight; and placing the settle directly under the window, he soon contrived to get into the opening, and kneeling in the deep wall, managed with some trouble to raise the heavy body of Groby, and place him in a sitting position on the edge, so that the moment he himself dropped down on the other side, the honest clothier could take his place and follow his example.

Turning round, Sir Osborne could perceive by the dim light of the night, the tall form of Longpole standing below, but he took care not to utter a sound, and bending his knees, he gradually stretched himself out, till he hung by nothing but his hands—then dropped, and in a moment stood silently by Heartley's side, who instantly placed in his hands the large double-edged sword of which he had been deprived in the morning.

It now became poor Jekin's turn, who managed the matter somewhat more slowly, and a good deal more clumsily, and at length, when he dropped, although the arms of the knight broke his fall, he uttered a tremendous "Oh!" and exhausted, leant against the wall.

At that moment a light appeared in a window above, passed by a second, and instantly the alarum bell rang out a peal enough to wake the dead.

"Run! run! every one his own way," cried Jekin, who seemed to trust mightily to the activity of his own legs, and plying them with vast rapidity, he fled up an alley before him.

"This way, my lord," cried Heartley; "quick, we shall distance them far," and darting off for the thick wood that almost touched the angle of the house, he led the knight into a deep forest path, crying, "Stoop!"

The sounds of pursuit were now loud on every side. Whoop, and halloo, and shout, floated on the wind, as the servants, dispersed in all directions, strove to give information or encouragement to their comrades, and one party especially seemed by the sound to come rapidly on their track. At length an alley, bounded by a wall, closed their course in that direction.

"We can vault?" said Heartley.

"On!" cried the knight, and in a moment both had cleared the wall and the dry ditch beyond, but at the same moment, the sounds of two parties of pursuers were heard in the parallel alley.

"Down in the ditch!" cried the knight, "they will see us if we take to the open field."

No sooner was it said than done, and immediately after they heard as they lay, the feet and voices of half a dozen men passing rapidly by.

"I was sure they did not take this way, Joe," cried one.

"And I am sure they did!" answered the other. "They're in the wood now. Let us——"

What he said more was lost, and after pausing for a moment or two till the sounds were but faintly heard in the wood, Longpole and his lord betook them to the open field, and soon were out of sight of the park.

CHAPTER VI.

"I do believe it : the common world
Teems out with things we know not ; and our mind,
Too gross for us to scan the mighty whole,
Knows not how busy all creation is."

SIR PAYAN WILETON, sitting in deep and earnest consultation with Sir Cesar the Magician, regarding the
teeming future, was only wakened to a full sense of the
present by the very resonant "oh!" uttered by Jekin
Groby as he fell from the window. His fury, his menaces, his orders, his promises to those who should retake
them may be imagined.

The servants, roused from their beds, beat the woods
in every direction, searching vainly for the young knight
and Richard Heartley, who, as we have seen, contrived
to evade their pursuit. Not such, however, was the fate
of poor Jekin Groby, who, running straight forward up
one of the avenues, was soon seen and overtaken by a
party of servants, who taking it for granted that he would
resist most violently, beat him unmercifully out of mere
expectation.

Roaring and grumbling, the unfortunate clothier was
brought back to the manor, and underwent Sir Payan's
objurgation with but an ill grace. "You are a villain!
you are!" cried Jekin. "You had better let me alone!
you had! You'll burn your fingers if you meddle with
me. You've stolen my bags already—but the king and
Lord Derby shall hear of it; ay, and the cardinal to boot
—and a deal more too. Did not I hear you promise to
murder him, you black-hearted vagabond?"

"Tie him hand and foot," said Payan, "and bring him
back again into the strong-room. Bring him along, I

would fain see how they reached the window." And
followed by the servants, hauling along poor Jekin, who
ever and anon muttered something about Lord Derby,
and the king, and his bags, he proceeded to the chamber
where the young knight had been imprisoned. There
the settle and the rope gave evidence of the manner in
which the escape had been affected, and were instantly
removed by order of the knight, to prevent the honest
clothier, though now bound hand and foot, from making
the attempt again.

"This man's evidence would damn me," thought Sir
Payan. "Fool that I was to forget that he was here,
and not look in that straw closet, before I committed
myself with the other! But he must be taken care of,
and never see England again. What is that?" continued
he aloud, pointing to the scroll which caught his eye on
the ground. "Give it me. Ha! All fair! Can old Sir
Cesar have aided in this trick?—we will see." And with
hasty strides he proceeded to the high chamber where
he had left the astrologer. He slackened his pace, however, with some feelings of awe, for as he approached
he heard a voice speaking high. "In the name of God
most high," it cried, "answer! Shall his head be raised
so high for good or for evil? Ha! thou fleetest away.
Let be! Let be!"

At this moment Sir Payan threw open the door, and
found the old man with his hair standing almost erect,
his eye protruded, and his arms extended, as if still ad-
juring some invisible being. "It is gone!" cried he, as
the other entered. "It is gone!" and he sunk back exhausted in his chair.

Notwithstanding the fund of dauntless resolution
which Sir Payan held, his heart seemed to grow faint
as he entered the apartment, in which there was a strange
sickly odor of incense and foreign gums, and a thin blue
smoke, that diffusing itself from a chafing-dish on the
table, rendered the various objects flickering and in-

distinct. Nor could he help persuading himself that something rushed by him as he opened the door, like a sudden gust of cold wind, that made him give an involuntary shudder.

When he had left the room below, he had determined to tax the old knight boldly, with having aided in the prisoners' escape; but his feelings were greatly changed when he entered, and accosting him with a mixture of awe and respect, he asked how it was that people discovered any characters written in a certain sort of ink he had heard of, which was quite pure and white, till the person who had the secret submitted it to some other process.

" Hold the paper to the fire!" said Sir Cesar feebly.

Sir Payan immediately extended the parchment over the chafing-dish, but in vain, no trace of any kind appeared, and vexed and disappointed he let it drop into the flame.

" Know ye that my prisoner has escaped?" said he, " and I am again insecure."

" Listen to what is of mightier moment," cried Sir Cesar with a great effort, as if his powers were almost extinct with some vast excitement just undergone. " Listen, and reply not; but leave me the moment you have heard. You besought me to ascertain the fate of Edward Duke of Buckingham, that you might judge whether to serve him as he would have you. I have compelled an answer from those who know, and I learn that, within one year, Buckingham's head shall be the highest in the realm. Mark! determine! and leave me!"

Sir Payan, aware that it was useless to remain when Sir Cesar had once desired to be alone, quitted the chamber in silence. " Yes!" said he thoughtfully, " I will serve him, so long as I do not undo myself—I will creep into his counsels—I will appear his zealous friend— but I will be wary. He aims at the crown—as he rises I will rise—but if I see him make one false step in that

proud ascent, I will hurl him down, and when the fair
lands of Buckingham are void——who knows? We shall
see. Less than I have risen higher!—Ho! who waits?
When the Portuguese returns, give the prisoner into
his hands—but first make the captain speak with me.—
Buckingham's head shall be the highest in the realm!
That must be king—never did I know his prophecies
fail, though sometimes they have a strange twisted meaning—highest in the realm—there can be none higher than
the king—Harry has no male heir.—Well, we shall see."

CHAPTER VII.

" Welcome, he said :
Oh, long expected, to my dear embrace !"
DRYDEN.

" WE must not think ourselves safe," said Longpole, when they had got about two miles from the park, " till we have put five estates between us and that double cunning fox, Sir Payan Wileton, for by break of day his horsemen will be out in every direction, and he will not mind breaking a little law to have us."

" Which way are we going now?" demanded the knight; " I should judge towards Canterbury."

" A little to the left we bear now," replied Longpole, " and yet the left is become the right, for by going left we get right off his land, my lord."

" Call me not my lord, Heartley," said Darnley. " Did I appear before the king as Lord Darnley, his grace might be offended, and especially the proud Wolsey; as, after many entreaties, made by the best in the land, the prelate refused to see either my father or myself, that we might plead our own cause; therefore, for the present, I am but Sir Osborne Maurice. Thou hast too much wit I know to give me my lord at every instant, like yon foolish clothier."

" Oh no, not I," replied Longpole, " I will Sir Osborne you, sir, mightily. But speaking of the clothier, your worship, how wonderfully the fellow used his legs. It seemed as if every step cried out ell-wide; and when he stumbled 'twas but three-quarters. I hope he escaped, if 'twere but to glorify his running."

" Even if they took him," said the knight, " Sir Payan would not keep him after he found I was gone."

"If 'twere not for avarice," said Longpole; "the fellow had all his better angels in his bags, and Sir Payan has store of avarice. I've seen him wrangle with a beggar for the change of a halfpenny, when the devil tempted him to commit a charity. And yet avarice, looked upon singly, is not a bad vice for a man to have either. It's a warm, a comfortable, solid sin; and if most men will damn their own soul to get money, he can't be much worse off who damns his to keep it. Oh, I like avarice! Give me avarice for my sin. But I tire your worship."

"No, no, faith," replied the knight. "Thy cheerfulness, together with the freedom of my limbs, gives me new spirit, Heartley."

"Oh, good your worship," cried Longpole, "call me something else than Heartley. Since the fit is on us for casting our old names, I'll be after the fashion, too, and have a new one."

"Well, then, I will call thee Longpole," said the knight, "which was the name we gave thee this morning, when thou wert watching us on the bank."

"Speak not of it, Sir Osborne," replied he: "that was a bad trick—the worst I ever was in. But call me Longpole, if your worship chooses. When I was with the army, they called me Dick Fletcher, because I made the arrows; and now I'll be Longpole, till such time as your honor is established in all your rights again, and then I'll be merry Master Heartley, my lord's man."

"I fear me, Dick, that thou wilt have but little beside thy merriment for thy wages," said the knight, "at least for a while, for yon same Sir Payan has my bags too in safe custody, and also some good letters for his grace of Buckingham. Yet I hope to receive in London the ransom of a knight and two squires, whom I made prisoners at Bouvines. Till then we must content ourselves on soldier's fare, and strive not to grow sad because our purses are empty."

"Oh, your worship, my merriment never leaves me," said Longpole. "They say that I laughed when first I came into the world; and, with God's will, I will laugh when I go out of it. But I think you said, Sir Osborne, that you had letters for the Duke of Buckingham: if we walk on at this pace, we shall soon be upon his land."

"What! has he estates in this county?" asked the knight; "my letters were addressed to him at Thornbury, in Gloucestershire."

"Oh, but he has many a broad acre too in Kent," answered Longpole; "and a fine house, windowed throughout with glass, and four chimneys at each end; not a room but has its fire. They say that he is there even now. And much loved is he of the commons, being no way proud, as some of our lords are, with their upturned noses, as if they scorned to wind their mother earth."

"Were I but sure that his grace were there," said the knight, "I would e'en venture without the letters; for much has he been a friend of my father, and he is also renowned for his courtesy."

"Surely, your worship," answered Longpole, "if his grace have any grace, he must be gracious; and yet I have heard that Sir Payan is the duke's good friend, and it might be dangerous to trust yourself."

"I do not fear," said the knight. "The noble duke would never deliver me into the hands of my enemy; and although, perhaps, Sir Payan may play the sycophant, and cringe to serve his own base purposes with his grace, I cannot believe that the duke would show him any further favor than such as we yield to a hound that serves us. However, we must find some place to couch us for the night, and to-morrow morning I will determine."

"Still, we must on a little further to-night," said Longpole. "That Sir Payan has the nose of a bloodhound, and I should fear to rest yet for a couple of hours. But the country I know well every path and field, so that I will not lead your worship wrong."

For nearly ten miles more, lighted by neither moon nor stars, did the two travellers proceed, through fields, over gates, and in the midst of woods, through which Longpole conducted with such unerring sagacity, that the young knight could not help a suspicion crossing his mind, that his guide must have made himself acquainted with the paths by some slight practice in deer-stalking, or other gentle employments of a similar nature. At length, however, they arrived in the bottom of a little valley, where a clear quick stream was dashing along, catching and reflecting all the light that remained in the air. On the edge of the hill hung a portion of old forest ground, in the skirts of which was a group of hay-stacks; and hither Longpole led his master, seeming quite familiar with all the localities round about. "Here, sir, leap this little ditch and mound. Wait! there is a young hedge— now between these two haystacks is a bed for a prince. Out upon the grumblers that are always finding fault with Fortune! The old lady, with her purblind eyes, gives, it is true, to one man a wisp of straw, and to another a cap and plume; but if he with the wisp wears it as gaily as the other does his bonnet, why fortune's folly is mended by content. I killed a fat buck in that wood not a month since," continued Longpole; "but, good your worship, tell not his grace of Buckingham thereof."

By such conversation Longpole strove to cheer the spirits of his young lord, upon whose mind all the wayward circumstances of his fate pressed with no easy weight. Laying himself down, however, between the two haystacks, while Heartley found himself a similar bed hard by, the young adventurer contrived soon to forget his sorrows in the arms of sleep.

It was bright daylight when the knight awoke, and all the world was gay with sunshine, and resonant with the universe's matin song. Longpole, however, was still fast asleep, and snoring as if in obstinate mockery of the birds that sat and sang above his head. Yet even in sleep there was a merry smile upon the honest Englishman's face, and the knight could hardly find the heart to wake him from the quiet blessing he was enjoying, to the cares, the fears, and the anxieties of active existence. "Wake, Richard," said he, at length, "wake; the sun has risen this hour."

Up started Longpole. "So he has," cried he; "well, 'tis a shame, I own, that that same old fellow, the sun, who could run alone before I was born, and who has neither sat down nor stood still one hour since, should still be up before me in the morning. But your worship and I did not go to bed last night so early as he did."

"Ay!" replied the knight, "but he will still run on, as bright, as vigorous, and as gay as ever, long after our short race is done."

"More fool he, then," said Longpole; "he'll be lag last. But how have you determined, sir, about visiting the noble duke?"

"I will go, certainly," replied the knight: "but, good Longpole, tell me, is it far from the manor? for all my food yesterday was imprisonment and foul words."

"Gods life! your worship must not complain of hunger, then, for such diet soon gives a man a surfeit. But, in troth, 'tis more than one good mile. However, surely we can get a muncheon of bread at some cottage as we go; so shall your worship arrive just in time for his grace's dinner, and I come in for my share of good things in the second or third hall, as it pleases master yeoman-usher. So let us on, sir, i' God's name."

Climbing the hill, they now cut across an angle of the forest, and soon came to a wide open down, whereon a shepherd was feeding a fine flock of sheep, singing lightly as he went along.

"This shepherd will have his hard-pressed curds and his brown bread," said Longpole; "and if your worship's hunger be like mine, no way dainty, we can man-

age to break our fast with him, though it be not on man-
chets and stewed eels."

The knight was very willing to try the shepherd's fare,
and bending their course towards him, they came up
just as he was placing himself under an old oak, leaving
his sheep to the care of his dogs, and found him well
disposed to supply their necessities. His pressed curds,
his raveled bread, and his leathern bottle, full of thin
beer, were cheerfully produced; and when the knight,
drawing from his pocket one of the few pieces that had
luckily not been placed in his bags, offered to pay for
their refreshment, the honest shepherd would receive no
payment; his good lord, he said, the Duke of Buckingham, let none of his people want for anything in their
degree, from his chancellor to his shepherd.

"Content is as good as a king," said Heartley, as they
proceeded on their way. "But there, does not your worship catch a glance of the house where those two hills
sweep across one another, with a small road winding in
between them—just as if under yon large mass of
chalky stone, that seems detached and hanging over the
path, with a bright gleam of sunshine seen upon the
wood beyond? Do you not see the chimneys, sir?"

"I do, I do," answered Sir Osborne. "But come, let
us on, it cannot be far."

"Not above half a mile," answered Longpole; "but
we must go round to the other side, for on this lie the
gardens, which, as I have heard, are marvellous rich and
curious. There may be seen all kinds of foreign fruit,
corn-trees, capers, lemons, and oranges. And they say,
that by a strange way they call graffing, making, as it
were, a fool of Dame Nature, they give her a parti-col-
ored coat, causing one tree to bring forth many kinds
of fruit, and flowers of sundry colors."

"I have seen the same in Holland," replied the knight,
"where the art of man seems boldly, as it were, to take

the pencil from Nature's hand, and paint the flowers with
what hues he will."

Walking rapidly on, they soon crossed the fields that
separated them from the park, and skirting round the
grounds, reached the high road. This ran along for
about a mile under the thick massy wall, which, supported
by immense buttresses, and partially overgrown with ivy,
inclosed the domain on all sides. The thick wall continued uninterrupted till towards the middle, where, turning abruptly round to the right, it was seen flanking on
both hands the wide road that led up to a pair of massy
iron gates before the house. On each side of these gates
appeared a square tower of brickwork, affording sufficient lodging for the porter and his men; and round
about the doors of which was a crowd of paupers already
collected, waiting for the daily dole which they received
from the table of the duke.

Through these Sir Osborne took his way, followed by
Longpole, yet not without a sort of murmur amongst the
beggar train, who, thinking all that remained from the
dinners in the various halls their own by right, grumbled
at every one who went in, as if they thereby received an
injury.

The gate being open, the knight entered, and looked
round for some one to answer his inquiries. The porter
instantly stepped forth from his house, and notwithstanding that the stranger's dress had lost the saucy freshness
of its first gloss, he doffed his cap with as much respect
as if he had been robed in ermines.

" Sir," said the porter, doffing his cap with a low bow,
imagining that the knight came to dine at the table in
the second hall, to which all strangers of respectable
appearance were admitted, " 'tis not yet eleven o'clock,
and the dinner is never served till noon."

" That will be more to my purpose," replied the knight,
" as I wish to have audience of his grace, if he be now in
Kent."

"His grace walks in the flower-garden," replied the porter, "and I know not whether he may be spoken with; but follow me, sir, and I will bring you to his chamberlain." So saying, he led the way across the court, and ascending the steps of the terrace on which the mansion was raised, he pushed open the hall-door, and conducted the knight through a merry group of servants, engaged in various sports, into a second hall, where were a number of ecclesiastics and gentlemen, of that intermediate grade, which raised them above the domestics, without giving them a title to associate with the persons admitted to the duke's own table.

Here the porter looked round, as if searching for some one amongst the various groups that tenanted the apartment; and then begging the knight to wait a moment, he left him.

Finding that all eyes were fixed upon him with that sort of glance of cool, impertinent inquiry, which few persons scruple to exercise upon a stranger, who comes new into a place where they themselves are at home, Sir Osborne went up to some fine suits of armor, which were ranged in order at the end of the hall. Amongst the rest, was one of those beautiful fluted suits of Milan steel, which are now so rarely met with. It was arranged as for use, and the arm extended, with the gauntlet resting on the pommel of an immense double-handed sword, which was supported by a small rail of iron, placed there as a guard.

The knight considered it all with the eyes of a connoisseur, and taking the sword from underneath the gauntlet, drew it partly out of the sheath.

"You are a bold gentleman," said one of the starers, coming up to the knight. "Do you know that these suits are my lord duke's? What are you going to do with that sword?"

"To slit the ears of any one who asks me impertinent

questions," answered the knight, turning suddenly round upon him.

"Cast him out! cast him out!" cried a dozen voices. "Who is the beggarly rascal, with his gray doublet? Cast him out!"

But the knight glanced round them with that sort of fierce determined look, which tells that an adversary would have no easy task to master the heart that so lights up the eye; and though some still cried to cast him out, no one thought fit to approach too near.

"Peace! peace!" cried an old ecclesiastic who had been sitting at the farther extreme of the hall, and who now advanced. "Peace! see ye not by his spurs the gentleman is a knight. My son," he continued, addressing Sir Osborne, "those arms are the noble Duke of Buckingham's, and, out of respect for our patron, those who are admitted to this hall refrain from touching his ten suits. That which seems to have excited your curiosity, was the prize at a tournament, given by an old friend of his grace some fifteen years ago, and it is one of the most handsome in his possession."

"I should not have touched those arms, my good father," answered the knight, "had I not thought that I recognized the suit; and was drawing the blade to see if it was the same."

"By what mark would you know it, young gentleman?" demanded the priest.

"If it be that I mean," replied Sir Osborne, "there is written on the blade—

> " ' I will win my right,
>   Or die in the fight.' "

"True, true!" said the clergyman. "There is so; but you must be too young to have been at that tourney."

"No matter," said the knight; "but, if I mistake not, here is his grace's chamberlain."

As he spoke, a gentleman, dressed in a black velvet

suit, with a gold chain round his neck, followed the porter into the hall, and addressed himself to the knight: " I
have communicated your desire," said he, " to my lord
duke, who has commanded me to say, that if your business with his grace be such as may pass through a third
person, he prays you to inform him thereof by me; but
if you must needs speak with him personally, he never
denies his presence to those who really require it."

Though he spoke with all courtesy, there was something in the manner of the chamberlain that Sir Osborne did not like; and he answered full haughtily : " Inform his grace that my business is for his private ear,
and that a moment will show him whether it be such as
he can hear with pleasure."

" Then I have nought left, sir, but to lead you to his
grace," replied the chamberlain; " though, I am sure, you
know that it is not well to trouble great men with small
matters."

" Lead on, sir," said the knight, observing the chamberlain's eye glance somewhat critically over his apparel:
" my doublet is not very new, you would say; but if I
judge it good enough for your lord, it is too good for his
servant's scorn."

The chamberlain led on in silence through one of the
side doors of the hall, and thence by a long passage to
the other side of the dwelling, where, issuing out upon
the terrace, they descended into a flower-garden, laid out
much after the pattern of a Brussels carpet.

As Darnley descended, he beheld at the farther end a
tall, dignified man, of about the middle age, walking
slowly up and down the longest walk. He was dressed
in one of the straight coats of the day, stiff with gold
embroidery, and the upper part of the sleeve puffed out
with crimson silk, and held down with straps of cloth of
gold. The rest of his attire was of the same splendid
nature: the high breeches of silken serge, pinked with
gold—the mirabaise, or small low-crowned bonnet, of

7

rich velvet, with a thin feather leaning across, fastened by a large ruby—the silken girdle, with its jewelled clasp,—all were corresponding: and though the dress might not be so elegant in its forms as that which we are accustomed to call the Vandyk, yet it was far more splendid in its materials, and had perhaps more of majesty, though less of grace. Two servants walked about ten paces behind, the one carrying in his hand his lord's sword, the other bearing an orange, which contained in the centre a sponge, filled with vinegar.

The duke himself was busily engaged in reading as he walked, now poring on the leaves of the book he held in his hand, now raising his eyes and seeming to consider what he had just collected. As the young knight approached, however, he paused, placed a mark between the leaves where he had left off, and advanced a step, with that affable smile and winning courtesy for which he was so famous.

"I give you good-morrow, fair sir," said he. "My chamberlain says that you would speak with me. Methinks my good fortune has made me see your face before —say, can Buckingham serve you?" and as he spoke, he considered the young stranger attentively, as if he did really remember him.

"Your grace is ever courteous," replied the knight; and then added, seeing that the chamberlain still stayed— "But in the first place let me say, that what I was unwilling to communicate to this your officer, I am equally unwilling to speak before him."

"Leave us!" said the duke. "In truth, I know not why you stay. Now, fair sir, may I crave your name?"

"'Tis now a poor one, my good lord," replied the knight—"Osborne Darnley."

"Rich, rich, dear youth! in virtue and in merit," cried the duke, taking him in his arms, and embracing him warmly—which accolade did not escape the reverted eyes of the chamberlain—"rich in honor and courage, and every good quality. The Lord of Surrey, my good son-in-law, to whom you are a dear companion in arms, wrote me from Ireland some two months past that I might expect you here; evolved to me the plans which you have formed to gain the favor of the king; and prepared me to aid you to the best of my poor power. Hold you the same purpose of concealing your name which you proposed when you wrote from Flanders to Lord Surrey, and which you observed when last in this our happy country?"

"I do, my good lord," replied the knight, "on every account; but more especially as it is the wish and desire of him, I am bound most to honor and obey—my father."

"My judgment goes with his and yours," said the duke, "more especially as for some cause that proud man Wolsey, when, not long since, I petitioned the king to see your noble father, stepped in and stayed the wavering consent that hung upon his grace's lips. But think not, my dear youth, that I have halted in your cause. Far from it; I have urged your rights with all the noblest and best of the land; while your own merits, and the high name you have acquired in serving with the emperor, have fixed your interest on the sure basis of esteem; so that, wherever you find a real English heart, and but whisper the name of Darnley, there you shall have a friend—yet, indeed, I have much to complain of in my lord, your father."

"Indeed, indeed, your grace!" cried the knight, the quick blood mounting into his cheek. "Some misconception must make you think so. My father, heaven knows, is full of gratitude and affection towards you."

"Nay, protest not," replied Buckingham, with a smile, "I have the strongest proof of his ingratitude and bad esteem; for what can be so great a proof of either as to refuse an offered kindness?"

"Oh, I understand your grace," said Sir Osborne.

" But though the noble, the princely offers of pecuniary
assistance which your grace held out to him were de-
clined, my father's gratitude was not the less. For five
long years I have not seen him, but in all his letters he
speaks of the noble Duke of Buckingham as one whose
virtues have shamed him from misanthropy."

" Well, well!" answered the duke. " At least remember you were counted once as my page, when you were
a child no higher than my knee: so now with you I will
command, whereas with your father I could but beg;
and I will say, that if you use not my house, my servants,
and my purse, you hold Buckingham at nought. But we
must be more particular: come into my closet till dinner
be served, and tell me all, for young soldiers are rarely
rich, and I will not have my purpose balked."

We shall not pursue the further conversation of the
Duke of Buckingham and the young knight: suffice that
the frank generosity of his noble friend easily drew from
Sir Osborne all his history, even to the very day.

" As to your enemy, Sir Payan Wileton," said the
duke, " I know him well—he is a desperate villain—and
yet such men are useful in great enterprises. You say
you met that strange but wonderful man Sir Cesar,—did
he not tell you anything concerning me? But no! he
was wise. His grace the king might die without issue
male—and then, God knows! However, we will not
think of that!" And with these dark hints of some more
remote and daring schemes, the Duke of Buckingham
contented himself for the time, and returned to the more
immediate affairs of him whose interest he now so
warmly embraced. But in the midst of their conversation, the controller of the household entered to marshal
the way to the banquet-hall.

" What said you, my dear youth, was the name you
had adopted?" demanded the duke; " for I must gain
you the acquaintance of my friends."

" Ever since the sequestration of our estates," replied

the knight, "and their transfer to Sir Payan Wileton, I have, when in England, borne the name of Osborne Maurice."

"Osborne Maurice!" said the duke, with some emphasis, as if he found something extraordinary in the name. "How came you to assume that?"

"In truth, I know not," answered the knight; "'twas fixed on by my father."

"Yes, I now remember," said the duke, after musing for a while. "He was a dear friend of my good lord, your father's—I mean the other Sir Osborne Maurice, who supported Perkyn Warbeck—but 'twill do as well as another—the name is forgotten now."

CHAPTER VIII.

" Born of noble state,
Well could he tourney, and in lists debate."
                                            SPENSER.

WHEN, as may be remembered, the porter led the knight into the second hall, our friend Longpole remained in the first, with those of his own degree; nor was he long in making acquaintance, and becoming intimate with every one round about, from the old seneschal, who took his place in the leathern chair by right of immemorial service, to the serving-man. For all, and each, Longpole had his joke and his quibble; he played with one, he jested with the other, and he won the hearts of all. In short, every one was in a roar of laughter when the porter returned from the second hall, followed by one of those inferior gentlemen, who had just found it inexpedient to follow up his purpose of casting Sir Osborne out.

Immediately on entering, the porter pointed out Longpole to the other, who advanced and addressed him, with a vastly supercilious air, which, however, did not produce any very awful effect upon the honest fletcher.*

" So, fellow," said he, " you are the servant of that gentleman in the old gray doublet."

" Yes, your worship, even so," answered Longpole. "My honored master always wears gray, for when he is not in gray cloth, he goes in gray iron—and as to its being old, better an old friend than a new foe."

" And who is your master? I should like to hear," asked the gentleman.

* A maker of arrows.

"Lord! does not your worship know?" demanded Longpole, giving a merry glance round the crowd, that stood already well-disposed to laugh at whatever he should say. "Bless you, sir! my master's the gentleman that beat Gog and Magog in single fight, slew seventy crocodiles of the Nile before breakfast, and played at pitch and toss with the cramp-bones of an elephant's hind-leg. For heaven's sake don't anger him, he'd eat a score such as you at a mouthful!"

"Come, fellow, no insolence, if you mind not to taste the stirrup leather," cried the other, enraged at the tittering of the menials. "You and your master both give yourselves too great airs."

"Odd's life, your worship, we are not the only ones!" answered Longpole. "Every Jack carries it as high as my lord, nowadays, so I'll not be out o' the fashion."

"You had better bid your master get a new doublet then," said the gentleman of the second hall, with a look of vast contempt.

"That your worship may have the old one?" asked Longpole, slyly.

What this might have produced it is impossible to say, for a most insupportable roar burst from the servants at Longpole's last thrust, but at that moment the chamberlain entered from the second hall, and beckoned to the gentleman, who was no other than his cousin.

"Take care what you say, William," whispered he; "that knight, with whom I find Master Wilmotswood quarrelled about touching the armor, is some great man, depend on it. The duke sent me away, and then he embraced him, and hugged him, as he had been his brother; and the old controller, who saw him go by, nods and winks, as if he knew who he is, and says that we shall see whether he does not dine at the first table, ay, and near his grace too, for all his old gray doublet. Hast thou found out his name?"

"No," replied the other. "His knave is as close as a

walnut, and does not scruple to break his jests on any
one—so I'll have no more of him."

Their further conversation was interrupted by a yeoman of the kitchen presenting himself at the door of the
hall, and a cry of " Sewers, sewers!" made itself heard,
giving notice that the noon repast was nearly ready to be
placed upon the table. The scene was at once changed
amongst the servants, and all was the bustle of preparation; the sewers running to serve the dinner, the yeomen
of the hall and the butler's men making speed to take
their places in the banquet-room, and the various pages
and servants of different gentlemen residing in the
manor, hurrying to wait on their masters at the table.

In the midst of this, our friend Longpole felt some
doubt what to do. Unacquainted with what had passed
between his master and the duke, and even whether the
knight had made known his real rank or not, Longpole
did not well know where to bestow himself.

" Odd's life!" said he, after fidgeting for a moment on
the thorns of uncertainty, " I'll e'en take my chance, and
go to the chief hall. I can but walk into the next, if my
young master does not show himself soon.—Ho, young-
ster!" he continued to a page he saw running by, " which
is the way to the lords' hall?"

" Follow! follow! quick!" cried the boy; " I'm going
there, to wait for my Lord Abergany, and we are too
late."

Longpole lost no time, and arrived in the hall at the
moment the controller was arranging the different servants round the apartment. " Stand you here, Sir
Charles Poynder's man, why go you higher than Sir
William Cecil's? Sir William is a Banneret. Harry
Mathers, you keep there. You Jim, by that cupboard—
and who are you? Who is your master, tall fellow?" he
continued, addressing Longpole.

" Oh, the gentleman that is with the duke," cried several of the servants, " the gentleman that is with the
duke,"

"Why, I know not where he will sit," said the controller, "but wait about, and stand behind his chair—Now, are you all ranged?—Bid the trumpets sound."

A loud flourish gave notice to the sewers to serve, and to the various·guests to descend to the hall, when in a few minutes appeared Lord Abergany and Lord Montague: and one by one dropped in Sir William Cecil, Sir Charles Poynder, and several other knights, who, after the various salutations of the morning, fell into groups of two and three, to gossip out the long five minutes which must pass while the controller informed the duke that the first dish was placed upon the table.

In the meanwhile honest Longpole stood by, too anxious to know the reception his lord had met with, even to jest with those around him, but instead, he kept examining all the splendid scene, the rich cloth of estate placed for the duke, the various cupboards of magnificent plate, the profusion of Venice glasses, and all the princely furnishing of the hall and table with feelings nearly allied to apprehension. At length the voice of the controller was heard crying, "The duke! the duke!—Make way there for the duke!" and in a moment after the Duke of Buckingham entered, leaning with familiar kindness on the arm of the young knight.

"My Lord Abergany," said the duke, "my son, and you my Lord Montague, my excellent good friend, before we fall to the cheer that heaven has given us, let me introduce to your love this much esteemed knight, Sir Osborne Maurice, of a most noble stock, and what is better still, ennobled by his deeds: and now let us to table. Sir Osborne, you must sit here on my right, so shall you enjoy the conversation of my Lord Abergany, sitting next to you, and yet I not lose yours. Our chaplain is not here—yet let some holy man bless the meat. Lord Montague, you will take my left."

That profound silence now succeeded which ought always to attend so important an avocation as that of din-

ing, and the whole worldly attention of every one seemed
fixed upon the progress of each dish, which being brought
up in turn to the Duke of Buckingham, first supplied
those immediately around him, and then gradually travelling down the table from person to person, according
to their rank, was at length carried out by a servant into
the second hall, where it underwent the same perambula-
tion, and was thence transferred to the third. Here, however, its journeys did not cease, for after having thus
completed the grand tour, and become nearly a finished
gentleman, the remnant was bestowed upon the paupers
without.

So great was the Duke of Buckingham's attention to
his new guest, that Longpole, who stood behind, to hand
his master drink, threw forward his chest, and raised his
head two inches higher than ordinary, as if all the stray
beams of the great man's favor that passed by the knight
lighted upon himself.

The duke, indeed, strove generously to distinguish his
young friend, feeling that misfortune has much greater
claims upon a noble mind than saucy prosperity. The
marks of regard which he gave were such as, in those
days, might well excite the wonder of Lord Abergany
who sat next to him. He more than once carved for him
himself, and twice invited him to drink, made him notice
those dishes which were esteemed most excellent, and
spoke to him far more than was usual during the course
of dinner.

At length the last service appeared upon the table, consisting entirely of sweets, then also came the finer sorts
of wines, Muscadel, Romanie, and Caprike; and the more
serious part of the banquet being over, the conversation
became animated and interesting. The young knight, as
a stranger to all, as well as from the marked kindness of
the duke, was of course a general object of attention;
and as the guests easily judged him a traveller lately
returned from abroad, many were the questions asked

him concerning the countries he had seen, and the wars he had been in.

Tilts and tournaments then became the subject of discourse; and at length the duke filled high a Venice glass with wine, and calling upon all to do the like, " Good gentlemen," said he, " 'tis seldom that Buckingham will stint his guests, but this is our last just now, for I would fain see a lance broken before night. I know not why, but methinks those sports and exercises, which are thus undertaken at a moment's notice, are often more replete with joy than those of long contrivance; and here is a good knight, who will balk no man of his humor, when 'tis to strike a strong blow, or to furnish good course. Sir Osborne, to your good health, and may all prosperity and success attend you. Good lords, and friends, join me in my health."

Sir Osborne expressed his willingness to do the duke any pleasure, and to furnish his course with any knight who thought him worthy of his lance. " But your grace knows," he continued, "that I have come here without arms, and that my horse I lost yesterday, as I explained to you."

" He would fain excuse himself the trouble," said the duke, smiling, " because we have no fair lady here to view his prowess; but, by heavens, I will have my will! Surely in my armory there is a harness that may suit you, Sir Knight, and in my stables a steed that will bear you stoutly. My lord of Montague, you are unarmed too; quick to the armory, and choose your arms. Sir Osborne shall maintain the field, and furnish two courses against each comer. We have not time for more; and the horse and harness which the good knight wears shall be the prize. Ho! call here the armorer! He is a Fleming most expert, and shall choose your suit, Sir Osborne."

All now rose, and Lord Montague proceeded to the armory to choose his arms, while the duke, taking Sir

Osborne and Lord Abergany into one of the recesses,
spoke to them apart for some moments, the effect of
which, as it appeared, was, that the duke's kinsman embraced the young knight heartily. While they were still
speaking, the armorer appeared, and with a low reverence approached the duke.

"Billenbach," said the duke, "thou hast an excellent
eye, and canst see, to the size of a straw, that a harness be
well adjusted. Look at this good knight, and search out
amongst the finest suits in the manor one that may be
convenient for him."

"'Tis a damage, your grace," replied the armorer,
with the sort of a bow a sledge-hammer might be supposed to make—"'tis a great damage that you are not at
Thornbury, for there is the armor that would have well
harnessed him. The gelt armor, that is all engrailed
with gelt—made for a tall man, and a strong, such as
his worship—very big upon the chest. Then there is the
polished suit upstairs, which might suit him, but I doubt
that the greaves be long enough, and I have taken away
the barbet and volant from the head-piece to give more
light, and 'twould take much time to fasten them on.
There are none but the ten suits in the second hall—one
of the tallest of them might do—but then they are for
your grace's own wear," and he looked inquiringly at
the duke, as if he doubted whether he might not have
offended by mentioning them.

"Nay, nay, thou art right, Billenback," exclaimed the
duke; "the fluted suit, above all others! I am sure it will
do. Call thy men, and fetch it here; we will arm him
amongst us."

The armorer obeyed; and in a few minutes returned
with his men bearing the rich suit of fluted armor,
which had attracted the knight's attention in the hall.
"Ha! Sir Osborne," said the duke, "do you remember
this armor? You were present when it was won; but
yet you were too young for that gay day to rest on your
memory."

"Nay, my good lord, not so," replied the knight; "I remember it well, and how gallantly the prize was won. I doubt not it will fit me."

"I feel full sure of it," said the duke, "and that you will fit it, for a better harness was never worn; and Surrey says, and I believe, there never was a better knight. Come, let us see; First, for the greaves. Oh, admirable! Does the knee move free? But I see it must. Now the corslet; that will fit, of course. How, fellow, you are putting the back-piece before! The breast-plate! The breast-plate!"

"This brassard is a little too close," said the knight. "If you loosen that stud, good armorer, 'twill be better."

"'Tis padded, good sir, near the elbow," said the man; "I will take out the padding. Will your worship try the head-piece? Can you see when the barbet is down?"

"Well enough to charge my lance," said the knight. "These arms are exquisite in beauty, my lord duke, but very light."

"There are none stronger in the world," said the duke, "and therein lies the excellence: though so light, that one moves in them more freely than in a coat of goldsmith's work, yet they are so well tempered, both by fire and water, and the juice of herbs, that the sword must be of fine steel indeed, that will touch them."

"One may see it by the polish that they keep," said the knight. "In each groove one may view oneself in miniature, as in a mirror. They are very beautiful."

"You must win them, my young soldier," whispered the duke. "Abergany has gone to arm, with Cecil, and Montague; but I know their force. And now for the horses. The strongest in my stable, with his chanfron, snaffle-bit, manifaire, and fluted poitrel (which I have all, point device corresponding with the suit), goes along as part of the prize. Billenback! take the casque, put a little oil to the visor, and bring it to the lawn of the four oaks. See that the other gentlemen be told that

we render ourselves there, where this knight will answer
all comers on horseback and I will judge the field. Send
plenty of light lances; and as we have not time to put
up lists, bid the porter bring seven men with staves to
mark the space."

Thus saying, the duke led the way towards the stable,
speaking to the knight, as they went, of various matters
which they had not discussed in the morning, and making
manifold arrangements for concentrating all sorts of
interest, to produce that effect upon the mind of the king
which might lead to the fulfilment of Sir Osborne's
hopes. Nor to the Duke of Buckingham, who was well
acquainted with the character of Henry, did the plan of
the young knight seem unlikely to be successful. The
sort of diffidence implied by concealing his name, was that
thing of all others calculated to win the monarch's good-
will; and there was also a kind of romantic and chivalrous
spirit in the scheme altogether, that harmonized well
with the tastes of the king, who would fain have revived
the days of the Round-Table, not contented with even
the wild, adventure-loving character of the times; and
yet, heaven knows! those who read the history of the
Chevalier Bayard, and the Memoirs of Fleurange, will
find scenes and details recorded of that very day, which
the novelist dare not venture to portray.

Only one thing made the duke anxious in regard to
his young protégé—the vast splendor and magnificence of
the court of England. He saw that the knight, accustomed alone to the court of Burgundy, where merit
was splendor, and valor counted for riches, was totally
unaware of the thoughtless expense required by Henry.
Sir Osborne had, indeed, informed him, that in London
he expected to receive from a Flemish merchant the
ransom of a knight and three esquires, amounting in all,
together with the value of their arms, to about three
thousand French crowns, which the duke well knew
would little more than pay for the bard and base of his

first joust; and yet he very evidently perceived it would be difficult to prevail upon him to accept of any purely pecuniary assistance, especially as he had no time to lay a plan for offering it with any very scrupulous delicacy, Sir Osborne purposing to depart after the beverage, or three o'clock meal.

"Now, Osborne," said the duke familiarly, after they had seen their horses properly accoutred, and were proceeding towards the place of rendezvous—"now you are once more armed at all points, and fit to encounter the best knight in the land; but we must have that tall fellow who serves you armed too, as your custrel, and mounted; for as you are a knight, and certainly errant, I intend to put you upon an adventure—but here come the counterparty. No one but Cecil will run you hard. I last year gave an harness and a purse of a thousand marks as a prize, which Cecil had nearly won from Surrey. But you must win."

"I will do my best, your grace," replied the knight, "both for the honor of your grace's friendship, and for this bright suit, which in truth I covet. To break two spears with all comers—I think your grace said, that was my task. And if I keep the field with equal success against all——"

"Of course you win the prize," interposed the duke. "And if any other gentleman make as many points as yourself, you furnish two more courses with him to decide. But here we are. Well, my lords, the horses will be here before the ground be marked. I stand by, and will be an impartial judge."

It is not easy to imagine, in these times, how the revenues of that age could support the nobles in the sort of unbounded expense in their houses, which has made old English hospitality a proverbial expression; but it is nevertheless a certain fact, that from fifty to sixty persons commonly sat to dinner each day in the various halls of every wealthy peer. The boards of those who, like

Buckingham, maintained a more than princely splendor, were generally much better furnished with guests; and when he looked round the spot that had been appointed for their morning's amusement, and beheld not more than a hundred lookers-on, all of whom had fed at his own tables, he felt almost disappointed at the scantiness of the spectators.

"We have more guests at Thornbury," said he; "and yet, porter, you do not keep the ground clear. Gentlemen, these four oaks are the bounds; I pray you do not come within. Here are our chargers."

The fine strong horse which Buckingham had chosen for the young knight was now led up, harnessed as if for war; and before mounting, Sir Osborne could not refrain from walking round to admire him, as he stood pawing the ground, eager to show his speed. The young knight's heart beat high, and laying his left hand on the neck, he sprang at once from the ground into the saddle, while the very clang of his new armor, and the feeling of being once more equipped as he was wont, gave him new life, and hope, and courage.

Ordered by a whisper from the duke, the groom beckoned Longpole from the ground, and the armorer taking the shield and lance, presented them to the young knight at the end of the course. A note or two was now sounded by the trumpet, and Lord Abergany offered himself on horseback opposite to Sir Osborne, who paused a moment, to observe if he charged his lance at the head-piece or the shield, that, out of compliment to the duke's relation, he might follow his example.

"Spur, spur, Sir Osborne!" cried the duke, who stood near; "Abergany comes."

The knight struck his spurs into the charger's sides; the horse darted forward, and the spear, aimed low, struck the fess-point of Lord Abergany's shield, and splintered up to the vantplate in Sir Osborne's hand; at the same moment Lord Abergany's broke upon the young knight's breast; and suddenly wheeling their chargers, they regained the opposite ends of the lawn.

The second lance was broken nearly in the same manner, with only this difference, that Sir Osborne, having now evinced his respect for his opponent, aimed at the head-piece, which counted a point more.

Lord Montague now succeeded, laughing good-humoredly as he rode towards his place and bidding Sir Osborne aim at his head, for it was, he said, the hardest part about him. The knight did as he was desired, and broke his spear twice on the very charnel of his helmet. It being now Sir William Cecil's turn, each knight charged his spear directly towards the other's head, and galloping on, both lances were shivered to atoms.

" Gallantly done! gallantly done!" cried the Duke of Buckingham, though he began to feel some little anxiety lest the knight banneret might carry off the prize, which he had fully intended for Sir Osborne. " Gallantly done! To it again, gentle knights."

The spears were now once more delivered, and setting out as before, each struck the other's head-piece, but Sir William Cecil's, touching obliquely, glanced off, while that of Sir Osborne was again splintered.

" Give me your voices, gentlemen all," cried the duke, turning to the spectators. " Who has the day?—Sir Osborne Maurice, I say."

" Sir Osborne! Sir Osborne!" cried a dozen voices; but one person, no other than he who had thought fit to quarrel with the knight about touching the very armor that he now wore, could not forbear shouting the name of Sir William Cecil, although, fearful of the duke's eye, he took care to keep back behind the rest while he did so.

" Some one says Sir William Cecil," cried the duke, both surprised and angry. " What say you yourself, Sir William?"

" I say, Sir Osborne Maurice," replied the banneret,

8

surlily, " because my lance slipped; but had it not, I
think I should have unseated him."

" He is not easily unseated," said the duke, " if report
speak true. However, the prize is yours, Sir Osborne.
Yet, because one voice has differed from my judgment, if
you two knights will furnish one more course for my
satisfaction, I will give a thousand marks for the best
stroke."

" Your grace knows that I must soon depart," said
Sir Osborne; " but nevertheless, I am quite willing, if
this good knight be so, for I am sure his lance slipped
merely by accident."

" Oh, I am very willing!" cried Sir William Cecil,
somewhat sharply. " A thousand marks, your grace
says?"

" Ay, sir," replied the duke, " I do."

" 'Tis a tough prize," cried Sir William, " so give me
a tough ash spear."

" To me the same," cried Sir Osborne Maurice, not
exactly pleased with the tone of his opponent—" 'tis for
the best stroke."

At this moment Longpole appeared, completely armed,
by Buckingham's command, as a custrel, or shield-bearer,
and hearing his master's demand, he searched amongst
the spears till he met with one that his practised eye,
long used in his quality of fletcher, or arrow-maker, to
select the hardest woods, instantly perceived was excellent, and bore it himself to the knight. The trumpet
sounded—both galloped forward, and Sir William Cecil's
lance, aimed as before at the knight's casque, struck hard:
but Sir Osborne was as immoveable as a rock, and though
of firm, solid wood, the spear shivered. Not so Sir Osborne's; borne forward by a steady, unerring hand, it
struck Sir William Cecil's head-piece just under the
crest, wrenched away the crest and plume, and still catching against the iron-work, bore him backwards upon the
croupier, and thence with his horse to the ground; for
though Sir Osborne pulled in his rein as soon as he could,

It was not before the weight of his charger had over-borne that of his opponent, and thrown him far back upon his haunches.

The servants of Sir William ran up to disentangle him; and finding him considerably hurt by the fall, they bore him away to his apartments in the manor.

In the meanwhile, the duke and his friends were not scanty of the praises which they bestowed upon the young knight; and indeed there might be some sensation of pleasure at Cecil's overthrow, mingled with their approbation of Sir Osborne; for though a good soldier and an honorable man, the banneret was overbearing in society with his equals, and insupportably proud towards those of an inferior rank, so that all the servants winked to each other, as he was borne past, taking no pains to conceal their pleasure in his humiliation.

"I am sorry that Sir William Cecil is hurt," said the knight, springing off his horse. "On, Longpole, after his men, and discover what is his injury."

"'Tis no great matter," said Lord Abergany, "and it will do Cecil no harm that his pride is lowered; for, in truth, he has lately become beyond all endurance vain. He spoke of quelling the mutiny of the shipwrights at Rochester, as if his single arm were capable of doing more than Lord Thomas and all his company. Well, fellow!" he continued to Longpole, who now returned, "what hurt has Sir William?"

"Why, please your lordship," replied he, "he is neither wholly beaten nor wholly strangled, but a little of both; for his casque has proved a cudgel, and given him a bloody nose; and his gorget a halter, and half hanged him."

"A merry knave!" said the duke. "Come, Sir Osborne, half an hour still rests before our beverage, that you shall bestow upon me, when you have taken off your casque. Gentlemen, amuse yourselves till three, when we will rejoin you in the hall."

Thus saying, the duke again led the way to his closet,

and concluded all his arrangements with the young knight, with the same generosity of feeling and delicacy of manner which had characterized all the rest of his conduct towards him. The prize Sir Osborne had won he paid to him as a mere matter of course, taking every means to conceal that it had been offered merely that he might win it. But he also exacted a promise, that whenever the young knight was in London, he would use his beautiful manor-house of the Rose in St. Lawrence Pountney, as if it were his own, and furnished him with a letter which gave him therein unlimited command over whomsoever and whatsoever it contained.

"And now," continued Buckingham, "let us speak, my young friend, of the means of introducing you to the king, without my appearing in it; for I am not well beloved of the butcher-begotten cardinal. My cousin, the abbot of the Benedictines, near Canterbury, writes me this morning, that his sister, the lady abbess, a most holy and devout woman, has with her, even now, a young lady of high station, a woman of the queen's, one Mistress Katherine Bulmer, who has lately been there to visit and cheer her relation the abbess, who has somewhat suffered from a black melancholy that all her holy piety can hardly cure; and also, as he hints, perhaps to tame down the young damsel's own light spirits, which, it may be, soar a pitch too high. However, the time has come that the queen calls for her lady, and the abbess must send her back; but this mutiny of the shipwrights at Rochester puts the good devotees in fear; and they must needs ask me (with an, if I be sending that way) to let the lady journey to the court at Greenwich, under escort of any of my retainers or friends. If you undertake the charge, our most excellent Queen Katherine will surely give you her best thanks, and make you know the king; and the mutiny of the shipwrights, who are still in arms, will be a full reason and excuse why you should ride armed. Three of my servants shall accompany you. Say, does the proposal please you? Will you accept it?"

" With many thanks," replied the knight; " your grace is ever kind and thoughtful for your poor friend's good."

" Your father once saved my life," answered the duke, " and I would almost give that life again to see him what he was. See, here is the letter to the lord abbot. Let us now back to our friends, or they will think we are plotting treason. Do you favor the bad habit of beverages? No! then we will drain one cup ere you mount, and bid you farewell."

The duke now led to the hall, called for a cup of wine, and then pledging the young knight, together with Lord Abergany and Lord Montague, conducted him to his horse, notwithstanding the opposition which he made to so marked an honor.

" 'Slife! " cried Lord Montague, seeing him still armed: " are you going to ride in harness? Three of his grace's servants armed too? Why, you are surely going to deliver some captive damsel from the power of a base ravager."

" Your lordship is not far wrong," replied the knight, springing on his horse. " But as it is a secret adventure put upon me by the noble duke, him you must ask if you would hear more."

" Oh, the history! the history! I pray thee, most princely Buckingham! " cried Lord Montague. " But the knight gallops off with his fellow, whom he calls Longpole; but I doubt me much that both Longpole and Osborne Maurice at times bear other names. Ha! my lord duke? Well, well! Keep your secret—nothing like a little romance. He seems a noble heart, whoever he be."

With this speech the whole party turned into the mansion; the generous-hearted duke congratulating himself on having thus found means to furnish his old friend's son with money and arms, and laying still further plans for rendering him more extensive and permanent service, and the two lords very well pleased with the little excitement which had broken in upon the sameness of their usual morning amusements,

CHAPTER IX.

" This is no Father Dominic—no huge overgrown
Abbey lubber."

SPANISH FRIAR.

WHO can depict the feelings of Sir Osborne Maurice
as he found himself riding on towards that court, where,
with the ardor of youthful hope, he doubted not to retrieve
the fortunes of his family by those qualities which had
already acquired for him an honorable fame? Clothed
once more in arms, which for five years had been his
almost constant dress, far better mounted than when he
first set out, supported by the friendship of some of the
best and noblest of the land, and furnished with a sum
which he had never dreamed of possessing; though but
starting for the race, he felt as if he already neared the
goal; and looking round upon his four attendants, who
were all, as they were termed in that day, especial stout
varlets, he almost wished, like a real knight-errant, that
some adventure would present itself, wherein he might
signalize himself for the first time in his native country.

Dame Fortune, however, was coy, and would not
favor him in that sort; and after having ridden on for
half an hour, enjoying almost to intoxication the deep
draughts of renewed hope, he brought to his side, by a
sign, our friend Longpole, who, now promoted to the
dignity of custrel, or shield-bearer, followed with the
armed servants of the duke, carrying Sir Osborne's tar-
get and spear.

"Tell me, Longpole," said the knight, who had remarked his faithful retainer in busy conversation with
his companions, "hast thou discovered why the duke's

servants have not his grace's cognizance or bearing, either
on the breast or arm?"

"Why, it seems, your worship, that they are three
stout fellows who attended the noble duke in the wars,
and they are commanded to wait upon your worship till
the duke shall have need of them. Each has his quiver
and his bow, besides his sword and pike; so if we should
chance to meet that wolf Sir Payan, or any of his under
wolves, we may well requite them for the day's board
and lodging which your worship had at the manor. We,
being five, could well match ten of them; and besides,
the little old gentleman in black velvet told me that your
worship would be fortunate in all things for two months
after you got out—but that after that he could not say
for——"

"What little gentleman in black are you speaking of?"
interrupted the knight. "You forget I do not know
whom you mean."

"Ay, true, your worship," answered Longpole. "I
forgot you were locked up all that while. But you must
know that when Sir Payan returned yesterday, he brought
with him a little gentleman dressed in a black velvet
doublet and crimson hose—but so small, so small, he
would be obliged to stand on tip-toe to look me into a
tankard. Well, Sir Payan sent for me, and questioned
me a great deal about the young lady who had been in
with you; and he thought himself vastly shrewd—for
certain he is cunning enough to cheat the devil out of a
bed and a supper any day; but I did my best to blind
him, and then he asked me for the key, and said he would
keep it himself. So I was obliged to give up the only
way I had of helping your worship; for I saw by that,
that Sir Payan suspected me, and would not trust me
any more near you, which indeed he did not. Well, he
made a speech to the little gentleman, and then left the
room; and I suppose I looked at the bottom of my wits,
for the little fellow says to me, 'Heartley! there's a

window as well as a door.' So I started, first to find
he knew my name, and secondly because he knew what
I was thinking about. However, I thought there was no
use to be angry with a man for picking my pocket of my
thoughts without my knowing it; so I took it quietly,
and answered, 'I know there is; but how shall I make
him understand what he is to do?'—'Tell me what it
is,' said he, 'and I will show you how.' So, I don't
know why, because he might have been a great cheat—
but I told him; and thereupon he took a bit of parchment
from his pocket—it might be half a skin, and a bit of
whitish wax, it looked like, out of a bottle, and made as
if he wrote upon the parchment; but the more he wrote,
the less writing I could see. However, he gave me the
piece of parchment, and told me to throw it in at the
window after dark, with a heap more. I resolved to try,
for I began to guess that the little old gentleman was a
conjuror; and when I got into the dark, I found that the
paper was all shining like a stinking fish; and your worship knows the rest."

"He is an extraordinary man," said Sir Osborne.
"But did you never hear your father speak of him?"

"I have heard my good dad talk about one Sir Cesar,"
said Longpole, "but I did not know that this was he.
If I had I would have thanked him for many a kind
turn he did for the two old folks while I was away.—
But does your worship see those heavy towers standing
up over the trees to the left? That is the Benedictine
Abbey, just out of Canterbury."

"That is where I am going," replied the knight, "if
that be Wilsbourne."

"Wilsbourne or St. Cummin," answered Longpole;
"they call it either. The abbot is a good man, they say,
which is something to say for an abbot, as days go. Your
abbey is a very silent discreet place; 'tis like purgatory,
where a man gets quit of his sins without the devil knowing anything about it."

" Nay, nay, you blaspheme the cloister, Longpole,"
said the knight; " I have heard a great deal spoken
against the heads of monasteries, but I cannot help thinking that as most men hate their superiors, some of the
monks would be sure to blazon the sins of those above
them, if they had so many as people say."

" Faith, they are too cunning a set for that," replied
Longpole; " they have themselves a proverb, which goes
to say—' Let the world wag, do your own business, and
always speak well of the lord abbot, so you shall feed
well, and fare well, and sleep, while tolls the matin bell.'
But your worship must turn up here, if you are really
going to the abbey."

The knight signified that such was certainly his intention, and turning up the lane that led across to the
abbey, in about a quarter of an hour he arrived at a
little open green, bordered by the high wall that surrounded the gardens. The lodge, forming, as it were,
part of the wall itself, stood exactly opposite, looking
over the green, with its heavy wooden doors and small
loop-hole windows. To it Longpole rode forward, and
rang the bell; and on the appearance of an old stupid-
faced porter, the knight demanded to see the lord abbot.

" You can see him at vespers in the church, if you like
to go any day," said the profound janitor, whose matter-
of-fact mind comprehended alone the mere meaning of
each word.

" But I cannot speak with him at vespers," said the
knight; " I have a letter for him from his grace of
Buckingham, and must speak with him."

" That is a different case," said the porter; " you
said you wanted to see the abbot, not to speak to him.
But come in."

" I cannot come in without you open the other gate,"
said the knight: " how can my horse pass, old man? "

" Light down then," said the porter; " I shall not let
in horses here, unless it be my lord abbot's mule, be you
who you will! "

"Then you will take the consequences of not letting me in," replied the knight, "for I shall not light down from my horse till I am in the court."

"Then you will stay out," said the old man, very quietly shutting the door, much to Sir Osborne's indignation and astonishment. For a moment he balanced whether he should ride on without further care, or whether he should again make an attempt upon the obdurate porter. A moment, however, determined him to choose the latter course, and, catching the bellrope, he rang a very sufficient peal. Nobody appeared, and angry beyond all patience, the knight again clapped his hand to the rope, muttering, "if you won't hear, old man, others shall;" and pulling for at least five minutes, he made the whole place echo with the din.

He was still engaged in this very sonorous employment, when the door was again opened by the porter, and a monk appeared, dressed simply in the loose black gown of St. Benedict, with the cowl, scapulary, and other vestments of a brother of the order.

"I should think, Sir Knight," said he, "that you might find some better occupation than disturbing myself and brethren here, walking in our garden, without offending you or any one."

"My good father," answered Sir Osborne, "it is I who have cause to be angry, rather than any one else. I came here for the purpose of rendering a slight service to my lord abbot, and am bearer of a letter from his grace of Buckingham; and your uncivil porter shuts your gate in my face, because I do not choose to dismount from my horse, and leave my attendants without, though I know not how long it may be convenient for your superior to detain me."

"You have done wrong," said the monk, turning to the porter; "first, in refusing to open the gate, next in telling me what was false about it. Open the great gates, and admit the knight and his train. I shall remember this in the penance."

The old porter dared not murmur, but he dared very well be slow, and he contrived to be nearly half an hour in the simple operation of drawing the bolts and bars, and opening the gates, which the good monk bore with much greater patience than the knight, who had fondly calculated upon reaching the village of Sithenburn that night, and who saw the day waning fast.

At length, however, the door unclosed, and he rode into the avenue that led through the gardens to the back of the abbey, the monk preparing to walk beside his horse. A feeling, however, of respect for a certain mildness and dignity in the old man's manner, induced him to dismount; and giving his horse to one of the servants, he entered into conversation with his conductor, while, as they went along, his clanging step and glistening arms called several of the brethren from their meditative sauntering, to gaze at the strange figure of an armed knight within their peaceful walls.

"Surely, father," said Sir Osborne, as they walked on, his mind drawn naturally to such thoughts, "the silent quietude of the scene, and the calm tranquillity of existence, which you enjoy here, would more than compensate for all the fleeting unreal pleasures of the world, without even the gratification of those holy thoughts that first call you to this retirement."

"There are many who feel it so, my son, and I among them," answered the old man; "but yet do not suppose that human nature can ever purify itself entirely of earthly feelings. Hopes, wishes, and necessities produce passions even here—pettier, it is true, because the sphere is pettier. But, depend upon it, no society can ever be so constructed, as to eradicate the evil propensities of man's nature, or even their influence, without entirely circumscribing his communion with his fellows. He must be changed, or solitary,—must have no objects to excite, or no passions to be excited,—he must be a hermit, or a corpse, have a desert, or the grave."

" 'Tis a bad account of human nature," said the knight.
" I had fancied that such feelings as you speak of were
unknown here,—that at all events religious sentiments
would correct and overcome them."

" They do correct, my son, though they cannot overcome them," said the monk. " I spoke of monastic life
merely as a human institution; and even in that respect
we are likely to meet with more tranquillity within such
walls as these, than perhaps anywhere else; because the
persons who adopt such a state from choice, are generally those of a calm and placid disposition, and religion
easily effects the rest. But there are others, driven by
disappointment, by satiety, by caprice, by fear, by remorse, by even pride; and urged by bad feelings from
the first, those bad feelings accompany them still, and
act as a leaven amongst those with whom they are thus
forced to consort. Even when it is but sorrow that,
weaning from worldly pleasure, brings a brother here,
often the sorrow leaves him, and the taste for the world
returns, when an irrevocable vow has torn him from it
forever; or else, if his grief lasts, it becomes a black and
brooding melancholy, as different from true religion, as
even the mad gaiety of the thoughtless crowd. There
was a youth here, not long ago, who was wont to call
the matin bell, the knell of broken hearts. Others, again,
circumscribed in the range of their feelings, become
irascible from the very restraint, and vent their irrita-
bility on all around them."

" But example in the superior does much," said the
knight; " and I have heard that your lord abbot——"

" Whether you are about to praise, or blame," said the
monk, " stop!—I am the abbot. If it were praise you
were about to speak, I could not hear it in silence; if
'twere blame, I would fain save you the pain of uttering
to my own ears what many doubtless say behind my
back."

" Indeed, my lord abbot," answered the knight, " I

had nothing to speak but praise; and had it been blame, I would sooner have said it to yourself than to one of your monks. But to the business which brings me hither. His grace the Duke of Buckingham, by this letter, commends him to your worship, and, knowing that I purpose journeying to the court, he has desired me to conduct, and protect with my best power, a young lady, whose name I forget, till I have rendered her safely to her royal mistress Queen Katherine."

"I thank you for the trouble you have already taken, my son. We will in to the scriptorium," said the abbot, "and when I have perused his grace's letter, will have the lady informed that you are here."

Although that art was rapidly advancing which soon after entirely superseded the necessity of manual transcription for multiplying books, yet the scriptorium, or copying-room, was still not only to be found, but was also still employed for its original purpose in almost every abbey or monastery of consequence. In that of the Benedictines of Wilsbourne, it was a large oblong chamber, vaulted with low Gothic arches, and divided into various small compartments by screens of carved oak. Each of these possessed its table and writing apparatus; and in more than one, when Sir Osborne entered, was to be seen a monk copying some borrowed manuscript, for the use of the abbey. The approach of the abbot, whose manners seemed to possess a great deal of primeval simplicity, did not in the least derange the copyists in their occupation; and it is probable that, when unengaged in the immediate ministry of his office, he did not exact that ceremonious reverence to which the mitred abbot was by rank entitled.

The abbot then sent some directions to the prior, concerning matters of discipline, and gave orders that the attendants of Sir Osborne should be brought to the hospitaler, whose peculiar charge it was to entertain guests and strangers; and this being done, he led the way

towards that part of the abbey which contained the
sisters of the order, preceded by a monk bearing a large
key.

Separated throughout by a wall of massive masonry, no
communication existed between the two portions of the
building, except by a small iron door, the key of which
always remained with the abbot, and by some under-
ground communications, as it was whispered, the knowledge of which was confined also to his own bosom. Of
these subterranean chambers, many dark tales of cruelty
and unheard-of penances were told, as having happened
in former ages, when monastic sway had its full ascendant; but even their very existence was now doubtful;
and when any one mentioned them before the abbot, he
only smiled, as a man will do at the tales of wonder that
amaze a child. However that may be, the way by which
he led the young knight to the female side of the monastery, was simply through the cloisters; and having
arrived at the door of communication, he took the key
from the bearer, unlocked it himself, and making the
knight pass into the cloister on the other side, he locked
the door and rejoined him.

The place in which they now were, was a gloomy
arcade, surrounding a small square court, in the centre
of which appeared a statue of Scholastica, the sister of St.
Benedict; and several almost childish ornaments evinced
the pious designs of the good sisters to decorate their
patroness. But notwithstanding all their efforts, it was
a dreary spot.

Another small door appeared on the left of the abbot,
who still held the key in his hand, but stopping, he pointed
along the cloister to the right, and said, " My son, I must
here leave you, for I go to my sister's apartment, to have
the lady called to the grate, and no layman must pass
here: but if you follow that arcade round the court, till
you see a passage leading again towards the light (you
cannot miss your way), you will come to the convent

court, as it is called, and exactly opposite you will find a
door which leads to the grate. There I will rejoin you."

The knight followed the lord abbot's direction, and
proceeding round the first side of the square, was turning into the second, when he thought he saw the flutter
of a white garment in the shadowy part of the inner
aisle. "It is some nun," thought he; but a moment's
reflection brought to his mind that the habit of the
Benedictines was always black; and it may be that
curiosity made him take a step or two somewhat faster
than he did before.

"Open the door, and make haste, Geraldine," said a
female voice in a low tone, but one that, nevertheless,
reverberated by the arches, reached the knight's ears
quite distinctly enough for him to hear the lady proceed.

"He must be on horseback, I think, by the quickness
of his pace, and the clanking of his hoofs. Cannot you
open it?"

"Run across the court then, silly wench, quick! or
Gogmagog will have you;" and with a light laugh, the
lady of the white robe darted out from the archway, and
tripped gracefully across the court, with her long veil
flowing back from her head as she ran, and showing fully
the beautiful brown hair with which it was mingled, and
the beautiful sunny face which it was meant to hide,
but which, fully conscious of its own loveliness, was now
turned with a somewhat playful, somewhat inquisitive,
somewhat coquettish glance, towards the knight.

Following close behind her, was a pretty young woman,
dressed as a servant maid, who ran on without looking
to the right or left, and who, probably being really
frightened, almost tumbled over her mistress, not perceiving that she slackened her pace as she reached the
other side of the court. It thus happened, that she trod
on the young lady's foot, who uttered a slight cry, and
leaned upon the servant for support.

As may be imagined, Sir Osborne was by her side in

a moment, expressing his hopes that she was not hurt, and tendering his services with knightly gallantry; but the lady suddenly drew herself up, made him a low curtsey, and stiffly thanking him for his attention, walked slowly to the door by which the abbot had entered.

Not very well pleased with the reception his politeness had met, the knight proceeded on his way, and easily found the passage which the abbot had described, leading, as he had been told, into the larger court exactly opposite the door by which visitors were usually admitted. This door, as usual, stood open; and mounting the steps, Sir Osborne proceeded on into a small room beyond, separated from the parlor by a carved oak partition, in the centre of which was placed the trellis work of gilded iron, called the grate.

Nobody appearing on the other side, Sir Osborne cast himself upon the bench, with which one side of the room was furnished, and waited patiently for the appearance of the lady, abandoning now, of necessity, the idea of proceeding farther that night. After having waited for a few minutes, a light step met his ear; and without much surprise, for he had already guessed what was the fact, he saw the same lady approach the grate whom he had met in the court. Rising thereupon from his seat, he advanced to the partition, and bowed low, as if to a person he had never seen. The lady, on her part, made him a low curtsey, and both remained silent.

"I am here," said the knight, after a long pause, " to receive the commands of Lady Katrine Bulmer, if I have now the honor of speaking to her?"

"My name is Bulmer, Sir Knight," replied the lady, "and also Katrine, and some folks call me lady, and some mistress; but by what my lord abbot and my lady abbess just tell me, it seems that I am to receive your commands rather than you to receive mine."

"Very far from it, madam," said the knight; "you have but to express your wishes, and they shall be obeyed."

"There now!" cried the lady, with an air of mock admiration; "Sir Knight, you are the flower of courtesy! Then you do not positively insist on my getting up at five to-morrow morning to set out, as my lord abbot informed me?—a thing I never did in my life, and which, please God, I never will do."

"I insisted upon nothing, madam," answered the knight; "I only informed my lord abbot that it would be more convenient to me to depart at an early hour; and I ventured to hint, that, if you knew of how much importance it might be for me to arrive at the court soon, you would gratify me by using all the despatch which you might, with convenience to yourself."

"Then it is of importance to you?" demanded the lady: "that changes the case; name the hour, Sir Knight, and you shall find me ready. But you know not what a good horsewoman I am; I can make long journeys and quick ones."

"Not less than two days will suffice, I fear," said the knight: "the first day we may halt at Gravesend——"

"Halt!" exclaimed the lady, laughing and turning to her woman, who stood at a little distance behind—"do you hear that? Halt! He talks to me as if I were a soldier. Tell me, Geraldine, is it possible that I look like a pikeman?"

"Not anyway like a soldier," replied the knight, sufficiently pleased with her liveliness and beauty to forget her pertness; "not any way like a soldier, unless it be one of heaven's host."

"Gracious God!" cried the lady, "he says pretty things! Only think of a man in armor being witty! But really, Sir Knight, it frightens me to see you all wrapped up in horrid steel. Can it possibly be that these Rochester shipwrights are so outrageous as to require a belted knight with lance in rest for the escort of a simple girl like me?"

"Men are wont to guard great treasures with even

9

superfluous care," replied Sir Osborne. The lady made him a very profound curtsey, and he proceeded: "This was most probably the lord abbot's reason for sending to request some escort from the Duke of Buckingham; for though I hear of some riot or tumult at Rochester, I cannot suppose it very serious. However, all I know is this, that the right reverend father did send, while I was there jousting in the park, and understanding that I was about to proceed to London, his grace resigned to me the honor of conducting you safely thither."

"What, then, you are not one of the duke's own knights?" exclaimed Lady Katrine.

"I am no one's knight," replied Sir Osborne with a smile, "except it be the king's and yours—if such you will allow me to be."

"Oh, that I will!" answered the lady. "I should like a tame knight above anything; but, in troth, I have spoken to you somewhat too lightly, sir." She proceeded more gravely:—"From what my lord uncle abbot told me, I judged the duke had sent me one of his household knights*—men who, having forty pounds a-year, have been forced to receive a slap on the shoulder, for the sake of the herald's fee; and then, having nought to do that may become the sir, they pin themselves to the skirts of some great man's robe, to do both knightly and unknightly service."

"Such am not I, fair lady," replied Sir Osborne, a little piqued that she could even have supposed so. "I took my knighthood in the battle-plain, from the sword

* It will be found in the description of Britain by Holinshed, that even in his days, it was held that any man possessing land producing an annual rent of forty pounds (called a knight's fee) could be called upon to undergo the honor of knighthood, or to submit to a fine. This was sometimes enforced, and the consequence was often what Lady Katherine insinuated, as few of the more powerful nobles of the day did not entertain more than one poor knight in their service. These, however, were looked upon in a very different light from those whose knighthood had been obtained by military service.

of a great monarch; and so long as I live, my service
shall never be given but to my lady, my king, or my
God!"

"Nay, nay, do not look so fierce, man in armor," answered Lady Katrine, relapsing into her merriment.
"Both from your manner and your mien, I should have
judged differently, if I had thought but for a moment;
but do not you see, I never think? I take a thing for
granted, and then go on acting upon it, as if it were
really true. But, as I said, you shall be my knight, and
before we reach the court, I doubt not I shall have a
task to give you, and a guerdon for your pains, if the
good folks of Rochester do not cut our throats in the
meanwhile. But what hour did you say, Sir Knight, for
setting out? for here my poor wenches have to make
quick preparations of all my habits."

"I have named no hour," replied Sir Osborne; "but
if you will do me the honor to let me know when you
are ready to-morrow, my horses shall stand saddled from
six in the morning."

"But how am I to let you know?" demanded the lady,
"unless I take hold of the bell-rope, and ring matins on
the convent bell; and then all the good souls will wink
their eyes, and think the sun has turned lie-a-bed. Dear
heart, Sir Knight, you do not suppose that the monks
and the nuns come running in and out between the two
sides of the abbey, like the busy little ants in their wonderful small cities? No, no, no, none comes in here but
my lord abbot and an old confessor or two, so deafened
with the long catalogue of worldly sins, that they would
not hear my errand, much less do it. But, now I think
of it, there is a good lay sister; her I will bribe with a
silver piece, to risk purgatory by going round to the
front gate of the abbey, and telling the monk when I
am ready. And now, good Sir Knight, I must go back
to my lord abbot, and fall down upon my knees and
beg pardon; for I left him so offended that he would

not come down with me, because I was pert about going early. Farewell! Judge not harshly of me till to-morrow; perhaps then I may give you cause—who knows?"

Thus saying, she tripped lightly away with a gay saucy toss of the head, like a spoiled child, too sure of pleasing to be heedful about doing so. As she turned away, the maid advanced to the grate, and informed Sir Osborne that the lord abbot would meet him at the place where they had parted; upon which information, the knight retraced his steps to the little court of the cloisters, where he found the abbot pacing up and down with a grave and thoughtful countenance.

"I am afraid, Sir Osborne Maurice," said he, as the knight approached, "that the young lady you have just left has not demeaned herself as I could have wished towards you; for she left me in one of those flighty moods which I had good hope would have been cured by her stay in the convent."

"She expected to find you still with the lady abbess," said Sir Osborne, avoiding the immediate subject of the abbot's inquiry; "and went with the intention of suing for pardon of your lordship, having given you, she said, some offence."

"I am glad to hear it, with all my heart," said the monk, "for then she is penitent, which is all that God requires of us, and all that we can require of others. Indeed, her heart is good, and though she commits many a fault, yet the moment after she repents, and would fain amend it. But come, Sir Knight, though our own rules are strict, we must show our hospitality to strangers, and I hope our refectioner has taken care to remember that you will partake the fare of my table to-night. But first you had better seek your chamber, and disencumber yourself of this armor, which, though very splendid, must be very heavy. Ho! Brother Francis, tell the hospitaller to come hither and conduct the knight to his apartment."

While this short conversation was taking place, the abbot had led Sir Osborne back into the cloisters on the male side of the building; and proceeding slowly along towards the wing in which was the scriptorium, and other apartments of general use, they were soon met by the hospitaller, who led the knight to a neat small chamber, furnished with a bed, a crucifix, and a missal.

Our friend Longpole soon made his appearance, and by his aid the knight freed himself from that beautiful armor, which we, who are in the secret of all men's minds, may look upon as in a great degree a present from the Duke of Buckingham.

After once more admiring for a moment or two the beauty of the suit, and having given directions for its being carefully cleansed of all damp that it might have acquired in the road, he descended to the table of the lord abbot, which he found handsomely provided for his entertainment.

To the wine, however, and the costly viands with which it was spread, the abbot himself did little justice, observing almost the rigid abstinence of an ascetic; but to compensate for his want of good-fellowship, the prior and subprior, who shared the same table, found themselves called upon to press the stranger to his food, and to lead the way.

CHAPTER X.

" I have dreamed
Of bloody turbulence."
SHAKSPEARE.

IN profound silence, will we pass over Sir Osborne's further entertainment at the abbey; as well as how Longpole contrived to make himself merry, even in the heart of a monastery.

The knight's horses were scarcely saddled and his four attendants prepared the next morning, than he was informed that the Lady Katrine Bulmer was ready to depart; and proceeding on foot to the great gates of the abbey, which fronted the high road, on the other side from that on which he had entered, he found her already mounted on a beautiful Spanish jennet, with her two women and a man, also on horseback. By her side stood the abbot, with whom she had now made her peace, and who, kindly welcoming Sir Osborne, led him to the young lady.

" Sir Knight," said he, " I give you a precious charge in this my dead sister's child, and I give her wholly to your charge, with the most perfect confidence, sure that you will guide her kindly and safely to her journey's end. And now, God bless you and speed you, my child," he continued, turning to the young lady; " and believe me, Kate, there is no one in the wide world more anxious for your happiness than your poor uncle."

" I know it, I know it, dear uncle," answered the lady, " and though I be whimsical and capricious, do not think your Katrine does not love you too: " a bright drop rose in her eye, and crying, " Farewell! farewell! " she made her jennet dart forward, to conceal the emotion she could not repress.

The knight sprang on his horse, bade farewell to the abbot, and galloped after Lady Katrine, who drew her rein in for no one, but rode on as fast as her steed would go. However notwithstanding her jennet's speed, Sir Osborne was soon by her side; but, seeing a tear upon her cheek, he made no remark, and, turning round, held up his hand for the rest to come up, and busied himself in giving orders for the arrangement of their march, directing the two women, with Lady Katrine's man, and Longpole, to keep immediately behind, while the three attendants given him by the duke concluded the array. The young lady's tears were soon dispersed, and she turned laughing to her women, who came up out of breath with the rapidity of their course.

"Well, Geraldine," she cried, "shall I go on as quick? Should I not make an excellent knight at a joust, Sir Osborne? Oh, I would furnish my course with the best of you. I mind me to try the very next jousts that are given."

"Where would you find the man," said Sir Osborne, "to point a lance at so fair a breast? unless it be Cupid's shaft."

"Ah, Sir Osborne Maurice," answered the lady, "you men jest when you say such things; but you know not sometimes what women feel. But trust me, that same Cupid's shaft that you scoff at, because it never wounds you deeply, sometimes lodges in a woman's breast, and rankling there will pale her cheek, and drain her heart of every better hope."

The lady spoke so earnestly that Sir Osborne was surprised, and perhaps looked it; for instantly catching the expression of his eye, Lady Katrine colored, and then breaking out into one of her own gay laughs, she answered his glance as if it had been expressed in speech.

"You are mistaken! quite mistaken!" said she, "I never thought of myself. Nay, my knight, do not look incredulous; my heart is too light a one to be so touched.

It skims like a swallow o'er the surface of all it sees, and the boy archer may spend his shafts in vain; its swift flight mocks his slow aim. But to convince you—when I spoke," she proceeded in a lower voice, " I alluded to that poor girl, Geraldine, who rides behind. Her lover was a soldier; who, when Tournay was delivered to the French, was left without employment, and after having won the simple woman's heart, and promised her a world of fine things, he went as an adventurer to Flanders, vowing that he would get some scribe to write to her of his welfare; and that as soon as he had made sufficient, what with pay and booty, they would be married; but eighteen months have gone, and never a word."

"What was his name?" asked the knight; " I would wish much to hear."

"Hal Williamson, I think she calls him," said the lady: " but it matters little; the poor girl has nigh broke her heart for the unfaithful traitor."

"You do him wrong," said the knight; " indeed, lady, you do him wrong. The poor fellow you speak of joined himself to my company at Lisle, and died in the very last skirmish before the death of the late emperor. With some money and arms, that I expect transmitted by the first Flemish ship, there is also a packet, I fancy for your maid, for I forget the address. From it she will learn that he was not faithless to her, together with the worse news of his death."

"Better! a thousand times better!" cried Lady Katrine energetically. " If I had a lover, I would a thousand times rather know that he was dead, than that he was unfaithful. For the first, I could but weep all my life, and mourn him with the mourning of the heart; but for the last, there would be still bitterer drops in the cup of my sorrow. I would mourn him as dead to me—I would mourn him as dead to honor; and I should reproach myself for having believed a traitor, almost as much as him for being one."

" So! " said the knight, with a smile, " this is the heart that defies Cupid's shaft—that is too light and volatile to be hit by his purblind aim! "

" Now you are stupid," said she, pettishly. " Now you are just what I always fancied a man in armor. Why I should have thought that, while your custrel carries your steel cap, you might have comprehended better, and seen that the very reason why my heart is so giddy and so light, is, because it is resolved not to be so wounded by the shaft it fears."

" Then it does fear? " said Sir Osborne.

" Pshaw! " cried Lady Katrine. " Geraldine, come up, and deliver me from him: he is worse than the Rochester rioters."

In such light talk passed they their journey, Sir Osborne Maurice sometimes pleased, sometimes vexed, with his gay companion, but, upon the whole, amused, and in some degree dazzled. For her part, whatever might be her more serious feelings, the lady found the knight quite handsome and agreeable enough to be worthy a little coquetry.

At length they approached the little town of Sittenbourne, famous even then for a good inn, where, even had they not been plagued themselves with that unromantic thing called hunger, they must have stopped to refresh their horses, amongst which the one that carried the baggage of Lady Katrine, being heavily laden, required at least two hours' repose.

The inn was built by the side of the road, though sunk two or three feet below it, with a row of eight old elms shadowing its respectable-looking front.

Here, when Lady Katrine had entered, while the knight gave orders for preparing a noon meal in some degree suitable to the lady's rank, she amused herself in examining all the quaint carving of the old oak pannelling, and having studied every rose in the borders, and every head upon the corbels, she dropped into a chair, crying

out, " Oh, dear! Oh, dear! what shall I do in the meanwhile? Bridget, girl, bring me my broidery out of the
horse-basket—I feel industrious. But make haste, for
fear the fit should leave me."

" Bless your ladyship," replied the servant, " the
broidery is at the bottom of all the things in the pannier.
It will take an hour or more to get at it—that it will."

" Then give me what is at the top, whatever it is,"
said the lady; " quick! quick! quick! or I shall be asleep."

Bridget ran out, according to her lady's command, and
returned in a moment with a cithren or mandolin, which
was a favorite instrument among the ladies of the day,
and placing it in Lady Katrine's hand, she cried, " Oh,
dear lady, do sing that song about the knight and the
damsel? "

" No, I won't," answered her mistress, " it will make
the man in armor yawn. Sir Knight," she continued,
holding up the instrument, " do you know what that
is? "

" It seems to me no very great problem," replied Sir
Osborne, turning from some orders he was giving to
Longpole; " it is a citharn, is it not? "

" He would fain have said, ' A thing that some fools
play upon, and other fools listen to,' " cried Lady Katrine;
" make no excuse, Sir Osborne, I saw it in your face, I'm
sure you meant it."

" Nay, indeed, fair lady," replied the knight, " it is an
instrument much used at the court of Burgundy, where
my days have lately been spent. We were wont to hold
it as a shame not to play on some instrument, and I know
not a sweeter aid to the voice than the citharn."

" Oh, then you play and sing! I am sure you do,"
cried the giddy girl. " Sir Osborne Maurice, good knight
and true, come into court—pull off your gauntlets, and
sing me a song."

" I will truly," answered the knight, " after I have
heard your ladyship, though I am but a poor singer."

"Well, well," cried Lady Katrine, "I'll lead the way, and if you are a true knight, you will follow."

So saying, she ran her fingers lightly over the strings, and commenced her song.

It may well be supposed that the music, and the execution, all met with their full share of praise, although Bridget declared that she liked better the song about the knight and the damsel.

"Now, your promise, your promise, Sir Knight," cried the lady, putting the instrument in Sir Osborne's hands; "keep your promise as a true and loyal knight."

"That I will do, to my best power," said Sir Osborne, "though my voice will be but rough after the sweet sounds we have just heard." And he sang with some skill and taste a ballad of the period.

"Alack! alack!" cried Lady Katrine, as Sir Osborne concluded his song, "you are not a knight, but a nightingale. Well, never did I hear a man in armor chirrup so before. Nay what a court must be that court of Burgundy! Why an aviary would be nothing to it—but here comes our host with dinner, for which I thank heaven."

As soon as the horses were refreshed, Sir Osborne, with his fair charge, once more set out on the longer stage, which he proposed to take ere they paused for the night. The news which he had received at Sittenbourne, leading him to imagine that the tumults at Rochester having been suffered, by some inexplicable negligence, to remain unrepressed, had become much more serious than he at first supposed, he determined to take a by-way, and avoiding the town, pass the river by a ferry, which Longpole assured him he would find higher up; but still this was longer, and would make them later on the road; for which reason he hurried their pace as much as possible, till they arrived at the spot where the smaller road turned off, at about two miles' distance from Rochester.

It was a shady lane which seemingly promised seclusion and safety but speedily the noise of a distant drum, and a variety of shouts and halloos came floating upon the gale, like the breakings-forth of an excited multitude.

As they advanced, the sounds seemed also to approach.

"My casque and lance," said Sir Osborne, turning to Longpole. "Lady, you had perhaps better let your jennet drop back to a line with your women."

"Nay, I will dare the front," said Lady Katrine; "a woman's presence will often tame a crowd."

"You are with a band of soldiers," said Sir Osborne, hearing the clamor approaching, "and must obey command. What, horse, back! back!" and laying his hand on the lady's bridle, he reined it back to a line with her women. "Longpole, advance!" cried the knight. "Left hand spear, of the third line, to the front! Archers behind, keep a wary eye on the banks;—shoot not, but bend your bows. I trust there is no danger, lady, but 'tis well to be prepared. Now on slowly."

And thus opposing what defence they could between Lady Katrine and the multitude, whose cries they now heard coming nearer and nearer, Sir Osborne, and the two horsemen he had called to his side, moved forward, keeping a wary eye on the turnings of the road, and the high banks by which it was overhung.

They had not proceeded far, however, before they descried the termination of the lane, opening out upon what appeared to be a village green beyond; the farther side of which was occupied by a motley multitude, whose form and demeanor they had now full opportunity to observe.

In front of all the host was a sort of extempore drummer, who with a bunch of cock's feathers in his cap, and a broad buff belt supporting his instrument of discord, seemed infinitely proud of his occupation, and kept beating with unceasing assiduity, but with as little regard to time on his part, as his instrument had to tune. Behind him, mounted on a horse of inconceivable ruggedness, appeared the general, with a vast cutlass in his hand, which he swayed backwards and forwards in menacing attitudes; while, unheedful of the drum, he bawled forth to his followers many a pious exhortation to persevering rebellion. On the left of this doughty hero was borne a flag of blue silk, bearing, inscribed in golden letters, "The United Shipwrights;" and on his right was seen a red banner, on which might be read the various demands of the unsatisfied crowd, such as "cheap bread," "high wages," "no taxation," etc.

The multitude itself did, indeed, offer a formidable appearance, the greater part of the men who composed it being armed with bills and axes, some also having possessed themselves of halberts, and some even of hackbuts and hand-guns. Every here and there appeared an iron jack, and many a prentice-boy filled up the crevices with his bended bow, while half a score of loud-mouthed women screamed in the different quarters of the crowd, and with the shrill trumpet of a scolding tongue urged on the lords of the creation to deeds of wrath and folly.

The multitude might consist of about five thousand men; and as they marched along, a bustle, and appearance of crowding round one particular spot in their line, led the knight to imagine that they were conducting some prisoner to Rochester, in which direction they seemed to be going, traversing the green at nearly a right angle with the line in which he was himself proceeding.

"Hold!" said Sir Osborne, reining in his horse. "Let them pass by. We are not enough to deal with such numbers as there are there. Keep under the bank—we must not risk the lady's safety by showing ourselves. Ah! but what should that movement mean? They have seen us, by heaven! Ride on then, we must not seem to shun them. See, they wheel! On, on, quick! Gain the mouth of the lane."

Thus saying, Sir Osborne laid his lance in the rest, and spurred on to the spot where the road opened upon the green, followed by Lady Katrine and her women, not a little terrified and agitated by the roaring of the multitude.

As soon as the knight had reached the mouth of the road, he halted; and seeing that the high bank ran along the side of the green guarding his flank, he still contrived to conceal the smallness of his numbers by occupying alone the space of the road, and paused a moment to watch the movements of the crowd, and determine its intentions.

Now, being quite near enough to hear great part of an oration which the general whom we have described was bestowing on his forces, Sir Osborne strained his ear to gather his designs; and soon found that his party was mistaken for that of Lord Thomas Howard, who had been sent to quell the mutiny of the Rochester shipwrights.

"First," said the ringleader, "hang up the priest upon that tree, then let him preach to us about submission if he will—and he shall be hanged, too, in his Lord's sight, for saying that he, with his hundreds, would beat us with our thousands; and let his Lord deliver him if he can. Then some of the men with bills and axes get up on the top of the bank. Who says it is not Lord Thomas? I say it is Lord Thomas, I know him by his bright armor."

"And I say you lie, Timothy Bradford!" cried Longpole, at the very pitch of his voice, much to the wonder and astonishment of Sir Osborne and all his party. "Please your worship," he continued, lowering his tone, "I know that fellow; he served with me at Tournay, and was afterwards a sailor. He's a mad rogue, but as good a heart as ever lived."

" Oh, then for God's sake speak to him!" cried Lady Katrine from behind, "and make him let us pass; for surely, Sir Knight, you are not mad enough, with only six men, to think of encountering six thousand?"

" Not I, in truth, fair lady," answered the knight. " If they will not molest us, I shall not meddle with them."

" Shall I on then, and speak with him?" cried Longpole. " See! he heard me give him the lie, and he's coming out towards us. He'd do the same if we were a thousand."

" Meet him, meet him then," said the knight; "tell him all we wish is to pass peaceably. The right hand man advance from the rear and fill up," he continued, as Longpole rode on, taking care still to maintain a good face to the enemy, more especially as their generalissimo had now come within half a bow-shot of where they stood.

As the yeoman now rode forward, the ringleader of the rioters did not at all recognize his old companion in his custrel's armor, and began to brandish his weapon most fiercely; but in a moment afterwards, to the astonishment of the multitude, he was seen to let the point of the sword drop, and seizing his antagonist's hand, shake it with every demonstration of surprise and friendship. Their conversation was quick and energetic; and a moment after Longpole rode back to Sir Osborne, while the ringleader raised his hand to his people, exclaiming, " Keep your ranks!—friends! these are friends!"

" Our passage is safe," said Longpole, riding back; "but he would fain speak with your worship. They have taken a priest, it seems, and are going to hang him for preaching submission to them. So I told him, if they did, they would be hanged themselves; but he would not listen to me, saying he would talk to you about it."

" Fill up my place," said the knight; " I will go and see

what can be done.   We must not let them injure the good
man."

So saying, he raised his lance, and rode forward to the
spot where the ringleader waited him; plainly discerning,
as he approached nearer to the body of the rioters, the
poor priest, with a rope round his neck, holding forth
his hands towards him, as if praying for assistance.

"My shield-bearer," said he, "tells me that we are
to pass each other without enmity, for though we are well
prepared to resist attack, we have no commission to
meedle with you or yours.   Nevertheless, as I understand
that ye have a priest in your hands, towards whom ye
meditate some harm, let me warn you of the consequences
of injuring an old man who cannot have injured you."

"But he has done worse than injured me, Sir Knight,"
said the ringleader; "he has preached against our cause,
and against redressing our grievances."

"Most probably, not against redressing your grievances," said Sir Osborne, "but against the method ye
took to redress them yourselves.   But listen to me.   It
is probable that the king, hearing of your wants and
wishes—he being known both for just and merciful—may
grant you such relief as only a king can grant; but if ye
go to stain yourselves with the blood of this priest—
which were cowardly, as he is an old man, which were
base, as he is a prisoner, and which were sacrilegious, as
he is a man of God—ye cut yourselves off from mercy
forever, and range all good men among your enemies.
Think well of this!"

"By the nose of the tinker of Ashford," said the man,
"your worship is right.   But how the devil to get him
out of their hands? that's the job; however, I'll make 'em
a 'ration.   But what I was wanting to ask your worship
is, do you know his grace the king?"

"Not in the least," was the laconic reply of the
knight.

"Then it won't do," said the man; "only as merry

Dick Heartley said you were thick with the good Duke of Buckingham, I thought you might know the king too, and would give him our petition and remonstrance. However, I'll go and make them fellows a 'ration—they're wonderful soon led by a 'ration." And turning his horse, he rode up to the front of the body of rioters, and made them a speech, wherein nonsense and sense, bombast and vulgarity, were all most intimately mingled. Sir Osborne did not catch the whole, but the sounds which reached his ears were somewhat to the following effect.

" He, the noble knight, is not Lord Thomas Howard, and so far from wishing to attack you, he would wish to do you good. Therefore he setteth forth and showeth—praise be to God for all things, especially that we did not hang the priest!—that if we were to hang the priest, it would be blasphemous, because he is an old man; and rascally, because he is a man of God; and moreover, that whereas, if we do not, the king will grant us our petition —he will infallibly come down, if we do, with an army of fifty thousand men, and hang us all with his own hands, and the Duke of Buckingham will be against us. Therefore, I give my vote, that Simon the cannon-founder, Tom the shipwright, and Long-chinned Billy the tinker, do take the priest by the rope that is round his neck, and deliver him into the hands of the knight and his men, to do with as they shall think fit. And that, after this achievement, we march straightway back to Rochester. Do you all agree? "

Loud shouts proclaimed the assent of the multitude; and with various formalities the three deputies led forth the unhappy priest, more dead than alive, and delivered him into the hands of Longpole; after which the generalissimo of the rioters drew up his men with some military skill upon the right of the green, leaving the road free to Sir Osborne. The knight then marshalled his little party as best he might, to guard against any sudden change in the minds of the fickle multitude; and having

10

mounted the poor exhausted priest behind one of the horsemen, he drew out from the lane, and passed unmolested across the green into the opposite road, returning nothing but silence to the cheers with which the rioters thought fit to honor them.

Their further journey to Gravesend passed without any interruption, and indeed without any occurrence worthy of notice.

Lady Katrine Bulmer was grave and pensive when she reached Gravesend; and then, without honoring the knight with her company even for a few minutes, as he deemed that in simple courtesy she might have done, she retired to her chamber, and, shutting herself up with her two women, the only communication which took place between her and Sir Osborne was respecting the hour of their departure the next morning.

The knight felt hurt and vexed; for though he needed no ghost to tell him, that the lovely girl he was conducting to the court was as capricious as she was beautiful, yet her gay whims and graceful little coquetry had both served to pique and amuse him, and he could almost have been angry at this new caprice, which deprived him of her society for the evening.

The next morning, however, the wind of Lady Katrine's humor seemed again to have changed; and at the hour appointed for her departure, she tripped down to her horse all liveliness and gaiety. Sir Osborne proffered to assist her in mounting, but in a moment she sprang into the saddle without aid, and turned round laughing, to see the slow and difficult manœuvres by which her women were fixed in their seats. The whole preparations, however, being completed, the cavalcade set out in the same order in which it had departed from the abbey the day before, and with the same number of persons; the poor priest whom they had delivered from the hands of the rioters being left behind, too ill to proceed with them to London.

"Well, Sir Knight," said the gay girl as they rode forward, "I must really think of some guerdon to reward all your daring in my behalf. I hope you watched through the livelong night, armed at all points, lest some enemy should attack our castle."

"'Faith, not I," answered Sir Osborne; "you seemed so perfectly satisfied with the security of our lodging, lady, that I e'en followed your good example, and went to bed."

"Now he's affronted!" cried Lady Katrine; "was there ever such a creature? But tell me, man in armor, was it fitting for me to come and sit with you and your horsemen, in the tap-room of an inn, eating, drinking, and singing, like a beggar or a ballad-singer?"

The knight bit his lip, and made no reply.

"Why don't you answer, Sir Osborne?" continued the lady, laughing.

"Merely because I have nothing to say," replied the knight, gravely; "except that at Sittenbourne, where you did me the honor of eating with me, though not with my horsemen, I did not perceive that Lady Katrine Bulmer was, in any respect, either like a beggar or ballad-singer."

"Oh! very well, Sir Knight; very well!" she said. "If you choose to be offended, I cannot help it."

"You mistake me, lady," said Sir Osborne. "I am not offended."

"Well then, sir, I am," replied Lady Katrine, making him a cold, stiff inclination of the head. "So we had better say no more upon the subject."

At this moment Longpole, who with the rest of the attendants followed at about fifty paces behind, rode forward, and put a small folded paper into Sir Osborne's hands. "A letter, sir, which you dropped," said he; "I picked it up this moment."

The knight looked at the address, and the small silken braid which united the two seals, and finding that it

was directed to Lord Darby at York House, Westminster, was about to return it to Longpole, saying it
was none of his, when his eye fell upon Lady Katrine,
whose head, indeed, was turned away, but whose neck
and ear were burning with so deep a red, that Sir Osborne
doubted not she had some deep and blushing interest in
the paper he held in his hand. " Thank you, Longpole!
thank you," he said, " I would not have lost it for an
hundred marks ; " and he fastened it securely in the fold-
ings of his scarf.

Though he could willingly have punished his fair companion for her little capricious petulance, the knight
could not bear to keep her in the state of agitation under
which, by the painful redness of her cheek, and the
quivering of her hand on the bridle, he very evidently
saw she was suffering. " I think your ladyship was
remarking," said he, calmly, " that. it was the height of
dishonor and baseness to take advantage of anything
that happens to fall in our power, or any secret with
which we become acquainted accidentally. I not only
agree with you so far, but I think even that a jest upon
such a subject is hardly honorable. We should strive,
if possible, to be as if we did not know it."

Lady Katrine turned her full sunny face towards him,
glowing like a fair evening cloud when the last rays of
daylight rest upon it: " You are a good—an excellent
creature," she said, " and worthy to be a knight. Sir
Osborne Maurice," she continued, after a moment's
pause, " your good opinion is too estimable to be lightly
lost, and to preserve it I must speak to you in a manner
that women dare seldom speak. And yet, though, on my
word, I would trust you as I would a brother, I know
not how—I cannot, indeed I cannot.—And yet I must, and
will, for fear of misconstruction.—You saw that letter.—
You can guess that he to whom it is addressed is not
indifferent to the writer.—They are affianced to each
other by all vows—but those vows are secret vows ; for

the all-powerful Wolsey will not have it so—and we must needs seem, at least, to obey. Darby has been some time absent from the court, and I was sent to the abbey.—What would you have more?—I promise to give instant information of my return; and last night I spent in writing that letter, though now I know not in truth how to send it, for my groom is but a pensioned spy upon me."

"Will you trust it to me?" said the knight. The lady paused. "Do you doubt me?" he asked.

"Not in the least," she said, "not in the least. My only doubt is, whether I shall send it at all."

"Is there a hesitation?" demanded the knight in some surprise.

"Alas! there is," answered she. "You must know all—I see it. Since I have been at the abbey, they have tried to persuade me that Darby yields himself to the wishes of the cardinal, and is about to wed another.—I believe it false—I am sure it is false! and yet, and yet" —and she burst into tears.—"Oh! Sir Osborne," she continued, drying her eyes, "I much need such a friend as you described yesterday."

"Let me be that friend, then, so far as I may be," said Sir Osborne. "Allow me to carry the letter to London, whither I go after I have left you at the court at Greenwich. I will ascertain how Lord Darby is situated—if I find him faithful (which doubt not that he is till you hear more), I will give him the letter— otherwise I will return it truly to you."

"But you must be quick," said Lady Katrine, "in case he should hear that I have returned, and have not written. How will you ascertain?"

"Many ways," answered the knight, "but principally by a person whom I hope to find in London, and who sees more deeply into the hidden truth, than mortal eyes can usually do."

"Can you mean Sir Cesar?" demanded Lady Katrine,

" I do," answered the knight: " do you know that very extraordinary being? "

" I know him as every one knows him," answered Lady Katrine, " that is, without knowing him. But if he be in London, and will give you the information, all doubt will be at an end; for what he says is sure,—though indeed I often used to tease the queer little old man, by pretending not to believe his prophecies, till our royal mistress, whom God protect, has rated me for plaguing him. He was much a favorite of hers—and I, somewhat a favorite of his; for those odd magical hop o' my thumbs, I believe, love those best who cross them a little. He gave me this large sapphire ring when he went away last year, bidding me send it back to him, if I were in trouble—quite fairy-tale like.—So now, Sir Osborne, you shall carry it to him, and he will counsel you rightly. Put it in your cap, where he may see it.—There, now, it looks quite like some fair lady's favor! so don't go and tilt at every one who denies that Katrine Bulmer is the loveliest creature under the sun."

" Nay, I must leave that to my Lord Darby," answered Sir Osborne.

" Now that was meant maliciously," cried Lady Katrine. " But I don't care—wait a little, and if there be a weak point in all your heart, Sir Knight, I'll plague you for your sly look."

Lady Katrine Bulmer's spirits were of that elastic quality, not easily repressed; and before ten minutes were over, all her gaiety returned in full force, nor did it cease its flow till their arrival at Greenwich.

When Sir Osborne and his party arrived at the brow of Shooter's Hill, the evening was as fair and lovely as if it had been summer—one of those sweet sunsets that sometimes burst in between two wintry days in the end of March, or the beginning of April, as a sort of herald to announce the golden season that comes on.

Sir Osborne Maurice impulsively reined-in his horse,

and seemed as if he could scarcely breathe when the whole magnificent scene rushed at once upon his view. " So this is London ! " cried he, " the vast, the wealthy, and the great; the throne of our island monarchs, from whence they sway a wide and powerful land. On! on!" and striking his horse with his spurs, he darted down the road as if he were afraid that the great city would, before he reached it, fade away like the splendid phantasms seen by the Sicilian shepards, showing for a moment a host of castles and towers and palaces, and then fleeting by, and leaving nought but empty air!

CHAPTER XI.

" Paracelsus and his chymistical followers are so many Prom-
ethei, will fetch fire from Heaven."
                    BURTON'S ANATOMY OF MELANCHOLY.

LADY KATRINE, having recalled to the knight's remembrance that his course lay toward Greenwich, and not
to London, as he seemed inclined to direct it, they turned
their horses to the right, at the bottom of the hill, and
soon reached the riverside, where, spreading along a little to the eastward of the spot on which Greenwich Hos-
pital at present stands, lay a large mass of heavy architecture, which, if judged by modern notions, would be
regarded as not very fit for the dwelling of a king.

The dull appearance of the building, however, was relieved by the gaiety of the objects round about; for
though the sun was now half below the horizon, yet
loitering round the various gates of the palace, or running to and fro on their separate errands, was seen a host
of servants and attendants in rich and splendid suits,
while multitudes of guards and henchmen, decked out to
pamper the costly whims of their luxurious lords, showed
forth their finery to the evening air. More than one
group of lords and ladies too, enjoying the fine sun-
set before the palace, made the parade a sort of living
pageant; while the river beyond, as if emulous of the gay
scene, fluttered and shone with the streamers and gilding of the various barges with which it was covered.

To every one they met, Lady Katrine seemed known,
and all, according to their rank, greeted her as she passed,
some with light welcome, some with respectful salutations, all stopping the moment after to turn and fix their
eyes upon Sir Osborne, with that sort of cold inquiring

glance which owns no affinity with its object but mere curiosity.

"Who is he?" demanded one; "What splendid armor!" cried another; "He must be from Rochester," said a third: but no word of gratulation met his ear, no kind familiar voice bade him welcome.

At one of the smaller doors in the western wing of the palace Lady Katrine reined in her horse, and Sir Osborne, springing to the ground, assisted her to dismount, while one of the royal servants, who came from within, held the bridle with all respect. In answer to her question, the attendant replied, that "Her highness Queen Katherine was at that moment dressing for the banquet which she was about to give to the king and the foreign ambassadors, and that she had commanded not to be interrupted."

"That is unfortunate, Sir Osborne Maurice," said the young lady, resuming somewhat of that courtly coldness which had given way to the original wildness of her nature while she had been absent;—"I am sure that her highness, who is bounty itself, would have much wished to thank you for the protection and assistance which you have given to me her poor servant. But—" and remembering the charge which the knight had taken of her letter to Lord Darby, she hesitated for a moment, not knowing how to establish some means of communication between them—"Oh! they will break all those things!" she cried, suddenly stopping and turning to the servant; "Good Master Alderson, do look to them for a moment, that groom is so awkward. Give him the horse.—Now, knight! quick! quick!" she continued, lowering her voice as the servant left them, "where do you lodge in London? I must have some way of hearing of your proceeding—where do you lodge?—Bless us, man in armor! where are your wits?"

"Oh, I had forgot," replied the knight: "it is called the Rose, in the Lawrence Poultney."

"At the Duke of Buckingham's!   Good, good!" she replied; and then making him a low curtsey as the servants again approached, she added with a mock gravity that nearly made the knight laugh, in spite of his more sombre feelings.   "And now, good Sir Knight, I take my leave of your worship, thanking you a thousand times for your kindness and protection; and depend upon it, that when her highness the queen shall have a moment to receive you, I will take care to let you know."

Thus saying, with another low curtsey, she retired into the palace; and Sir Osborne, mounting his horse, bade adieu to the precincts of the court, bearing away with him none of those feelings of hope with which he had first approached it.

After having ridden on for some way, giving full rein to melancholy fancies, he found himself in the midst of a small town, whose narrow streets, running along by the river, shut out almost all the daylight that was left; and not knowing if he was going in the right direction, he called Longpole to his side, asking whether he had ever been in London.

"Oh, yes, sir," replied the custrel, "and have stayed in it many a month.   'Tis a wonderful place for the three sorts of men—the knaves, the fools, and the wise men; and as far as I can see, the one sort gets on as high as the other.   The fool gets promoted at court, the knave gets promoted at the gallows, and the wise man gets promoted to be Lord Mayor, and has the best of the bargain."

"But tell me, Longpole," said Sir Osborne "where are we now? for night is falling, and, in sooth, I know not my way."

"This is the good town of Deptford," said Longpole; "but if your worship ride on, we shall soon enter into Southwark, where there is an excellent good hostel, called the Tabard, the landlady of which may well be esteemed a princess for her fat, and a woman for her tongue. God's blessing is upon her bones, and has well covered them. If your worship lodge there, you shall be treated like a prince."

"It may be better," said Sir Osborne, "for to-night; but you must lead the way, good Longpole, for this is my first sight of the great city."

Longpole readily undertook the pilotage of the knight and his company, and in about half an hour lodged them safely in the smart parlor of the Tabard.

The knight supped well, and found himself happier— slept well, and rose with renewed hope. So he was but of flesh and blood after all.

As soon as he was up, and before he was dressed, the door of his chamber flew open, and in rushed a thing called a barber, insisting upon his being shaved.

Sir Osborne acquiesced in the operation, of which, indeed, he stood in some want; and the barber pounced upon his visage in a moment. "The simple moustache, I see, the simple moustache!" he cried; "well, 'tis indeed the most seemly manner, though the pique-devant is gaining ground a leetle a leetle: not that I mean to say, fair sir, that the beard is not worn any way, so it be well trimmed—and the moustache is of a sweet comely nature —the simple moustache!—We use, indeed, to cut beards all ways, to suit the nature of the physiognomy; supplying, as it were, remedies for the evil tricks of nature.—Now, my good Lord Darby gives in to the pique devant, for it is a turn that ladies love; and doubtless you have heard his marriage spoken of—to a lady—Oh! such a beautiful lady! though I cannot remember her name— but a most excellent lady.—Your worship would not wish me to leave the pique devant?"

"No, no!" cried Sir Osborne, much in the same manner as the young man of Bagdad: "Cease your babbling, and make haste and shave me."

The operation, however, was finally brought to an end, and being free from his chattering companion, the knight took one or two turns in his apartment in deep thought.

"So," said he, "this light of love, Lord Darby, does play
the poor girl false; and, as she said, the arrow will rankle
in her heart, and rob her of every better hope. But still
it is not sure—I will not believe it. If I had the love of
such a creature as that, could I betray it?" and the
thought of Lady Constance de Grey darted across his
mind. "I will not believe it—there must be better assurance than the babbling fool like that.—Oh, Longpole,"
he continued, as the man entered the room, "I have
waited for you. Quick! As you know London, speed
to the house of an honest Flemish merchant, William
Hans—ask him if he have received the packages from
Anvers for me—give him my true name, but bid him be
secret. Bring with you the leathern case containing
clothes, and see if he have any letters from Wales. Greet
the old man well for me, and tell him I will see him soon.
—Stay! I forgot to tell you where he lives—'tis near the
Conduit, in Gracious Street, any one near will tell you
where. William Hans is his name."

Longpole was soon gone, but, to the mind of Sir Osborne, long before he returned. When, however, he did
once more make his appearance, he not only brought
the news that all the packages which Sir Osborne expected had arrived, but he also brought the large leathern
case containing the apparel in which the knight was wont
to appear at the court of the Duchess Regent of Burgundy, and a letter, which Sir Osborne soon perceived
was from his father, Lord Fitzbernard.

Being privileged to peep over men's shoulders, we
shall make no apology for knowing somewhat of the
contents of the old earl's epistle. It conveyed in many
shapes the gratifying knowledge to the son, that the
father was proud of the child, together with many ex-
hortations, founded in parental anxiety, still carefully to
conceal his name and rank. But the most important
part of the letter was a short paragraph, wherein the earl
laid his injunctions upon his son, not to think of coming

to see him till he had made every effort at the court, and their fate was fully decided. "And then, my son, continued Lord Fitzbernard, " come hither unto me, whether the news thou bringest be of good or bad comfort, for, of a certain, thy presence shall be of the best comfort; and if still our enemies prevail, I will pass with thee over sea into another land, and make my nobility in thy honor, and find my fortune in thy high deeds."

Sir Osborne's wishes would have led him into Wales, for, after five long years of absence, he felt, as it were, a thirst to embrace once more the author of his birth; but still he saw that the course which his father pointed out was the one that prudence and wisdom dictated, and therefore at once acquiesced. For awhile he paused, meditating over all the feelings that this letter had called up; but, well knowing that every moment of a man's life may be well employed, if he will but seek to employ them, he cast his reveries behind him, and dressing himself in a costume more proper to appear at the house of the Duke of Buckingham, he commanded his armor to be carefully looked to, and paying his score at the Tabard, departed to fulfil his noble friend's hospitable desire, by taking up his lodging at the manor-house of the Rose, in Saint Lawrence Poultney.

Passing through Southwark, he soon arrived at London Bridge, which, as every one knows, was then but one long street across the water, with rich shops and houses on each side, and little intervals between, through which the passenger's eye might catch the flowing of the Thames, and thence only could he learn that he was passing over a large and navigable river. The shops, it is true, were unglazed and open, and perhaps to a modern eye might look like booths; but in that day the whole of Europe could hardly furnish more wealth than was then displayed on London Bridge.

Passing, then, over London Bridge, the knight and his followers took their way up Gracious Street (now

corruptly Gracechurch Street), and riding through the
heart of the city, soon arrived at the gates of the Duke
of Buckingham's magnificent mansion of the Rose. As
they approached the garden entrance, they observed a
man covered with dust, as from a long journey, dismount from his horse at the door, bearing embroidered
on his sleeve the cognizance of a swan: from which, with
the rest of his appearance, Sir Osborne concluded that
he was a courier from the duke. This supposition proved
to be correct; the considerate and liberal-minded nobleman having sent him forward to prepare the household
to receive his young protégé, and also for the purpose
of conveying various other orders and letters, which
might tend to the advancement of his views. But it so
unfortunately had happened, the man informed the knight,
that he had been attacked on the road by four armed
men, who had taken from him his bag with the letters;
and that therefore the only thing which remained for
him to do, was to deliver the verbal orders which he
had received to his grace's steward, and then to return
to his lord, and inform him of the circumstances as they
had occurred.

The profound respect with which he was treated, very
soon evinced to Sir Osborne what those verbal orders
were.

He found the retinue of a prince ready to obey his
command, and a dwelling, that in decoration, if not in
size, certainly surpassed that of the king. It was not,
however, the object of the young knight to draw upon
himself those inquiries which would certainly follow any
unnecessary ostentation; nor would he have been willing,
even had it coincided with his views, to have made his
appearance at court with so much borrowed splendor.
He signified, therefore, to the chamberlain, his intention
of requiring merely the attendance of the three yeomen
who, with his own custrel, had accompanied him from
Kent; and added, that though he might occupy the apart-

ments which had been allotted to him when he was in London, and dine at the separate table which, by the duke's command, was to be prepared for himself, he should most probably spend the greater part of his time at Greenwich.

Having made these arrangements, he determined to lose no time in proceeding to seek for Dr. Butts, the king's physician, at whose house he had good hope of hearing of his old tutor, Dr. Wilbraham, and of discovering what credit was to be given to the reported marriage of the young Earl of Darby.

Sir Osborne knew that the physician was one of those men who had made and maintained a high reputation at the court by an honest frankness, which, without deviating into rudeness, spared not to speak the truth to king or peasant. He was greatly loved and respected at the court; and from his character and office, was more intimately acquainted with all the little private secrets and lies of the day, than any other person perhaps, except Sir Cesar the astrologer, with whom he was well acquainted, and upon whom he himself looked with no small reverence and respect, shrewdly suspecting that in his magical studies he had discovered the grand secret.

Towards his house, then, Sir Osborne directed his steps, taking with him no one but a foot-boy of the duke's, to show him the way; for as the good physician lived so far off as Westminster, it became necessary to have some guide to point out the shortest and most agreeable roads. Passing by York Place, where bustling menials and crowding courtiers announced the ostentatious power of the proud prelate who there reigned, they left the royal mansions also behind them, and entering into some of the narrower and more intricate streets in Westminster, soon reached a house with a small court before it, which, as the boy informed Sir Osborne, was the dwelling of the physician.

Seeing a door open opposite, the knight entered, and

found himself in a sort of scullery, where a stout servant-girl was busily engaged in scrubbing some pots and crucibles, with such assiduity that she could scarcely leave off even to answer his inquiry of whether her master was at home.

"Yes, sir, yes! he is at home," replied she at length; "but he cannot be spoken with, unless you are very bad, for he is busy in the laboratory."

The knight signified that he had a great desire to speak with him; and the girl, looking at him somewhat more attentively, said, that "if he were from abroad, the doctor would see him, she was sure, for he had a great many foreign folks with him always."

The knight replied, that though he was not a foreigner, he certainly had come from abroad very lately; upon which assurance the damsel relinquished her crucible-scrubbing, and went to announce his presence. Returning in a few minutes, she ushered him through a long dark passage, into a large low-roofed room, at the further end of which appeared a furnace, with the chimney carried through the ceiling, and near it various tables covered with all sorts of strange vessels and utensils.

The principal curiosity in the room yet remained. Standing before the furnace, holding in one hand a candle sweltering in the heat of the fire, and in the other a pair of chemical tongs embracing a crucible, was seen a stout portly man, of a rosy complexion, with a fur cap on his head, and his body invested in a long coarse black gown, the sleeves of which, tucked up above his elbows, exhibited a full puffed shirt of very fine linen, much too white and clean for the occupation in which he was busied.

"Sir, my servant tells me you are from abroad," said he, advancing a little, and speaking quick. "From Flanders, I see, by your dress.—Pray, sir, do you come from the learned Erasmus or from Meyerden? However, I am glad to see you. You are an adept, I am sure—I see it in your countenance."

An explanation now ensued, which at last enlightened the ideas of the worthy physician.

"Bless my soul!" cried he; "so you are the young gentleman that my excellent good uncle Wilbraham was concerned about; and well he might be, truly, seeing what a lover you are of the profound and noble science. He came here yesterday to inquire for you, and finding that I had heard nothing of you, I thought he would have gone distracted. But tell me, fair sir, have you met with any of the famous green water of Palliardo? Ha! I see you were not to be deceived—I procured some, and truly on dipping the blade of the knife therein, it appeared gilt. But what was it? A mere solution of copper."

"You mistake, I see, still," replied the knight; "in truth, I know nothing of the science to which you allude. I doubt not that it is both one of the most excellent and admirable inquiries in the world, but I am a soldier, my dear sir, and have as yet made but small progress in turning anything into gold."

"'Slife! I know not how I came to think so," cried the doctor; "sure, the servant told me so. Ho, Kitty! But who is this I see? Oh, Uncle Wilbraham:—Come in! come in!"

No words can express the joy of the good tutor when he beheld the knight. He embraced him a thousand times; he shook him by the hand; he shed tears of joy, and he made him repeat a thousand times every particular of his escape. "The villain! the wretch!" cried he, whenever the name of Sir Payan was mentioned; "the dissembling hypocrite! We have had news since we left Canterbury that the posse, which I obtained with great difficulty from the magistrates, when they arrived at the manor-house, found every one in bed, but were speedily let in, when Sir Payan sent word down that, though he was much surprised to be so visited, being a magistrate himself, yet the officers might search where they pleased, for that he had had no prisoners during the day but two deer-stealers, whom he had liberated that evening on their penitence. They searched, and found no one, and so sent me a bitter letter this morning for putting them on the business."

" I am glad to hear they found no one," said the knight; " for then my poor companion, Jekin Groby, has escaped. But, let me ask, how is Lady Constance?"

" Alas! not well, my lord, not well!" answered the clergyman. " First, the anxiety about you: in truth, she has never looked well since, not knowing whether you were dead or alive, and having known you in her youth. Then this sudden news, that my lord cardinal will have her marry her noble cousin, Lord Darby, has agitated her."

The knight turned as pale as death, for feelings that had lain unknown in the deepest recesses of his heart swelled suddenly up, and nearly overpowered him.

" Umph!" said Dr. Butts, at once comprehending all that the changes of the knight's complexion implied; " umph! it's a bad business."

" Nay, my good nephew, I see not that," answered the clergyman; who, a great deal less clear-sighted than the physician, had neither seen Sir Osborne's paleness, nor for a moment suspected his feelings—" I see not that. 'Tis the very best marriage in the realm for both parties, and the lady is only a little agitated from the anxiety and hurry of the business."

" If that be all," said the doctor, " I'll soon cure her. But tell me, why did you call him my lord, just now?"

Dr. Wilbraham looked at the knight with a glance that seemed to supplicate pardon for his inadvertence; but Sir Osborne soon relieved him. " I am going, Dr. Butts," said he, " to ask your advice and assistance, and therefore my secret must be told you. I ask your advice, because you know the court thoroughly; and because having, I am afraid, lost one good means of introducing myself to his grace the king, I would fain discover some other; and I tell you my secret, because I am sure that it is as safe with you as with myself."

"It is," said the physician. "But if you would have me to serve you well, and to some purpose, you must tell me all. Give me no half-confidence. Let me know everything, and then, if I can do you good, I will; if not, your counsel shall not be betrayed, my lord, I suppose I must say."

"You had better tell him all your history, my dear Osborne," said Dr. Wilbraham. "He can, and I am sure will, for my sake, serve you well."

"My dear Osborne!" echoed the physician. "Then I have it! You are my Lord Darnley, my good uncle's first pupil. Your history, my lord, you need not tell me—that I know. But tell me your plans, and I will serve you heart and hand, to the best of my power."

The plans of our hero need not be again detailed here. Suffice it that he laid them all open to the worthy physician, who, however, shook his head. "It's a mad scheme!" said he, in his abrupt manner. "His grace, though right royal, bountiful, and just, is often as capricious as a young madam in the honeymoon. However, if Buckingham, Abergany, Surrey, and such wise and noble men judge well of it, I cannot say against it. A straw, 'tis true, will balance in one way or t'other. However, give me to-day to think, and I will find some way of bringing you to the king, so as to gain his goodwill at first.—And now I will go to see Lady Constance de Grey."

"We will go along, good doctor," exclaimed the tutor: "for I must be back to speak with her, and Osborne must render her a visit, to thank her for her good wishes and endeavors in his behalf. She will be so charmed to see him free and unhurt, that 'twill make her well again."

" Will it?" said the doctor, dryly. " Well, you shall give her that medicine after I have ordered her mine. But let me have my turn first. Thus saying, the learned physician left them, to proceed on his visit to Lady Constance de Grey.

CHAPTER XI.

"Though Heaven's inauspicious eye
Lay black on love's nativity,
Her eye a strong appeal shall give:
Beauty smiles, and love shall live."
CRASHAW.

WHEN Dr. Butts had left them, the knight would fain
have excused himself from accompanying his old tutor
on the proposed visit. He had encountered many a
danger in the " imminent deadly breach " and the battle-
field with as light a heart as that which beats in beauty's
bosom, when she thinks of sunning herself in admiring
looks at the next ball; but now his courage failed him,
at the thought of meeting the person he loved best, and
so much did his spirit quail, that "you might have
brained him with a lady's fan."

Dr. Wilbraham, however, pressed, and insisted so intently upon the pleasure it would give Lady Constance
to see him after his escape, and the rudeness which might
be attributed to him if he did not wait upon her soon,
that he at length consented to go; and shortly after the
physician had left them, they themselves took the way
towards the dwelling of the lady. In this happy age,
when choice is as free as thought, we can hardly imagine
the generous nobility of England submitting to yield the
selection of a companion for life to the caprice of a king
or of his favorite; yet such was frequently the case in
the times whereof we write, and dangerous would it
have been to have opposed the will of the despotic Henry,
or his tyrant minister, when the whim of the one, or the
interest of the other, led them to seek the union of any
two families. Nor at that time was Wolsey's will less
potent than the king's; so that, to the mind of the young

knight, the marriage of Lady Constance with Lord Darby
seemed fixed beyond recall.

"If I dared but think she loved me," thought Sir
Osborne, "I should fear nothing;" and he felt as if his
single arm could conquer a world. But then came the
remembrance, that as equivalent for her rich lands and
lordships, he had nothing—absolutely nothing! and with
a sigh he entered the house which Wolsey had taken care
to provide for his fair ward as near his own palace as
possible.

Most doors in that day standing open, Dr. Wilbraham,
whose sacred character gave him much freedom of
access, took no pains to call servant or attendant to
announce them, but leading the way up the narrow winding stairs, opened the door at the end of the flight, and
brought Sir Osborne into a large room, wherein were
sitting several of the young lady's women, occupied in
various tasks of needle-work and embroidery. One of
these rose, and in silence gave them entrance to a chamber
beyond: into which the clergyman conducted his former
pupil, without even the ceremony of announcing him.

Lady Constance, at the moment, was seated somewhat
listlessly on a pile of oriental cushions, holding her arm
extended, while Dr. Butts kept his hand upon her pulse.
She was dressed in white, after the mode of the French
of that day: the upper part of her robe, except the
sleeves, which were large and floating, fitting close to
her figure round the waist and shoulders, but falling
back, just above the bosom, into a beautiful standing
ruff, or fraise, as the French termed it, of fine Italian
lace. The skirt of the robe was wide and loose, and
dividing at the girdle, showed part of a satin dress
beneath, as well as the beautiful small foot and delicate
ankle, which, hanging over the edge of the cushions,
indicated, fully as much as the heaviness of her eyes,
the languor of sickness and want of rest. A few yards
behind her stood her waiting-woman, who remained in

the room, fully as much in capacity of duenna, as for the purpose of serving her mistress.

As Lady Constance did not raise her head when the door opened, thinking that it was some of the domestics who entered, the eyes of the waiting-maid were those that first encountered Sir Osborne; and as she bore him no small good-will for having given up with such alacrity the tapestry chamber at the inn to herself and lady, immediately on perceiving him she burst forth with a pleasurable " Oh dear! "

Lady Constance looked up, and seeing who entered, turned as red as fire, then pale, then red again; and starting up from the cushions, drew her hand suddenly away from Dr. Butts,—advanced a step—hesitated—and then stood still.

" Umph! " muttered the physician, " it's a bad business."

" Oh, Sir Osborne Maurice," said the lady, her eyes sparkling with pleasure, although she struggled hard to compose herself, to seem disembarassed, and to hide the busy feelings at her heart—" I am most delighted to see you safe; for indeed I—that is, Dr. Wilbraham, began to be very seriously alarmed—and though he told me there was no danger, yet I saw that he was very much frightened, and—and—I hope you got away easily.— Will you not take that seat? "

The young knight took the chair to which she pointed, and thanked her for the interest and kindness she had shown towards him, with some degree of propriety, though at first he felt his lip quiver as he spoke; and then he fancied that his manner was too cold and ceremonious, so, to avoid that, he made it somewhat too warm and ardent, and in the end, finding that he was going from one extreme to the other, without ever resting at the mean, he turned to Dr. Butts, and said, with a sort of anxiety, which went thrilling to the heart of Lady Constance, that he hoped he had not found his patient really ill.

"Indeed I did though," answered the physician, "a great deal worse than I had expected, and therefore I shall go directly and tell my good lord the reverend father cardinal, that the lady must be kept as tranquil as possible, and as quiet."

"Nay, nay," said Lady Constance, "I am not so ill, indeed, my good physician—I feel better now. However, you may go to my lord cardinal if you will—but I really am better."

"Umph!" said Dr. Butts, "now I think you are worse. But tell me, lady, why do you quit the habits of your country, to dress yourself like a Frenchwoman?"

Lady Constance smiled. "Do you not know," said she, "that I am a French vassal?—do you not know that all the estates that belonged to my mother, of the Val de Marne and Boissy, are held from the French crown?"

"Go and see them, lady," said Dr. Butts; "the French air would suit you better than the English, I've a notion; for a year or two, at least."

"Nay, Dr. Butts," said Sir Osborne, "why deprive England of Lady Constance's presence?—There are so few like her," he added, in an under voice, "that indeed we cannot spare her."

Lady Constance raised her eyes for an instant to his face—they met his, and though it was but for a moment, that look was sufficient to determine his future fate. A thousand such looks from Lady Katrine Bulmer would have meant nothing; from Lady Constance de Grey, that one meant everything, and Sir Osborne's bosom beat with renewed hope. True, the same obstacle existed as heretofore; but it mattered not. Nothing, he thought—nothing now could impede his progress; and he would dare all—defy all—win her, or die.

Nor in truth was the heart of Lady Constance de Grey less lightened, although she still felt that trembling fear which a woman perhaps does not wholly lose for long, long after the lips of the man she loves have made pro-

fession of his attachment; yet still she was almost sure
that she was loved. There had been something in
Darnley's manner, in his agitation, in his anxiety about
her, in his very glance, far, far more eloquent than words;
and Lady Constance's certainty that he loved her, was
more, perhaps a sensation of the heart, than a conviction
of the mind—she felt that she was loved.

While these thoughts, or feelings, or what you will,
were busy in the bosom of each, a servant entered, and
with much more ceremony than the good chaplain had
used to usher in the young knight, announced that Lord
Darby waited in the antechamber to inquire after her
ladyship's health.

"Bid him come in," said the young lady, and in a
moment after, Sir Osborne had his rival before his eyes.

He was a slight, elegant young man, dressed with
great splendor of apparel and possessed of that sort of
calm, easy self-possession, and gay, nonchalant bearing,
that made the knight instantly conceive a violent inclination to cut his throat.

"Good-morrow, my fair cousin!" cried he, advancing;
"good-morrow, gentles all—God gi' ye good-morrow,
Mrs. Margaret," to the waiting woman—"what, have you
been standing there ever since I left you yesterday?"
(The woman tossed her head pettishly, much to the
young lord's amusement.) "Gad! you must do like the
hens then—stand upon one leg while you rest the other.
But say, my fair cousin, how dost thou do?"

"I am not well, my lord," replied the lady, "at least,
so Dr. Butts would fain have me believe, and he says I
must have quiet; so, by your leave, I will not have you
quarrel with my woman Margaret, as you did yesterday."

"Faith, not I," answered he; "I love her dearly, bless
the mark! But cousin, his reverend grace the cardinal
commends him, by your humble slave, to your most sublime beauty, and adviseth (that is, you know, com-
mandeth) that you should betake yourself, for change of

air (which means for his pleasure and purposes), to the court at Greenwich, to which you are invited by our royal mistress and queen. And if it seemeth fit to you (which would say, whether you like it or not), he will have his barge prepared for you to-morrow at noon."

" Present my thanks unto the very reverend father," replied Lady Constance, " and say that I will willingly be ready at the hour he names.

" Nay, if you are so sweetly obedient to all his commands," said Lord Darby, more seriously, " faith, Constance, our plan of yesterday will fall to the ground; for I cannot be rude enough to take it all on myself." Then darting off into a thousand other subjects, the young peer laughed and spoke with light facility of various indifferent matters; while Dr. Butts looked on, keenly observing all that passed, and Sir Osborne bent his eyes sternly upon the ground, biting his lip and playing with the hilt of his sword, more irritated, perhaps, with the confident gaiety of his rival, than he would have been with a more serious and enthusiastic passion, and certainly not appearing to advantage where he wished most to please.

" That sword, I think, must be of Spanish mounting," said Lord Darby, at length turning calmly towards the knight.

" Sir!" replied Sir Osborne, raising his eyes to his face.

" I asked whether that sword was not mounted in Spain, Sir Knight?" said Lord Darby quietly. " Will you let me look at it?" and he held out his hand.

" I am not in the habit, my lord," replied Sir Osborne, " of giving my weapon out of my own hands; but in answer to your question—it was mounted in Spain."

" I never steal folk's swords," said the peer, with the same imperturbably nonchalant air; and then turning to Dr. Wilbraham, he went on—" Dear Dr. Wilbraham, do let me see that book you talked of yesterday; for as you go to Greenwich to-morrow, I shall never behold any of you again, I am sure."

The good chaplain, who had remained silent ever since he had been in the room, not at all understanding what was the matter between Lady Constance and the young knight, although he evidently saw that they had from the first been both agitated and embarrassed, now rose, and went to search for the book which Lord Darby required, very willing to get away from a scene he did not in the least comprehend. To make way for him, however, Sir Osborne raised his cap and plume, which had hitherto lain beside him; and as he did so, the sapphire ring, that had been given him by Lady Katrine Bulmer, met the eye of Lord Darby, and instantly produced a change in his whole demeanor. His cheek burned, his eye flashed, and, starting upon his feet, he seemed as if he would have crossed over towards Sir Osborne; but then recovering himself, he relapsed into his former somewhat drawling manner, took leave of Lady Constance, and, without waiting, for Dr. Wilbraham's return, left the apartment.

A moment after, the physician also rose, in his usual quick, precipitate manner, saying that he must depart.

"But, doctor! doctor!" cried Mrs. Margaret, the waiting-woman, seeing him proceeding towards the door, "you have not told me how I am to manage my mistress."

"I can't stop! I can't stop!" said the physician, still walking on out of the room. "What is it? what is it?"

"Nay but, doctor, you must tell me," cried she, running after him. "Indeed, I shall not know what to do with my lady." Still the doctor walked on, giving her, however, some necessary directions as he went, and Mrs. Margaret following, for a moment, left the two lovers alone.

Darnley felt that it was one of those precious instants, which, once lost, rarely if ever return; but an irresistible feeling of anxiety tied his tongue, and he could but gaze at Lady Constance, with a look that seemed to plead for pardon, even for what he felt. The fair girl trembled in every limb, and, as if she knew all that was passing in his mind, dared not look up but for a single glance, as she heard the last words hang on the physician's lip when he began to descend the stairs.

Darnley raised the glove that lay beside her. " May I, may I nave it? " said he.

" Oh, Darnley! " she replied; and happy almost to delirium, he placed the glove in his bosom, and pressed an ardent kiss upon her hand.

" Go! " cried she; " for heaven's sake! Go if you love me! We shall meet again soon."

The knight obeyed, almost as agitated as herself; and passing out of the room just as Mrs. Margaret entered, he followed Dr. Butts, whose steps he heard descending the stairs before him. Scarcely knowing what he did, Sir Osborne sprang after Dr. Butts, and walked on with him for a minute or two in silence, while his brain turned, and all his thoughts and feelings whirled in inextricable confusion.

" Ah! " muttered the physician to himself, seeing the absent agitated air of his young companion. " Ah! you've been making a fool of yourself, I see, though you've not had much time either."

The murmuring of the good doctor, however, did not disturb in the least the young knight's reverie, which might have lasted an indefinite space of time, had he not been roused therefrom by a smart tap on the shoulder. Laying his hand upon his sword, he turned suddenly round, and beheld Lord Darby, who, seeing him grasp the hilt of his weapon, pointed to it coolly, saying, " Not here, sir, not here; but anywhere else you please."

" What would you with me, sir? " demanded· the

knight, not exactly understanding his object, though quite ready to quarrel upon any provocation that might occur.

"But a trifle," replied the earl. "You looked at me some five minutes past as if I had offended you in something. Now, that being the case, I am ready to make reparation at the sword's point when and where it may suit your convenience."

"But, my good lord," said Dr. Butts, who had turned back, "this is a mistake. How can you have offended this good knight, who never saw you till to-day?"

"Oh, the problem, the problem, my good doctor," replied Lord Darby. "Why does a farmer's cur bark at a beggar, and let a ruffling gallant swagger by? Perchance the knight may not like my countenance—my complexion—my nose may not please him—my mouth—the cut of my beard."

"Faith! neither one nor the other please me particularly," answered Sir Osborne. "At all events, my lord, if your wish be to quarrel with me, I will not balk your humor. So say your will, and have it."

"Oh, if that be the case," said Lord Darby, "and you'd rather be quarrelled with than quarrel, the offence shall come on my part. Fair sir, I dislike that scar upon your brow so much, that I shall not be content till I make its fellow on your heart; therefore, when your good-humor serves to give me an opportunity of tilling at your nose, you will find me your very humble servant."

"Nay, now, my lord," cried Dr. Butts, "I must witness that you have given the provocation; for under any other circumstances, this gentleman is so situated that 'twould be mere madness to meet you as you wish."

"If it be provocation he desires," cried the earl, "he shall have a dish of it, so cooked as to serve an emperor. He is a gentleman, I suppose, and worth a gentleman's sword?"

"Your equal in every respect, and your better in many,"
replied the knight. "And in regard to provocation, I
have had as much, my lord, as your body may well bear
in repayment. How do you choose to fight?"

"Quietly! quietly!" answered the earl. "A few inches
of tough steel are as good as a wagon load. A double-
edged sword, sir, such as we both wear, may serve our
turn, I should suppose; and as it may be unpleasant to
both of us to make the monster multitude busy with
our little affair, we will be single—hand to hand—I do
detest the habit of making the satisfaction of private
wrongs the public amusement. We'll have no crowd,
sir, to look on and criticise our passados, as if we were
gladiators on a stage. Where shall it be?"

"Why, faith, my lord," answered the knight, "as I
am a mere stranger here, I know but of one place. The
gardens of my lord of Buckingham, at the Rose, are
large; and I remarked this morning a grove, where there
must be good space and quiet. If, therefore, you will
inquire for me at his grace's dwelling this evening, at
four of the clock, you will find me prepared to receive
you."

Lord Darby waved his hand for his page to come up,
who stood chattering with the footboy that had accompanied the knight, and taking from him a case of tablets,
he wrote down the name of Sir Osborne, and the place
and the hour he had appointed. "And now, fair sir,"
said he, "I will leave you. I shall not miss my hour.
Good doctor, your profession has doubtless taught you
secrecy—and so farewell."

So saying, Lord Darby walked away, leaving Sir Osborne with Dr. Butts. "Ah!" cried the physician, "a
bad business! a bad business! Yet it cannot be helped;
if two people will fall in love with the same woman, what
can be done? But it's a bad business for you. If he
kills you—why, that is not pleasant; and if you kill him,
you must fly your country. A bad business! a bad busi-

ness! But fare ye well. Don't kill him if you can help it; for he's not bad, as times go—wound him badly, then it may be mended. Fare ye well! fare ye well!" and turning away, he left Sir Osborne, not appearing to take much heed of the approaching duel, though in reality deeply occupied with the means of preventing it, without betraying the trust that had been reposed in him.

Sir Osborne was not displeased to be left to his own meditations; and, plunged in thought, followed his young guide down a narrow lane, running between the gardens of York and Durham House. "I thought, sir, you might like to take boat," said the boy, who was himself completely wearied out with waiting for the knight, "and so brought your worship down here, where there is always a boatman. "'Twill save three miles, your worship."

Sir Osborne signified his assent, and the boat being procured, he was soon after landed within a short distance of St. Lawrence Poultney, where he was received with great respect by the duke's household, and formally marshalled to his apartment. Two hours still remained to the time of rendezvous, which he spent in writing to his father; never thinking, however, of alluding to his approaching rencontre; for in truth, though not vain either of his skill or strength, he had enjoyed so many opportunities of proving both, that he well knew it must be a strong and dexterous man indeed, who would not lie greatly at his mercy in such an encounter as that which was to ensue.

In the meanwhile, Lord Darby, carried away by passion, thought of nothing but his approaching meeting; and though he looked upon Sir Osborne as some knight attached to the Duke of Buckingham, he was very willing to pass over any little difference of rank for the sake of gratifying the rage and jealousy by which he was possessed. He was, however, very greatly surprised, when, on presenting himself, towards four o'clock, at the manor-house of the Rose, he found that the same attendance and respect waited Sir Osborne Maurice, a man he had never even heard of, as he had seen paid to the Duke of Buckingham himself. Two servants marshalled the way to the knight's apartments, one ran on before to announce him, and with a deference and attention, which evidently did not proceed from his own rank, for he had not given his name, but rather, apparently, from the station of the person whom he went to visit, he was ushered into the splendid apartments which had been assigned to the knight.

Sir Osborne rose from the table where he had been writing, and with graceful but frigid courtesy, invited him to be seated, which was complied with by the earl, till such time as the servants were gone.

"Now, my lord," said Sir Osborne, as soon as the door was shut, "I am at your service; I will finish my writing at my return. Will you examine my sword? 'tis apparently somewhat longer than yours; but here is one that is shorter. Now, sir."

"That is shorter than mine," said Lord Darby. "Have you not another?"

"Not here," replied the knight; "but this will do, if you are satisfied that it is not longer than your own. By this passage we shall find our way to the garden privately, as I am informed. Pardon me, if I lead the way."

Lord Darby followed in silence, perhaps not quite so contented with the business in which he was engaged as when he first undertook it. There was a sort of calm determination in Sir Osborne's manner, that had something in it very unpleasantly impressive, and the young peer began to think it would have been better to have sought some explanation ere he had hurried himself into circumstances of, what might be, unnecessary danger. However, he felt that it was now too late to make any advance towards such a measure; and there, too, in the knight's cap, still stood the identical large sapphire ring, which, if he might believe his eyes, he had seen a thou-

"What devil has tempted ye," said Sir Cesar, as he sprang between them, parting their swords with his bare hands.   Page 177.

Darnley.

sand times on the hand of his promised wife. The sight thereof served marvellously well to stir up his anger, and striding on, he kept equal pace with Sir Osborne down the long alley which led from the house into a deep grove near the side of the river. The knight paused at a spot where the trees concealed them from the view of the house, and opening out into a small amphitheatre, gave full space for the deadly exercise in which they were about to be engaged.

"Now, Lord Darby," said he drawing his sword, and throwing down the scabbard before him, "you see me as I stand; and as a knight and a gentleman, I have no other arms, offensive or defensive, but this sword, so help me God!"

"And so say I," replied Lord Darby, "upon my honor;" and following the knight's example, he drew his sword, cast the sheath away from him, and brought his blade across that of his adversary.

"Madmen! what are ye about to do?" cried a stern voice from the wood. "Put up, put up!" and the moment after, the diminutive form of Sir Cesar the astrologer stood directly between them. "What devil," he continued, parting their drawn swords with his bare hand—"what devil has tempted ye—ye, of all other men, destined to bring about each other's happiness—what devil, I say, has tempted ye to point these idle swords at each other's life?"

"Sir Cesar," said Lord Darby, "I am well aware that you possess the means of seeing into the future by some method, for which they hint that you are likely to be damned pretty heartily in the next world—so you are just the person to settle our dispute. But tell us, which it is of us two that is destined to slay the other, and then the one who is doomed to taste cold iron this day, will have nothing to do but offer his throat, for depend upon it, only one will leave this spot alive."

"Talk not so lightly of death, young lord," replied the

old man, " for 'tis a bitter and unsavory cup to drink, as
thou shalt find when thy brain swims, and thy heart grows
sick, and thine eye loses its light, and thy parting spirit
reels upon the brink of a dim and shadowy world. But
I tell thee, that both shall leave this spot alive; though if
any one remained upon this sward, full surely it were thyself, for thou art as much fitted to cope with him, as the
sapling with the thunderbolt of heaven. But listen—each
of you, I adjure you, state what you demand of the other,
and if, after that, ye be still bent upon blood, blood ye
shall have. But full sure am I that now neither knows
what the other seeks."

Both the antagonists stood silent, gazing first on each
other, and then on Sir Cesar, as if they knew not what to
reply, and both feeling that there might be some truth
in what the old man advanced. At length, however,
Lord Darby broke forth—" God's life, what he says is
true! Sir Osborne Maurice, what do you seek of me?"

" Speak! speak!" cried Sir Cesar, turning to the
knight, who seemed to hesitate—" speak, if the generous
blood of a thousand noble ancestors be still warm in your
veins! be candid, and charge him like a man."

Sir Osborne's cheek burned; " The quarrel is of his
own seeking," said he, " and what I have to say, I know
not how to speak, without violating the confidence of a
lady, which cannot be."

" Then I will speak for you," said Sir Cesar. " Lord
Darby, he demands that you shall yield all claim and all
pursuit of Lady Constance de Grey. This is his demand
—now for yours. Oh! if I am deceived in you, woe to
you and yours forever!"

" I can scarcely suppose," replied the earl, with bitter
emphasis, " that such be this knight's demand, when I
see the ring of another lady borne openly in his bonnet—
a lady that shall never be his, so long as one drop of
blood flows in my veins."

" This ring, my lord," replied Sir Osborne, taking it

from the plume of his hat, " was only trusted with me as a deposit to transmit to the person to whom it originally belonged, claiming his advice for a lady, whose affianced lover was, as report said, about to wed another—Sir Cesar, I give it unto you for whom it was intended."

" Faith, I have been in the wrong," cried Lord Darby, extending his hand frankly to Sir Osborne; " in the first place, pardon me, Sir Knight, for having insulted you; and next, let me say, that in regard to Lady Constance de Grey, I have no claim, but that of kindred, upon her affection, and none upon her hand. Farther, if you can show that your rank entitles you to such alliance, none will be happier than myself to aid you in your suit. Though, let me observe, without meaning offence, that the name of Sir Osborne Maurice is unknown to me, except as connected with the history of the last reign. And now, sir, having said thus much, doubtless you will explain to me how that ring came into your possession, and by what motives Lady Katrine Bulmer could be induced to confide her most private affairs to a gentleman who can but be an acquaintance of a month."

" Most willingly," replied the knight; and after detailing to Lord Darby the circumstances which we already know, he added, " The letter of which I speak is still in my possession, and if you will return with me to the house, I will deliver it to you; as I cannot doubt, from what you say, that the report of a marriage being in agitation between yourself and Lady Constance de Grey originated in some mistake."

" 'Faith, not a whit!" cried the earl; " the report is unhappily too true. The lord cardinal, whom we all know to be one degree greater than the greatest man in England, has laid his commands upon me to marry my cousin Constance, although both my heart and my honor are plighted to another, and has equally ordered my cousin to wed me, although her heart be, very like, fully as much given away as mine. However, never supposing we could think of disobeying, he has already sent to Rome for all those permissions and indulgences which are necessary for first cousins in such cases; and on my merely hinting in a sweet and dutiful manner, that it might be better to see first whether it pleased the lady, he replied, meekly, that it pleased him, and that it pleased the king, which was quite enough both for her and me."

This information did not convey the most pleasing sensations to Sir Osborne's heart, and in a moment there flashed through his mind a thousand vague but evil auguries. Danger to Constance herself, the ruin of his father's hopes, the final destruction of his house and family, and all the train of sorrows and of evils that might follow, if Wolsey were to discover his rash love, hurried before his eyes like the thronging phantoms of a painful dream, and clouded his brow with a deep shade of thoughtful melancholy.

"Fear not, Osborne Darnley," said Sir Cesar, seeing the gloomy look of the young knight. "This cardinal is great, but there is one greater than he, who beholds his pride, and shall break him like a reed. Nor in this thing shall his will be obeyed. Believe what I say to you, for it is true—I warned you once of coming dangers, and you doubted me; but the evils I foresaw came upon your head. Doubt me not then now—but still I see fear sits upon your eyelids. Come, then, both of you with me, for in this both your destinies are linked for a time together. Spend with me one hour this night, and I will show you that which shall ease your hearts," and he turned towards the house, beckoning them to follow.

"I suppose, then, your lordship is satisfied," said Sir Osborne, taking up the scabbard of his sword, and replacing it, with the weapon, in his belt, as the astrologer moved away.

"I shall be more satisfied," said Lord Darby, laying his hand on the knight's arm with a frank smile, "if you would confide in me. Indeed, I have no title to pry

into your secrets," he added, " nor into those of Constance either, though I think she might have told me of
this yesterday, when I made her a partaker of all mine.
However, I cannot believe that the profound reverence
in which all the duke's servants seem to hold you, can
be excited by the unknown Sir Osborne Maurice. Besides, Sir Cesar called you but now Osborne Darnley.—
Can it be, that I am speaking to the Lord Darnley, who
from his feats at the court of the princess dowager, goes
amongst us by the surname of the Knight of Burgundy? " *

" I shall not deny my name, Lord Darby," replied the
knight. " I am, as you say, Lord Darnley ; but as this has
fallen into your knowledge by mere accident, I shall hold
you bound in honor to forget it."

" Nay ! " replied the earl, " I shall remember it, to
render you, if possible, all service.—But come, Darnley,
as, by a mistake, we began bitter enemies, now let us
end dear friends. I can aid you much, you can aid me
much, and between us both surely we shall be able to
break the trammels with which the cardinal enthrals us.
We will put four young heads against one old one, and
the world to nothing we shall win ! "

There was a frankness in Lord Darby's manner that
it was impossible to resist, and taking the hand he
tendered him, the young adventurer met his offered
friendship with equal candor. With the openness natural
to youth, the plans of each were soon told, the sooner,
indeed, that their future prospects and endeavors so
greatly depended for success upon their sincere coöpera-
tion, and thus they sauntered back to the house, with very
different feelings from those with which they had left it.
Before they had arrived at the steps of the door, they had
ran through a thousand details, and were as much prepared to act together as if their acquaintance had been of

* Every knight of that day had his subriquet, or nickname ; thus the
famous Bayard was generally called Piquet.

many years' duration. No sooner did the young earl hear
that his new friend had not yet been introduced to the
king, than he at once proposed to be the person to do it,
offering to call for him in his barge the next day but one,
and convey him to the court at Greenwich, where he
undertook to procure him a good reception.

"It may be difficult," he said, "to find private audience
of those two persons whom we both feel most anxious
to meet. Dame Fortune, however, may befriend us; but
we must be cautious even to an excess, for Wolsey has
eyes that see where he is not present, and ears that hear
over half the realm, and the first step to make our plans
successful, depend upon it, is to conceal them. But lo!
where Sir Cesar stands at the window of the hall. Now,
in the name of fortune, where will he lead us to-night?
'Tis strange that there should be men so gifted with rare
qualities as to see into the deepest secrets of nature, to
view things that to others are concealed, and yet seemingly to profit little by their knowledge; for never did I
meet or hear of one of these astrologers that were either
happier or more fortunate than other men. And yet,
what were the good to Sir Cesar to boast a knowledge
that he did not possess? For he seeks no reward, will
accept of no recompense, and hourly exposes what he
says to contradiction if it be not true. But doubtless it
is true, for every day gives proofs thereof. That man is
a riddle, which would have gained the Sphinx a good
dinner off Œdipus.—You seem to know him well, but I
dare say know no more of him than any one else does;
for no one that I ever met knows who he is, nor where he
comes from, nor where he goes to; and yet he is well received everywhere, courted, ay, and even loved, for he
is beneficent, charitable, and humane—is rich, though it is
unknown whence his wealth arises, and possesses wonderful knowledge, though, I fear me, wickedly acquired.—
I have heard that those poor wretches, who have mastered forbidden secrets, often strive to repair, by every

good deed, the evil that their presumptuous curiosity has
done to their own souls—God knows how it is. But come,
let us join him. The information we gain from him, at
all events, is sure."

Entering the manor-house, they passed on into the
hall, where they found Sir Cesar buried in deep thought;
and while the young knight proceeded to his own apartments, to procure the letter which Lady Katrine Bulmer
had entrusted to him, the Earl of Darby approached the
old knight with that sort of gaiety which, like a spoiled
servant, would very often play the master with its lord.
"Well, Sir Cesar," cried he, "where are your thoughts
roaming? In the world above, or the world below?"

"Farther in heaven than you will ever be," replied the
old man.

"Nay, then," continued the earl, "as you can tell
everything, past, present, and to come, could you divine
what we were talking but now in the gardens?"

"At first you were talking of what did concern yourselves, and afterwards of what did not concern you,"
answered the knight.

"Magic, by my faith!" cried the earl; "and in truth,
your coming just in the nick of time, as folks have it,
to save us from slicing each other's weasands, must have
had a spice of magic in it too."

"If one used magic for so weak a purpose as that of
saving an empty head like thine," replied the knight, "it
would be worthy the jest with which you treat it. Fools
and children attribute everything to magic that they do
not comprehend—but, however, my coming here had
none. Was it not easy for one friend to tell another that
he had heard two mad young men name a place to slaugh-
ter each other, they knew not for what?—But here comes
thy companion. Read thy letter, and then come with
me; for the light is waning, and the hour comes on when
I can show ye both some part at least of your destiny."

Lord Darby eagerly cut the silk which fastened Lady

Katrine's letter, and read it with that sort of intent
earnestness, that would have removed from the mind of
Sir Osborne any doubt of the young earl's feelings, even
if he had still continued to entertain such. This being
done, they prepared to accompany Sir Cesar, who insisted that not even a page should follow them, and accordingly Lord Darby's attendant was ordered to remain
behind, and wait his lord's return.

Passing, then, out into the street, they soon found
themselves in the most crowded part of the city of London, which was at that time of the evening filled with the
various classes of mechanics, clerks, and artists, returning to their homes from their diurnal toil. Gliding
through the midst of them, Sir Cesar passed on, not in
the least heeding the remarks which his diminutive size
and singular apparel called forth, though Lord Darby did
not seem particularly to relish a promenade through the
city with such a companion, and very possibly might
have left Sir Osborne to proceed with him alone if he
liked it, had not that strong curiosity, which we all experience, to read into the future, carried him on to the
end.

Darkness now began to fall upon their path, and still
the old man led them forward through a thousand dark
and intricate turnings, till at length, in what appeared to
be a narrow lane, the houses of which approached so
closely together, that it would have been an easy leap
from the windows on one side of the way into those of
the other, the old knight stopped, and struck three strokes
with the hilt of his dagger upon a door on the left hand.

It was opened almost immediately by a tall meagre
man, holding in his hand a small silver lamp, which he
applied close to the face of Sir Cesar before he would permit any one to pass. " Il maestro," cried he, as soon as
he saw the dark small features of the astrologer, making
him at the same time a profound inclination, " Entra
dottissimo! Benvenuto, benvenuto sia."

Sir Cesar replied in an undertone, and taking the lamp from the Italian, motioned to Sir Osborne and the earl to follow. The staircase up which he conducted them was excessively small, narrow, and winding, bespeaking one of the meanest houses in the city; and what still more excited their surprise, they mounted near forty steps without perceiving any door or outlet whatever, except where a blast of cold air through a sort of loophole in the wall announced their proximity to the street.

At length the astrologer stopped opposite a door, only large enough to admit the passage of one person at a time, through which he led the way, when to the astonishment of both Sir Osborne and the earl, they found themselves in a magnificent oblong apartment, nearly forty feet in length, and rather more than twenty in breadth. On each side were ranged tables and stands, covered with various specimens of ancient art, which, rare in any age, were then a thousand times more scarce.

Although the taking of Constantinople, about seventy years before, by driving many of the Greeks, amongst whom elegance and science long lingered, into other countries, had revived already, in some degree, the taste for the arts of painting and sculpture, still few, very few, even of the princes of Europe, could boast such beautiful specimens as those which that chamber contained.

Here stood a statue, there an urn; on one table was an alabaster capital of exquisite workmanship, on another a bas-relief whose figures seemed struggling from the stone; medals, and gems, and specimens of curious ores, were mingled with the rest; and many a book, written in strange and unknown characters, lay open before their eyes. There, too, were various instruments of curious shape and device, whose purpose they could not even guess; while here frowned a man in armor, there grinned a skeleton, and there, swathed in its historic bands, stood an Egyptian mummy, resting its moldering and shapeless head against the feet of a figure, in which some long

dead artist had labored skilfully to display all the exquisite
lines of female loveliness.

To observe all this the two young men had full opportunity, while Sir Cesar proceeded forward, stopping between each table, and bringing the flame of the lamp he
carried in contact with six others, which stood upon a
row of ancient bronze tripods ranged along the side of
the hall. At the end of the room hung a large black
curtain, on each side of which was a clock of very
curious manufacture; the one showing, apparently, the
year, the day, the hour, and the minute; and the other
exposing a figure of the zodiac, round which moved a
multitude of strange hieroglyphic signs, some so rapidly
that the eye could scarcely distinguish their course, some
so slow that their motion was hardly to be discerned.

As Sir Osborne and Lord Darby approached, Sir Cesar
drew back the curtain, and exposed to their sight an
immense mirror, in which they could clearly distinguish
their own figures, and that of the astrologer, reflected at
full length.*

" Mark," said Sir Cesar, " and from what you shall see,
draw your own inference. But question me not—for I
vowed when I received that precious gift, which is now
before you, never to make one comment upon what it
displayed. Mark, and when you have seen, leave me."

" But I see nothing," said Sir Osborne, " except my
own reflection in the glass."

" Patience! patience! impetuous spirit! " cried the old
man; " will an hundred lives never teach thee calmness?
Look to the mirror."

Sir Osborne turned his eyes to the glass, but still
nothing new met his view, and after gazing for a minute

---

* Since writing the above, I have seen a most beautiful sketch by
Sir Walter Scott, of a scene precisely similar. The coincidence of even
the minute points is distressingly striking; but I know, that Sir Walter,
and I trust the public also, will believe me, when I pledge my word
that the whole of this book was written before I ever saw " My Aunt
Margaret's Mirror,' and I believe before it was even published.

or two, he suffered his glance to wander to the clock by his side, which now struck eight with a clear, sweet, musical sound.

At that moment Lord Darby laid his hand on his arm. "God's my life!" cried he, "we are vanishing away! Look! look!"

Sir Osborne turned to the glass, and beheld the three figures he had before seen plain and distinctly, now growing dimmer and more dim. He could scarcely believe his sight, and passing his hand before his eyes, he strove, as it were, to cure them of the delusion. When he looked again, all was gone, and the mirror offered nothing but a dark shining blank. Presently, however, a confusion of thin and misty figures seemed to pass over the glass, and a light appeared to spring up within itself: gradually the objects took a more substantial form; the interior of the mirror assumed the appearance of a smaller chamber than that which they were in, lighted by a lattice window, and in the centre was seen a female figure leaning in a pensive attitude on a table. Sir Osborne thought it was like Lady Katrine Bulmer, but the light coming from behind cast her features into shadow. The moment after, however, a door of the chamber seemed to open, and he could plainly distinguish a figure, resembling that of Lord Darby, enter, and clasp her in his arms, with a semblance of joy so naturally portrayed, that it was hardly possible to suppose it unreal.

While he yet gazed, the outlines of the figures began to grow confused and indistinct, and various ill-defined forms floated over the glass; gradually, however, they again assumed shape and feature; the mirror represented a princely hall hung with cloth of gold, and a thousand gay and splendid figures ranged themselves round the scene. Princes, and prelates, and warriors, moved before their eyes, as if 'twas all in life. There might be seen the slight significant look, the animated gesture, the whisper apart, the stoop of age, the high, erect carriage of knight and noble, and the graceful motion of youth and beauty.

"By heavens!" cried Lord Darby, "there is the Earl of Devonshire, and the Duke of Suffolk, and the Princess Mary. It is the court of England! But no! Who are all these?"

Gradually the crowd opened, and two persons appeared, whose apparel, demeanor, and glance bespoke them royal.

"Henry himself, as I live!" cried Lord Darby.

"Which? which?" demanded Sir Osborne.

"The one to the right," answered the earl; "the other I know not."

It was the other, however, which advanced, leading forward by the hand a knight, in whom Sir Osborne might easily distinguish the simulacre of himself. The prince, whoever he was, seemed to speak, and a lady came forth from the rest. By the graceful motion, by the timid look, by the rich light brown hair, as well as by all a lover's feelings, Sir Osborne could not doubt that it was Constance de Grey—the monarch took her hand, placed it in that of the knight—the figures grew dim, and the glass misty—but gradually clearing away, it resumed its original effect, and reflected the hall in which they were, their own forms standing before the mirror, and the old man, Sir Cesar, sitting on the ground, with his hands pressed over his eyes. The moment they turned round he started up.—"It is done!" cried he; "so now begone. We shall meet again soon," and putting his finger to his lip, as if requiring silence, he led them out of the hall, and down the stairs, signed them with the cross, and left them.

CHAPTER XII.

"There grows
In my most ill-composed affection,
A quenchless avarice, that were I king
I should cut off the nobles for their lands."

MACBETH.

EARLY in the morning of the day after that on which Sir Osborne had left the manor-house to proceed to the Benedictine abbey, near Canterbury, Sir Payan Wileton, with a large suit, rode up to the gates and demanded an audience of the duke, which was immediately granted. As the chamberlain marshalled him on the way to the duke's closet, the knight caught a glance of the old man, Sir Cesar, passing out, from which he augured favorably for his purposes; doubting not that the discourse of the astrologer had raised the ambition and vanity of the duke, and fitted him to second the schemes with which he proposed to tempt him.

When the knight entered, the princely Buckingham was seated, and with that cold dignity which he knew well how to assume, he motioned his visitor to a chair, without, however, deigning to rise.

"He thinks himself already king," thought Sir Payan. "Well, his pride must be humored. My lord duke," he said, after a few preliminary words on both parts, "I come to tender your grace my best service, and to beg you to believe, that should ever the occasion offer, you shall find me ready at your disposal, with heart and hand, fortune and followers."

"And what is it that Sir Payan Wileton would claim as his reward for such zealous doings?" demanded the duke, eying him coolly. "Sir Payan's wisdom is too well known to suppose that he would venture so much without proportionate reward."

"But your grace's favor," replied the knight, somewhat astonished at the manner in which his offers were received.

"Nay, nay, Sir Payan," replied the duke, "speak plainly. What is it you would have? Upon what rich lordship have you cast your eyes? Whose fair estate has excited your appetite? Is there any new Chilham Castle to be had?"

"In truth, I know not well what your grace means," answered the knight, "though I can see that some villain behind my back has been blackening my character in your fair opinion. I came here frankly to tender you, of my own free will, services that you once hinted might be acceptable. Men who would climb high, my lord duke, must make their first steps firm."

"True, true, Sir Knight," replied the duke, moderating the acerbity of his manner; "but how can I rise higher than I am? Perhaps, indeed, my pride may soar too high a pitch, when I fancy that in this realm, next to his grace the king, my head stands highest."

"True," said Sir Payan, "but I have heard a prophecy, that your grace's head should be of all the highest, without any weakening qualification of next to any man's. His grace King Henry may die, and I have myself known the Duke of Buckingham declare, that there were shrewd doubts whether the king's marriage with his brother's wife were so far valid as to give an heir to the English crown. Kings may die, too, of the sharp sword and the keen dagger. Such being the case, and the king dying without heirs male, who will stand so near the throne as the Duke of Buckingham? Who has so much the people's love? Who may command so many of the most expert and powerful men in England?"

The duke paused and thought. He was not without ambition, though he was without the illness that should

accompany it. No one did he more thoroughly abhor
than Sir Payan Wileton, and yet, rich, powerful, unscrupulous, full of politic will and daring stratagem, Sir
Payan was a man who might serve him essentially as a
friend, might injure him deeply as an enemy, and he was,
moreover, one that must be treated as one or the other—
must be either courted or defied. While a thousand
thoughts of this kind passed through the mind of the
duke, and connecting themselves with others, wandered
far on the wild and uncertain tract that his ambition
presented to his view—while the passion by which angels
fell was combating in his bosom with duty, loyalty, and
friendship, the eye of Sir Payan Wileton glanced from
time to time towards his face, watching and calculating
the emotions of his mind, with that degree of certainty
that long observation of the passions and weaknesses of
human nature had bestowed.

At length, he saw the countenance of the duke lighted
up with a triumphant smile, while fixing his eyes upon
the figure of an old king in the tapestry, he seemed busily
engaged in anticipations of the future. " He has them
now," thought Sir Payan, " the crown, the sceptre, and
the ball. Well, let him enjoy his golden dream; " and
dropping his eyes to the table, he gathered the addresses
of the various letters which Buckingham had apparently
been writing—" The Earl of Devonshire—The Lord
Dacre—Sir John Morton—The Earl of Fitzbernard, to
be rendered to the hands of Sir Osborne Maurice—The
Prior of Langley."

" Ha ! " thought the knight, " Lord Fitzbernard ! Sir
Osborne Maurice ! So, so, I have the train. Take heed,
Buckingham, take heed, or you fall ! " and he raised his
eyes once more to the countenance of the duke, whose
look was now fixed full upon him.

" Sir Payan Wileton," said Buckingham, " we have
both been meditating, and perhaps our meditations have
arrived at the same conclusion."

"I hope, my lord duke," answered Sir Payan, returning to the former subject of conversation, "that your grace finds that I may be of service to you."

"Not in the least!" replied the duke, sternly, for it had so happened that his eyes had fallen upon Sir Payan just at the moment that the knight was furtively perusing the address of the letter to Lord Fitzbernard, and the combinations thus produced in the mind of the noble Buckingham had not been very much in favor of Sir Payan. "Not in the least, Sir Payan Wileton. Let me tell you, sir, that you must render back Chilham Castle to its lord; you must reverse all the evil that you have done and attempted towards his son; you must abandon such foul schemes, and cancel all the acts of twenty years of your life, before you be such a man as may act with Buckingham."

"My lord duke! my lord duke!" cried Sir Payan, "this is too much to bear. Your pride, haughty peer, has made you mad, but your pride shall have a fall. Beware of yourself, Duke of Buckingham, for no one shall ever say that he offended Sir Payan Wileton unscathed. Know ye, that you are in my power?"

"In thine, insect?" cried the duke. "But begone! you move me too far. Ho! without there! Begone, I say, or Buckingham may forget himself."

"He shall not forget me," said Sir Payan. "Mark me, lord duke;—you wisely deem, that because you have not shown me your daring schemes in your handwriting, you are safe. But you have yet to know Sir Payan Wileton. We shall see, lord duke! we shall see! So farewell," and turning on his heel, he left the duke's closet, called for his horse, and in a few minutes was far on the road homeward.

"Guilford," cried he, turning towards his attendants, "Guilford, ride up."

At this order, a downcast, sneering-looking man, drew up from the rest of the servants, and rode up to the side of his master, who fixed his eyes upon him for a moment, shutting his teeth hard, as was his custom when considering how to proceed. " Guilford," said he at last—" Guilford, you remember the infant that was found dead in Ashford ditch last year, that folks supposed to be the child of Mary Bly—eh?" The man turned deadly pale. " I have found an owner for the kerchief in which it was tied with the two large stones," proceeded Sir Payan. " A man came to me yesterday morning, who says he can swear to the kerchief, and who it belonged to —fie, do not shake so! Do you think I ever hurt my own?—Guilford, you must do me service. Take three stout fellows with you, on whom you can depend; cast off your liveries, and ride on with all speed to the hill on this side of Rochester. Wait there till you see a courier come up with a swan embroidered on his sleeve. Find means to quarrel with him; and when you return to Elham Manor, if you bear his bag with you, you shall each have five George nobles for your reward—but leave not the place! Stir not till you have met with him. And now be quick; take the three men with you. There will be enough to return with me. Mark me! let him not escape with his bag, for if you do, you buy your-self a halter."

" Which of them shall I take?" said the man. " There is Waldelsham and Black John, who together stole the Prior of Merton's horse, and sold it at Sandwich. They would have been burned i' the hand, if your worship had not refused the evidence. Then there is Simpkin, the deer-stealer——"

" That will do," said Sir Payan, " that will do— 'tis said he set Raper's barn on fire—but be quick, we waste time."

It was late the next day before the party of worthies whom Sir Payan entrusted with the honorable little com-mission above stated returned to his house at Elham Manor: but, to his no small satisfaction, they brought the

13

Duke of Buckingham's letter-bag along with them, which Master Guilford deposited on the table before Sir Payan, in his usual sullen manner, and only waited till he had received his reward, which was instantly paid; for the honest knight, well knowing by internal conviction that rascality is but a flimsy bond of attachment, took care to bind his serviceable agents to himself, by both the sure ties of hope and fear—if they were useful and silent, their hopes were never disappointed; if they were negligent or indiscreet, their fears were more than realized.

The moment he was alone, the knight put his dagger into the bag, and ripped it open from side to side. This done, his eye ran eagerly over the various letters it contained, and paused on that to Lord Fitzbernard. In an instant the silk was cut, and the contents before his eyes.

"Ha!" said Sir Payan, reading, "so here it is—the whole business—so, so, my young knight, the real name to be told to nobody till the king's good-will is gained. But I will foil you, and blast your false name before your real one is known—good Duke of Buckingham, I thank you!—A villain! If I am, you shall taste my villainy. Oh! so he had charge to conduct the Lady Katrine Bulmer to the court. His feats of arms and manly daring shall much approve him with the king—ay! but they shall damn him with the cardinal, or I'll halt for it. Now for the rest.

With as little ceremony as that which he had displayed toward the letter addressed to Lord Fitzbernard, Sir Payan tore open all the rest, but seemed somewhat disappointed at their contents, gnawing his lips and knitting his brow, till he came to the last, addressed to Sir John Morton—"Ha!" exclaimed he, as he read, "Duke of Buckingham, you are mine—now, proud Edward Bohun, stoop! stoop! for out of so little a thing as this will I work thy ruin. But what means he by this? Sir Osborne Maurice! It cannot be him he speaks of—it matters not

—it shall tell well too, and in one ruin involve them both. Sir Osborne Maurice—I have it! I have it! Sure the disclosure of such a plot as this may well merit Wolsey's thanks! ay! and even, by good favor, some few acres off the broad estates of Constance de Grey. We shall see— but first let us track this young gallant, we must know his every step from Canterbury to Greenwich."

Proud in supreme villainy, Sir Payan trod with a larger stride, confidently calculating that he held all his enemies in his power; but, subtle as well as bold, he did not allow his confidence to diminish in the least his care, and calling to his aid one of his retainers, upon whose cunning he could count with certainty, he laid him upon the path of our hero, like a hound upon the track of a deer, with commands to investigate, with the most minute care, every step he had taken from Canterbury to Greenwich.

"And now," said Sir Payan, "to-morrow for Greenwich—I must not fail the party of Sir Thomas Neville. When enemies grow strong, 'tis time to husband friends;" and, springing on his horse, he proceeded to put in train for execution some of those minor schemes of evil, which he did not choose to leave unregulated till his return.

CHAPTER XIII.

"Traffic is thy God."

CIMON.

"By my faith," cried the Earl of Darby, as soon as they found themselves in the street, or rather lane, before the dwelling of Sir Cesar, "I know not in the least where we are; and if I had known it before, my brain is so unsettled with all this strange sight, that I should have forgotten it now. Which way did we turn?"

"The other way, the other way!" cried Sir Osborne, "and then to the right."

"Pray, sir, can you tell me where the devil I am?" demanded the earl, when they had reached the bottom of the lane, addressing a man who was walking slowly past.

"I'll tell you what, my young gallant," answered the man, "if you don't march home with your foolery, I'll lock you up—I am the constable of the watch."

"It is my way home that I want to know, friend constable," replied the earl. "For, 'fore God, I know not where I am any more than a new-born child, who, though he comes into the world without asking the way, finds himself very strange when he is in it."

"Why, marry, thou art at the back of Baynard's Castle, Sir Fool," replied the constable.

"Ay, then I shall find my road," said the earl. "Thank thee, honest constable—thou art a pleasant fellow, and a civil—and hast risked having thy pate broken to-night more than thou knowest. So, fare thee well!" and, turning away, he led his companion through various winding lanes into a broader street, which at length conducted them to the mansion of the Duke of Buckingham.

" Now, by my faith, Darnley, or Maurice, or whatever you please to be called," said the earl, " if you have any hospitality in your nature, you will give me board and lodging for a night. May you make so free with the good duke's house?"

" Most willingly will I do it," said Sir Osborne, " and find myself now doubly happy in his grace's request, to use his mansion as if it were my own."

" Were I you," said Lord Darby, " and had so much of Buckingham's regard, I would hear more of that strange man—if he be a man—Sir Cesar; for 'tis said, that the duke and Sir John Morton are the only persons that know who and what he really is. God help us! we have seen as strange a sight to-night as mortal eyes ever beheld."

" I have heard one of my companions in arms relate, that a circumstance precisely similar happened to himself in Italy," replied the knight. " The famous magician, Cornelius Agrippa, showed him out of friendship a glass, wherein he beheld the lady of his love reading one of his own letters, which thing she was doing, as he ascertained afterwards, at the very minute and day that the glass was shown to him. I never thought, however, to have seen anything like it myself."

It may be easily supposed that various were the remarks and conjectures of the two young noblemen during the rest of the evening, but with these it will be unnecessary to trouble the reader; suffice it, that we have translated as literally as possible the account which Vonderbrugius gives of the circumstances, nor shall we make any comment on the facts, leaving it to the reader's own mind to form what conclusions he may think right. The effect upon the mind of Sir Osborne, was to give him new hope and courage, for so ·completely had the former prediction of Sir Cesar been fulfilled, that though he might still doubt, yet his very hesitation leant to the side of hope.

Lord Darby laughed, and vowed 'twas strange, 'twas passing strange, and wrote it down in his tablets, lest he should not believe a word of it the next morning. When the morning came, however, he found that his belief had not fled; and before leaving Sir Osborne, he talked over the business with more gravity than he could usually command. Many arrangements, also, were necessary to be made in regard to the knight's introduction to the court; at length, it was agreed, that the earl should account for his acquaintance with Sir Osborne, by saying that their parents had been friends: and that, having been educated in the court of Burgundy, the knight was then in England for the first time since his youth.

"All this is true," said Lord Darby, "for my father was well known to yours, though, perhaps, they could hardly be called friends—but, however, there are not above two grains of lie to an ounce of truth, so it will poison no one."

When all their plans were finally settled, Lord Darby took leave of the knight, and left him to make his preparations for the next morning. As soon as he had departed, Sir Osborne called for his horse, and accompanied by Longpole, of whom he had seen little since his arrival in London, set out for the house of the honest Flemish merchant, William Hans.

As they proceeded, the worthy custrel, who, for the purpose of showing him the way, rode by his side (permitting him, nevertheless, to keep about a yard in advance) did not fail to take advantage of their proximity, to regale the knight's ears with many a quaint remark upon the great bee-hive, as he called it, in which they were.

"Lord, Lord!" said he, "to think of the swarm of honey-getting, or, rather, money-getting insects, that here toil from morn to-night, but to pile up within their narrow cells that sweet trash, which, after all, is none of theirs; for ever and anon comes my good lord king, the

master of the hives, and smokes them for a subsidy.
Now to the left, your worship, up that paved court."

The house of the merchant now stood before them, and
Sir Osborne dismounting from his horse, advanced to the
door of what seemed to be a small dark counting-house,
in which he found an old man, with many a book and a
slate before him, busy employed in adding to the multitude
of little black marks with which the page under his eyes
was cumbered.

In answer to the knight's inquiry for Master William
Hans, he replied, that he was in the warehouse, where he
might find him, if he wished to see him. " Stay, stay,
I will show you the way," cried he, with ready politeness.
" Lord, sir, our warehouse is a wilderness, wherein a
man might lose himself with blessed facility. Thanks be
to God therefore, for on May-day, three years last past,
called Evil May-day, we should have lost our good master,
when the 'prentices, and watermen, and pick-purses, and
vagabonds broke into all the aliens' houses, and injured
many; but, happily, he hid himself under a pile of stockfish, which was in the far end of the little warehouse, to
the left of the barrel-room, so that they found him not."

While he pronounced this oration, the old clerk locked
carefully the door of the counting-house, and led the
knight into an immense vaulted chamber, wherein were
piled on every side all kinds of things, of every sort and
description that human ingenuity can apply to the supply
of its necessities, or the gratification of its appetites.

Making his way through all, Sir Osborne proceeded
directly towards the spot where a small window in the
roof poured its light upon a large barrel, the contents of
which were undergoing inspection by the worthy Fleming whom he sought. In Flanders, the knight had
known the good burgess well, and had been sure to receive a visit from him whenever business had called his
steps from his adopted to his native country. There
might be both an eye to gratitude and an eye to interest

in this proceeding of Master William Hans, for the knight had twice procured him a large commission for the army, and, what was still more in those days, had procured him payment.

On perceiving his visitor in the present instance, the merchant caught up his black furred gown, which he had thrown off while busied in less dignified occupations, and having hastily insinuated his arms into the sleeves, advanced to meet the knight with a bow of profound respect. " Welcome back to England, my lord," cried he, in very good English, which could only be distinguished as proceeding from the mouth of a foreigner by a slight accent and a peculiar intonation. " Cood now, my lord, I hope you have not given up your company in Flanders. I have such a cargo of beans in the mouth of the Schelt, it would have suited the army very well indeet."

" But, my good Master Hans," answered the knight, " the army itself is given up since the peace. When I left Lisle, there were scarce three companies left."

After a good deal more of such preliminary conversation, in the course of which the knight explained to the merchant the necessity of keeping his name and title secret for the present, they proceeded to the arrangement of those affairs which yet remained unconcluded between them. Conducting the knight back to the counting-house, William Hans turned over several of his great books, looking for the accounts. " Here it is, I think," he cried at length. " No, that is the Lady de Grey's."

" Lady Constance de Grey?" demanded Sir Osborne, in some surprise.

" Yes, yes!" answered the merchant. " I receive all the money for her mother's estate, who was a French lady —did for her father, too, till the coot old lord died. Oh! it was hard work in the time of the war; but I got a Paris Jew to transmit the money to a Flemish Jew, who sent it over to me. They cot ten per cent., the thieves, for commission, but that very thing saved the estates; for they would have been forfeited by the old king Louis, if the Jew, who had given him money in his need, had not made such a noise about it, for fear of losing his ten per cent., that the king let it pass. Ah! here is the account. First, we have not settled since I furnished the wine for the companie, when they had the fever. Five hundred chioppines of wine, at a croat the chioppine, make just twenty-five marks—received thirty marks—five carried to your name. Then, for the ransom of the Sire de Beaujeu; you put him at a ransom of two thousand crowns, not knowing who he was, but he has sent you six thousand; because, he says, he would not be ransomed like an ecuyer. Creat fool! Why the devil, when he could get off for a little, pay a much?"*

"No true knight but would do the same," replied Sir Osborne. "It was only by my permission that he got away at all, therefore he was bound in honor to pay the full ransom of a person of his condition."

"Well, then," said the Fleming, "here comes the ransom of two esquires, gentlemen they call themselves, five hundred crowns each, making in the whole seven thousand crowns, or two thousand six hundred and twenty-five marks. Then, there is against you freight and carriage of armor and goods, four marks: exchange and commission, three marks; porterage, a croat; warehouse-room, two croats—balance for you, two thousand six hundred and seventeen marks, five shillings, and two croats,—which I am ready to pay you, as well as to deliver the two suits of harness and the packages."

"The money, at present, I do not want," replied Sir

---

* I have not been able to discover at what precise period the custom of exacting a ransom from each prisoner taken in battle was dropped in Europe. It certainly still existed in the reign of Elizabeth, and perhaps still later, for Shakespeare (writing in the days of James I.) makes repeated mention of it. Some centuries before the period of this tale, Edward the Black Prince fixed the ransom of Du Guesclin at 100 francs, which the constable considered degrading, and rated himself at the sum of 70,0000 florins of gold.

Osborne, " but I will be glad if you would send the arms, and the rest of the packages, to the manor of the Rose, in St. Lawrence Poultney."

" To the coot Duke of Buckingham's? Ah, that I will, that I will! But I hope you will stay and take your noon-meal with me; though I know you men of war do not like the company of us merchants. But I will say I have never found you any way proud."

" I would most willingly, Master Hans," answered the knight, " but I go to the court to-morrow for the first time, and I have no small preparation to make with tailors and broiderers."

" Oh, stay with me, stay with me, and I will fit you to your desire," answered the Fleming. " There is a tailor lives hard by, who will suit you well. I am not going to give you a man who can make nothing but a burgo-master's gown, or a merchant's doublet. I know your coot companions would laugh, and say you had had a merchant's tailor; but this is a man who, if you like it, shall stuff out your breeches till you can't sit down, make all the seams by a plumbline, tighten your girdle till you have no more waist than a wasp; and, moreover, he is tailor to the Duke of Suffolk."

The knight found this recommendation quite sufficient: and, agreeing to dine with the honest Fleming, the tailor was sent for, who, with a great display of sartorial learn-ing, devised several suits, in which Sir Osborne might ap-pear at court, without being either so gaudy as the butter-flies of the day, or so plain as to call particular attention. The only difficulty was to know whether the tailor could furnish a complete suit for the knight, and one for each of his four attendants, by the next morning; but after much calculation, and summing up of all the friendly tailors within his knowledge, he undertook to do it, and, what is wonderful for a tailor, kept his word.

" The luckiest accident for you in the world has just happened!" cried Lord Darby, entering Sir Osborne

Maurice's apartment two full hours before the time he had appointed; "order your men to choose your best suit of harness, to pack it on a strong horse; to load your own courser by the bridle, and to make all speed to the foot of the hill at Greenwich, there to wait till they be sent for; and you come with me, my barge waits at the duke's stairs."

"But what is the matter, my lord?" demanded Sir Osborne; "at least, tell me if my horse must be barded."

"No, no; I think not," replied the earl, "at all events, we shall find bards,* if he want them. But be quick, we have not a moment to lose, though the tide be running down as quick as a tankard of ale over the throat of a thirsty serving-man; I will tell you the whole as we go."

"Longpole," cried the knight to his follower, who at the moment the earl entered, was in the room, putting the last adjustment to his master's garments—"Longpole, quick! you hear what Lord Darby says—take the fluted suit—"

"Oh, the fluted, the fluted by all means," interrupted the earl, "it shows noble and knightly. So shall we go along as in a Roman triumph, with flutes before, and flutes behind. The fluted by all means, good Longpole, and lose no time on the road—for every flagon you do not drink, you shall have two at Greenwich.—Now, Maurice, are you ready?—By heaven! you make a gallant figure of it—your tailor deserves immortality.—'Tis well! 'tis mighty well!—But, to my taste, the cuts in your blue velvet had been better lined with a soft yellow than a white—the hue of a young primrose. The feather might have been the same, but 'tis all a taste: white does marvellous well—the silver girdle and scabbard too! But come, we waste our moments, let two of your men come with us."

Lord Darby conducted his new friend to the barge, and

* A suit of horse armor and housings.

as they proceeded towards Greenwich with a quick tide, he informed him, that some knights, Sir Henry Poynings, Sir Thomas Neville, and several others, having agreed to meet, for the purpose of trying some new-invented arms, the king had been seized with a desire of going unknown to break a lance with them on Blackheath, and had privately commanded the Earl of Devonshire to accompany him as his aid: but that very morning, at his house in Westminster, the earl had slipped, and so much injured his leg, that his surgeon forbade his riding for a month.

"As soon as I heard it," continued Lord Darby, "I flew to his lodging, and prayed him to let me be his messenger to the king—to which petition he easily assented, provided I set off with all speed, for his grace expects him early. Now, the moment that the king hears that the earl cannot ride, he chooses him another aid, and I so hope to manage, that the choice may fall upon you. If you break a lance to his mind, you shall be well beloved for the next week at least; and during that time you must manage to fix his favor. But first, let me give you some small portraiture of his mind, so that by knowing his humor, you may find means to fit it."

The character which Lord Darby gave of Henry the Eighth shall here be put in fewer words. He was then a very, very different being from the bloated despot which he afterwards appeared. All his life had hitherto been prosperity and gladness; no care, no sorrow, had called into action any of the latent evil of his character, and he showed himself to those around him as an affable and magnificent prince; proud without haughtiness, and luxurious without vice. Endowed with great personal strength, blessed with robust health, and flourishing in the prime of his years, he loved with a degree of ostentation all those manly and chivalrous exercises which were then at their height in Europe; and placed, as it were, between the age of chivalry and the age of learning, he in his own person combined many of the attributes of each. In temper and in manner he was hasty but frank, and had much of the generosity of youth unchilled by adversity. Yet he was ever wilful and irritable, and in his history even at that time may be traced the yet un-stated luxurist, and the incipient tyrant, beginning a career in splendor and pride that was sure to end in des-potism and blood.

It may well be supposed that the young knight's heart beat as the boat came in sight of the.palace at Greenwich. It had nothing, however, to do with that agitation which men often weakly feel on approaching earthly greatness. Accustomed to a court, though a small one, if Sir Osborne had ever experienced those sensations, they had long left him, but he felt, that on what was to follow from the present interview, perhaps on that interview itself, de-pended his father's fortune and his own—more, his own happiness forever.

Lord Darby's rowers had plied their oars to some purpose, and before ten o'clock the barge was alongside the king's stairs at Greenwich. "Come, Sir Osborne," cried the earl; "bearing a message which his grace will think one of great consequence, I shall abridge all cere-mony, and find my way as quickly to his presence as I can."

The two young men sprung to the shore, followed by their attendants, and passed the parade, which was quite empty, the king having taken care to disperse the principal part of his court in various directions, that his private expedition might pass unnoticed, feeling a sort of ro-mantic interest in the concealment and mystery of his proceedings. The earl led the way across the vacant space to one of the doors of the palace, which opened into a sort of waiting hall, called the "Hall of Lost Steps," where the two friends left their servants, and proceeding up a staircase that seemed well known to Lord Darby, they came into a magnificent saloon, wherein an idle page was gazing listlessly from one of the windows.

" Ha! Master Snell," cried the earl, " may his grace be spoken with? "

" On no account whatever, my noble lord," replied the page; " I am placed here expressly to prevent any one from approaching him—his grace is at his prayers."

" Go then, good Master Snell," said the earl, " and bid our royal master add one little prayer for the Earl of Devonshire, who has fallen in his house at Westminster, and is badly hurt; and tell his grace that I bear an humble message from the earl, who dared not confide it to a common courier."

" I go directly, my noble lord," said the page; " the king will find this bad news; and making all haste he left the room by a door on the other side of the apartment.

" This is indeed a kingly chamber," said Sir Osborne, gazing round upon the rich arras mingled with cloth of gold which covered the walls. " How poor must the court of Burgundy have seemed to the king, when he visited the princess regent at Lisle. And yet, perhaps, he scarcely saw the difference."

Even while he spoke, the door by which the page had gone out was again thrown open, and a tall, handsome man entered the apartment, with haste and peevishness in his countenance. He was apparently about thirty years of age, broad-chested and powerfully made, muscular but not fat, and withal, there was an air of dignity and command in his figure that might well become a king. He seemed to have been disturbed half-dressed, for under the loose gown of black velvet which he wore, was to be seen one leg clothed in steel, while the other remained free of any such cumbersome apparel. The rest of his person, as far as might be discovered by the opening of the gown, was habited in simple russet garments, guarded with gold, while on his head he wore a small-brimmed black bonnet and a jewelled plume. Lord Darby and Sir Osborne immediately doffed their hats as the king entered, the young knight not very well pleased to see the irritable spot that glowed on his brow.

"How now, lord? how now?" cried Henry, as they advanced. "What is this the page tells me?—Devonshire is hurt—is ill.—What is it? what is it, man? speak!"

"I am sorry to be the bearer of evil news to your grace," replied Lord Darby, with a profound inclination; "but this morning, as my Lord of Devonshire was preparing to set out to render his duty to your highness, his foot slipped—heaven knows how! and his surgeons fear that he has dislocated one of the bones of the leg. He, therefore, being unwilling to trust an ordinary messenger, begged me humbly, in his name, to set forth his case before you, and to crave your gracious pardon for thus unintentionally failing in his service."

"Tut! he could not help it," cried Henry. "The man broke not his bones and wrenched not his leg to do me a displeasure—and yet, in this, is fortune crossgrained, for where now shall I find an aid who may supply his place?—But, how now! What is this? Who have you with you? You are bold, young lord, to bring a stranger to my privy chamber!—Ha! how now! Mother of God, you are too bold!"

Hope sickened in Sir Osborne's bosom, and bending his head, he fixed his eyes upon the ground, while Lord Darby replied, nothing abashed by the king's reproof—

"Pardon me, my liege, but trusting to the known quality of your royal clemency, which finds excuses for our faults, even when we ourselves can discover none, I made bold to bring to your grace's presence this famous knight, Sir Osborne Maurice, who being himself renowned in many courts for feats of arms, has conceived a great desire to witness the deeds of our most mighty sovereign, whose prowess and skill, whether at the tourney or in the joust, at the barriers or with the battleaxe, is so noised over Europe, that none, who are themselves skilful, can refrain from coveting a sight of his royal daring. Allow me to present him to your grace."

Sir Osborne advanced, and kneeling gracefully before

the king, bent his head over the hand that Henry extended
towards him; while pleased with his appearance and demeanor, the monarch addressed him with a smile: " Think
not we are churlish, Sir Knight, or that we do not welcome you freely to our court; but, by St. Mary! such
young gallants as these must be held in check, or they
outrun their proper bounds. But judge not of our poor
doings by Darby's commendation, he has of a sudden
grown eloquent."

" On such a theme who might not be an orator? " said
Sir Osborne, rising. " Were I to doubt Lord Darby, I
must think that fame herself is your grace's courtier,
acting as your herald in every court, and challenging a
world to equal you."

" Fie, fie! I must not hear you! " cried the king.
" Darby, come hither, I would speak with you. Come
hither, man, I say! "

Sir Osborne drew a step back, and the king, taking the
young earl into the recess of a window, spoke to him for
a moment in a low tone but still sufficiently loud for
great part of what he said to be audible to the knight,
especially towards the conclusion.

" A powerful man," said the king; " and if he be but as
dextrous and valiant as he is strong, will prove a knight
indeed. Think you he would? "

" Most assuredly, my liege," replied the earl. " He
is your grace's born subject; only his father having fallen
into some unhappy error in the reign of our last royal
king, Sir Osborne has had his training at the court of
Burgundy, and received his knighthood from the sword
of Maximilian, the late emperor.

" Good, good," said Henry: " I remember hearing of
his father; 'twas either Simnel, or Perkyn Warbeck, or
some such treacherous cause he espoused. But all that
is past. Sir Knight," he continued, turning to Sir Osborne, " what if in my armory we could find a harness
that would fit you, are you minded to break a lance as

consort with the king, eh? This very morning—ay, this very hour? What say you, eh?"

"That I should hold it an honor never to be forgot, my liege," replied the knight. "And for the arms, my own are here in Greenwich. They might be brought in a moment."

"Quick, quick, then!" cried the king. "But we must be secret. Stop, stop! You go, Lord Darby. Send for the arms quick. Is your horse here, Sir Knight? By St. Mary, 'tis happy you came! Darby, bid them take the knight's horse into the small court, and shut the gates. Quick with his armor. Bid them put no bards on the horses, and be secret. I'll go arm. You arm here, Sir Knight. Snell, stand firm at that door; let no one pass but Lord Darby and the knight's armorer. Be quick, Sir Knight, I charge you be quick—and, above all, let us be secret. Remember, we will never raise our vizors. These knights think of no such encounter, but fancy to have it all amongst themselves. They have kept their joust mighty secret, but we will break their lances for them, eh?"

The king now left Sir Osborne, who delighted with the unexpected turn which his humor had taken, waited impatiently for Lord Darby's return, expecting every minute to see the other door open and Henry re-appear before he had even received his armor. At length, however, Lord Darby came, and with him our friend Longpole, who, as the page would only allow one person to enter with the earl, received that part of the armor which he did not carry himself from the attendant without, and then flew to assist his lord. Sir Osborne lost no time, and expert by constant habit, he put on piece by piece with a rapidity that astonished the young earl, who, accustomed alone to the tiltyard, was unacquainted with the facility acquired by the unceasing exercises of the camp.

At length while Longpole was buckling the last strap,

14

the king re-entered alone, completely armed, and with his beaver down.

"What! ready, Sir Knight," cried he; "nay, 'faith, you have been expeditious."

"Lord bless you, sir," cried Longpole, never dreaming that he spoke to the king, "my master puts on his arms as King Hal took Terouenne."

"How now!" cried Sir Osborne, afraid of what might come next; but the king held up his hand to him to let the man speak. "How is that, good fellow?" demanded he.

"Why he just puts his hand on it, and it is done," replied Longpole.

"Thou art a merry knave," said Henry, better pleased perhaps with the unquestionable compliment of the yeoman, than he would have been with the more refined and studied praise of many an eloquent oration. "Thou art a merry knave. Say, canst thou blow a trumpet?"

"Ay, that I can, to your worship's contentment," replied Longpole, who began to see by the looks of Lord Darby and his master that something was wrong. "I hope I have not offended."

"No, no," answered Henry, "not in the least, Snell, fetch him a trumpet with a blanche banner. Now, fellow, take the trumpet that the page will bring you, and, getting on your horse, follow us. When you shall come to a place where you see lists put up, blow me a defiance. Hast thou never a vizard to put thy muzzle in? Darby, in that chamber you will find him a masking vizard, so that we may not be recognized by his face hereafter."

Longpole was soon furnished with one of the half masks of the day, the long beard of which, intended to conceal the mouth and chin, as it had been worn by the king himself, was composed of threads of pure gold; so that the yeoman bore an ample recompense upon his face for the duty the king put him on. He would fain have had his remark upon the vizard, but beginning to entertain a suspicion of how the matter really stood, he wisely forbore, and followed his master and Lord Darby, who, preceded by the king, passed down a narrow back-staircase into the smaller court, wherein stood the horses prepared for their expedition.

All now passed in almost profound silence. The king and his aid mounted, and, followed by Longpole with his trumpet, issued forth through two gates into the park; where, taking the wildest and most unfrequented paths, they made a large circuit, in order that their approach might seem from any other quarter than the palace. After gaining the forest on Shooter's Hill, the king led the way through one of the roads in the wood, to what we may call the back of Blackheath, on the very verge of which they might behold a group of gentle-men on horseback, with a crowd of lookers-on a-foot, disposed in such sort as to show that their exercises were begun. The spot which they had chosen was a very convenient one for their purpose; shaded on the south by a grove of high elms, whose very situation has not been traceable for now more than two centuries, but which then afforded a width of shade sufficient for several coursers to wheel and charge therein, without the eyes of the riders being dazzled by the morning sunshine. At the foot of these trees extended an ample green, soft, smooth, and even, round which the tilters had pitched the staves, and drawn the ropes, marking the limits of the field; and at the northern end was erected a little tent for them to arm before, and rest after, the course. The four knights themselves, who had met to try their arms, together with several grooms, an armorer, a mule to bear the spears, and two horses for the armor, with their several drivers, formed the group within the lists, which in the wide-extended plain whereon they stood, looked but a spot, and would have seemed still less had it not been for the crowd of idlers

that hung about the ground; and the four knightly
pennons, which, disposed in a line, with a few yards
distance between them, caught the eye as it wandered
over the heath, and attracted it to the spot by their
flutter, and their gaudy hues.

The king paused for a moment to observe them, and
then beckoning Longpole to come up, " Now ride on,
trumpet," cried he; " blow a challenge, and then say
that two strange knights claim to break two lances each,
and pass away unquestioned."

At this command Longpole rode forward, and while
Henry and his master followed more slowly, blew a
defiance on his trumpet at the entrance of the lists, and
then in a loud voice, pronounced the message with which
the king had charged him.

As he finished, Henry and Sir Osborne presented
themselves, and Sir Thomas Neville, the chief of the
other party, after some consultation with his companions,
rode up and replied, " Though we are here as a private
meeting, for our own amusement only, yet we will not
refuse to do the pleasure of the stranger knights; and
as there are four of us, we will each break a spear with
one of the counter-party, which will make the two lances
a-piece that they require. Suffer the knights to enter,"
he continued to the keeper of the barrier; and Henry,
with the young knight, taking the end of the ground in
silence, waited till their lances should be delivered to
them.

Whether the tilters suspected or not who was the
principal intruder on their sport, matters not, though
it is indeed more than probable that they did, for it was
well known to everybody, that if Henry heard of any
rendezvous of the kind, he was almost certain to be
present, either privately or avowedly; and indeed on one
occasion, recorded by Hall, the chronicler of that day,
this romantic spirit had almost cost him dear, the sport
being carried on so unceremoniously, as nearly to slay

the gentleman by whom he was accompanied, and to bring his own life in danger.

On the present occasion no words passed between the two parties, and after a few minutes' conversation amongst the original holders of the ground, as to who should first furnish the course to the strangers, Sir Thomas Neville presented himself opposite to the king, and Sir Henry Poynings, one of the best knights of the day, prepared to run against Sir Osborne. " Now do your best, my knight," said the king, to his aid; " you have got a noble opponent."

The spears were delivered, the knights couched their lances, and galloping on against each other like lightning, the tough ash staves were shivered in a moment against their adversaries' casques.

" Valiantly done! " said Henry, to Sir Osborne, as they returned, to their place; " valiantly done! You struck right in the groove of the basnet, and wavered not an inch. Who are these two, I wonder? They have their beavers down."

While he spoke the spears were again delivered, and upon what impulse, or from what peculiar feeling would be difficult to say, but Sir Osborne felt a strong inclination to unhorse his opponent; and couching his lance with dextrous care as far as possible to prevent its splintering, he struck him in full course upon the gorget, just above its junction with the corslet, and bore him violently backwards to the ground, where he lay apparently deprived of sense.

By this time the king had shivered his lance, and some of the attendants ran up to unlace the fallen man's helmet, when, to his surprise, Sir Osborne beheld the countenance of Sir Payan Wileton. He appeared to be much hurt with his fall, but that was a thing of such common occurrence in those days, that no further notice was ever taken of an accident of the kind, than by giving the injured person all the assistance that could be administered at the time.

However, it may well be supposed that Sir Osborne Maurice felt no ordinary interest in the sight before him. By an extraordinary coincidence, overthrown by his hand, though without intention, and apparently nearly killed, lay the persevering enemy who had swallowed up the fortunes of his house, and had sought so unceasingly to sweep it forever from the face of the earth; and while he lay there prostrate at his feet, with the ashy hue of his cheek paler than ever, and his dark eye closed, as if in death, Sir Osborne still thought he could see the same determined malignity of aspect with which he had declared that he would found his title to the lordship of Chilham Castle on the death of its heir.

Still holding the lance in his hand, the knight bent over the bow of his saddle, and through the bars of his volant-piece contemplated the face of his fallen adversary, till he began to unclose his eyes and look round him, when Sir Thomas Neville, thinking that the stranger was animated merely by feelings of humanity, turned to him, saying that Sir Payan had only been a little stunned, and would do very well now.

"Gentlemen," continued he, addressing the king and Sir Osborne, "we must, according to promise, let you pass away unquestioned; but I will say, that two more valiant and skilful knights never graced a field, nor is it possible to say which outdoes the other; but ye are worthy companions, and true knights both, and so fare ye well."

The king did not reply, lest he should be recognized by his voice, but bending low in token of his thanks, rode out of the lists, accompanied by Sir Osborne, and followed by Longpole.

"Now, by my fay, Sir Knight!" cried Henry when they had once more reached the cover of the wood, "you have far exceeded my expectations and I thank you heartily, good faith, I do! for your aid. But I must have you stay with me. Our poor court will be much graced by the addition of such a knight: what say you, eh?"

"To serve your grace," replied Sir Osborne, "is my first wish; to merit your praise my highest ambition. It is but little to say, that you may command me, when you may command all; but if my zeal to obey those commands may be counted for merit, I will deserve some applause!"

"Wisely spoken," answered the king, "we retain you for ours from this moment; and that you may be ever near our person, we shall bid our chamberlain find you apartments in the palace. How say you, Sir Knight? are you therewith contented?"

"Your grace's bounty outstrips even the swift wings of hope," replied Sir Osborne; "but I will try to fly gratitude against it, and though perhaps she may not be able to o'ertop, she shall, at least, soar an equal pitch."

The knight's allusion to the royal sport of falconry, was well adapted to the ears that heard it. Sir Osborne, without knowing it, drew his metaphor from a sport in which the king delighted, and more convinced of his zeal by these few words, than if the young knight had spoken for an hour, the king replied, "I doubt ye not —'Faith, I doubt ye not! But this night we give a mummery unto our lady queen, when I will bring you to her knowledge; 'tis a lady full of graciousness, and though 'tis I who say it, one that will love well all that I love. But now, let us haste, for the day wears, and as you shall be my masking peer, we must think of some quaint disguise; Darby shall be another; and being all light of foot, we will tread a measure with the fair ladies. You are a proper man, and may, perchance, steal some hearts, wherein you shall have our favor; if 'tis for your good advancement. But turn we down this other path; in that I see some strangers. Quick! Mary Mother! I would not be discovered for another kingdom!"

CHAPTER XIV.

"Not vain she finds the charmful task,
In pageant quaint, in motley mask."
                                            COLLINS.

DURING this expedition of Henry and Sir Osborne,
Lord Darby had acted with more prudence than might
have been expected from one so light and volatile as
himself; but with all the levity of youth, he had a great
fund of shrewdness and good sense, which enabled him
keenly to perceive all the weaknesses of the king's character, and adapt his own behavior exactly to the circumstance whenever he was brought particularly in contact
with the monarch.

In the present instance, seeing that the spirit of mystery
had seized upon Henry, he consented to forego all more
active amusement; so that when the king and his young
companion returned, they found the earl seated in the
saloon wherein Sir Osborne had been armed, never
having quitted it during their absence.

Henry was in high spirits. All had gone well with
him; his expedition had been both successful and secret,
and he was not a little pleased to find that the earl had
not joined any of the gay parties of the court while he
had been away.

"Ha, my lord!" cried he, as he entered, "still here;
you have done well. You have done well—'tis a treasure
you have brought me, this good knight—Snell, unlace my
casque—I must thank you for him as a gift, for he is
now mine own. He outdoes all expectation—nay, say
naught against it, Sir Osborne; I should be able to judge
of these matters, I have broken spears enow, and I pronounce you equal to any knight at this court. Call some
one to undo these trappings. But. Darby, you must not

quit the court to-night. Dine here; 'tis time, i' faith, near one o' the clock! and take Sir Osborne Maurice with you. Make him known to the best of the court. Say the king holds him highly—but stay," he added—" I had forgot "—and sending for the sub-controller of the household, he gave commands that the young knight should be furnished with apartments in the palace from that moment, and receive the appointments of a gentleman of the privy-chamber. "The number is complete," he continued, turning to Sir Osborne; " but, nevertheless, you shall be rated as such, and yourself and men provided in the palace. See it be done, Sir John Harvey. Darby, return hither privately with your friend at nine to-night; we have a mask and revel afoot. But take no heed to send to London for disguise, we will be your furnishers."

"I hope, sir," said the sub-controller, as the knight and his friend followed him from the presence, "you are aware that only three servants are allowed to a gentleman of the privy-chamber."

"Three will be as much as I have occasion for," answered the knight; "the other shall remain in London."

"If you will follow me then," said the officer, "I will show you to the apartment. Ho! send me a yeoman usher there," he continued, speaking to a servant that passed. "This way, sir, we shall find the rooms."

"What!" cried Lord Darby, after they had ascended a good many steps in one of the wings of the building, "are you going to put my friend in a third story?— Think, Sir John Harvey, may not the king find it strange, when he hears that a knight he honors with his regard has been so lodged."

"I can assure you, my lord," answered the controller, "they are absolutely the only ones in the palace vacant, which are at all equal to the knight's quality—and, in truth, were it not for the height, are amongst the best in the place. They are large and spacious, exactly the same size as those which were appointed yesterday by

the queen's command for Lady Constance de Grey, and
which are immediately underneath."

"I was going to offer Sir Osborne the use of mine,"
said Lord Darby, with a laughing glance towards the
knight, "till you could find him better; but if they are
so very good as you say, maybe he will prefer having
his own at once. Eh! Sir Osborne?"

The controller looked solemn, seeing there was some
joke, and not understanding it; but, however, he was
joined in a moment after by a yeoman usher, bearing a
bunch of keys, from which he selected one, and opened
the door at which they had been standing while the earl
spoke. A little ante-chamber conducted into three others
beyond, all very well furnished according to the fashion of
the day, with a beautiful view of the wild park from the
windows of some of the rooms, and of the river from the
others; on which advantages the worthy sub-controller
descanted with much the tone and manner of a lodging-
house keeper at a watering place, little knowing that one
word regarding the proximity of Constance de Grey,
would have been higher recommendation to the young
knight than all the prospects in the world, though he·
loved the beautiful and varied face of earth as much as
any one.

"Go to the wardrobe of beds, usher," said the officer,
when he had promenaded the knight and Lord Darby
through the apartment; "go to the wardrobe of beds,
and tell the under-master to come hither and garnish
this apartment with all speed. As I do not know the
honorable knight's face," continued he, "it is probable
that he is new to this court, and is not aware of the
regulations, which, therefore, I will make bold to tell
him. Dinner and supper are served at the board of estate
every day at noon and at night-fall. No rare suppers
are given, nunchions, beverages or breakfast; but to
each gentleman of the privy-chamber, his grace commands a livery every night.

" A livery ! " said Osborne; "pray, Sir John, what is that?"

" Its value, sir," said the controller, " depends upon the station of the person to whom it is given. I have known it cost as much as ten pounds; such was sent every night to the gentlemen who came to seek the Princess Mary for the French king; but the livery given by his grace the king, to the gentlemen of the privy-chamber, and others bearing the same rank, is a cast of fine manchet bread, two pots of white or red wine at choice, one pound weight of sugar, four white lights, and four yellow lights of wax, and one large staff torch, which is delivered every evening at seven of the clock."

Without proceeding farther with such discourse, we shall merely say that the arrangement of Sir Osborne's apartment was soon completed, himself unarmed, his servants furnished with what modern Johnnys would call dog-holes, and with truckle beds; and having, by inter-cession with a gentleman wearing black velvet and a gold chain, and calling himself the chief cook, obtained some dinner, for the board of estate had long been cleared, Lord Darby and Sir Osborne sauntered forth on the parade, where the young gallants of the court were beginning to show themselves; some taking, as it were, a furtive walk across, afraid to be seen there before the moment of fashion sanctioned their appearance, and some, who, from either ignorance or boldness, heeded no mode but their own convenience.

The presence of Lord Darby, however, who gradually gathered round him a little multitude as he walked, soon rendered the parade more populous. Sir Osborne was introduced to all who were worthy of his acquaintance; and the same persons who three days before might hardly have given him a courteous answer if he had asked them a question, were now mortified at not being numbered with his acquaintance. The knight himself, however, was absent and inattentive, his eye continually seeking

Lady Constance de Grey through the crowd, and his
mind, sometimes occupied with pleasing dreams of love,
and hope, and happiness to come, and sometimes pondering over his unexpected encounter with Sir Payan
Wileton and its probable results.

So strange is the world, that this very abstractness of
manner and carelessness in regard to those about him
had its grace in the eyes of the court. They seemed to
think that he who cared so little about anybody, must
be somebody of consequence himself; and when, after a
prolonged saunter the two friends re-entered the palace,
Sir Osborne's name had acquired a degree of éclat which
the most attentive politeness would scarcely have obtained.
Still no Constance de Grey had he seen, and he sat down
in the apartments of Lord Darby not peculiarly satisfied
with their walk.

The young earl himself had also suffered a similar
disappointment, for in the midst of all the nonchalant
gaiety which he had displayed to the crowd, his eye had
not failed to scan every group of ladies that they met,
for the form of Lady Katrine Bulmer, and he felt a good
deal mortified at not having seen her. But very different
was the manner in which his feelings acted, from the
deeper and more ardent love of Darnley. He laughed,
he sung, he jested his companion upon his gravity, and
in the end consoled him, by assuring him that they should
meet with both their lady-loves that night at the queen's,
so that if he was not in a very expiring state, he might
hope to live to see her once more.

The hours quickly flew, and a little before nine the
knight and his companion presented themselves at the
door of the king's private apartments, where they were
admitted by a page. When they entered Henry was
reading, and pursued the object of his study without
taking any notice of their approach by word or sign.
Nothing remained to be done but to stand profoundly
still before him, waiting his good pleasure, which remained full a quarter of an hour unmanifested.

"Well, gentlemen both," cried the king at last, starting up and laying down the book. "I have kept ye long—eh? But now to make amends, I will lead ye to the fair ladies. Oh, the disguises! the disguises! Bring the disguises, Minton; the three I chose but now. You, Darby, shall be a Muscovian; you, Maurice, a Polacco, and I an Almaine. Say, Darby did you see my good lord cardinal this morning, ere you came? Holds he his mind of going to York, as he stated yesterday?"

"I did not see the very reverend lord this morning," replied Lord Darby, who was, as well as his ward, the chief lord of Wolsey's household. "But his master of the horse informed me that he still proposed going at ten this morning. Your grace knows that he never delays when business calls him, and in the present case he thinks that his presence may quell the murmurers of Yorkshire, as well as Lord Howard has put down the Rochester fools."

"Ah, 'twas a shrewd business that of Rochester," said the king. "Now would I give a thousand marks to know who 'twas that set that stone a-rolling. Be you sure, Darby, that the brute shipwrights would ne'er have dreamed such a thing themselves. They were set on! They were set on, man! Ha, the disguises. Quick, come into this closet, and we will robe us. 'Tis late, and our lady has promised to give, as well as to receive, a mask."

So saying, Henry led the way to a cabinet at the side of the saloon, in which they were; and here the two young lords offered to assist in dressing him, but of this he would not permit, bidding them haste with their own robes, or he would be ready first. The disguise assigned to Sir Osborne was a splendid suit of gold brocade trimmed with fur, intended to represent the dress of a Pole; having a sort of pelisse with sleeves of rich gold damask, and sables thrown over the back, and held by a baldrick, crossing from the right shoulder under the left arm. His head was covered with a square bonnet of cloth of gold, like his dress, with an edge of fur; and his face concealed by a satin mask with a beard of golden threads.

The dress of Lord Darby was not very dissimilar, with only this difference, that in place of the pelisse, he was furnished with a robe with short sleeves, and wore on his head a sort of turban, or toque, with a high feather. In a very different style was the king's disguise, being simply a splendid German dress of cloth of gold, trimmed with crimson velvet, but certainly not so unlike the garments he usually wore, as to afford any great degree of concealment. All being masked and prepared, Henry sent the page to see if the torch-bearers were ready, and issuing out of the palace, the three maskers, preceded by half a dozen attendants, crossed the greater quadrangle, passed out at the gate, and making a circuit round the building, came immediately under the windows of the queen's great hall, from each of which a broad blaze of light flashed forth upon the night, and cast a line of twinkling splendor across the river, that otherwise flowed on, dark and indistinct, under a clouded and moonless sky.

" Sir Osborne," said Henry, in a low voice, as they entered the open doors, and turned into a suite of apartments anterior to the room where the queen held her assembly—" Sir Osborne, your voice being unknown, you shall be our orator, and in your fine wit, seek a fair compliment for our introduction."

Had his face been uncovered, perhaps the young knight might have sought to excuse himself, but there is wonderful assurance in a mask, and feeling a boldness in his disguise, which perhaps the eye of Constance de Grey might have robbed him of, had he not been concealed from its glance, he at once undertook the task, saying, that he would do his best.

As he spoke, a couple of hautboys, by which Henry

was preceded, paused at the entrance of the great hall,
and placing themselves on each side, began a light duet,
to announce that some masks were coming. The doors
were thrown open, and a splendid scene burst on the view
of Sir Osborne, full of bright and glittering figures,
fleeting about in the blaze of innumerable lights, like the
gay phantasms of a brilliant dream. The knight in-
stinctively paused, but Henry urged him on.

"Quick! quick!" whispered he, "To the lady, to the
lady! You forget your task."

Sir Osborne instantly recollected himself, and seeing
a lady who, standing unmasked at the farther end of
the hall, bore about her that air of royalty, and that
majestic beauty, scarcely touched by time, for which the
noble Catherine was famous, he advanced directly towards her, and bent one knee to the ground. Nature
had given him somewhat of a poet's inspiration, which
now came happily to his aid, and if his verses were not
very good, they were at least ready.

> " Lady of beauty, queen of grace,
>   Strangers three have come to thee,
> To gaze on thine unclouded face,
>   Where so many maskers be.
> Oh! never shade that brow so high,
>   With the mummers' painted wile,
> Sure you keep that lip and eye,
>   Welcome on your slaves to smile."

"I thank you, fair sir, I thank you," replied the queen,
with a pleased and gracious smile; "be most welcome,
you and your company—I should know you, and yet I
do not. But will you not dance? Choose you fair ladies;
and, chamberlain, bid the music sound."

Sir Osborne passed on, and the king and Lord Darby
followed.

"Excellent well, my knight! excellent well!" whispered Henry. "Now show your wit in choice of a fair
dame. I' faith one must be keen in these same masks to

tell the foul from the fair. However, let us disperse and
find the jewels, though they be hid in such strange rinds."

At the word the three maskers took different paths
amongst the various figures with which the hall was
now nearly filled; Lord Darby and the knight, each in
search of the object of their love; while Henry, as yet
unrecognized, glided through the apartment, it might be
in quest of some particular fair one also.

For some time Sir Osborne sought in vain, bewildered
amongst the crowd of quaint disguises with which he
was surrounded. Now he thought he beheld the form
of Lady Constance here, and after following it for a
moment was called away by the sight of one that re-
sembled her more. That again he gave up, convinced
by some turn or some gesture that it was not her. Another presented itself, which perhaps he might have mistaken, but the gay flutter of her manner at once showed
that it was not the person he sought. He saw that
already Lord Darby had found his partner,—the tuning
of the musical instruments was over,—and, mentally
cursing his own stupidity, or his own ill-fortune, he was
proceeding once more towards the part of the room
where stood the queen, with his heart beating between
eagerness and vexation, when he beheld a lady, dressed
in silver brocade, with a plain satin mask, glide into
the hall, and, passing by several who spoke to her, approach that spot, as if to take a seat which stood near.
Sir Osborne darted forward. He felt that it was her;
and, eager to prevent any one intercepting him, almost
startled her with the suddenness of his address.

" Fair mask," said the knight, in a voice that trembled
with delight and hope, " will you tread a measure with a
stranger, for courtesy's sake ? "

" I should know your voice," said the lady, in a low
tone; " but I can scarce believe I see you here. But one
word, to tell me who you are ? "

" My motto," replied the knight, " is Constanc-y—my
crest a lady's glove."

The lady instantly put her hand into his. "Darnley," said she, in a voice so low as to be inaudible to any one but himself, who, bending his head over her, trembled to catch every accent.

"Ah, Constance," he replied, in the same subdued tone, "what is it I have dared to say to you? what is it I have dared to hope? Friendless and fortuneless as I am, can you ever pardon my boldness?"

"Hush!" she said, "for pity's sake speak not in that way. Now I know you love me, that is enough. Friendless you are not, and fortuneless you cannot be when all that is Constance's is yours. But see, they are going to dance, afterwards we will speak more. Do not think me bold, Darnley, or too easily won; but were I to affect that reserve which still perhaps might be right, we are so circumstanced that we might be ruined before we understood each other."

The knight poured forth a thousand thanks, and strove to explain to Lady Constance how deeply grateful he felt for that generous candor which is ever the companion of the truest modesty; and the music now beginning, he led her through the dance, with calm and graceful ease. As soon as the measure was ended, the queen's chamberlain pronounced, with a loud voice, that, in the other halls, the knights and ladies who had danced, would find cool air and shady bowers; and, gladly taking advantage of this information, Sir Osborne led his partner into the chamber beyond, which, by the queen's device, had been divided into a thousand little arbors, where artificial trees and shrubs, mingled with real ones, and often ornamented with gilt fruit or flowers, formed a sort of enchanted garden, for the dancers to repose themselves, not very exquisite in its taste, indeed, but very much to the taste of the day.

Singling out the farthest of all the arbors, and the one which permitted its occupants most easily to observe the approach of any other party, Darnley led Lady Constance to one of the seats which it contained, and placing himself by her side, paused for a moment in silence, to enjoy the new delights that came thrilling upon his heart. "Oh, Constance!" said he at length, looking up to the sweet hazel eyes that gazed upon him through the meaningless mask; "never, never did I think to know such happiness on earth. Could I have dreamed of this when I left you for Flanders?"

"I do not know," replied Constance, "I have done nothing but think ever since—ever since—you took my glove—and I have fancied that my dear father foresaw this, and wished it, as you tell me he was aware who you were, for never, even at that age, was I permitted to know, and converse with, and see intimately, any young cavalier but yourself. And then, do not you remember when you used to teach me to shoot with the bow, how he would stand by and praise your shooting. Oh! I can call to mind a thousand things to make me think so."

"Could I but believe it," said Darnley, "I should be even happier than I am. But still, dear Constance, I hope, I trust, that in the end I may be enabled to seek your hand, not as an outcast wanderer. Your good cousin, Lord Darby, has brought me to the knowledge of the king, whose favor I have been happy enough to gain. He had retained me as one of the gentlemen of his privy chamber, appointed me apartments in the palace, which are just above your own, and I hope so far to win his regard by this opportunity, that he may be induced to hear my cause against the villain who has seized our inheritance, and do justice to us at last. And then, Constance, with rank and fortune, and favor, all restored, Darnley may hope."

"And what, if not restored, Darnley?" said Lady Constance. "Do you think that rank, or fortune, or favor will make any difference in the regard of Constance de Grey? No, Darnley: if—but I won't say if—you love me, and the cardinal may do what he will, but I will never wed another, He may find means, as they hint, to forfeit my English lands—yet he cannot take my French ones, and even if he did, I would rather be beggar and—free, than married to a man I do not love. Not that I do not love Darby as my cousin—he is kind, and generous, and frank, but oh! it is very, very different. But you say that he introduced you to the king, I did not know you were even acquainted."

"It is a long story, dear Constance," replied the knight; "I will give it you some other time; but now tell me, while we are yet uninterrupted, how may I see you. To watch for you, even to catch a word during the day, certainly were delight, but still 'tis hard, situated as we are, not to be able to communicate together more freely. May I not come to see you?"

"Certainly," replied Lady Constance: "but you know that I can hardly have any private conversation with you even when you do, for good Dr. Wilbraham is with me the greater part of the morning, and one of my women always." She paused for a moment in thought, and raising her eyes to his, "Darnley," she said, "I never could love a man in whose honor I could not entirely confide, therefore I do not think it shows me either weak or wrong, when I say that I will be entirely guided by you. We are not situated as people in general, and therefore we cannot act as people in general do. Tell me, then, what you think right, and I will do it. But here are two of the maskers coming directly towards us; say, what must I do?"

"It is necessary, Constance," said the knight, quickly, "absolutely necessary, that I should sometimes be allowed half an hour's conversation alone, especially at the present moment. I will come to-morrow early, very early, if it can be then. May I?"

"Yes," said Lady Constance, "I will see. But who are these? They are coming to us!"

"It is Lord Darby," said the knight; "and, if I mistake not, Lady Katrine Bulmer."

"Dear Polacco," cried Lord Darby, approaching with a lady, who, to use an old writer's description, was wondrous gay in her apparel, with a marvellous strange and rich tire on her head—"dear Polacco, I am but now aware of how much I have to thank you for. What, you were near tilting at the Rochester host?—and broaching me half a dozen plank-shavers on your spear in defence of a fair lady, and also took my part, even before you knew me?—Now will I guess who is this silver fair one by your side—she's blushing through her mask, as if I were going to pronounce her name with the voice of a trumpet. Well, sweet cousin, will you own that you have a wild and rattle-pated relation in the good town of Westminster; and if so, though you cannot love him, will you love a very lovable creature for his sake?"

"Hush, mad-cap, let me speak," said the voice of Lady Katrine Bulmer. "Lady," she continued, placing herself by the side of Lady Constance, "will you hate one, that would fain love you very much, and have your love again?"

"Heaven forbid!" replied Lady Constance; "'tis so sweet to be loved ourselves, that feeling it, we can scarce refuse it again to those that love us—with a reservation, though," she added.

"Granted the reservation, that there is still a one must be loved best," said Lady Katrine; "we all four know it," and she glanced her merry eyes round the circle. "Oh what a happy thing is a mask! Here one may confess one's love, or laugh at one's friends, or abuse one's relations, without a blush; and surely, if they were worn always, they would save a world of false smiles, and a world of false tears. Oh, strange economy! What an ocean of grimaces might be spared if man were but to wear a pasteboard face!"

"I am afraid that he does so more than you think, lady," replied Sir Osborne. "You will own that his countenance is hollow, and that its smiles are painted, in short, that it is all a picture, though a moving one."

" Listen to him," cried Lady Katrine, raising her look to Lord Darby; " think of his having the impudence to moralize in the presence of two women! Would you have believed it?"

" Nay, fair lady, it was you who led the way," replied Sir Osborne. " But what means that trumpet in these peaceful halls?"

" 'Tis either a sound to supper," replied Lord Darby, " or the entrance of one of those pageants, of which our gracious king is so fond; at all events, let us go and see."

Thus speaking, he led away Lady Katrine gaily to the door, towards which all the other parties from the enchanted garden were now proceeding. Sir Osborne and Lady Constance followed more slowly. " Darnley," said the fair girl, as she leaned on his arm, " I know not what sort of presentiment led me hither to-night, for I have been so vexed and so distressed with much that has happened since my arrival in London, that I can hardly call myself well—I am now much fatigued, and if I can escape, I will hie me to my bed.—When you come to-morrow, you shall answer me a thousand questions that I have to ask. Oh, I see I can pass round by that other door—farewell, for this night."

" Oh, that I dared hope it had been a happy one to you as it has been to me," said the knight, still holding her hand with a fond and lingering pressure.

" It has, Darnley—it has," replied Lady Constance! " it has been one that I shall never forget—farewell!" and turning away, she passed out of the door at the side, which led to the apartments on that wing of the building, not, however, without one look more into the room, where her lover stood gazing still, to catch the last glance of that graceful figure, ere it left his sight.

When she was gone, the young knight, with a high beating heart, turned to the door of the great hall, and entered with some of the last lingerers, who were now changing their slowness into speed, in order to get a place before the pageant entered. The thoughts of Sir Osborne, however, were employed on so much more engrossing subjects, that he took no pains to hasten his steps till he was fairly within the chamber, when, seeing the whole of the guests arranged on the farther side of the hall, with the queen in the centre, under her canopy, or cloth of estate, he felt the impropriety of standing there alone, and hastened to seek a place.

At that moment, he observed Henry, who, still disguised, was seated amongst the rest, and who made him a sign to take a place beside him. Notwithstanding his mask, however, it was very evident that the king was known; for, on his sign to Sir Osborne, all around made way for the young knight to approach the monarch. Scarcely had he taken his seat, when through the great doors of the hall, a huge machine was rolled in, before which extended a double cloth of arras, so arranged as to hide every part of the gewgaw within, only leaving a twinkling light here and there, seen through the crevices, like the lamps that, through the cracks of the last scene in a pantomime, announce the brilliant change that is soon to take place, to the temple of Love or Venus, or some other such sweet power, that deals in pasteboard and spangles.

When the eye of Henry, pampered with such gaudy food from day to day, had taken in enough of the pageant, he rose from his seat, and waving his hand for the musicians to cease, " Thanks, gentle lords and ladies, thanks," he cried, and taking off his own mask, added, " Let us ease our faces of their vizards."

As he spoke, every one rose and unmasked, and Henry, taking Sir Osborne by the hand, led him forward to the queen, while all eyes naturally fixed upon him.

" Fair lady mine," said the king, " I bring you a good knight, Sir Osborne Maurice, who, as you see, has wit at will; and who, I can vouch, is as keen a champion in the saddle, as he is a graceful dancer in the hall; in short, he is 'A very gentle perfect knight,' whom you must cherish and receive for my love."

While Sir Osborne knelt and kissed the hand that she extended to him, Katherine replied, " Indeed, my lord, you have brought me one that I have longed to see. This is the good knight who, on his journey towards London, took charge of my giddy girl and namesake, Katrine Bulmer, and defended her from the Rochester rioters. Come hither, Kate, and in our presence thank the knight for all the trouble, I am sure, he had with them upon the road."

" Nay, your grace," said Lady Katrine, advancing, " I have thanked him once already, and men are all too saucy and conceited to thank them twice."

" 'Tis thou art saucy, my fair mistress," said the king, laughing, and then bending down his head to the queen, who was still seated, he whispered something to her which made her smile and raise her eyes to the knight and Lady Katrine. " A handsome pair, indeed ! " said she, in reply to what the king had whispered. " But the banquet is ready."

" Lords and ladies," said Henry, raising his voice, "our royal mistress will not let us part without our supper. All, then, come in pairs, for in the white hall is prepared a banquet—Sir Osborne, lead in Lady Katrine there, you shall be coupled, for an hour at least."

Sir Osborne glanced his eye to Lord Darby, but the earl was perfectly master of his countenance, and looking as indifferent as if nothing had happened, led in some other lady, while the knight endeavored to entertain Lady Katrine as well as he might, laboring under the comfortable assurance that she would very much have preferred another by her side.

CHAPTER XV.

Would I a house for happiness erect,
Nature alone should be the architect.

                                        COWLEY.

WE must now pass over a brief space of time with but
little commemoration. At the foot, of one of the old oaks
in Richmond Park sat Lady Constance de Grey while her
woman Margaret stood at a little distance with a page,
and Sir Osborne Maurice leaned by her side. They had
met by chance—really by chance—at that early hour in
that remote part of the park; though it is more than probable that the same thoughts, acting on hearts so nearly
allied, had led them both forth to meditate on their fate.
And even after they had met, the stillness of the scene
seemed to have found its way to their souls, for they
remained almost in silence watching the clouds, and
gazing at the view, content to feel that they enjoyed
together the same sweet morning, and the same lovely
scene.

It may be as well, however, before proceeding farther,
to give some slight sketch of what had occurred since the
close of the last chapter, though were we to account for
every day, it would be but detail of joust after joust,
tourney after tourney, revel upon revel, wearisome from
their repetition, and sickening from their vain splendor.
Suffice it, that Sir Osborne still maintained his place in
the king's favor. His lance was always held by the
judges of the field as next to the king's; his grace in the
hall, or at the court, his dexterity in martial exercises,
his clerkly learning, and his lighter accomplishments,
won him much admiration, while a sort of unassuming-
ness, which seemed to hold his own high qualities as

light, silenced much envy, in short, it became the fashion to praise him.

There was, however, many a curious whisper of, Who was he? Whence did he come? What was his family? and some of the knights who had served abroad, and had been with the king at Terouenne and Tournay, conferred together, and shook the wise head; but still it was remarked that they were amongst those who most praised and sought the young knight. Sir Osborne marked with a keen and observing eye all that passed about him, and seeing that he was recognized by more than one, he felt that he must hasten to prevent his secret being communicated to the king by any lips but his own; and now high in favor, he only waited a fitting opportunity to hazard all by the avowal of his name and rank.

Wolsey had been absent for nearly a month in his diocese at York, and removed from the influence of his presence, Lord Darby and Lady Katrine Bulmer, Sir Osborne and Constance de Grey, seemed to have forgot his stern authority, and given course to the feelings of their hearts. The knight had seen Lady Constance almost every day, and good Mrs. Margaret her woman, with whom Sir Osborne was no small favorite, took care not to exercise towards him that strict etiquette which she practised upon all other visitors, leaving them full opportunity to say all that the heart sought to communicate, as she very well perceived what feelings were busy in their breasts.

Thus everything between them was explained, everything was known; there was no coldness, there was no reserve, there was none of that idle and base coquetry which delights in teasing a heart that loves. Constance de Grey loved, sincerely, openly, and she had too high an esteem for the man she had chosen, to suppose that the acknowledgment of that love could make it less worthy in his eyes. Happy, indeed, it was for them both that the most perfect confidence did exist between them, for

Henry had conceived the project of marrying the young knight to Lady Katrine; and though the queen, with the instinctive perception of a woman in those matters, soon saw that such a plan would very little accord with the feelings of either party, and quickly discouraged it; yet Henry, giving way to all his own impetuosity, hurried it on with precipitation, took every occasion to force them together, and declared that he would have them married as soon as the court returned from the meeting with the French king at Guisnes.

The situation of Sir Osborne was not a little embarrassing, the more especially as Lady Katrine, in her merry malice, often seemed to give in entirely to the king's schemes, having a threefold object in so doing—if object can be attributed to such heedless gaiety; namely, to coquet a little with Sir Osborne, which she did not dislike with anybody, to enjoy his embarrassment, and at the same time to tease Lord Darby.

With these three laudable motives she might have contrived to make Sir Osborne and Lady Constance unhappy, had not that mutual confidence existed between them which set all doubts at defiance. Nor, indeed, was it Lady Katrine's wish to do harm; whimsical, gay, and thoughtless, she gave way to the impulse of the moment. If she was in good-humor, she was all liveliness and spirit; running as close to the borders of direct flirtation as possible with whomsoever happened to be near; but, on the contrary, if anything went wrong with her, she would be petulant and irritable, showing forth a thousand little contemptible airs of dignity which she did not possess, and reserve which was not natural to her. No one's good regard did she seek more than that of Lady Constance de Grey, and yet she seemed to take every way to lose it. But Constance, though so different herself, understood her character, appreciated the good, made allowance for the faults, and, secure in Darnley's affection, forgave her little coquetry with her lover.

In regard to Lord Darby, he knew Lady Katrine too; and if ever he gave himself a moment's uneasiness about her waywardness, he did not let it appear. If she flirted, he flirted too; if she was gay, he took care not to be a wit behind; if she was affectionate, he was gentle: and if she was cross, he laughed at her. She never could put him out of humor; though, to do her all manner of justice, she tried hard, and thus finding her attempts to tease ineffectual, she gradually relaxed in the endeavor.

In the meantime the days of Sir Osborne and Lady Constance flew by in a sweet calm, that had something ominous in its tranquillity. He had almost forgotten Sir Payan Wileton; and in the mild flow of her happiness, Constance scarcely remembered the schemes with which the avaricious haughty Wolsey threatened to trouble the stream of her existence. But, nevertheless, it was to be expected, that if the dispensation had not yet arrived from Rome, it could not be delayed more than a few days; and that at the return of the minister from York, the command would be renewed for her to bestow her hand upon Lord Darby. Such thoughts would sometimes come across Constance's mind with a painful sensation of dread; and then, with a spirit which so fair and tender an exterior seemed hardly to announce, she would revolve in her mind a plan for baffling the imperious prelate at all risks, and yet not implicate her lover, at the very moment that his " fortunes were a-making."

The scene in Richmond Park, to which the court had now removed from Greenwich, as well as the bright gentleness of the May morning in which she met Sir Osborne there, was well calculated to nurse the most pleasing children of hope.

" This is very, very lovely, Darnley," said Lady Constance, after they had gazed for long in silence; " oh, why are not all days like this; why must we have the storm, and the tempest, and the cloud?"

" Perhaps," replied the knight, " if all days were so

fair, we might not esteem them so much; we should be like those, Constance, who in the world have gone on in a long course of uninterrupted prosperity, and who have enjoyed so much, that they can no longer enjoy."

"Oh no, no," cried she; "there are some pleasures that never cloy, and amongst them, are those that we derive from contemplating the loveliness of nature. I cannot think that I should ever weary of scenes like these—no, let me have a fairy sky, where the sunshine scarcely knows a cloud, and where the air is always soft and sweet like this."

At this moment Mistress Margaret approached, with some consternation in her aspect. "Good now, lady," cried she; "look! who is this that is coming? Such a strange-looking little man, no bigger than an atomy— oh, I'm so glad the knight is with us, for it is something singular, I am sure."

"You are very right, Mistress Margaret," said Sir Osborne; "this is, indeed, a most singular being that approaches. Constance, you have heard the queen and her ladies speak of Sir Cesar, the famous alchymist and astrologer. He is well known to good Dr. Wilbraham, and seems, for some reason, to take a strange interest in all my proceedings. Depend on it, he comes to warn us of something that is about to happen, and his warning must not be slighted; for, from wheresoever his knowledge comes, it is very strange."

Lady Constance and the knight watched the old man as he came slowly over the green towards them, showing little of that vivacity of demeanor by which he was generally characterized. On approaching near, he bowed to Lady Constance with courtly ease, saluted the knight in a manner which might be called affectionate, and without apology for his intrusion, seated himself at the lady's feet, and began a gay and easy conversation upon the jousts of the day before.

"There is no court in the world," said he after a little

—" and there are few courts I have not seen—where such sports are carried to the height of luxury that they are here. I never saw the tournaments, the jousts, the pageants of the eighth Henry King of England exceeded but once."

"And when was that, may I ask?" demanded Lady Constance, whose feelings towards the old man were strangely mingled of awe and curiosity, so much had she heard of him and his strange powers during her residence at the court.

"It was in Germany," replied Sir Cesar, "at the city of Ratisbon, and it was conducted as all such displays should ever be conducted—each knight wore over his armor a motley suit, and on his casque a cap and bells; the hilt of his sword was ornamented with a bauble, and as they made procession to the lists, the court fools of all the electors in the empire followed behind the knights, and whipped them on with blown bladders."

"Nay, nay, you are a satirist," said Lady Constance; "such a thing, surely, could never happen in reality."

"In truth, it did, lady" answered Sir Cesar; "it was called the tournament of fools, though I wot, not to distinguish it from other tournaments, which are all foolish enough. Osborne," he continued, turning abruptly to the young knight, "you will ride no more at this court."

"How mean you?" demanded Sir Osborne: "why should I not?"

"I mean," replied the old man, "that I come to forewarn you of approaching evil. Perhaps, you may turn it aside, but there is much that threatens you. Are you not losing time? The king's regard is gained—wherefore, then, do you delay? While Wolsey is absent— mark me! while Wolsey is absent—or you are lost, for the moment."

"Oh, say not so," cried Lady Constance, clasping her hands; "oh say not so, for I hear that he returns to-morrow."

"Fear not, lady," said Sir Cesar, who had now risen, "the danger will last but for a time, and then pass away. So that, whatever happens to either of you, let not your hearts sink; but be firm, steadfast, and true. All the advice that I can give you, is but the advice of an ordinary mortal like yourselves. Men judge rashly when they think that even those who see clearest can yet see clear. All that I know, all that I behold, is but a dim shadowing forth of what will be, like the indistinct memory of long gone years—a circumstance without a form; I see in both your fates an evil and a sorrowful hour approaching, and yet I cannot tell you how to avoid it; but I can descry that 'twill be but for a while, and that must console you."

"Good Sir Cesar," said the young knight, "I will ask you no questions, for I have now learned that you were a dear friend of my father, and I feel sure that you will give all knowledge that may be useful to me, and if you will tell me what is good to do in this conjuncture, I will follow it."

"Good, now!" said Sir Cesar, with a gratified look: "good! I see you are overcoming your old fault, though you have been a long while about it. Three thousand years! three thousand years to my remembrance."

Constance turned an inquiring look to her lover, who, however, was not capable of giving her any explanation. "Think you," demanded he, addressing Sir Cesar, "that it would be best to inform his grace of everything at once?"

"I think it would," said the old man, "I think it would, but I scarcely dare advise you. Osborne, there is conviction pressing on my mind, which I have perhaps learned too late. Can it be, that those who are permitted to read certain facts in the book of fate, are blinded to the right interpretation of that which they discover? Perhaps it may be—I have reason to believe it—nought that I have ever calculated has proved false, but often,

often, it has been verified in a sense so opposite to my expectations, yet so evident when it did appear, that it seems as if heaven held the search presumptuous, and baffled the searcher even with the knowledge he acquired. Never will I more presume to expound aught that I may learn. The fact I tell you; an evil and a bitter hour is coming for you both, but it shall not last—and then you shall be happy, when I am no more;" and turning away, without other farewell, he left them, and took the way to the palace.

Lady Constance gazed on the face of her lover with a look of apprehensive tenderness that banished all thought of himself. "Oh, my Constance," said he, "to think of your having to undergo so much for me is too, too painful! But fear not, dear Constance; we are still in a land where laws are above all power, and they cannot, they dare not ill-treat you!"

"For myself, Darnley," replied Constance, "I have no fear. They may threaten, they may wrong me, they may do what they will, but they can never make me marry another. It is for you I fear. However, he said that we should be happy at last, though he hinted that you would be driven from the court. Oh, Darnley, if that be the case; if you find there be the least danger, fly without loss of time—"

"And leave behind me," said Darnley, "all I love in the world! Oh, Constance, would not the block and axe itself be preferable? It would! it would, a thousand times preferable to leaving you forever."

"It might," said Constance; "I feel myself it might, if you feel as I feel. But, Darnley, I tell you at once—I boldly promise to follow."

"But still, Constance, dear, excellent girl," said the knight, "would it be right, would it be honorable in me to accept such a sacrifice?"

"Darnley," said Lady Constance, firmly, "my happiness is in your hands, and what is right and honorable, is not to throw that happiness away. Now that my love is yours, now that my hand is promised to you, you have no right to think of rank, or fortune, or aught else. If I were obliged to fly, would you not follow me? and wheresoever you go, there will I find means to join you; all I ask, all I pray in return is, that if there be the least danger, you will instantly fly. Will you promise me? If you love me you will."

"I will," said Sir Osborne. "What would I not do to prove that love? But, I trust, dear Constance, there may be no need of hasty flight. All they can do will be to banish me the court, for I have committed no crime, but coming here under a feigned name."

"I know not—I know not," said the lady; "'tis easy, where no crime is, to forge an accusation; and, if report speak truth, such has been Wolsey's frequent policy, when any one became loved of our gracious king—so that even the favor you have gained may prove your ruin. But you have promised to fly upon the first threatening of danger, and I hold as a part of that promise that you will stay for no leavetaking."

"Well, well, Constance," replied the knight, "time will show us more. But at all events I will try to anticipate Wolsey's return, and, by telling Henry all, secure my fate."

"Do so! do so!" said Lady Constance, "and oh, lose no time. Fly to him, Darnley, he must be risen by this time. Farewell! farewell!"

Sir Osborne would fain have lingered still, but Constance would not be satisfied till he went. At last, then, he left her, and proceeded with quick steps to the palace; while she, with a slower pace, pursued another path through the park, having been rejoined by Mistress Margaret, who, not liking the appearance of old Sir Cesar, had removed to secure distance on his approach, and who now poured forth no inconsiderable vituperation on his face, his figure, and his apparel. On arriving at the palace,

Sir Osborne found that he had been sent for by the king, and hurrying his steps towards the privy chamber, he was met by Henry himself, bearing a hawk upon his hand, and armed with a stout leaping pole, as if prepared for the field. "Come, Sir Knight," cried the king, "if you would see sport, follow quick. Bennet has just marked a heron go down by the side of the river, and I am resolved to fly young Jacob here, that his wings may not rust. Follow quick!"

Thus speaking, the king made all speed out of the palace, and cutting partly across the park, and round the base of the hill, soon reached the edge of the river, where slower progress became necessary, and he could converse with the young knight, without interrupting his sport. Their conversation, however, was solely about hawking and it accessories, and winding along by the side of the sedges with which the bank was lined, they tried to raise the game by cries, and by beating the rushes with the leaping pole.

For a long way no heron made its appearance, and Henry was beginning to get impatient, just in the same proportion as he had been eager in setting out. Unwilling, however, to yield his sport, after persisting some time in endeavoring, with the aid of Sir Osborne, to make the prey take flight, he sent back the only attendant that had followed him for a dog, and went on slowly with the knight, pursuing the course of the river. When they had proceeded about two hundred yards, and had arrived at a spot where the bank rose into a little mound, the knight paused, while Henry, rather crossed with not having instantly met with the amusement he expected, sauntered on, bending his eyes upon the ground.

"Hist, your grace! Hist!" cried Sir Osborne: "I have him!"

"Where, man? Where?" cried Henry, looking round without seeing anything. "God's life, where?"

"Here, your grace! Here!" replied the knight. "Do

16

you not see him?—with one leg raised, and the claw
contracted, gazing on the water as intently as a lady in a
looking-glass,—by that branch of a tree that is floating
down."

"Ha! Yes, yes!" cried Henry. "The long neck
and the blue back! 'Tis he—Whoop! Sir Heron!
Whoop! Cry him up, Maurice! Cry him up!"

Sir Osborne joined his voice to the king's, and their
united efforts reaching the ears of the long-legged fowl
they were in search of, he speedily spread his wings,
stretched out his neck, and rose heavily from the water.
With a whoop and a cry the king slipped the jesses of his
falcon, and flew him after the heron, who, for a moment,
not perceiving the adversary that pursued him, took his
flight over the fields, instead of rising high. On went the
heron, on went the falcon, and on went Henry after
them; till coming to a little muddy creek, which there-
abouts found its way into the river, the king planted his
pole with his accustomed activity, and threw himself
forward for the leap. Unfortunately, however, at the
very moment that his whole weight was cast upon the
pole, in the midst of the spring, the wood snapped, and in
an instant Sir Osborne saw the king fall flat on his face,
and nearly disappear in the ooze and water with which
the creek was filled. Henry struggled to free himself, but
in vain, for the tenacity of the mud prevented his raising his head, so that in another minute he must inevitably
have been drowned, had not Sir Osborne plunged into
his aid, and lifted his face above the water, thus giving
him room to breathe. Short as had been the time, however, that respiration had been impeded, the king's powers
were nearly exhausted, and even with the knight's assist-
tance, he could not raise himself from the position in
which he had fallen.

Though an unsafe experiment for both, considering the
mud and slime with which they were entangled, nothing
remained for Sir Osborne but to take the king in his

arms, and endeavor to carry him to the bank: and this at length he accomplished, sometimes slipping, and sometimes staggering, with the uncertain nature of the footing and the heavy burden that he carried; but still supported by his vast strength, he contrived to keep himself from falling, proceeding slowly and carefully forward, and assuring himself of the firmness of each step before he took another.*

With a feeling of inexpressible gladness, he seated Henry on the bank, and kneeling beside him, expressed his hopes that he had received no injury. "No," said the king, faintly: "no—but, Maurice, you have saved my life. Thank God! and thank you!"

A pause now ensued, and the young knight endeavored, as well as circumstances would permit, to cleanse the countenance and hands of the monarch from the effects of the fall. While he was thus employed, the king gradually recovered his breath and strength, and from time to time uttered a word or two of thanks, or directions, till at last Bennet, the attendant, was seen approaching with the dog.

"Stay, stay, Sir Osborne," said the monarch, "here comes Bennet. We will send him for fresh clothes. Where is the falcon? By my faith, I owe you much—ay, as much as life! Whistle for the falcon, I have not breath."

Sir Osborne uttered a long falconer's whistle, and in a moment the bird hovered above them, and perched upon the hand the monarch extended for it, showing by its bloody beak and claws that it had struck the prey. Nearly at the same time came up Bennet, who, as may be supposed, expressed no small terror and surprise at beholding the king in such a situation, and was preparing

---

* Hall gives an account of this event with very little variation in the circumstances, stating that only a footman was with the king, one Moody; but, of course, Vonderbrugius may be relied on as the most correct.

to fill the air with ejaculations and lamentations, when Henry stopped him in the midst.

"No, Bennet, no!" cried he, "keep all that for when I am dead quite! Ha, man! 'twill be time enough then. Thanks to Sir Osborne, I am not dead at present. Here, take this bird. I have lost both hood and jesses in that foul creek. Hie to the manor, Bennet, and fetch me a large cloak with a hood, and another for Sir Osborne. We will not return all draggled with the ooze, eh, Maurice? Quick, Bennet! But mind, man, not a word of this misadventure, on your life!"

"Ah! your grace knows that I am discreet," replied the footman.

"Ay, as discreet as the babbling echo, or a jay, or a magpie," cried Henry; "but get thee gone, quick! and return by the path we came, for we follow slowly. Lend me your arm, Sir Osborne. We will round by yon little bridge. A curse upon the leaping pole, say I. By my fay, I will have all the creeks in England stopped. I owe my life to you, but hereafter we will speak of that—I will find means to repay it."

"I am more than repaid, your grace," said Sir Osborne, "by the knowledge that, but for my poor aid, England might have lost her king, and within a few hours the whole realm might have been drowned in tears."

"Ay, poor souls! I do believe they would regret me," said the monarch; "for, Heaven knows! it is my wish to see them happy. A king's best elegy is to be found in the tears of his subjects, Sir Osborne, and every king should strive to merit their love when living, and their regret when dead."

Discoursing on the unlucky termination of their sport, Henry proceeded with Sir Osborne into the park, and there waited the coming of the servant with their cloaks; feeling a sort of foppish unwillingness to enter the palace in the state in which his fall had left him, his whole dress being stiff with mud, and both face and hands in anything but a comely condition. Many men might have taken advantage of Sir Osborne's situation, to urge their suit; but notwithstanding the very great claim that the accident of the morning had given him upon Henry, the knight was hardly satisfied that it had occurred. He deemed that, in common decency, he should be obliged to delay the communication which he had proposed to make that very evening, and thereby allow Wolsey to arrive before the event was decided, which for every reason he had hoped to avoid. Were he to press his suit now, it would seem, he thought, surprising, from the king's gratitude, what his justice might have denied, and indelicately to solicit a high reward for an accidental service. His great hope, however, was, that in the course of the evening the king might himself renew the subject, and by offering some token of his thanks, afford an opportunity of pleading for justice for his father and himself.

The discomfited falconers waited not long in the park before they were rejoined by the servant bearing the cloaks, which the king had commanded, but notwithstanding that they soon reached the palace, the clammy wetness of his whole dress caused several slight shiverings to pass over the limbs of Henry, and after some persuasion by Sir Osborne, he was induced to ask the counsel of his surgeon, who recommended him instantly to bathe, and then endeavor to sleep.

This was, of course, a signal for the young knight to withdraw, and taking leave of the king, he retired to his apartments to change his own dress, which was not in a much more comfortable state than that of the monarch. Our old friend Longpole soon answered to his call, and while aiding him in his arrangements, without any comment upon the state of his clothes, which he seemed to regard as nothing extraordinary, the honest custrel often paused to give a glance at his master's face, as one who has something to communicate, the nature of which may not be very palatable to the hearer.

"Well, Longpole," said the knight, after observing several of these looks, "when you have trussed these three points, you shall tell me what is the matter, for I see you have something on your mind."

"I only wished to ask your worship," said the custrel, "if you had seen him; for he's lurking about here, like a blackbird under a cherry-tree."

"Seen who?" demanded the knight.

"Why, the devil, your worship," replied Longpole. "I've seen him twice."

"Indeed!" said Sir Osborne; "and pray what did his infernal highness say to you, when you did see him? or, rather, what do you mean?"

"Why I mean, sir," replied the other, "that I have seen Sir Payan Wileton twice here in the park during yesterday, if it was not his ghost; for he looked deadly pale, and I fancy I could smell a sort of brimstony smell. Now, I wot, a cunning priest would have told by the flavor whether 'twas purgatory half and half, or unadulterated hell—though, if he's not there, hell's empty."

"Hush!" said Sir Osborne; "speak not so lightly. When was this?"

"The first time I saw him, sir," answered the yeoman, "was yesterday in the forenoon, just after the jousts, when I took a stroll out into the park with Mrs. Geraldine, the Lady Katrine's maid, for a little fresh air after the peck of dust I had broken my fast upon in the field. We had got, I don't know how, your worship, into that lonely part under the hill, when beneath one of the trees hard by I saw Sir Payan, standing stock still, with his hand in the bosom of his doublet. His color was always little better than that of a turnip, but now it looked like a turnip boiled."

"Did he speak to you?" demanded Sir Osborne; "or give any sign that he recognized you?"

"He did not speak," replied Longpole; "but when he saw me, he quietly slipped his hand out of the bosom of his doublet, and getting it down to the hilt of his poniard, kept fingering it with a sort of affectionate squeeze, as much as to say, ' Dearly-beloved, how I should like to pluck you out of your leathern case, and furnish you with one of flesh and blood.' He was ever fond of playing with his poniard, and when he spoke to you, if it were but of sousing a toast, he would draw it in and out of the scabbard all the time, as though he were afraid of losing the acquaintance, if he did not keep up the intimacy."

" You neither spoke, nor took any notice, I hope," said Sir Osborne.

" Oh no, your worship," answered the custrel; " I did not even give him bon jour, though he was fond of talking French to me when he wished to say something privately. I only twitched Mistress Geraldine over to the other side, and passed him by close; thinking to myself, if I see your dagger in the air, I'll go nigh to sweep your head off with my broadsword, if I have to run to France for it; but seeing that I looked him in the face, he turned him round upon his heel, with a draw down of the corner of his mouth, which meant a great deal, if it were rightly read."

" Ah! and what would be your translation thereof, good Longpole?" demanded his master.

" Why first, it meant—I hate you sufficiently to pretend to despise you. Then—I'll murder you whenever I can do so safely; and again, it went to say—give my best love to your master, and tell him he'll hear more of me soon."

" By my faith, a good reading, and, I doubt not, a true one," replied the knight; " but we must try and render his malice of no avail. And now tell, me when did you see him the second time?"

" The second time was after dinner, sir," said Longpole, " when his grace the king, yourself, and the Duke of Suffolk kept the barriers against all comers."

" He did not try the field, did he?" demanded Sir Osborne.

"Oh, no!" replied Longpole; "he stood looking on at a great distance, wrapped up in a cloak, so that it needed sharp eyes to recognize him; but I saw him all the time fix his eyes upon you, so like a cat before a mousehole, that I thought every minute to see him overspring the barrier and take you by the throat. Depend upon it that good and honest knight, like his german cousin, Satan, never travels for any good, and we shall hear more of him."

"I doubt it not," answered Sir Osborne; "and we must guard against him. But now, Longpole, a word or two to you. Did you give the packet, as I directed you, to Mistress Geraldine, Lady Katrine's woman?"

"I did, your worship," answered Longpole, somewhat surprised at the serious air that came over his lord's countenance: "I gave it immediately I received it from your hands."

"That was right," replied Sir Osborne. "And now let me say to you, my good Heartley, that I have remarked you often with this same girl Geraldine, and it seems to me that you are seeking her love."

"Oh, good now; your worship," cried Longpole; "if you prohibit me from making love, it's all over with me. Indeed, your worship, I could not do without it—it is meat, drink, and sleep to me—better than a stirrup cup when I rise in the morning, or a sleeping cup when I go to bed at night. 'Faith! I could not sleep without being in love. There, when I was with Sir Payan, where there was nothing to fall in love with but the portrait of his grandmother against the wall, I could not sleep o' nights at all, and was forced to take to deer stealing, just for amusement. Odds life! your worship is hard on me. There, you have overmuch of love, all day long, from the highest ladies of the court, and you would deny me as much as will lay in the palm of a serving woman."

"Nay, nay, Longpole," said Sir Osborne, laughing, "you have taken me up too hastily. All I meant to say was merely, that seeing you are evidently seeking this poor girl's love, you must not play her false. I mean, you must not win her love, and then leave her for another."

"Dear heart, no!" cried Longpole; "I would not for the world. Poor little soul, she has suffered enough! So I'm now consoling her, your worship. It's wonderful how soon a broken heart is patched up with a little of the same stuff that broke it. It is the very reverse of piecing a doublet; for in love you mend old love with new, and it's almost as good as ever. However, some day soon we intend to ask your worship's leave, and the priest's blessing, and say all those odd little words that tie two folks together."

"My leave and good wishes you shall have, Longpole," replied the knight, "and all I can do to assist your purse. Hark! is not that the trumpet to dinner? Give me my bonnet, I will down and dine at the board of estate to-day, as I was not there yesterday."

On descending to the hall, Sir Osborne was instantly assailed by a thousand questions respecting the accident which had befallen the king; for what between the diligent exertions of the attendants, and those of the surgeon, the news had already spread through the whole court. In reply, the knight gave as brief and exact an account of the whole occurrence as possible, endeavoring to stop the lying tongue of rumor by furnishing her with the truth at least. After dinner he returned to his own apartments, and only left them once for a momentary visit to Constance de Grey, remaining in hopes all the evening that the king might send for him when he arose. Such hopes, however, were in vain: day waned, and night fell, and the knight's suit was no farther advanced than when Sir Cesar warned him to hasten it in the morning.

CHAPTER XVI.

"—— He, full of fraudful arts,
This well-invented tale for truth imparts."

DRYDEN.

WE must now for a while change our place of action, and endeavor to carry the mind of the reader, from the sweeter and more tranquil scenes of Richmond Park, one of the most favored residences of Henry the Eighth, to York Place, the magnificent dwelling of that pampered child of fortune Cardinal Wolsey.

York Place, which, as every one knows, was afterwards called Whitehall, though it offered an appearance very different from the building at present known by that name, stood nearly on the same spot which it now occupies. Surrounded by splendid gardens, and ornamented with all that the arts of the day could produce, of luxurious or elegant, so far from yielding in any degree to the various residences of the king, it surpassed them all in almost every respect. The combination also of ecclesiastical pomp, with the magnificence of a lay prince, created in the courts and round the gates of the palace a continual scene of glitter and brilliancy. Whether it were deputations from abbeys and monasteries—the visits of other bishops—the attendance of noblemen and gentlemen come to pay their court—the halt of military leaders with their armed bands, prepared for service and waiting for command—still bustle, activity, and splendor were always to be met with in the open space before the building, on every morning when the fineness of the weather permitted such display. There, were to be seen passing to and fro, the rich embroidered robes of the

clergy, in all the hues of green and purple, and of gold;
the splendid liveries of the cardinal's own attendants,
and the followers of his visitors; the white dresses of
the soldiery, traversed with the broad red cross of England; the arms of the leaders, and the many colored
housings of the horses; while above the rest was often
displayed the high wrought silver cross, or the glittering
crook, of bishop or mitred abbot, borne amongst banners
and pennons and fluttering plumes.

It was on a morning when the scene before the palace
was full of more than usual life, owing to the arrival of
the cardinal the night before from York (which was, be
it remarked, one day earlier than he had been expected),
that Sir Payan Wileton rode through the crowd to the
grand entrance. He was followed by ten armed attendants, the foremost of whom were Cornish men, of
that egregious stature which acquired for their country-
men in the olden time the reputation of sprouting out into
giants. These two, Sir Payan had sent for expressly
from his estates in Cornwall, not without a purpose; and
now having dressed them in splendid liveries, he gave
orders for his train to halt at such a distance, as to be
plainly visible from the windows of the palace.

Dismounting from his horse at the door, he gave him
to his page, and entering the hall, passed through the
crowd of attendants with which it was tenanted, and
mounted the grand staircase, with that sort of slow, determined step, which is almost always to be found in
persons, whose reliance on their own powers of mind, is
founded in long experience and success.

The number of people whom he met running up and
down the wide staircase with various papers in their
hands, announced at once the multitude of affairs which
the cardinal was obliged to despatch after his long absence
at York, and betokened some difficulty of obtaining an
audience.

Entering the waiting-hall, at the top of the staircase,

Sir Payan found it crowded almost to suffocation with persons staying for an audience, either from Wolsey himself or from one of his secretaries. Above their heads appeared a misty atmosphere of condensed human breath, and all around was heard the busy buzz of many voices murmuring in eager but whispered consultation.

The hall was a large chamber, cutting directly through the centre of the house with a high Gothic window at each end, to the right and left of which, at both extremities, appeared a door. The one opposite to that by which Sir Payan entered, stood open, though a small wooden bar prevented the entrance of the crowd into the room beyond, which was occupied by six or seven ordinary clerks, busily employed in filling up various papers, and speaking from time to time to the persons who presented themselves on business. At each of the doors, at the other end, stood an usher with his rod, and a marshall with his staff, opposing the ingress of any but such as the highest rank, or personal interest, entitled to enter beyond the porch of the temple; for there, the right hand path led to the privy chambers of Wolsey himself, and the left to the offices of his principal secretaries. It was round this left-hand door that the crowd took its densest aspect, for many who were hopeless of obtaining a hearing from the cardinal himself, fondly flattered themselves that their plaint or petition might reach his ear through his secretary, if either by bribe or flattery they could secure the interest of the secondary great man.

Winding in and out through the meandering path left by the various groups in the hall, Sir Payan approached the door which led to the cardinal's apartments, and demanded admission. There was something in his tone which implied right, and the usher said, that if he would give his name, he would inquire; though an applicant who had remained long unlistened to, audibly murmured his indignation, and claimed to be admitted first.

Sir Payan turned to look at him while the usher was

gone, and at once encountered the eyes of a near neighbor of his own, who, under his fostering care, had dwindled from a rich landholder to a poor farmer, and thence had sunk to beggary, while his possessions one by one had merged into the property of Sir Payan; which, like the Norwegian whirlpool, seemed to absorb everything that came within its vortex. No sooner did the old man's eyes fall upon his countenance, and beheld who it was that still kept him from the light, than giving way to his rage, he clasped his hands, and stamping upon the ground, cursed him with the energy of despair.

Sir Payan cast upon him a cold look, mingled of pity and contempt, and passed through the door, which the usher now held open for his entrance. The room at which he arrived was a large ante-room, occupied by various groups of lords and gentlemen attached to the household of the cardinal, who, prouder than royalty ever needs to be, would, at least, be equal with the king himself in the rank of his various officers. These were scattered about in various parts of the room, talking with the select visitors whom the ushers had permitted to enter, or staring vacantly at the figures on the rich tapestry by which they were surrounded; wherein, though scrutinized a thousand times, they still found sufficient to occupy their idle eyes, while waiting till the minister should go forth. With almost every one he saw, Sir Payan was in some degree acquainted; but in their bow or gratulation, as he passed, there was none of the frank, cordial welcome of regard or esteem; it was simply the acknowledgment of a rich and powerful man, whose only title to reverence was in his influence and his wealth.

About the centre stood Lord Darby, and to him Sir Payan approached with a " good-morrow, my good lord."

" Sir ! " said the earl, looking him steadfastly in the face for a moment,—then, turning on his heel, he walked to the other end of the room. Nothing abashed, Sir Payan kept his ground, tracing the young lord with his

eyes, in which no very amicable expression was visible;
and then, after a moment, he approached a small table,
near the door of the minister's cabinet, whereat was
seated a clerk, whom, as it so happened, Sir Payan himself had recommended to the Cardinal.

"Can his grace be spoken with, Master Taylor?" demanded the knight, as the clerk bowed low, at his approach.

"He is busied, honored sir," replied the man, with a
second profound reverence, "in conversation with the
prior of his abbey of St. Albans, on matters of deep importance—" a loud laugh from the chamber within
reached Sir Payan's ear, through the door by which he
stood, but he took no notice of this comment on the important business which Wolsey was transacting, and the
clerk went on. "I am sorry to say, sir, also, that there
are five or six persons of distinction, who have waited on
his grace's leisure for near an hour."

"But the cardinal sent for me," said Sir Payan; "and
besides—" and he whispered something to his former
servant which seemed convincing. In a minute or two
after, the door opened, and the Prior of St. Albans issued forth. Rustling up to the table in his rich silk
robes, he said to the clerk in a low and important voice,
"His grace commands you to send in the person of the
highest rank that came next."

"Well, holy father!" said the clerk rising; and then
appearing to search the room with his eyes, he waited
till the prior was gone, when turning to Sir Payan, he
added in a loud voice, "Sir Payan Wileton, the lord
cardinal is waiting for you."

The knight instantly proceeded to the door, which was
opened by one of the ushers who stood near, and passing
on, he found himself directly in the presence of the cardinal, who, seated in a chair of state, waited the next
comer, with a countenance prepared to yield a good or
bad reception, according to their rank and purpose.

As Sir Payan entered, Wolsey's brow gradually contracted into a frown. Page 255.

Darnley.

He was, at that time, not apparently much above fifty-five, tall, erect, and dignified, with a face replete with thought and mind and a carriage at once haughty and graceful. His dark eye was piercing and full of fire, and lurking about the corners of his mouth, might be seen the lines of unbounded pride, striven against and repressed, but still existing with undiminished force. The robes of bright scarlet satin, which he wore without any other relief than a tippet of rich sables, made his cheek look almost ashy pale, and the shade of the broad hat, which covered his brow, gave an air of pensive solemnity to his features, which, joined with the fire of his eye, the pride of his lip, and the knowledge of his power, invested his presence with a magnificence not devoid of awe.

As Sir Payan entered, Wolsey's brow gradually contracted into a frown, and fixing his glance full upon him, he let him stand for several moments before he motioned him to a seat. At length, however, he spoke.

"Sir Payan Wileton," said he, "I have sent for you to speak on many subjects that may not be very agreeable for you to discuss. However, as they concern the welfare of society, and the fame of the king's justice, they must be inquired into; nor must any man's rank or wealth shelter him from the even eye of equity."

"Your grace hardly does me justice," replied Sir Payan, resolving to keep to vague professions, till he had ascertained, as far as possible, what was passing in Wolsey's mind. "Had I been unwilling to discuss any part of my conduct with your grace, should I have importuned your gates every day for the last week, in hopes of your return? and if, on the most minute investigation, I found any of my acts which would not meet the eye of equity itself, should I voluntarily present myself before the Cardinal of York?"

"You were sent for, Sir Payan," replied Wolsey. "Last night the messenger set out."

" By your grace's pardon," said the knight, " if you but
calculate, you will find that I could not have come from
a far part of Kent in so short a space of time. It is true,
that I have received the packet, but that was only by
sending last night to know if you had then returned. My
servant met your messenger at the very door, and received
the letter intended to be sent to Chilham. But every day,
as I have told your grace, since I have risen from a
bed of sickness, where a cross accident had thrown me,
I have not ceased to seek your presence on business of
some import."

Wolsey, long ascustomed to encounter every species of
wily art, was not to be led away by the exhibition of a
new subject, and pursuing his first object, he proceeded.

" We will speak of that anon. At present, it is my
task to inform you, sir, that various are the complaints,
petitions, and accusations against you, that daily reach my
hand. And many prayers have been addressed to his
royal grace the king, by the very best and noblest of the
land, to induce him to re-establish the house of Fitzbernard in the lordship and estates of Chilham Castle. All
these things have led me to inquire—as indeed is but
my duty, as chancellor of this kingdom—into the justice
of your title to these estates, when I find that the case
stands thus :—The Earl of Fitzbernard, in the last year of
his late majesty's reign, was accused by those two in-
famous commissioners, Empson and Dudley, and was,
upon the premises, condemned to the enormous fine of
one hundred thousand pounds, under the penal statutes ;
and as a still farther punishment, for some words lightly
spoken, the king, then upon his death-bed, recalled the
stewardship of Dover Castle, which involved as was supposed the forfeiture of Chilham Castle and its lands.
Was it not so ? "

" It was so far, your grace," replied Sir Payan; " but
allow me to observe——"

" Hush ! " said the cardinal, waving his hand; " hear

me, and then your observations, if you please. Such
being the case, as I have said, and the wide barony of
Chilham supposed to be vacant—the stewardship of
Dover Castle, with those estates annexed, is bestowed
upon you—how or why, is not very apparent, though the
cause alleged is service rendered in the time of Perkyn
Warbeck. Now it appears, from some documents placed
in the hands of Lord Dacre, of the North, by the Duke
of Buckingham, that Chilham Castle was granted to
Fulbert de Douvre, at a period much subsequent to the
grant of the stewardship of Dover, that it was totally
distinct, and held by tenure of chivalry, in fee and unalienable, except under attainder or by breach of tenure.
What say you now, Sir Payan?"

"Why simply this, your grace," replied Sir Payan
boldly, "that the good Duke of Buckingham—the noble
Duke of Buckingham, as the commons call him—seems
to be nearly as much my good friend, as he is to the king
his royal master, or to your grace;" and, knitting his
brow, and clenching his teeth, he fixed his eyes upon the
rose in his shoe, remaining sternly silent, to let what he
had said, and what he had implied, work fully on the
mind of the cardinal.

Wolsey's hatred to the princely Buckingham was well
known, and Sir Payan easily understood that it was of
that most maddening kind of hatred, called jealousy; so
that not a word he had said, but was meeted to the taste
and appetite of the cardinal with a skilful hand. The
minister's cheek flushed while the knight spoke, and
when, after implying by tone, and look, and manner that
he could say more, Sir Payan suddenly stopped, and bent
his eyes upon the ground, Wolsey had nearly burst forth
in that impatient strain of question, which would have
betrayed the deep anxiety he felt, to snatch at any accusation against his noble rival. Checking himself, however,
the politic churchman paused, and seemed to wait for
some further reply, till finding that Sir Payan still main-

17

tained his silent attitude of thought, he said, " Have you
any reason, sir, to suppose that the duke is ill-disposed
towards his grace the king?—of myself, I speak not.
His envy touches me not, personally; but where danger
shows itself towards our royal master, it becomes a duty
to inquire—your insinuations, Sir Payan, were strong—
you should be strongly able to support them."

" I know not, your grace," replied the knight, with the
unhesitating daring that characterized all his actions,
" how far a man's loyalty should properly extend; but this
I know, that I am not the tame and quiet dog that fawns
upon the hand that snatches its mess from before its
muzzle. What I know, I know; what I suspect remains
to be proved: but neither knowledge, nor suspicion, nor
the clue to guide judgment through the labyrinth of
wicked plotting, will I furnish to any one, with the prospect before my eyes of being deprived, for no earthly
fault, of my rightful property, granted to me by the free
will of our noble King Henry the Seventh."

An ominous frown gathered upon Wolsey's brow, and
fain would he have possessed the thunder to strike dead
the bold man who dared thus withhold the information
that he sought, and oppose him in the plenitude of his
power. " You are gifted with a strange hardihood, sir,"
cried he, in a voice, the slight trembling of whose tone
told the boiling of the soul within. " Did you ever hear
of misprision of treason—say?"

" I have, your grace," replied Sir Payan, whose bold
and determined spirit was not made to quail even before
that of Wolsey. Acting, however, coolly and shrewdly,
he was moved by no heat as the cardinal; and though
calculating exactly the strength of his position, he knew
that it was far from his interest to create an enemy in
the powerful minister, who, sooner or later, would find
means to avenge himself. At the same time, he saw that
he must make his undisturbed possession of Chilham
Castle, the price of any information he could give, or

that he might both yield his secret and lose his land. "I have heard, your grace," he said, "of misprision of treason, but I know not how such a thing can affect me. First, treason must be proved, then it must be shown that it was concealed with full knowledge thereof. Doubts and suspicions, your grace knows, are not within the meaning of the law." Sir Payan paused, and Wolsey remained in silence, as if almost disdaining to reply. The knight clearly saw what was passing in his mind, and continued, after an affectation of thought, to give the appearance of a sudden return of affectionate submission to what he was about to say.

"But why, your grace, why," cried he, "cast away from you one of your most faithful servants? Why must it be, when I have waited at your door, day after day, to give you some information, much for the state's and for your grace's benefit to know—that the very first time I am admitted to your presence, I find my zeal checked and my affection cooled, by an express intention to deprive me of my estates?"

"Nay, Sir Payan," said Wolsey, glad of an opportunity of yielding, without compromising either pride or dignity, "no such intention was expressed. You have mistaken entirely—I only urged these reasons, that you might know what had been urged to me; and I was about to put it to you what I could do, if the young Lord Darnley came over to this country and claimed these estates, for, probably, the old earl will not have energy enough to make the endeavor. What could I do, I say?"

"Let him proceed by due course of law, my lord," replied Sir Payan; the calculation in whose mind was somewhat to the following effect, though passing more rapidly than it could when embodied in words. "Before his claim is made in law (thought he), he shall taste of the axe of the Tower, or I am mistaken. However, I will not let Wolsey know who he is, for then my interest in the business would be apparent, and I could claim no high recompense for ridding myself of my own enemy. No, I will crush him as Osborne Maurice, a perfect stranger to me; then will my zeal seem great. Pride will prevent him from owning his name till the death, and if he does own it, his coming here concealed, joined to the crimes that I will find means to prove against him, shall but make him appear the blacker." Such was the train of thought that passed instantly through his mind; while with an affectation of candor, he replied, " Let him proceed by due course of law, my lord; then if he succeed, let him have it, in God's name. All I ask is, that your grace will not moot the question; for one word of the great Wolsey throws more weight into one or other of the scales of justice, than all the favor of a dozen kings."

Wolsey was flattered, but not deceived. However, it was his part not to see, at least for the time; and though he very well understood that Sir Payan would take special means to prevent the young lord from seeking justice by law, he replied, " All that I could ever contemplate, Sir Payan, was to do even right to any one that should bring their cause before me. It is not for me to seek out occasions for men to plunge themselves in law; and be you very sure, that without the matter be brought before me in the most regular manner, I shall never agitate the question—which is one, that even should it be discussed, would involve many, many difficulties. From what I say now, you may see, sir, that your haste has hurried you into unnecessary disrespect, which, heaven knows, I feel not as regards my person, but as it touches my office I am bound to reprove you."

" Most deeply do I deplore it," replied Sir Payan, " if I have been guilty of any disrespect to one whom I reverence more than any other on the earth; but I think that the information which I have to communicate will at least be some atonement. I have then, my lord," he proceeded, lowering his voice, " I have then discovered, by a most singular and happy chance, as dangerous a con-

spiracy as ever stained the annals of any European kingdom; and I hold in my hand the most irrefragable proofs
thereof, together with the names of the principal persons,
the testimony of several witnesses, which bear upon the
subject, and various letters, which are in themselves conviction. I will now, with your grace's leave——"

At that moment one of the ushers opened the door of
the cabinet, and with a profound reverence, informed
Wolsey that the Earl of Knolles desired to know when he
could have an audience, as he had been waiting long
without.

"Ha! what!" exclaimed the cardinal, his eye flashing,
and his lip quivering with anger at the interruption—
"am I to be disturbed each moment? Tell him I cannot
see him—I am busy—I am engaged—occupied on more
important things. Were he a prince, I would not see him.
And you, beware how you intrude again. Now, Sir
Payan, speak on. This is matter of moment, indeed.
What was the object of this conspiracy?"

"Nothing less, I can conceive, my lord, than to make
the commons dissatisfied with the government under
which they live, to incite them to various insurrections,
and, if possible, into general rebellion, under favor of
which my lord Duke of Buckingham might find his way
to the throne; at least, there are fixed his eyes."

"Ha, ha! my proud lord of Buckingham!" cried
Wolsey, with a triumphant smile; "what! hast thou wired
thine own feet? But you say you have proofs, Sir
Payan. We must have full proof: but you are not a man
to tread on unsteady ground—your proofs are sure?"
he reiterated, with a feverish sort of anxiety, to ascertain that his great rival was fully in his power.

"In the first place, read that, my lord," said Sir
Payan, putting in his hand one out of a bundle of papers
that he had brought with him. "That is the first step."

"Why, what is this?" cried Wolsey. "This is but
the deposition of Henry Wilson, of Pencriton, in the

duchy of Cornwall, who maketh oath and saith, that the
prisoner Osborne Maurice, alias Sir Osborne Maurice, is
the man whom he saw at the head of the Cornish miners,
in insurrection, on the 3d of January last, and who in-
cited them, by cries and words, to burn and destroy all
that came in their way, till they should have satisfaction in
everything that they required: but for the farther acts of
the said Osborne Maurice, he, the deponent, begs leave
to refer to his former depositions, taken before Sir John
Balham, knight, of the city of Penzance, in Cornwall;
only upon oath he declareth, that the said Osborne
Maurice now present, is the ringleader or conductor of
the mob, mentioned in his former deposition, in witness
whereof——Ha!" said Wolsey, thoughtfully, "there is
one, I find, of this same name, Sir Osborne Maurice, who,
during my absence, has crept into the king's favor.
Surely it may be the same!"

"On my life, my lord, the very same," replied Sir
Payan. "'Twas but the morning before last, that, at the
jousts at Richmond, I saw him with our noble king, his
chosen companion, with the Duke of Suffolk, to keep
the barriers against all comers: and there he ruffled it
amongst the best, swimming, as 'twere, on the top of the
wave."

"Then will we lay this on his head," said Wolsey, laying emphatically his forefinger on the paper, "and that
shall sink him. But how does this touch the Duke of
Buckingham?"

"Your grace shall hear," replied Sir Payan. "This
Wilson, who made the deposition you there hold, came
to me one day in the last of March—you must know he is
my bailiff—and told me a sad story of his woful plight,
how in a cottage hard by he had met the man whom he
had seen burn down his father's house in Cornwall, and
who was here employed in the same devilish attempt, to
instigate the peasants to revolt. Wilson, it seems, accused him; whereon, being a most powerful and atrocious

traitor, he struck the bailiff to the ground, and left him for dead. This being sworn on oath before me, as a magistrate, I sent forth and had the villain arrested, after a most desperate struggle. With the intention of sending him to Cornwall, I had him committed to the strong room of the manor, but somehow, during the night, he contrived to escape through a window, and made his way to the court—"

"But still, Sir Payan," interrupted the cardinal, "this does not implicate the Duke of Buckingham, who, as I have good reason to believe, is but a scant lover of our royal king, and towards myself bears most inveterate malice—I have heard many a rumor of his plots and schemes—but it is proof, Sir Payan—it is proof that we must have!"

"And proof your grace shall have," replied the knight, counting the hatred that Wolsey bore towards the duke as his own gain, and enjoying the inveteracy of his malice, not only with the abstract satisfaction of fellow-feeling, but as a fisherman delights to see the voracious spring of the trout at the fly he casts before his snout. "Let your grace listen to me, for my story, though somewhat long, is nevertheless conclusive. This Osborne Maurice, in his escape, left behind him the leather horse-bags with which he rode when he was taken, and, in my capacity as magistrate, I made free to open them—"

"You did right, you did right," cried Wolsey, almost forgetting his dignity in eagerness. "What did you find? Say, Sir Payan! What did you find?"

"I found several letters from his grace the Duke of Buckingham," answered Sir Payan, "being principally written to bring this Sir Osborne Maurice to the knowledge of persons about the court, recommending him as one that may be trusted. Your grace will mark those words, 'may be trusted.' But amongst the rest was one, which shows for what he may be trusted. Behold it here, my lord! You know the duke's hand and style," and he presented the letter to Wolsey.

The cardinal snatched it eagerly, but remembering himself, he turned more composedly to the address, and read, "' Sir John Morton.'—Ah!" cried he, "So! an old Perkyn Warbeckist!—the last I believe alive—but for the contents;—' Trusty and well-beloved friend '— um—um—um—' everlasting friendship '—of course, one traitor loves another—but let us see. How! the daring villain!—' to inform you, that before another year arrive my head shall be the highest in the realm—at least so promises Sir Osborne Maurice, whose promises are not such as fail!'—Ha, Sir Payan! ha! Did you read it? This is treason—is it not? By my life, the duke's own hand!—But what says he farther. Ha! 'The butcher's cur Wolsey has long wanted the lash, and he shall have it soon.' See you how rank is his malice; we will read no farther. This condemns him; and as for Sir Osborne Maurice, to-night he shall have his lodging in the Tower."

"Though other proof might be deemed superfluous," said Sir Payan, "yet, my lord, when I came to the part where he calls your grace a butcher's cur," and the knight dwelt maliciously on the words, "my zeal and affection for your grace's service made me instantly resolve to track this Osborne Maurice on his journey, after escaping from prison. In person I could not do it, for a fall from my horse laid me in my bed for three weeks. But I took care that it should be done, and found that he returned straight to my lord of Buckingham's, from thence he went to the Benedictine Abbey, at Canterbury, where he seems to have been sent to escort a Lady Katrine Bulmer to the court. Then, passing by Rochester, he had an interview with the chief of the rioters at Hilham-green. Your grace will now be at no loss to know how, and by whom, that memorable tumult was instigated. There he pretended to save a good simple priest from the mob; but, by the clergyman's own account, they gave him up at a single word from this Maurice, which shows what was his influence with them, for they were the mo-

ment before about to hang the man they yielded so
quietly after. The priest is at my lodging here. This
was the traitor's last adventure before arriving at the
court; where, either by some sorcery, or other damned
invention, he has bewitched the better judgment of the
king, so that none is so well loved as he. Perhaps he
waits but an opportunity to put his dagger in our royal
master."

"Heaven forbid!" cried Wolsey. "We will instantly
set off for Richmond. Without there! Let the barge be
prepared directly: Sir Payan, you have saved the realm,
and may claim a high reward."

"The reward I most affect," replied the knight in a
well acted tone of moderation, "is simply to remain in
quiet possession of that which I have. Life is now wearing with me, your grace, and I covet not greater charges
than those which I enjoy. Let me but be sure of them."

"Rest tranquil on that point," replied Wolsey. "I
will look thereto."

"There are, indeed," continued Sir Payan, "some
hereditary estates, which, though they should be mine,
are held by another; and on that score I may claim your
grace's assistance before I endeavor to recover them; for
I put my whole actions in your grace's hands, that, like
a mere machine, I may move but as you please."

"What estates are these, Sir Payan?" demanded
Wolsey, with something very near approaching to a smile,
at the peculiar line of the knight's cupidity. "If they be
truly yours, doubt not but you shall have them."

"They are those estates in Cornwall," replied the
knight, "lately held by my cousin, the Earl de Grey,
which have since passed to Constance, his daughter;
though by all custom of succession, according to their
tenure, I hold them to pass directly in the male line."

"Nay, nay, Sir Payan," cried Wolsey, with a curl of
his lip; "this is too much! Constance de Grey is my
ward, and shall not lose her estates lightly. She is, in-

deed "—added he thoughtfully, and speaking to himself more than to the knight, though not a word was lost to his attentive ears—" she is, indeed, somewhat wilful. That letter, in which she refuses to wed her cousin, though calm and humble, was full of rank obstinacy. The fear of losing her estates, however—but we shall see. Sir Payan, I must hold my opinion suspended till such time as you lay before me some proofs of the matter. —And now tell me—think you, in this plot of Buckingham's, is there any other person of high rank implicated? Indeed there must be, for he would never undertake such daring schemes without some sure abettors. Sir Payan, these lords are all too proud. We must find means to humble them—it may be as well to let this arch traitor, Buckingham, proceed for some short time, till we find who are his accomplices. But for this Sir Osborne Maurice, he shall to the Tower to-night, for therein is the king's life affected."

" Might it not be better, in your grace's good judgment," said Sir Payan, " to take the duke's person at once; for, assuredly, as soon as he hears that his minion is committed, he will become alarmed, and find his security in some foreign land."

" He shall be so well watched," said Wolsey, closing his hand tightly, as if he grasped his enemy, " that were he no larger than a meagre ermine, he should not escape me;—no! we must let him condemn himself full surely. But, Sir Payan, are you prepared to accompany me to Richmond?"

" If by any chance this Maurice were to see me with your grace," replied Sir Payan, " he would lose no time, but fly instantly, before you had speech of his grace the king. If you think it necessary, my lord, that I should attend you, it may be well to arrest the traitor immediately on your arrival."

" Nay, nay, nay!" said Wolsey, shaking his head. " You know not Henry, Sir Payan—he is hard and difficult to rule, and were I to arrest Sir Osborne, would take for insult what was meant a service. But you shall not go—there is, indeed no need—these papers are quite enough, with the testimony of the priest. Let him be sent down post-haste to Richmond after me."

"He shall, my lord," replied Sir Payan. "But one word more your grace. If the Duke of Buckingham be condemned, his estates, of course, are forfeited to the crown. Near me lies his beautiful manor of the Hill, in Kent, and I know your grace will not forget your faithful servants." Wolsey paused, and Sir Payan went on. "To show how constantly present your grace is to all my thoughts, you told me some time ago, that you desired to have two of the tallest men in the realm for porters of the gate. Cast your eyes through that window, my lord, and I think you will see two that no prince in Europe can match in his hall."

No service that Sir Payan could have rendered, either to the state or to himself, would have given half so much pleasure to Wolsey as the possession of the two gigantic Cornishmen we have before mentioned, for amongst all his weaknesses, his passion for having tall men about him was one of the most conspicuous. As soon as, for a moment or two, he had considered them attentively through the window, and compared them with all the pigmy-looking race around, he thanked Sir Payan with infinite graciousness for his care; and hinted, though he did not promise, that Buckingham's manor in Kent might be the reward. While he yet spoke, a gentleman-usher entered, to announce that the barge was ready; and giving some more directions to Sir Payan, in regard to sending the priest, Wolsey rose to proceed on his journey. The procession, without which he never moved, was already arranged in the antechamber, consisting of marshals and gentlemen-ushers, with two stout priests bearing the immense silver crosses of his archbishopric and his legacy; and the moment he moved towards the

door, the ushers pressed forward, crying, " On before,
my lords and masters; on before! Make way for the
lord cardinal! Make way for my lord's grace! On before! on before!"

Wolsey immediately followed, and proceeded to his
barge; while Sir Payan returned to his own house in
Westminster, and despatched the priest to Richmond,
after which he sat himself down to write. What he did
write consisted of but a few lines, but they were of some
import; and as soon as they were finished, he entrusted
them to one of his shrewdest and most assured servants,
with many a long direction, and many an injunction to
speed.

CHAPTER XVI.

"This hour's the very crisis of your fate."
THE SPANISH FRIAR.

IF any one will look in the almanack for the year 1520, they will find, marked opposite the 4th day of May, the following curious piece of information, " High-water at London-bridge at half-past three," and, if they calculate rightly, they will discover, that as Wolsey set out from what was then called the Cardinal's-bridge at high noon, he had the most favorable tide in the world for carrying him to Richmond. His rowers, too, plied their oars with unceasing activity, and his splendid barge with its carved and gilded sides, cut rapidly through the water but still not rapidly enough for his impatience.

Sitting under an awning, with a table before him, at which was placed a clerk, he sometimes read parts of the various papers that had been presented during the morning, and sometimes dictated to the secretary; but more frequently gave himself up to thought, suffering his mind to range in the wild chaos of political intrigue; which was to him like the labyrinth a man makes in his own garden, in which a stranger might lose his way, but where he himself walks for his ease and pleasure.

No surer road to Wolsey's hatred existed than the king's favor; and since his return to London, though but one evening had passed, yet often had his heart rankled at hearing, from those who watched for him in his absence, that a young stranger, named Sir Osborne Maurice, had won the king's regard, and become the sharer of all his pleasures. The information given him by Sir Payan Wileton had placed in his hand arms against this incipient rival, as he deemed him, which were sure to crush him; and, with a sort of pride in the conquest he anticipated, he muttered to himself, as he saw the narrowing banks of the river, approaching towards Richmond, " Now, Sir Osborne Maurice, now ! "

The boat touched the shore, and while the chief yeoman of the barge, as his privilege supported the arm of the cardinal, the two stout priests bearing the crosses hurried to land with the other attendants, and ranged themselves in order to proceed before him. Two of his running footmen sped on to announce his approach, and the rest, with the form and slowness of a procession, traversed the small space that separated them from the court, reached the gate and entering the palace, Wolsey, more like an equal prince than a subject, passed towards the king's privy-chamber, amidst the profound bows and reverences of all the royal attendants, collected to do honor to his arrival.

Many had been the rumors in the palace during the morning respecting the king's health, and it was generally reported that the accident of the day before had thrown him into a fever. This, however, was evidently not the case, for a little before noon Sir Osborne Maurice had received a message by one of the royal pages, to the effect, that at three o'clock the king would expect him in his privy chamber. That hour had nearly approached, and the young knight was preparing to obey Henry's commands, when a note was put into his hands by Mrs. Margaret, the waiting woman of Lady Constance de Grey. It was a step which Sir Osborne well knew she would not have taken had it not been called for by some particular circumstance, and with some alarm he opened the paper, and read—

" The lord cardinal is here—remember your promise. Tarry not rashly, if you love—Constance."

As Wolsey had been ever a declared enemy to his father, and a steady supporter of Sir Payan Wileton, Sir Osborne felt that the prospect was certainly in some degree clouded by his arrival; and while at the court, he had heard enough of the jealousy that the favorite entertained towards all who often approached the king, to make him uneasy with regard to the future. But yet he could not imagine that the regard of Henry would be easily taken from him, nor the service he had rendered immediately forgotten; and strong in the integrity of his own heart, he would not believe that any serious evil could befall him; yet the warning of Sir Cesar still rung in his ears, and made an impression which he could not overcome. Nevertheless, he felt a hesitation, an uneasiness, a sort of presentiment of evil, as he approached the privy-chamber of the king.

At the door of the antechamber, however, he found stationed a page, who respectfully informed him that the king was busy on affairs of state with the cardinal lord chancellor, and that his grace had bade him say, that as soon as he was at leisure he would send for him to his presence.

Sir Osborne returned to his own apartment, and after calling for Longpole, walked up and down the room for a moment or two, while some curious vague feelings of doubt and apprehension passed through his mind.

" 'Tis very foolish! " said he, at length; " and yet 'tis no harm to be prepared. Longpole, saddle the horses, and have my armor ready. 'Tis no harm to be prepared," and quitting his own chambers, he turned his steps towards those of Lady Constance, which here, not like the former ones in the palace at Greenwich, were situated at the other extremity of the building. His path led him again past the royal lodgings, and as he went by, Sir Osborne perceived that the page gave entrance to a priest, whose figure was in some degree familiar to his eye. Where he had seen him he did not know, but, however, he stayed not to inquire, and proceeded onward to the door of Lady Constance's apartments. One of her women gave him entrance, and he soon reached her sitting-chamber, where he found her calmly engaged in embroidery. But there, also, was good Dr. Wilbraham, who of late had shrewdly begun to suspect a thing that was already more than suspected by half the court, namely, that Sir Osborne Maurice was deeply in love with Constance de Grey, and that the lady was in no degree insensible to his affection. The doctor never for a moment imagined, that either Constance or her lover might in the least wish his absence, and therefore, with great satisfaction at beholding their mutual love, he remained all the time that Sir Osborne dared to stay, and conducted him to the door with that affectionate respect which he always showed towards his former pupil. While the old clergyman stood bidding Sir Osborne farewell, a man habited like a yeoman approached, inquiring for the lodging of Lady Constance de Grey, and on being told that it was before him, he put a folded note into the hands of Dr. Wilbraham, begging him to deliver it to the lady, which the chaplain promised to do, and the man departed.

And now, leaving the good clergyman to perform this promise, and Sir Osborne to return to his apartment, somewhat mortified at not having had an opportunity of conversing privately with Constance, even for a moment, we will steal quietly into the privy-chamber of the king, and seating ourselves on a little stool in the corner, observe all that passes between him and his minister.

"God save your royal grace!" said Wolsey, as he entered, "and make your people happy in your long and prosperous reign."

"Welcome back again, my good lord cardinal," replied the king; "you have been but a truant of late. We have in many things wanted your good counsel. But your careful letters have been received, and we have to thank you for the renewed quiet of the West Riding."

"Happily, your grace, all is now tranquil," replied the cardinal, "and the kingdom within itself blessed with profound peace; but yet, my lord, even when this was accomplished, it was necessary to discover the cause and authors of the evil, that the fire of discord and sedition might be totally extinguished, and not, being only smothered, burst out anew where we least expected it. This has been done, my liege. The authors of all these revolts, the instigators of their fellow-subjects' treason, have been discovered, and if your grace have leisure for such sad business, I will even now crave leave to lay before you the particulars of a most daring plot, which, through the activity of good Sir Payan Wileton, I have been enabled to detect."

"Without there!" cried the king, somewhat impatiently. "See that we are not interrupted. Tell Sir Osborne Maurice that we will send for him when we are free. Sit, sit, my Wolsey!" He continued, "Now, by the holy faith, it grieves me to hear such things! I had hoped that tranquillity being restored, I should have sped over to France to meet my royal brother Francis, with nothing but joy upon my brow. However, you are thanked, my good lord, for your zeal, and for your diligence. We must not let the poisonous root of treason spread, lest it grow too great a tree to be hewn down. Who are these traitors, eh? Have you good proof against them?"

"Such proof, my liege, that however willing I might be to doubt, uncertainty, the refuge of hope, is denied me, and I must needs believe. When we have nourished anything with our grace, fostered it with kindly care, taught it to spread and become great, heaped it with favors, loaded it with bounty, we naturally hope that, having sowed all these good things, our crop will be rich in gratitude and love; but, sorry I am to say, that your grace's royal generosity has fallen upon a poisoned soil, and that Edward Duke of Buckingham, who might well believe himself the most favored man in the realm, now proves himself an arrant traitor."

18

"By heaven!" cried the king, "I have lately much doubted of his loyalty. He has, as you once before made me observe, much absented himself from the court, keeping, as I hear, an almost royal state in the counties; and lately, on the pretence that he is sick, that his physicians command him quiet, he refuses to accompany us to Guisnes. I fear me, I fear me, that 'tis his loyalty is sick. But let me hear your reasons, my good lord cardinal. Fain would I still behold him with an eye of favor; for he is in many things a noble and a princely peer, and by nature richly endowed with all the shining qualities both of the body and mind. 'Tis sad! indeed 'tis sad, that such a man should fall away, and lose his high renown! But your reasons, Wolsey. Give me the history!"

It were needless in this place to recapitulate all that we have seen in the last chapter, advanced by Sir Payan Wileton, to criminate the Duke of Buckingham. Suffice it, that Wolsey related to the king the very probable tale that had been told him by the knight; namely, that Buckingham, aspiring to the throne, affected an undue degree of popularity with the commons, and by his secret agents rendered them dissatisfied with the existing government, exciting them to various tumults and revolts, of which he cited many an instance; and that still farther, he had contrived to introduce one of the most active agents of his treason into the court, and near to the king's own person.

"Who do you aim at?" cried the king. "Quick! give me his name; I know of no such person. All about me are men of trust."

"Alas! no, my liege," answered Wolsey: "the man I mean calls himself Sir Osborne Maurice."

"Ha!" cried Henry, starting—and then, after thinking for a moment, he burst into a fit of laughter. "Nay, nay, my good Wolsey," he said, shaking his head; "nay, nay, nay, Sir Osborne saved my life no longer ago than yesterday, which looks not like treason," and he related to the cardinal the accident that had befallen him while hawking.

Wolsey was somewhat embarrassed, but he replied, " We often see that, taken by some sudden accident, men act not as they proposed to do; and there is such a nobility in your grace's nature, that he must be a hardened traitor indeed who could see you in danger, and not by mere impulse hasten to save you. Perhaps such may have been the case with this Sir Osborne, or perhaps his master's schemes may not yet be ripe for execution; at all events, my liege, doubt not that he is a most assured traitor."

" I cannot believe it! " cried Henry, striking the table with his hand. " I will not believe it! By heaven, the very soul of honor sparkles in his eye! But your proofs, lord cardinal! Your proofs! I will not have such things advanced against my faithful subjects without full and sufficient evidence."

The more eagerness that Henry showed in defending his young friend, the more obnoxious did Sir Osborne become to Wolsey, and he laid before the king, one by one, the deposition of Wilson, Sir Payan's bailiff, several letters which Buckingham had written in favor of the young knight, and lastly, the duke's letter to Sir Thomas Morton, where, either by a forgery of Sir Payan Wileton's, or by some strange chance, it appeared that Sir Osborne Maurice had promised that within a year the duke's head should be the highest in the realm.

While he read, Henry's brow knit into a heavy frown, and, biting his lip, he went back to the beginning, and again read over the papers. " Cardinal," said he, at length, " bid the page seek Pace, my secretary, and ask him for the last letter from the Duke of Buckingham."

Wolsey obeyed; and, while waiting for the return of the page, Henry remained, with his eyes averted, as if in deep thought, beating the papers with his fingers, and gnawing his lip in no very placable mood, while the cardinal wisely abstained from saying a word, leaving the irritation of the king's mind to expend itself, without calling it upon himself. As soon as the letter was brought, Henry laid it side by side with those that Wolsey had placed before him, and seemed to compare every word, every syllable, to ascertain the identity of the handwriting. "True! by my life!" cried he, casting down the papers. "The writing is the same; and now, my lord cardinal, what have you farther to say? Are there any farther proofs, eh?"

"Were there none other, your grace," replied Wolsey, "than the duke's handwriting, and the deposition of a disinterested and respectable witness, who can have no enmity whatever against this Sir Osborne Maurice, and who probably never saw him, but on the two occasions that he mentions, I think it would be quite sufficient to warrant your grace in taking every measure of precaution. But there is another witness, whom, indeed, I have not seen, but who can give evidence, I understand, respecting the conduct of the person accused, towards the Rochester rioters. Knowing how much your grace's wisdom passeth that of the best in the realm, I have dared to have this witness (a most honorable priest) brought hither, hoping that the exigency of the case might lead you to examine him yourself, when perhaps, your royal judgment may elicit more from him than others could do."

"You have done wisely, my good lord cardinal," replied Henry, whose first irritation had now subsided. "Let him be called, and bid your secretary take down his desposition, for 'tis not fitting that mine be so employed."

At the command of Wolsey, one of the pages went instantly to seek the priest, who, by the care and dispatch of Sir Payan, had been sent down with all speed, and was now waiting with the cardinal's attendants, in no small surprise and agitation, not being able to conceive why he was thus hurried from one place to another, and breathing also with some degree of alarm in the unwonted atmosphere of a court. On being ushered into the royal presence, the worthy man fell down upon both his knees before Henry, and clasping his hands, prayed for a blessing on his head, with such fervor and simplicity, that the monarch was both pleased and amused.

" Rise, rise, good man! " said the king, holding out his hand for him to kiss: " we would speak with you on a business of import. Nay, do not be alarmed. We know your worth, and purpose to reward you. Place yourself here, master secretary, and take down his replies. Sit, my good lord cardinal; we beg you to be seated." As soon as Wolsey had taken a low seat near the king, and the secretary, kneeling on one knee before the table, was prepared to write, Henry again proceeded, addressing the priest, who stood before him, the picture of a disquieted spirit.

" Say, do you know one Sir Osborne Maurice? " demanded the king.

" Yes, surely, please your royal grace," replied the priest. " At least that was the name which his attendants gave to the noble and courageous knight that saved me from the hands of the Rochester shipwrights."

" First," said Wolsey, " give us your name, and say how you came to fall into the hands of those rebellious shipwrights."

" Alas, your grace," answered the priest; " I am a poor priest of Dartford, my name John Timeworthy, and hearing that these poor misguided men at Rochester were in open rebellion against the government, from lack of knowledge and spiritual teaching, I resolved to go down amongst them and preach to them peace and submission. I will not stay to say how, and where, I found them; but getting up, upon a bench that stood hard by, under an apple-tree, I gathered them round me like a flock of sheep, and began my discourse, saying—Woe! woe! woe!

Woe unto ye, shipwrights of Rochester, that you should arm yourselves against the king's grace. You are like children, that must fain eat hot pudding, and burn their mouths withal; for ye will cry, and ye will cry, till the sword fall upon you, and then, when Lord Thomas comes down with his men-at-arms, ye will turn about and fly; and the spears will stick in your hinder parts, and ye shall be put to shame: for though he have but hundreds, and ye have thousands, his are all men of the bow and of the spear, and ye know no more of either than a jackass does of the harp and psaltery. And thereupon, your grace, they that I took for strayed sheep, showed themselves to be a pack of ravening wolves, for they took me down from the bench, and beat me unmercifully, and putting a halter round my neck, led me along to hang me up, as they vowed, in sight of Rochester Castle: when just as they were dragging me along, more dead than alive, across a little green, the knight, Sir Osborne Maurice, came up, and, as I said, rescued me: and for a surety, he is a brave and generous knight, and well deserving your grace's favor."

"By my faith, I have always thought so," said Henry. "What say you now, cardinal? Question him yourself, man."

Wolsey eagerly snatched at the permission, for he plainly saw that the matter was not proceeding to his wish. "Pray, my good Master Timeworthy," said he, "how was it that this Sir Osborne rescued you? Did he put his lance in rest, and charge the whole multitude, and deliver you from their hands?"

"Not so! not so!" cried the priest. He did far more wisely, for there would have been much blood spilt; but he sent forward one, who seemed to be his shield-bearer, who shook hands with the chief of the rioters, and spoke him fair; and then the knight came forward himself, and spoke to him; and the chief of the rioters cried with a loud voice to his people, that this was not Lord Thomas, as they had thought, but a friend and well-beloved of the good Duke of Buckingham; and it was wonderful how soon the eloquence of that young man worked upon the multitude, and made them let me go. He was, indeed, a youth of a goodly presence, and fair to look upon, and had something noble and commanding in his aspect; and his words moved the rioters in the twinkling of an eye, and made them wholly change their purpose."

Henry's brow, which had cleared during the former part of the priest's narration, now grew doubly dark and cloudy; and he muttered to himself, "Too clear! too clear!" While Wolsey proceeded to question the priest more closely.

"Indeed, your grace," replied he, in answer to the cardinal's more minute questions, "I can tell you no more than I have told; for, as I said, I was more dead than alive all the time, till they gave me up to the knight, and did not hear half that passed."

"And what did you remark after you were with the knight?" demanded Wolsey. "Was there no particular observation made on the whole transaction?"

"Not that I can call to mind," answered the priest. "All I remember is, that they seemed a very merry party; and laughed and joked about it; which I, being frightened, thought almost wicked, God forgive me! for it was all innocency, and high blood of youth."

"Well, sir," said Wolsey, "you may go. Go with him, secretary; and see that he be well tended, but allowed to have speech of no one."

The priest and the secretary withdrew in silence; and no sooner were they gone, than, abandoning his kingly dignity, Henry started from his seat, and strode up and down the room in one of those fits of passion which, even then, would sometimes take possession of him. At length, stopping opposite Wolsey, who stood up the moment the king rose, he struck the table with his clenched hand, "He shall die!" cried he. "By heaven he shall die! Let him be attached, my Wolsey."

" My sergeant-at-arms is with me, your grace," replied
the cardinal, " and shall instantly execute your royal
will. Better arrest him directly, lest he fear and take
flight."

" Whom mean you?" cried the king. " Ha! I say
attach Edward Bohun, Duke of Buckingham."

" In regard to the Duke of Buckingham, my liege," replied Wolsey, less rudely than he had before spoken,
" will you take into your royal consideration, whether it
may not be better to suffer him to proceed awhile with
his treasonous schemes, for I question if the evidence we
have at present against him would condemn him with the
peers."

" But he is a traitor," cried Henry, " an evident traitor; and, by my faith, shall suffer a traitor's death."

" Most assuredly he is a black and heinous traitor,"
answered Wolsey. " And yet your grace will think what
a triumph it would be for him, if his peers should pronounce him innocent. He has store of friends among
them. Far better let him proceed yet awhile, and, with
our eyes upon him, watch every turn of his dark plot,
and seize him in the midst, when we shall have such
proof, that even his kindred must, for very shame, pronounce his guilt. In the meantime, I will ensure that he
be so strictly guarded that he shall have power to do no
evil."

" You are right, my Wolsey, you are right," cried the
king, seating himself, and laying his hand upon the
papers, " let it be conducted as you say. But see that he
escape not, for his ingratitude adds another shade to
what is black itself. As to this Sir Osborne Maurice,
'tis a noble spirit perverted by that villain Buckingham;
I have seen and watched the seeds of many virtues in
him."

" It must be painful, then, for your grace to command his arrest," said Wolsey; " and yet he is so near
your royal person, and his treason is so manifest, that the

very love of your subjects requires that he should suffer death."

"And yet," replied Henry, fixing his eye upon the cardinal, and speaking emphatically, "and yet, even now, I feel the warm blood of the English kings flowing lightly in my veins, which, but for him would have been cold and motionless—and shall I take his life that has saved mine? No, Wolsey, no! It must not be! He has been misled, but is not wicked."

"Still, your grace's justice requires," said Wolsey, "(pardon me my boldness) that he should undergo his trial. Then, if condemned, comes in your royal mercy to save him; saying to him, you are judged for having been a traitor, you are pardoned for having saved your king."

"But be assured, my Wolsey," replied Henry, "that if his trial were to take place now, the great traitor Buckingham will take alarm, and either endeavor to do away all evidence of his treason, or take to flight and shelter himself from justice."

"No need that his trial be immediate," answered the cardinal; "if your grace permits, he shall be committed privately to the Tower, and there await your return from France; by which time, depend on it, the Duke of Buckingham will have given farther tokens of his mad ambition, and both may be tried together. Then let the greater traitor suffer, and lesser find grace, so that your royal justice and your clemency be equally conspicuous."

"Be it so, then," said the king; "though, in truth, good cardinal, it grieves me to lose this youth. He is, without exception, the best lance in Christendom, and would have done our realm much credit in our journey to France—I say it grieves me! Ay, heartily it grieves me!"

"Nay, your grace," said Wolsey, "you will doubtless find a thousand as good as he."

"Not so! not so, lord cardinal!" cried Henry; "these

are things not so easily acquired as you churchmen think. I never saw a better knight. When his lance breaks in full course, you shall behold his hand as steady as if it held a straw—nor knee, nor thigh, nor heel shall shake; and when the toughest ash splinters upon his casque, he shall not bend even so much as a strong oak before a summer breeze.—But his guilt is clear, so the rest is all naught."

"Then I have your grace's command," said Wolsey, "to commit him to the Tower. He shall be attached directly, by the sergeant-at-arms, and sent down by the turn of the tide."

"Hold, hold!" cried the king; "not to-night, good Wolsey. Before we fly our hawk, we cry the heron up, and he shall have the same grace. To-morrow, if he be still found, arrest him where you will; but for to-night he is safe, nor must his path be dogged. He shall have free and fair start, mark me, till to-morrow at noon; then slip your greyhounds on him, if you please."

"But your grace," cried Wolsey, "if you let him——"

"It is my will," said the king, his brow darkening— "who shall contradict it? Ha! See that it be obeyed exactly, lord!"

"It shall, your grace," said Wolsey, bending his head with a profound inclination. "Your will is law to all your faithful servants; but only let your noble goodness attribute to my deep love for your royal person, the fear I have that this traitorous agent of a still greater traitor may be tempted in despair, if he find that he is discovered, to attempt some heinous crime against your grace."

"Fear not, man! fear not!" replied the king. "He, that when he might have let me die, risked his own life to save mine, will never arm his hand against me—I fear not, cardinal. So be you at ease. But return to London; see that Buckingham be closely watched; and be sure that no preparation be wanting for the meeting with

Francis of France. Be liberal, be liberal, lord cardinal!
I would not that the nobles of France should say they
had more gold than we. Let everything be abundant,
be rich, and in its flush of newness: and as to Sir Osborne Maurice, arrest him to-morrow, if he be still here—
let him be fairly tried, and if he come out pure, well!
Yet still, if he be condemned, his own life shall be given
him as a reward for mine. However, till to-morrow let
it rest. It is my will!"

Though Wolsey would have been better pleased to
have had the knight safely in the Tower, yet, even in
case of his making his escape before the next morning,
his great object was gained, that of banishing from the
court forever, one, whose rapid progress in the king's regard, bade fair, with time, to leave every one behind in
favor. He therefore ceased to press the king upon the
subject, especially as he saw, by many indubitable signs,
that Henry was in one of those imperious moods which
would bear no opposition. A few subjects of less import
still remained to be discussed, but the monarch bore these
so impatiently, that Wolsey soon ceased to importune him
upon them, and resolving to reserve all farther business
for some more auspicious day, he rose, and taking leave
with one of those refined, yet high-colored compliments,
which no man was so capable of justly tempering as himself, he left the royal presence, and proceeded to another
part of the palace on business, whose object is intimately
allied to the present history, as we shall see hereafter.

CHAPTER XVII.

"Away! though parting be a fretful corrosive,
  It is applied to a deathful wound."
                                SHAKSPEARE.

WHEN Wolsey had left him, Henry once more raised
the papers which lay upon the table, and read them
through; then leant his head upon his hand, and passed
some moments in deep and frowning meditation. "No!"
said he, "no! I will not show them to him, lest he warn
the traitor Buckingham. Ho, without! Tell Pace to
come to me," and again falling into thought, he remained
musing over the papers, with bent brows, and an absent
air, till the secretary had time to obey his summons. On
his approach, the good but timid Pace almost trembled
at the angry glow he saw upon the king's face; but he
was relieved by Henry placing in his hands the papers,
which Wolsey had left, bidding him have good care
thereof.

Pace took the papers in respectful silence, and waited
an instant to see whether the king had farther commands;
but Henry waved his hand, crying, "Begone! leave me!
and send the page."

The page lost not a moment in appearing; for the
king's hasty mood was easily discernible in his aspect,
and no one dared, even by an instant's delay, to add fuel
to the fire which was clearly burning in his bosom; but
still Henry allowed him to wait for several minutes.
"Who waits in the antechamber?" demanded he, at
length.

"Sir Charles Hammond, so please your grace," replied
the page.

"And where is Denny?" asked the king. "Where
is Sir Anthony Denny, ha?"

"He has been gone about an hour, your grace," replied the page.

"They hold me at naught!" cried Henry. "Strike
his name from the list! By my life, I will teach him to
wait! Go call Sir Osborne Maurice to my presence,"
and rising from his seat, he began again to pace the apartment.

The page, as he conducted the young knight to the
hall in which Henry awaited him, took care to hint that
he was in a terrific mood, with that sort of eagerness
which all vulgar people have to spread evil tidings. The
knight, however, asked no question, and made no comment, and passing through the door which he had seen
give admission to the priest about an hour before, he
entered the antechamber, in which was seated Sir Charles
Hammond, who saluted him with a silent bow. Proceeding onward, the page threw open the door of the
privy chamber, and Sir Osborne approached the king, in
the knitting of whose brow, and in the curling of whose
lip, might be plainly seen the inward irritation of his
impetuous spirit. As he came near, Henry turned round,
and fixed his eye upon him; and the knight, not knowing
what might be the cause, or what the consequence of his
anger, bent his knee to the ground, and bowing his
head, said, "God save your grace!"

"Mary, thou sayest well!" cried Henry. "We trust
he will, and guard us ever against traitors! What say
you? ha?"

"If ever there be a man so much a traitor to himself,"
replied Sir Osborne, "as to nourish one thought against
so good a king, oh, may his treason fall back upon his
own head, and crush him with the weight."

"Well prayed again," said Henry, more calmly. "Rise,
rise, Sir Osborne, we must speak together. Give me your
arm. We cannot sit and speak when the heart is so
busy. We will walk. This hall has space enough," and
with a hurried pace he took one or two turns in the

chamber, fixing his eyes upon the ground, and biting his lip in silence. " Now, by our Lady," cried he at length, " there are many men in this kingdom, Sir Osborne Maurice, who, seeing us here, holding your arm, and walking by your side, would judge our life in peril."

Sir Osborne started, and gazed in Henry's face with a look of no small surprise.

" Did I but know of any one," said he, at length, " who could poison your royal ear with such a tale, were it other than a churchman or a woman, he should either confess his falsehood, or die upon my sword. But your grace is noble, and believes them not. However," he continued, unbuckling his sword and laying it on the table as far away as possible—" on all accounts I will put that by. There lays the sword that was given me by an emperor, and here is the hand that saved a king's life—and here," he continued, kneeling at the king's feet, " is a heart as loyal as any in this realm, ready to shed its best blood if its king command it. But tell me, only tell me, how I have offended."

" Rise, Sir Knight," said the king. " On my life, I believe you so far, that if you have done wrong, you have been misled; and that your heart is loyal, I am sure—yet listen. You came to this court a stranger; in you I found much of valor and knightly worth—I loved you, and I favored you; yet now I find that you have in much deceived me. Speak not, for I will not see in you any but the man who has saved my life; I will know you for none other. Say, then, Sir Osborne, is not life a good return for life—it is? ha?"

" It is, my liege," replied Sir Osborne, believing his real name discovered. " Whatever I have done amiss has been but error of judgment, not of heart, and surely cannot be held as very deep offence in eyes so gracious as my noble king's."

" We find excuses for you, sir, which rigorous judges might not find," replied the monarch; " yet there are many who strive to make your faults far blacker than they are, and doubtless may urge much against you; but hitherto we stand between you and the law, giving you life for life. But see you use the time that is allowed you well, for to-morrow, at high noon, issues the warrant for your apprehension, and if you make not speed to leave this court and country—your fate upon your head, for you have warning."

Sir Osborne was struck dumb, and for a moment he gazed upon the king in silent astonishment. "I know not what to think," he cried, after a while; "I cannot believe that a king, famous for his clemency, can see in my very worst crime aught but an error. Your grace has said that many strive to blacken me, still humbly at your feet let me beseech you to tell me of what they do accuse me?"

"Of many rank offences, sir!" replied the king, somewhat impatiently; "offences of which you might find it hard to wash yourself so clear, as not to leave enough to weigh you down. However, 'tis our will that you depart the court, without farther sojourn; and if you are wise, you'll speed to leave a country where you may chance to find worse entertainment and a harder lodging if you stay. Go to the keeper of our privy purse, who will give a thousand marks to clear your journey of all cost; and God befriend you for the time to come."

"Nay, your grace," replied Sir Osborne; "poor as I came, I'll go; but thus far richer, that for one short month, I won a great king's love, and lost it without deserving; and if to this, your grace will add the favor, to let me once more kiss your royal hand, you'll send me grateful forth."

Henry held out his hand towards him. "By my faith," cried he, "I do believe him honest. But the proofs! the proofs! Go, go, Sir Osborne—I judge not harshly of you. You have been misled—but fly speedily, I command you—for your own sake fly."

Sir Osborne raised himself, took his sword from the table, and with a low obeisance to the king quitted the room, his heart far too full to speak with any measure what he felt.

His hopes all broken, his dream of happiness dispelled, like a wreath of morning mist in the sunshine, the young knight sought his chamber, and casting himself in a seat, leant his head upon his hands, in an attitude of total despondency.

After much consideration, he resolved that he would fly to Flanders, once more to try the fortune of his sword; for though peace nominally subsisted between the French king and the new emperor, it was a peace which could be but of short duration, and was even then interrupted by continual incursions upon each other's territories, and incessant violation of the frontier by the various garrisons of France and Burgundy. Once arrived, he would write, he thought, to his father, who would surely join him there, and they would raise their house and name in a foreign land. But Constance de Grey—could she ever be his? He knew not; but at her very name, hope relighted her torch, and he began to dream again.

As he thought thus, he raised his eyes, and perceived his faithful attendant Longpole watching him with a look of anxious expectation, waiting till his agitated reverie should end. "How! Longpole!" said he. "You here? I did not hear you come in."

"I have been here all the time, your worship," replied the yeoman. "And I've made some noise in the world, too, while you have been here, for I let all the armor fall in that closet."

"I did not hear you," said the knight. "My thoughts were very busy. But, my good Heartley, I am afraid the time is come that we must part."

"By my faith, it must be a queer time, then, your worship," answered Longpole: "for it is not every-day weather that will make me quit you—specially when I see you in such a way as you were just now."

" But, my good Longpole," answered the knight, " I am ruined. The king has discovered who I really am, Wolsey has whetted his anger against me, and he has banished me his court, bidding me fly instantly, lest I be to-morrow arrested, and perhaps committed to the Tower. I must therefore quit this country without loss of time, and take my way to Flanders, for my hopes here are all at an end—Wolsey is too powerful to be opposed."

" Well, then, my lord," said Longpole—" I will call you by your real name now—and so I'll go and saddle our horses, pack up as much as I can, and we'll be off in a minute."

" But, my good Longpole," said his master, " you do not think what you are doing. Indeed you must not leave your country and your friends, and that poor girl Geraldine, to follow a man ruined in fortune and expectations, going to travel through strange lands, where he knows not whether he may find friends or enemies."

" More reason he should have a companion on the road," replied Longpole. " But, my lord, my determination is made. Where you go, there will I go too; and as to little Mistress Geraldine, why, when we've made a fortune, which I am sure we shall do, I'll make her trot over after me. But, as I suppose there is but little time to spare, I will go get everything into order as fast as possible. Carpe diem, as good Dr. Wilbraham used to say to me when I was lazy. There is your lordship's harness. If you can manage to pop on the breast and back pieces, I will be back directly."

" Nay," said the knight, " there is yet one person I must see. However, be not long, good fellow, for I shall not stay. Give me that wrapping cloak with the hood."

Longpole obeyed, and enveloping himself in a large mantle, which he had upon a former occasion used to

19

cover his armor, in one of those fanciful jousts where every one appeared disguised, the knight left his own apartments, and proceeded to those of Lady Constance de Grey. Hurrying on he approached the suite of rooms appropriated to Lady Constance, and was surprised at finding the door open. Entering, nothing but confusion seemed to reign in the ante-chamber, where her maids were usually found employed in various works. Here stood a frame for caul work, there one for embroidery; here a cushion for Italian lace thrown upon the ground, there a chair overturned: while two of the maids stood looking out of the window, (to make use of the homely term) crying their eyes out.

"Where is your mistress?" demanded Sir Osborne, as he entered; the agitation of his own feelings, and the alarm he conceived from the strange disarray of the apartment, making him stint his form of speech to the fewest words possible.

"We do not know, sir," replied one of the desolate damsels. "All that we know is, that she is gone."

"Gone!" cried Sir Osborne. "Gone! In the name of heaven where is she gone? Who is gone with her?"

"Jesu Maria, sir! don't look so wild," cried the woman, who thought herself quite pretty enough, even in her tears, to be a little familiar,—"Dr. Wilbraham is with the Lady Constance, and so is Mistress Margaret, and therefore she is safe enough, surely."

"But cannot you say where she is gone?" cried the knight. "When did she go? How?"

"She went but now, sir," replied the woman. "She was sent for about an hour or more ago to the little tapestry-hall, to speak with my lord cardinal; and after that she came back very grave and serious, and made Mrs. Margaret pack up a great parcel of things, while she herself spoke with Dr. Wilbraham; and when that was done, they all three went away together; but before she went she gave each of us fifty marks a-piece, and said that she would give us news of her."

" Did she not drop any word, in regard to her destination?" demanded Sir Osborne. " Anything that might lead you to imagine whither she was gone? "

" Mrs. Margaret said they were going to London," said the other girl, turning round from the window, and speaking through her tears. " She said that they were going, because such was my lord cardinal's will. But I don't believe it, for she said it like a lie—and I'm sure I shall never see my young lady again. I'm sure I shan't! So now, Sir knight, go away and leave us, for we can tell you nothing more."

The knight turned away. " Oh, Constance! Constance! " thought he, as he paced back to his apartments; " will you ever be able to resist all the influence they may bring against you? When you hear, too, of your lover's disgrace! Well, God is good; and sometimes joy shines forth out of sorrow, like the sun that dispels the storm." As he thought thus, the prediction of Sir Cesar, that their misfortune should be but of short duration, came across his mind. " The evil part of his prophecy," thought he, " is already on my head. Why should I doubt the good? Come, I will be superstitious, and believe it fully; for hope is surely as much better than fear, as joy is better than sorrow. Will Constance ever give her hand to another? Oh, no, no! And surely, surely, I shall win her yet."

On returning to his apartment, he found his faithful attendant ready prepared; and there was a sort of easy, careless confidence in the honest yeoman's manner, that well seconded the efforts of reviving hope in his master's breast.

" Longpole," said the knight, " give me my armor; I will put it on, while you place what clothes you can in the large horsebags. But, my good custrel, we must put something over our harness—give me that surcoat. You have not barded my horse, I trust."

" Indeed I have, my lord," replied he; " and depend

on it you may have need thereof. Remember how dear
the barding of a horse is—I speak of the steel, which is,
in fact, the true bard, or bardo, as the Italians call it;
for the cloth that covers it is not the bard—and if you
carry the steel with you, you may as well have the silk
too."

" But 'twill weary the horse," said Sir Osborne; " however, as 'tis on, let it stay; only it may attract attention,
and give too good a track to any that follow; though,
God knows, I can hardly determine which way to turn
my rein."

" To London! to London! to be sure, your worship,"
cried Longpole; " that is the high road to every part on
the earth. What would you think of just paying a visit
to good Master William Hans, the merchant, to see if
he cannot give us a cast over to Flanders? A thousand
to one he has some vessel going, or knows some one that
has."

" Well bethought," answered Sir Osborne, slowly
buckling on his armor; " it will soon grow dusk, and
then our arms will call no attention—my hands refuse
to help me on with my harness. I am very slow. Nay,
good Longpole, if you have already finished, take a hundred marks out of that bag, which will nearly empty it,
and seek the three men the Duke of Buckingham gave
me. Divide it between them, for their service: and,
good Longpole, when you have done that, make inquiries
about the palace, as to what road was taken by Lady Constance de Grey and Dr. Wilbraham—do not mention the
lady—name only Dr. Wilbraham, as if I sought to speak
with him."

Longpole obeyed, and after about half an hour's absence returned, tolerably successful in his inquiries; but
much to his surprise and disappointment, he found his
young lord very nearly in the same situation in which
he had left him, sitting in his chair, half armed, with his
casque upon his knee, his fine head bare, and his eye
fixed upon the fading gleams of the evening sky.

"Well, Longpole," cried he, waking from his reverie, "what news? Have you heard anything of Lady Constance?" and, as if ashamed of his delay, he busied himself to finish the arrangement of his armor.

"Let me aid you, my lord," said Longpole, kneeling down, and soon completing, piece by piece, what his master had left unfinished, replying at the same time to his question. "I have spoken with the man who carried the baggage down to the boat, my lord, and he says that Dr. Wilbraham, Lady Constance, and one of her women took water about half an hour after the lord cardinal, and seemed to follow his barge."

Sir Osborne fell into another reverie, from which, at last, he roused himself with a sigh. "Well, I can do nothing," said he; "like an angry child I must rage and struggle, but I could do no more. Were I to stay, 'twould but be committing me to the Tower, and then I must be still per force—"

Longpole heard all this with an air of great edification; but when he thought that his master had indulged himself enough, he ventured to interrupt him, by saying, "The sun, sir, has gone to bed, had we not better take advantage of his absence, and make our way to London? Remember, sir. He is an early riser at this time of year, and will be up looking after us to-morrow before we are well aware."

"Ay, Longpole, ay!" replied the knight, "I will linger no longer, for it is unavailing. The trumpet must have sounded to supper by this time, has it not? So we shall have no idlers to gaze at our departure."

"The trumpet sounded as I went down but now," said Longpole, "and I met the sewer carrying in a brawn's head so like his own, that I could not help thinking he had killed and cooked his brother—they must be hard at his grace's liege capons even now."

"Well, I am ready," said the knight; "give me the surcoat of tawny velvet—now—no more feathers!" he continued, plucking from his casque the long plume that, issuing from the crest in graceful sweeps, fell back almost to his girdle, taking care, however, at the same time, to leave behind, a small white glove wrought with gold, that had surrounded the insertion of the feather, and which he secured in its place, with particular attention. " Some one will have rare pillage of this apartment," he added, looking round; " that suit of black armor is worth five hundred marks—but it matters not to think of it—we cannot carry them with us—the long sword and baldrick, Longpole, and the gold spurs—I will go as a knight, at least—now, take the bags—I follow. Farewell, King Henry, you have lost a faithful subject!"

Thus saying, he proceeded down the stairs after Longpole, and following a corridor, passed by one of the small doors of the great hall, through the partial opening of which was to be heard the rattle and the clatter of plates, of dishes, and of knives, and the buzz of many busy jaws. There was a feeling of disgust came over Sir Osborne as he heard it—he scarce knew why, and stayed not to inquire, but striding on, came speedily to the stable-yard, and was crossing towards the building in which his horses stood, when he observed a man loitering near the door of the stable, whom he soon discovered to be one of the yeomen given him by the Duke of Buckingham.

" On, Longpole," cried the knight, " on, and send him upon some errand, for I am in no fit mood to speak with him now."

While Sir Osborne drew back into the doorway, Longpole advanced, and in a moment after the man was seen traversing the court in another direction. The knight then proceeded, the horses were brought forth, and springing into the saddle, Sir Osborne, with a sigh given to the recollection of lost hopes, touched his charger with the spur, and rode out of the gates. Longpole followed, and in a few minutes they were on the high road to London.

It was hardly night when Sir Osborne departed. For some time the knight indulged in vague dreams, then he spurred forward his horse, and proceeded as fast as he could towards London. Longpole followed in silence, for in spite of all his philosophy, he felt a sort of qualm at the idea of the long period which must intervene ere he could hope to see his pretty Geraldine, that took away several ounces of his loquacity.

London, at length, spread wide before them, and they at length reached Gracious Street, and discovered the small square paved court, long since built over, which then afforded a sort of area before the dwelling of the Flemish merchant, William Hans. While Longpole dismounted, and knocked with the hilt of his dagger against a little door by the side of that which led to the counting-house, the knight watched a light in the window; but he watched, and Longpole knocked, in vain; for neither did the light move, nor the door open, till Sir Osborne bethought him of a stratagem to call the merchant's attention.

"Make a low knocking against the windows of the counting-house, Longpole," said he, "as if you were trying to force them. I have known these money-getters as deaf as adders to any sound but that which menaced their mammon."

Longpole obeyed, and the moment after the light moved. "Hold, hold!" cried the knight, "he hears;" and the next moment the casement window was pushed open, through which the head of the good merchant protruded itself, vociferating, "Who's tere? What do you want? I'll call the watch—Watch! watch!"

"Taisez vous!" cried the knight, addressing him in French, not being able to speak the Brabant dialect of the merchant, and yet not wishing to proclaim his errand aloud in English. "Nous sommes amis—descendez, Guillaume Hans—c'est le Sire de Darnley."

"Oh, I'll come down! I'll come down!" cried the

merchant. "Run, Skippenhausen, and open te door. I'll come down, my coot lord, in a minute."

The two travellers had not now long to wait, for in a moment or two the little door at which Longpole had at first in vain applied for admission, was thrown open by the merchant, himself, who was informed as succinctly as possible of what had occurred. Good Master Hans was prodigal of his astonishment, which vented itself in various exclamations in Flemish, English, and French, after which, coming to business, as he said, he told the knight that he could put up his horses in the same stable where he kept his drays, and that after that they would talk of the rest. "But on my wort, my coot lord," said he, "I must go with your man myself, for there is not one soul in the place to let him in or out of the stable, which is behind the house."

The most troublesome part of the affair for the moment, was to take off the bard or horse armor, that covered the knight's charger, as it could not be left in the stable till the next morning, when the merchant's carters would arrive, and poor William Hans was desperately afraid that the round of the watch would pass while the operation was in execution, and suppose that he was receiving some contraband goods, which might cause a search the next day.

The business, however, was happily accomplished, and the knight was conducted upstairs into the room where he had first discovered the light, and invited him to be seated. By the appearance of the chamber, it seemed that Master Hans had been preparing to make great cheer, for various were the flagons and bottles that stood upon the table, together with trenchers and plates unused, and a pile of manchet and spice bread, with other signs of an elaborate supper; not to mention an immense bowl which stood in the midst, and whose void rotundity seemed yearning for some savory mess not yet concocted.

It was not long before the merchant reappeared, ac-

companied by a certain Dutch sea captain and Longpole, who, according to the custom of those days, when
many a various rank might be seen at the same board,
seated himself at the farther end of the table, after having
taken his master's casque, and soon engaged the Dutch
captain in conversation, while the knight consulted with
William Hans, regarding the means of quitting England
as speedily as possible.

"It is very unlucky you did not let me know before,"
said the merchant, "for we might easily have cot the
ship of my goot friend Skippenhausen there, ready to-
day, and you could have sailed to-morrow morning by
the first tide. You might trust him! you might trust
him with your life! Bless you, my coot lord, 'tis he that
brings me over the Bibles from Holland."

"But cannot he sail the day after to-morrow," said
the knight, "if one day will be sufficient to complete his
freight?"

"Oh, that he can," answered the merchant; "but what
will you do till then?" He added, with a melancholy
shake of the head, "You will never like to lie in warehouse, like a parcel of dry goods."

"Why, it must be so, I suppose," said the knight, "if
you have any place capable of concealing me."

"Oh, dear life, yes!" cried William Hans; "a place
that would conceal a dozen. I had it made on purpose
after that evil May-day, when the wild rabblement of
London rose, and nearly murdered all the strangers they
could find. I thought what had happened once might
happen again, and so I had in some of my own country
people, and caused it to be made very securely."

The matter was now soon arranged. It was agreed
that the knight and Longpole should lie concealed at the
merchant's till the ship was ready to sail, and that then
Master Skippenhausen was to provide them a safe passage to some town in Flanders, which being finally settled
between all parties, it only remained to fix the price of
their conveyance with the Dutchman.

The door opened, and in bustled a servant-maid, of about two or three and thirty, whose rosy tinge had acquired a deeper tinge by the soft wooing of a kitchen fire, and whose sharp eyes shot forth those brilliant rays, generally supposed to be more animated by the wrathful spirit of cookery and of ardent coals, than by any softer power or flame. Immediately she beheld two strangers, forth burst upon the head of William Hans the impending storm. She abused him for telling her that there would only be himself and the captain; she vowed that she had not cooked half salmon enough for four; she declared that she had only put down plates and bread for two; and she ended, by protesting that she never in her life had seen anybody so stupid as he himself, William Hans.

To the mind of Sir Osborne, the lady somewhat forgot the respect due to her master; but, however, whether it was from one of those strange mysterious ascendencies, which cooks and housekeepers occasionally acquire over middle-aged single gentlemen, or whether it was from a natural meekness of disposition in the worthy Fleming, he bore it with most exemplary patience; and when want, of breath for a moment pulled the check-string of the lady's tongue, he informed her that the two strangers had come unexpectedly. Thereupon, muttering to herself something very like, " Why the devil did they come at all! " she set down on the table a dish of hot boiled salmon; and, after flouncing out of the room, returned with the air of the most injured person in the world, bringing in a platter-full of dried pease, likewise boiled.

These various ingredients (the salmon was salted) William Hans immediately seized upon, and emptied them into the great bowl we have already mentioned. Then casting off his gown, and tucking up the sleeves of his coat, he mashed them all together; adding various slices of some well preserved pippins, a wooden spoon's capacity of fine oil, and three of vinegar.

Sir Osborne resisted the tempting viands, and con-

tented himself with some of the plain bread, although
both the merchant and the captain pressed him several
times to partake.

Sweetmeats and wines, which were all of peculiar
rarity and excellence, came next.

As the wine diffused itself over Hans' stomach, it
seemed to buoy up his heart to his lips. Prudence too
slackened her reins, and on went his tongue, galloping,
as a beggar's horse is reported to do, on a way that shall
be nameless. Many were the things he said, which he
should not have said, and many were the things he told,
which would have been better left untold.

Sir Osborne soon began to be weary of the scene, and
begged to know where he should find his chamber, upon
which Master Hans rose to conduct him, with perfect
steadiness of limb, the wine having affected nothing but
his tongue. Lighting a lamp, he preceded the knight
with great reverence and while Longpole followed with
the armor, he led the way up a little narrow stairs, to a
small room, whose walls, though not covered with arras,
were hung with painted canvas, after a common fashion
of the day, representing the whole history of Jonah and
the whale; wherein the fish was decidedly cod, and the
sea undoubtedly parsley and butter, notwithstanding anything that the scientific may say to such an assemblage.

The whole of the room, however, was cleanliness itself:
the little bed that stood in the corner, with its fine linen
sheets, the small deal table, even the very sand upon the
floor, all were as white as snow. " I am afraid, my coot
lord," said the merchant, who never lost his respect for
his guest, " that your lordship will be poorly lodged; but
these three chambers along in front, are what I keep
always ready, in case of any of my captains arriving unexpectedly, and it is all clean and proper, I can assure you.
I will now go and bring a cushion for your head, and
what the French call the coupe de bonne nuit, and will
myself call your lordship to-morrow, before any one is

up, that you may take to your hiding-place without being seen."

The knight was somewhat surprised to find his host's recollection so clear, notwithstanding his potations; but he knew not what much habit in that kind will do, and still doubted whether his memory would be active enough to remind him that he was to call him when the next morning should really come.

However, he did Master Hans injustice, for without fail, at the hour of five, he presented himself at the knight's door, and soon after rousing Longpole, he conducted them both down to the warehouses, through whose deep obscurity they groped their way, amidst tuns and bags, and piles and bales, with no other light than such straggling rays as found their way through the chinks and crevices of the boards which covered the windows for the night.

At length an enormous butt presented itself, which appeared to be empty, for without any great effort the old merchant contrived to move it from its place. Behind this appeared a pile of untanned hides, which he set to put on one side as fast as possible, though for what purpose Sir Osborne did not well understand, as he beheld nothing behind them but the rough planks which formed the wall of the warehouse. As the pile diminished, a circumstance occurred which made all parties hurry their movements, and despatch the hides as fast as possible. This was nothing else than a loud and reiterated knocking at the outer door, which at first induced Master Hans to raise his head and listen, but then, without saying a word, he set himself to work again harder than ever, and with the assistance of the knight and Longpole, soon cleared away all obstruction, and left the fair face of the boarded wall before them.

Kneeling down, the merchant now thrust his fingers under the planks where the apparently rude workmanship of the builder had left a chink between them and the ground—then applied all his strength to a vigorous heave, and in a moment three of the planks at once slid up, being made to play in a groove, like the door of a lion's den, and discovered a small chamber beyond, lighted by a glazed aperture towards the sky.

"In! in! my coot lord!" cried the merchant, "don't you hear how they are knocking at the door? They will soon rouse my maid Julian, though she sleeps like a marmot. What they want I don't know."

Sir Osborne and Longpole were not tardy in taking possession of their hiding-place, and having themselves pulled down the sliding door by means of the cross-bars, which in the inside united the three planks together, they fastened it with a little bolt, whereby any one within could render his retreat as firm, and, to all appearances, as immovable as the rest of the wall. They then heard the careful William Hans replace the hides, roll back the butt, and pace away; after which, nothing met their ear but the unceasing knocking at the outer door, which seemed every minute to assume a fiercer character, and which was perfectly audible in their place of refuge.

The merchant appeared to treat the matter very carelessly, and not to make any reply till it suited his convenience, for during some minutes he let the knockers knock on. At length, however, that particular sound ceased, and from a sort of rush, and clatter of several tongues, the knight concluded that the door had been at length opened. At the same time the voice of the Fleming made itself heard, in well-assumed tones of passion, abusing the intruders for waking him so early in the morning, bringing scandal upon his house, and taking away his character.

"Seize the old villain!" cried another voice; "we have certain information that they are here. Search every hole and corner, they must have arrived last night."

Such, and various other broken sentences, pronounced by the loud tongue of some man in office, reached the

ears of Sir Osborne, convincing him—notwithstanding
Henry's assurance that till noon of that day he should
remain unpursued—that Wolsey, taking advantage of the
king's absence at Richmond, had lost no time in issuing
the warrant for his arrest.

Sitting down on a pile of books, which was the only
thing that the little chamber contained, he listened with
some degree of anxiety to the various noises of the search.
Now it was a direction from the chief of the party to
look here or to look there,—now the various cries of the
searchers, when they either thought they had discovered
something suspicious, or were disappointed in some expectation—now the rolling of the butts, the overturning
of the bales, the casting down of the skins and leathers—
now the party was far off, and now so near, that the
knight could hear every movement of the man who examined the hides before the door of his hiding-place.
Even at one time, in the eagerness of his search, the
fellow struck his elbow against the boarding, and might
probably have discovered that it was hollow underneath,
had not the tingling pain of his arm engaged all his attention, passing off in a fit of dancing and stamping, mingled
with various ungodly execrations.

At length, however, the pursuers seemed entirely
foiled, and after having passed more than two hours, some
in examining the dwelling-house, and some the warehouse
—after having tumbled over every article of poor William
Hans' goods, their loud cries, and insolent swaggering,
dwindled away to low murmurs of disappointment; and
growing fainter and fainter as they proceeded to the
door, the sounds at length ceased entirely, and left the
place in complete silence. Not long after the workmen
arrived and began their ordinary occupations for the day,
.and Sir Osborne and Longpole thanked their happy stars,
both for having escaped the present danger, and for their
enemy's search being now probably turned in some other
direction.

CHAPTER XVIII.

"NORFOLK,—What, are you chafed?
  Ask God for temperance; that's the appliance only
  Which your disease requires."

                                        SHAKSPEARE.

As the day passed on, Sir Osborne grew more and more impatient under his confinement. He felt a sort of degradation in being thus pent up, like a wild beast in a cage; and though, with invincible patience, he had lain a thousand times more still, in many an ambuscade, he felt an almost irresistible desire to unbolt the door, and assure himself that he was really at large, by going forth and exercising his limbs in the free air. But then came the remembrance that such a proceeding would almost infallibly transfer him to a still stricter prison; where, instead of being voluntary, and but for one day, his imprisonment would be forced and long continued. The thought, too, of Constance de Grey, and the hope of winning her yet, gave great powers of endurance; and he contented himself with every now and then marching up and down the little chamber, which, taken transversely, just afforded him space for three steps and a half; and, at other times, with speaking in a whisper to Longpole, who, having brought the armor down with him, sat, in one corner, polishing off any little dim spots that the damp of the night air might have left upon it.

At length the knight taking up one of the books, on which he had been sitting, found that it was an English version of the Bible, with copies of which it appears that Master William Hans was in the habit of supplying the English Protestants. Our mother Eve's bad old habit of prying into forbidden sources of knowledge, affects

us all more or less; and as the Bible was at that time
prohibited in England, except to the clergy, Sir Osborne
very naturally opened it, and began reading. What effect
its perusal had upon his mind matters little; suffice it
that he read on, and found sufficient matter of interest
therein to occupy him fully.· Hour after hour fled, and
day waned slowly, but having once laid his hand upon
that book the knight no longer felt the tardy current of
the time, and night fell before the day, which he anticipated as so tedious, seemed to have half passed away.

A long while elapsed after the darkness had interrupted
Sir Osborne in his study, before the warehouse was
closed for the night; which, however, was no sooner
accomplished, than good Master Hans, accompanied by
his friend Skippenhausen, came to deliver them from
their confinement.

"He, he, he!" cried the merchant, as they came forth.
"Did you hear what a noise they made, my coot lord,
when they came searching this morning? They did not
find them though, for they were all in beside you."

"What do you mean?" demanded the knight. "Who
were in beside us? Nobody came here."

"I mean the Bibles; I mean the Word of God," cried
the merchant; "the bread of life, that those villains came
seeking this morning, which, if they had got, they would
have burnt most sacrilegiously, as an offering to the
harlot of their idolatry."

"Then I was wrong in supposing that they searched
for me?" said the knight, with a smile at his own mistake.

"Oh, no, not for you at all!" replied the merchant.
"It was the Bibles that Skippenhausen brought over
from Holland, for the poor English Protestants, who are
here denied to eat of the bread, or drink of the water of
salvation. But now, my lord, if you will condescend to
be weighed, you will be ready to sail at four in the morning, for your horses and horse-armor are all weighed and

aboard, and the cargo will be complete, when your lord-ship and your gentleman are shipped."

Finding that Master Skippenhausen was bent upon ascertaining his weight, Sir Osborne consented to get into the merchant's large scales, and being as it were lotted with Longpole, his horse-bags, and his armor, he made a very respectable entry in the captain's books. After this, Master Hans led him into his counting-house, and displayed his books before him; but as the items of his account might be somewhat tedious, it may be as well merely to say, that the young knight found he had expended, in the short time he had remained in Henry's luxurious court, more than two thousand five hundred marks; so that of the two thousand seven hundred which he had possessed, in the hands of the Fleming, and the thousand which he had won at the Duke of Buckingham's, but one thousand two hundred and a trifle remained.

Sir Osborne was surprised, but the accurate merchant left no point in doubt, and the young knight began to think that it was lucky he had been driven from the court before all his funds were completely expended. He found, however, to his satisfaction, that a great variety of arms and warlike implements, which he had gathered together while in Flanders, and had left in the warehouses of the merchant since he had been in England, had been shipped on board Skippenhausen's vessel, whose acknowledgment of having received them, William Hans now put into his hand; and having paid him the sum due, and received an acquittance, he led him once more upstairs to his former apartments.

The next morning Sir Osborne was awakened by the seaman; and dressing himself as quick as possible, he followed to William Hans' parlor, where the worthy mer-chant waited, to drink a parting cup with his guests, and wish them a prosperous voyage.

As the easiest means of carrying their harness, Sir Osborne and Longpole had both armed themselves, and

20

as soon as they had received the Fleming's benediction, in a cup of sack, they donned their casques, and followed the captain towards the vessel.

It was a dull and drizzly morning, and many was the dark foul street, and many the narrow tortuous lane through which they had to pass. Wapping, all dismal and wretched as it appears even nowadays, to the unfortunate voyager, who, called from his warm bed in a wet London morning, is rolled along through its long hopeless windings, and amidst its tall spiritless houses, towards the ship destined to bear him to some other land; and which with a perversion of intellect only to be met with in ships, stage-coaches, and other wooden-headed things, is always sure to set out at an hour when all rational creatures are sleeping in their beds.

A narrow lane brought them to the side of the river, where waited a boat to convey them to the Dutchman's ship, which lay out some way from the bank. Beside the stairs, stood a man apparently on the watch, but he seemed quite familiar with Master Skippenhausen, who gave him a nod as he passed, and pointing to his companions, said, "This is the gentleman and his servant."

"Very well," said the man; "go on!" and the whole party taking their places in the boat without further question, were speedily pulled round to the vessel by the two stout Dutchmen who waited for them. As soon as they were on board, the captain led the knight down into the cabin, which he found in a state of glorious confusion, but which Skippenhausen assured him, would be the safest place for him, till they had got some way down the river; for that they might have visitors on board, whom he could not prevent from seeing all that was upon the deck, though he would take care that they should not come below.

"Ay, Master Skippenhausen," cried Longpole, "for God's sake fetter all spies and informers with a silver ring, and let us up on deck again as soon as possible, for

I am tired of being hid about in holes and corners, like a crooked sixpence in the box of a careful maid; and as for my lord, he looks more weary of it than even I am."

The master promised faithfully, that as soon as the vessel had passed Blackwall, he would give them notice, and then proceeded to the deck, where almost immediately after, all the roaring and screaming made itself heard, which seems absolutely necessary to get a ship under weigh. In truth, it was a concert as delectable as any that ever greeted a poor voyager on his outset; the yelling of the seamen, the roaring of the master and his subordinates, the creaking and whistling of the masts and cordage, together with volleys of clumsy Dutch oaths, all reached the ears of the knight, as he sat below in the close foul cabin, and joined to his own painful feelings, made him almost fancy himself in the Dutch part of Hades. Still the swinging of the vessel told, that, though not as an effect, yet at least as an accompaniment to all this din, the ship was already on her voyage, and after a few minutes, a more regular and easy motion began to take place, as she glided down what is now called the Pool.

However, much raving, and swearing, and cursing, to no purpose, still went on, whenever the vessel passed in the proximity of another; and, as there were several dropping down at the same time, manifold were the opportunities which presented themselves for the captain and the pilot to exercise their execrative faculties. But at length, the disturbance began to cease, and the ship held her even course down the river, while the sun, now fully risen, dispelled the clouds that had hung over the early morning, and the day looked more favorably upon their passage.

Sir Osborne gazed out of the little window in the stern, noticing the various villages that they passed on their way down, till the palace at Greenwich, and the park sweeping up behind, met his eye, together with many a little object associated with hopes, and feelings, and happiness gone by, recalling most painfully all that expectation had promised, and disappointment had done away. It was too much to look upon steadily, and turning from the sight, he folded his arms on the table, and burying his eyes on them, remained in that position, till the master descending, told him that they were now free from all danger.

On this information the knight gladly mounted the little ladder, and paced up and down the deck, enjoying the free air, while Longpole jested with Master Skippenhausen, teasing him the more perhaps, because he saw that the seaman had put on that sort of surly domineering air, which the master of a vessel often assumes, the moment his foot touches the deck, however gay and mild he may be on shore.

The wind was in their favor, and the tide running strongly down, so that passing one by one, by Woolwich, Purfleet, Erith, Gravesend, and sundry other places, in a few hours they approached near the ocean limits of the English land.

Before they had reached the mouth of the river, they beheld a vessel which had preceded them, suddenly take in sail and lay to under the lee of the Essex shore: the reason of which was made very evident the moment after, by the vane at the mast-head, wheeling round, and the wind coming in heavy squalls right upon their beam. The Dutchman's ship was not one at all calculated to sail near the wind, and paying little consideration to the necessity of Sir Osborne's case, he followed the example of the vessel before him, and gave orders for taking in sail and laying-to, declaring that the gale would not last. The knight remonstrated, but he might as well have talked to the wind itself. Skippenhausen was quite inflexible, not even taking the pains to answer a word, and contenting himself with muttering a few sentences in High Dutch, interspersed with various objurgatory addresses to the sailors,

By day-break the next morning, the wind was rather more favorable, and at all events by no means violent, so that the vessel was soon once more under weigh. Still, however, they made but little progress; and even the ship that was before them, though a faster sailor, and one that could keep nearer the wind, made little more way than themselves. While in this situation, trying by a long tack to mend their course, with about the distance of half a mile between them and the other vessel, they perceived a ship of war apparently run out from the Essex coast some way to windward, and bear down upon them with all sail set.

"Who have we here, I wonder?" said the knight, addressing Skippenhausen, who had been watching the approaching vessel attentively for some minutes.

"'Tis an English man-of-war," replied the master. "Coot now, don't you see the red cross on her flag. By my life, she is making a signal to us!—It must be you she is wanting, my lord, for, on my life, I have nothing contraband but you aboard—I will not understand her signal though, and as the breeze is coming up I will run for it. Go you down in the cabin and hide yourself."

"I will go down," replied the knight. "But hide myself, I will not—I have had too much of it already."

Skippenhausen, who, as we before hinted, had, by the long habit of smuggling in a small way, acquired a taste for the concealed and mysterious, tried in vain to persuade the knight to hide himself under a pile of bedding. On this subject Sir Osborne was as deaf as the other had been the night before, in regard to proceeding on their voyage; and all that the master could obtain was, that the two Englishmen would go below, and wait the event, while he tried by altering his course, and running before the wind, to weary the pursuers if they were not very hearty in the cause.

"Well, Longpole," said Osborne, "I suppose that we must look upon ourselves as caught at last."

"Would your worship like us to stand to our arms?" demanded the yeoman. "We could make this cabin good a long while in case of necessity."

"By no means," replied the knight. "I will on no account resist the king's will. Besides, it would be spilling good blood to little purpose, for we must yield at last."

"As your lordship ·pleases," answered the custrel. "But knowing how fond you are of a good downright blow of estoc at a fair gentleman's head, I thought you might like to take advantage of the present occasion, which may be your last for some time."

"Perhaps it may be a mistake still," answered the knight, "and pass away like the search for the Bibles when we were concealed in the warehouse. However, we shall soon see; at all events, till it comes I shall take no heed about it," and casting himself into a seat, with a bitter smile, as if wearied out with Fortune's caprices, and resolved to struggle no longer for her favor, he gazed out of the little stern window upon the wide expanse of water that rolled away towards the horizon. The aperture of this window not being more than six inches either in height or width, and cut through the thick timbers of the Dutch vessel for considerably more than a foot in depth, was in fact little better than a telescope without a glass, so that the knight's view was not a little circumscribed in respect to all the nearer objects, only being able to see, as the ship pitched, the glassy green waves, mingled with white foam, rushing tumultuously from under her stern, as she now scudded before the wind, leaving a long, glistening, frothy track behind, to mark where she had made her path through the midst of the broad sea. As he looked farther out, however, the prospect widened, and at the extreme verge, where the sea and sky, almost one in unity of hue, showed still a faint line of light to mark their boundary, he could perceive, rising up as it were from the bosom of the deep, the light tracery of masts and rigging, belonging to far-dis-

tant vessels, whose hulls were still concealed by the con-
vexity of the waters. Nearer, but yet within the range
that the narrowness of the window allowed his sight, appeared the vessel that had dropped down the river just before them, and the English ship of war, which, crowding
all sail before the wind, seemed in full chase—not of their
companion, but of themselves, for the other, in obedience
to the signal, had hauled her wind and lay-to.

Sir Osborne now watched to ascertain whether the
man-of-war gained upon them, but an instant's observation put an end to all doubt. She evidently came nearer
and nearer, and soon approached so far, as to be scarcely
within the range of his view, being lost and seen alternately at every motion of the ship. At length, as the
vessel pitched, she disappeared for a moment, then came
in sight again—a quick flash glanced along her bow, and
the moment after, when she was no longer visible to his
eye, the sullen report of a cannon came upon the wind.

By a sudden change in the motion of the vessel, together with various cries upon the deck, the knight now
concluded that the Dutchman had at length obeyed this
peremptory signal, and lay-to, which was in fact the
case, for passing over to the window on the other side,
he again got a view of the English ship, which sailed
majestically up, and then when within a few hundred
yards, put out, and manned a boat, which rowed off
towards them. Sir Osborne had not long an opportunity
of observing the boat in her approach, as she soon passed
out of the small space which he could see, but in a few
minutes after the voice of some one, raised to its very
highest pitch, made itself heard from a distance, hardly
near enough for the knight to distinguish the words,
though he every now and then caught enough to perceive,
that the whole consisted of a volley of curses discharged
at Master Skippenhausen, for not having obeyed the signal.

The Dutchman replied in a tone of angry surliness,

that he had not seen their signal, and in a minute or two more, a harsh grating rush against the vessel, told that the boat was alongside.

"I will teach you, you Dutch son of a dogfish, not to lay-to when one of the king's ships makes the signal," cried a loud voice by the side. "Have you any passengers on board?"

"Yes, five or six," answered the Dutchman.

"Stop! I will come on board," cried the voice, and then proceeded, as if while climbing the ship's side, "Have you one Sir Osborne Maurice with you?"

"No!" answered Skippenhausen, stoutly.

"Well, we will soon see that," cried the other, "for I have orders to attach him for high treason. Come, bustle! disperse, my boys!—You, Wilfred, go forward; I will down here and see who is in the cabin; and if I find him, Master Dutchman, I will slit your ears."

CHAPTER XIX.

"My conscience will serve me to run from this Jew."
MERCHANT OF VENICE.

WE will now return to Lady Constance de Grey whose
fate must no longer be left in uncertainty; and taking up
the thread of our narrative at the moment Sir Osborne
quitted her, on the eventful evening which destroyed
all his fond expectations, we will, in our homely way, re-
cord the events that followed.

It may be remembered, that at the very instant the
knight parted from good Dr. Wilbraham, at the door of
the young lady's apartment in the palace at Richmond, a
letter was put into the clergyman's hands, to be delivered
to the heiress of De Grey, for such was the style of the
address. No time was lost by Dr. Wilbraham, in giving the letter to his lady's hands; and, on being opened,
it proved to be one of those anonymous epistles, which are
seldom even worth the trouble of deciphering, being
prompted always by some motive which dares not avow
itself.

However, as Lady Constance was very little in the
habit of receiving letters from any one, and certainly
none to which the writer dared not put his name, mere
curiosity would have prompted her, if nothing else, to
read it through; the more especially as it was written
in a fine and clerkly hand, and in a style and manner
to be acquired alone by high and courtly education. The
letter professed to be a warning from a friend, and informed the young lady, that the most rigorous measures
were about to be adopted towards her, in case of her still
refusing to comply with Wolsey's command, in respect to

her marriage with Lord Darby. The writer then hinted that perpetual seclusion in a convent, together with the forfeiture of all her estates, would be the consequence, if she could not contrive to fly immediately; but that, if she could, her person, at least, would be at liberty, and that a friend would watch over her property; and, as a conclusion, he advised her to leave Richmond by water, as the means which would leave the least trace of her course.

So singularly did this letter anticipate, not only her own fears, but also her own plans, that it instantly acquired, in the eyes of Lady Constance, an authenticity which it did not otherwise possess; and placing it in the hands of Dr. Wilbraham, she asked his opinion upon its contents.

"Pshaw!" cried the clergyman, when he had read it; "Pshaw! lady, it is all nonsense! The very reverend lord cardinal will never try to make you marry against your will. Do not frighten yourself about it, my dear lady; depend on it, 'tis all nonsense. Let me see it again." But after he had read it over once more, Dr. Wilbraham's opinion seemed in some degree to change. He considered the letter, and re-considered it, with very thoughtful eyes, and then declared that it was strange that any one should write it, unless it were true; and yet he would not believe that either. "Pray, lady, have you any idea who wrote it?" demanded he.

"I can imagine but one person," said Lady Constance, "who could possess the knowledge and would take the pains.—Margaret, leave us," she continued, turning to the waiting-woman. "I have heard, my dear Dr. Wilbraham," she proceeded, as soon as they were alone, "that you were in former times acquainted with an old knight, called Sir Cesar—I met him yesterday when I was out in the park—" Lady Constance paused, and a slight blush came into her cheek, as she remembered that the good clergyman knew nothing of the affection which subsisted between herself and Darnley; and feeling a strong repugnance to say that he was with her at the moment, she hesitated, not knowing how to proceed.

Dr. Wilbraham relieved her, however, by exclaiming, the instant she stopped: " Oh, yes, lady, in truth I know him well! He was the dearest and the best friend of my Lord Fitzbernard; and though unhappily given to strange and damnable pursuits—God forgive him—I must say, he was a friend to all the human race, and a man to be trusted and esteemed. But think you this letter came from him?"

" He is the only one," replied Constance, " on whom my mind could for a moment fix, as having written it."

" It is very likely," answered the clergyman: " it is very likely; and if it comes from him, you may believe every word that it contains. His knowledge, lady, is strange—is very strange—and is more than good—but it is sure. He is one of those restless spirits that must ever be busy; and human knowledge not being sufficient for his eager mind, he has sought more than he should seek, and found more than is for the peace of his soul."

" But if he make a good use of his knowledge," said Constance, " surely it cannot be very wicked, my dear sir?"

" It is presumptuous, lady," replied the clergyman: " it is most presumptuous, to seek what God has concealed from our poor nature."

" But if this letter be from him," said the lady, " and the bad tidings that it brings be true, what ought I to do? You, whom my dear father left with me, asking you never to quit me! you must be my adviser, and tell me what to do in this emergency; for sure I am, that you will never advise me to marry a man that I do not love, and who does not even love me."

" No, no, Heaven forbid! especially when you would rather marry Osborne," said the good clergyman with the utmost simplicity, looking upon it quite as a matter of course, which required no particular delicacy of handling. "And a much better thing, too, lady, in every respect," he continued, seeing that he had called up a blush in Constance's cheek, and fancying that it arose from a fear of his disapproving her choice. "If you will tell the lord cardinal all the circumstances, depend upon it he will not press you to do anything you dislike. Let him have the whole history, my dear lady: tell him that you do not love Lord Darby, and that he loves another; and then show him how dearly Darnley loves you, and how you love him in return; and then—"

"Oh, hush, hush! my dear Dr. Wilbraham," cried the lady, with the blood glowing through her fair clear skin, over neck, and face, and forehead. "Impossible! indeed, quite impossible! You forget."

"Oh yes, yes, I did forget," replied the chaplain; "Osborne does not wish his name to be known—I did forget. Very true! That is unfortunate. But cannot you just insinuate that you do love some one else, but do not like to mention his name?"

Lady Constance now endeavored to make the simple clergyman understand that under any circumstances she would be obliged to limit her reply to the cardinal to a plain refusal to wed Lord Darby; and though he could not enter into any feelings of reluctance on her part to avow her regard for Darnley, yet he fully comprehended that she was bound to hold undivulged the confidence of others. However, he did not cease to lament that this was the case, fully convinced in his own mind, that if she had been able to inform Wolsey of everything, the prelate, whom he judged after his own heart, would have unhesitatingly accorded his sanction to all her wishes: whereas, at present, her refusal might be attributed to obstinacy, being unsupported by any reason: and thus indeed, he observed, Sir Cesar's prediction might be fulfilled, and she obliged to fly to screen herself from the consequences. Dr. Wilbraham having admitted that there might be a necessity for flight, the mind of Constance was infinitely quieted; that being a point on which she had long, long wished to ascertain his opinion, yet had timidly held back, believing him to be unacquainted with the most powerful motive that actuated her. Nothing now remained but to learn whether he would so far sanction her proceedings as to accompany her; and she was considering the best means of proposing it to him, when she received a message to inform her that the cardinal waited her in the little tapestrial hall.

The moment which was to decide her fate, she plainly perceived to be now arrived; but, with all the gentle sweetness of her character, a fund of dauntless resolution had descended to her from a long line of warlike ancestors, which failed not to come to her aid in moments of danger and extremity; and though she had long dreaded the interview to which she was now called, she prepared to undergo it with courage and firmness. In obedience to the cardinal's command, then, she descended to the hall, accompanied by two of her women, who, though neither likely to suffer anything themselves, nor informed of their mistress's situation, yet felt much more alarm at the thoughts of approaching the imperious Wolsey, than even she did herself, burthened as her mind was with the certainty of offending a man the limit of whose power it was not easy to define.

At the door of the hall stood two of the cardinal's ushers, by whom she was introduced into the chamber to which Wolsey had retired after leaving the king, and where, seated in a chair of state, he waited her approach with many an ensign of his power and pomp about him. As she entered, he fixed his eye upon her, scarcely rising from his seat, but still slightly bending his head in token of salutation. The high blood of De Grey, however, though flowing in a woman's veins, and one of the gentlest of her sex, was not made to humble itself before the upstart prelate; and moving forward unbidden, Lady Constance calmly seated herself in a chair opposite to that of the cardinal, while her women placed themselves behind her; and thus, in silence, she waited for him to speak.

"Lady," said Wolsey, when she was seated, "at the time I saw you last, I proposed to you a marriage, which in point of rank, of fortune, and of every other accessory circumstance, is one which may well be counted amongst the best of the land, and for which I expected to have your thanks. Instead thereof, however, I received, at the moment of my departure for York, a letter wherein with a mild obstinacy and an humble pride, you did reject what was worthy of your best gratitude. A month now has waned since then, and I trust that calm reflection has restored you to your sense of what is right; which being the case, all that is past shall be pardoned and forgot."

"Your proposal, my lord cardinal," replied Lady Constance, "was doubtless intended for my happiness, and therein you have my most sincere gratitude; but yet I see not how I can have merited either reproof or pardon, in a matter which, alone concerning myself, no one can judge of but myself."

"You speak amiss, lady," said Wolsey haughtily; "ay, and very boldly do you speak. Am I not your guardian by the English law, and are you not my ward?—say, lady, say!"

"I am your ward, my lord," replied Lady Constance, her spirit rising under his oppression, "but not your slave—you are my guardian, but not my master."

"You are nice in your refinements, lady," said the cardinal; "but if I am your guardian, I am to judge what is good for you, till such time as the law permits you to judge for yourself."

"That time is within one month, my lord," answered Constance; "and even were it longer, I never yet did hear that a guardian could force a ward to wed against her will; though I at once acknowledge his right to forbid her marriage, where he may judge against it."

"Nay!" exclaimed Wolsey, "this is somewhat too much. This bold spirit, lady, becomes you not, and must be abated. Learn, that though I, in gentleness, rule you but as a ward, and, for your own good, control your stubborn will, the king, your sovereign, may act with a stronger hand, and, heedless of your idle fancies, compel you to obey."

"Then to the king, my sovereign, I appeal," said Constance, "sure that his justice and his clemency will yield me that protection which, God help me, I much need."

"Your appeal is in vain, proud girl!" cried the cardinal, rising angrily, while the fiery spirit flashed forth from his dark eye. "I stand here armed in his case with the king's power, and commissioned to speak his will; and 'tis in his name that I command you, on Thursday next, at God's altar, to give your hand to your noble cousin, Lord Darby—ay! and gratefully to give it, without which you may fall to beggary and want; for know, that all those broad lands which now so swell your pride, are claimed by Sir Payan Wileton, in right of male descent, and may pass away like a shadow from your feeble hand, leaving you naught but your vanity for dowry."

"Then let them pass," said Constance firmly; "for I would sooner a thousand times be landless, friendless, hopeless, than wed a man I do not love."

"And end your days in a nunnery, you should have added to the catalogue of woes you call upon your head," said the cardinal sternly; "for as I live, such shall be your fate. Choose either to give your vows to your cousin, or to heaven, lady; for no other choice shall be left you. Till Thursday next I give you to decide; and while you ponder, York Place shall be your abode. Lady, no more," he added, seeing her about to speak; "I have not time to argue against your fine wit. To-night, if I reach Westminster in time, I will send down your litter; if not, to-morrow, by eight of the clock; and be you prepared—I have done."

Constance would not trust her voice with any reply, for the very efforts she had made to conceal her agitation had but served to render it more overpowering; and it was now ready to burst forth in tears. Repressing them, however, she rose, and bending her head to the cardinal, returned to her own apartments. Here Dr. Wilbraham awaited her in no small anxiety, to know the event of her conference with Wolsey, which, as it had been so short, he judged must be favorable. Lady Constance soon undeceived him, however; and shocked and indignant at the cardinal's haughty and tyrannical conduct, he agreed at once with the lady that she had no resource but flight.

"It is very strange! very strange indeed!" cried the good man; "I have often heard that the lord cardinal is haughty and cruel,—and indeed men lay to his charge that he never does anything but for his own interests; but I would never believe it before. I thought that God would never have placed so much power in the hands of so bad a man: but His ways are inscrutable; and His name be praised! Now, my dear lady, what is to be done? Where are we to go? Had not I better go and tell Osborne, that he may know all about it?"

"On no account," replied Constance; "however painful it may be, my good friend,—and painful indeed it is I acknowledge,"—and while she spoke the long-repressed tears burst forth, and rolled rapidly over her face,—"I must go without even bidding him adieu. I would not for the world involve him at this time in a business which might bring about his ruin. He shall be innocent even of the knowledge of my flight, so that Wolsey shall have no plea against him. When his fate is fixed, and the storm is blown away, I will let him know where I am; for I owe him that at least. Even for you, my good Dr. Wilbraham, I fear," she continued. "If you fly with me, may it not bring down upon your head some ecclesiastical censure? If so, for heaven's sake, let me go with Margaret alone."

" Why it may, indeed," answered the chaplain thoughtfully. " I had forgot that. It may indeed. What can
be done?"

" Then you shall stay," replied Lady Constance with
some degree of mournfulness of accent at the thought
of the friendless loneliness with which she was going to
cast herself upon the wide inhospitable world. " Then
you shall stay indeed."

" What! and leave you to wander about alone, I
know not whither?" cried the good clergyman. " No,
my child, no! Did all the dangers in the world hang
over my head, where you go, there will I go too. If I
cannot protect you much, which, God help me! is not in
my power, at least I can console you under your sorrows,
and support you during your pilgrimage, by pointing continually to that Being who is the protector of the widow
and the orphan, the friend of the friendless and the desolate—Lady, I will go with you. All the dangers in the
world shall not scare me from your side."

A new energy semed to have sprung up in the bosom
of the clergyman; and by his advice and assistance Lady
Constance's plans and arrangements for her flight were
very soon completed.

It was agreed that herself, Dr. Wilbraham, and Mistress Margaret, the waiting-woman, should immediately
take boat, and proceed by water to the little village of
Tothill, from whence a walk of five minutes would bring
them to the house of the physician Dr. Butts, who, as
the old chaplain observed, was, though his nephew, a
man of an active and piercing mind, and would probably
find some means to facilitate their escape to France. By
landing some little way from his house, they hoped to
prevent their route from being traced afterwards, and
thus to evade pursuit; as to be overtaken and brought
back, would involve far more danger than even to remain where they were and dare the worst.

All this being determined between Lady Constance

and the clergyman, Mistress Margaret was called in, and informed of as much of the plan as was necessary to enable her to make up her mind whether she would accompany her young lady or not. Without a moment's hesitation, she decided upon going, and having received her orders, proceeded to arrange for their journey such articles of apparel as were absolutely necessary, together with all her lady's money and jewels. She also was deputed to inform the other servants that Lady Constance thought it best to follow the lord cardinal to York Place immediately, instead of waiting for the litter which he had promised to send, and that she only permitted herself and Dr. Wilbraham to accompany her.

Everything being ready, a man was sought to carry the two large bags, to which their baggage was restricted; and Constance prepared to put in execution the very important step on which she had determined. Her heart sank, it is true, and her spirit almost failed, as Dr. Wilbraham took her by the hand to lead her to the boat; but remembering to what she would expose herself if she stayed, she recalled her courage, and proceeded on her way.

In the antechamber, however, she had a painful scene to go through, for her women, not deceived by Mrs. Margaret's tale, clung round their mistress for what they deemed might be a last farewell. All of them, born upon her father's lands, had grown up as it were with her; and, for some good quality, called from amongst the other peasantry to the honor of serving the heiress De Grey, had become attached to her by early habit, as well as by the affection which her gentle manners and sweet disposition were certain to produce in all those by whom she was surrounded. Many a bitter tear was shed by the poor girls as they saw their lady about to leave them; and Constance herself, unable to refrain from weeping, thereby not only encouraged their grief, but confirmed their fears. Angry with herself for giving way to her feelings when she felt the absolute necessity of governing them strictly, Constance gently disengaged herself from her maids, and promising to let them hear of her soon, proceeded to the water-side, where they easily procured a boat to convey them down the river.

The irrevocable step was now taken, and Constance and the chaplain both sat in silence, contemplating the vague future, and striving, amidst all the dim uncertain shapes that it presented, to ascertain even, as far as probability went, what might be their own fate.

Long before arriving at Tothill, the sun had gone down; and the cold wind blowing from the river, chilled Lady Constance as she sat in the open boat without any other covering than a long veil added to her ordinary apparel. Notwithstanding this, she judged it best to bid their two rowers continue their course as far as Westminster, fearing that the little knowledge of the localities possessed either by Dr. Wilbraham or herself, might cause them to lose their way if they pursued their original intention of landing at Tothill, and hoping that the darkness, which was now coming thick upon them, would at least conceal their path from the boat to the house of Dr. Butts. To insure this, as soon as they had landed, Mrs. Margaret took one of the bags, and the good clergyman the other, and having satisfied the boatmen for their labor, the whole party began to thread the narrow tortuous lanes and streets, constituting the good town of Westminster.

After various turnings and windings, however, they discovered that they were not on the right track, and were obliged to ask their way of an old locksmith, who was just shutting up his shop. The direction they received from the worthy artificer was somewhat confused, and contained so many rights and lefts, that by the time they had taken two more turnings, each person of the three had got a different reading of the matter, and could in no way agree as to their farther proceeding.

"He said we were to go on, in this street, till we came to a lantern, I am sure," said Dr. Wilbraham.

"No, no, sir," cried Mrs. Margaret, "it was the next street after we had turned to the left. Did he not say, take the first street to the right, and then the first again to the right, and then the second to the left, and then go on till we came to a lantern?"

Dr. Wilbraham denied the position; and the matter was only terminated by Constance proposing that they should proceed to the second turning at least. "Then if we see a light in the street to the left," she continued, "we may reasonably suppose that that is the turning he meant, unless before that we find a lantern here too, and then we can but ask again. But make haste, my dear Dr. Wilbraham, for there is a man behind who seems as if he were watching us!"

This last observation quickened all their motions, and proceeding as fast as possible, they found that Mrs. Margaret was in the right; for immediately in the centre of the second turning to the left appeared a lantern, shedding its dim small light down the long perspective of the street; which, be it remarked, was highly favored in having such an appendage; few and scanty being the lights that, in that age, illuminated the streets of London after dark. Pursuing their way, then, towards this brilliant luminary, with many a look behind to ascertain whether they were followed, which did not appear to be the case, they found another street diverging to the right which shared in the beneficent rays of the lantern, and which, also, conducted into a known latitude, namely a little sort of square, that the chaplain instantly recognized as being in the immediate proximity of his nephew's dwelling.

The house of Dr. Butts now soon presented itself; and entering the little court before it, the clergyman was just about to knock against a door which fronted them, when some one entering the court from the street, laid hold of his arm, saying, "Stop, stop! If you please! you must come with me to my lord cardinal."

Worthy Dr. Wilbraham, finding somebody take him by the arm, turned round in a state of vexation and worry, if I may use the word, which overcame the natural gentleness of his disposition, and made him demand, rather sharply, what the stranger wanted with him.

"Why, doctor," replied the man, "you must come instantly to my lord cardinal, who has been struck with the pestilent air in returning from Richmond, and desires to consult with you on the means of preventing its bad effects."

"Pshaw!" cried the good chaplain pettishly, "I am not Dr. Butts! How could you frighten me so? We come to see the doctor ourselves."

"Stand out of the way, then, if you are not him," cried the man, changing his tone, and rudely pushing between the clergyman and Lady Constance. "The cardinal must be served first, before such as you, at least;" and knocking loudly against the door, he soon brought forth a page, who informed him that the physician was at the house of old Sir Guy Willoughby farther down in the same street.

On this news, the messenger immediately set off again, leaving Dr. Wilbraham to discuss what matters he liked with the page, now that his own insolent haste was satisfied. The servants instantly recognized their master's uncle, and permitted him, with his fair companions, to enter and take possession of his book-room, while awaiting his return; and the rosy maid, whom Sir Osborne had found scrubbing crucibles, now bustled about with good-humored activity to make the lady comfortable.

Long seemed the minutes, however, to the mind of poor Constance, till the physician's return. Her path was now entirely amidst uncertainties, and at each step she knew not whether it would lead her to safety or destruction.

Though it seemed to her an age, Dr. Butts was not really long in returning; but no language can depict the astonishment of his countenance, when he beheld Lady Constance with his uncle. " Odds life ! " cried he ; " what is this ? lady, are you ill, or well, or wise ? Uncle, are you mad, or drunk, or foolish ? "

The good clergyman informed him that he was in neither of the predicaments that he alluded to ; and then proceeded to relate the circumstances and motives which had induced them to resolve upon leaving the court of England and flying to France, to claim the protection of the French king, who was in fact the lady's sovereign as far as regarded her maternal estates.

" It's a bad business ! " cried Dr. Butts, who still stood in the middle of the floor, rubbing his chin, and not yet recovered from his surprise.

" It's a bad business ! I always thought it would be a bad business ! nay, nay, lady, do not weep," continued the kind-hearted mediciner, seeing the tears 'that began to roll silently over Constance's cheek ; " it is not so bad as that. Wolsey will doubtless claim you at the hands of the French king ; but Francis is not a man to give you up. However, take my advice—retire quietly to one of your châteaux, and live like a nun, till such time as this great friendship between the two courts is past. It will not last long," he added, with a sententious shake of the head ; " it will not last long. But, nevertheless, you keep yourself in France, as secretly as may be, while it does last."

" But how to get to France is the question," said Dr. Wilbraham. " We shall do well enough when we are there, I doubt not. It is how to get to France, that we must think of."

" Oh, we will manage that," replied Dr. Butts ; " we will manage that ; though, indeed, these are not things that I like to meddle with ; but nevertheless, I suppose I must in this case. Nay, nay, my dear lady, do not grieve. 'Slife ! you a soldier's daughter and afraid ! Nay, cheer up, cheer up. It shall all go right, I warrant."

The doctor now seated himself, and observing that Constance looked pale and cold, he insisted on her swallowing a Venice glass of mulled sack, and going to bed. As to the sack, he said, he would insure it for the best in Europe: and in regard to the beds in his house, he could only say, that he had once entertained the four most famous alchymists of the world, and they were not men to sleep on hard beds. "Taste the sack, lady; taste the sack!" he continued. "Believe me, it is the best medicine in the pharmacy, and certainly the only one I ever take myself. Then, while you go and court your pillow, I will devise some scheme with this good uncle of mine, to help you over the Frenchman's shore."

The physician's rosy maid was now called, and conducted Lady Constance and Mrs. Margaret to a handsome bed-chamber, where we shall leave them for the present; and without prying into Dr. Butts's household furniture, return to the consultation that was now going on below.

"Well, uncle," said the physician, as soon as Lady Constance had left them, "you have shown your wisdom truly, in running away with an heiress, for another man. On my life, you have beaten the man who was hanged for his friend, saying that he would do as much for him another time. Why, do you know, you can never show your face in England again?"

"My good nephew," replied Dr. Wilbraham quietly, "for all your fine words, if you had been in my situation, you would have done just as I have done. I know you, Charles."

"Not I, i'faith," cried Dr. Butts; "I would not have budged a foot."

"What! when you saw her cast upon the world, friendless, and helpless," cried the old man, "with nobody to advise her, with nobody to aid her, with nobody to console her? So sweet a girl, too! such an angel in heart, in mind, in disposition—all desolate, and alone, in this wide rough world!—Fie, Charles, fie! You would have gone with her!"

"Perhaps I might, perhaps I might," replied the physician; "however, let us now think of the best means of serving her. What can be done?"

As usual in such cases, fifty plans were propounded, which, on examination, were found to be unfeasible. "I have it," cried Dr. Butts, at last, after discarding an infinite variety; "There was a nun's litter came up yesterday, to the inn hard by. It will hold three; and you shall set off to-morrow by daybreak, as nuns."

"But how?" cried Dr. Wilbraham, with horror and astonishment depicted in his face. "You don't mean me to go as a nun?"

"Faith, but I do!" replied the physician: "it would be fully as bad for you to be discovered, as for Lady Constance. Now, there is no dress in the world, that I know of, but a nun's, that will cover your face, and hide your beard. Oh, you shall be a nun, by all means. I will get the three dresses this very night, from a frippery in Poole Street. I will knock them up, and you shall be well shaven to-morrow morning, and will make as fine an old Sister Monica as the best of them."

Dr. Wilbraham still held out stoutly, declaring that he would not so disguise himself, and disgrace his cloth, on any account or consideration; nor was it till the physician showed him plainly, that by this means alone Lady Constance's safety could be insured, that he would at all hear of the travesty thus proposed.

"Where, then, do you intend us to go?" asked Dr. Wilbraham, almost crying with vexation, at the bare idea of being so metamorphosed. "I cannot, and I will not, remain long in such a dress."

"Why, you must go down to Sandwich," answered the physician. "There is a religious house there, under a sub-prioress, about a mile out of the town, looking out over the sea. I know the dame, and a little money will do much with her. Nay, look not shocked, good uncle. I mean not to say that she is wicked, and would endanger her soul's repose for mammon; but she is one of those that look leniently on small faults, and would not choke at such an innocent sin, as helping you out of the cardinal's power. The time is lucky, too, for the cold wind last night has given his haughty lord cardinalship a flow of humors to the head, and he is as frightened about himself as a hen before a dray horse; so that, perhaps, he may not think of sending to Richmond so soon as he proposed."

"But, Charles," said Dr. Wilbraham, whose abhorrence of the nun's dress was not to be vanquished, and who would have been right glad to escape the infliction on any excuse; "will not your servants, who have seen us come in one dress, think it very strange when they see us go away in another?—and may they not betray us?"

"Pshaw!" cried Dr. Butts, "they see a thousand odder things every day, in a physician's house. Do you think I let my servants babble? No, no! They know well, that they must have neither eyes, ears, nor understanding for anything that passes within these doors. If I were to find that they ever did so much as to recollect a person they had once seen with me they should troop. But stay: go you to bed and rest. I will away for these dresses, and bespeak the litter for to-morrow, at five. At Sandwich, you are sure to find a bark for Boulogne."

The next morning, Dr. Wilbraham was awoke before it was light, by the physician entering his room with a candle in his hand, and followed by a barber; who, taking the good priest by the nose, shaved him most expeditiously, before he was out of bed, having been informed by Dr. Butts, that the person under his hands was a poor insane patient, who would not submit to any very tedious tonsorial operation.

When this was done, much to the surprise of the chaplain, who was, in truth, scarcely awake, the barber was

sent away, and the physician produced the long black
dress of a Benedictine nun, into which, after much en-
treaty, he persuaded Dr. Wilbraham to get: not, however, without the rest of his clothes; for no argument
would induce him to put on the woman's dress, without
the man's under it. First, then, he was clothed with his
ordinary black vest, and silk hose, above which came
a full and seemly cassock; and then, as a superstructure,
was placed on the top of all, the long black robes of the
nun, which swelled his bulk out to no inconsiderable size.
This, however, was not a disadvantage, for being tall
and thin, he had great need of some supposititious contour,
to make his height seem less enormous, when conjoined
with his female habiliments. Upon the whole, with the
rope tied tight round his middle, and the coif and veil, he
made a very respectable nun, though there was in the
whole figure, a certain long-backed rigidity of carriage,
and straggling wideness of step, that smacked infinitely of
the masculine gender.

When all was completed, the physician led his transformed uncle down to a little hall, to which Lady Constance and Mrs. Margaret had already found their way,
habited in similar garments to those which Dr. Butts had
furnished for the chaplain.

In point of beauty, Constance had never, perhaps,
looked better than now, when her small exquisite features,
and clear delicate complexion, slightly shaded by the
nun's cap, had acquired an additional degree of softness,
which harmonized well with the pensive, melancholy expression that circumstances had communicated to her
countenance. However, she was, perhaps, even more sad
and agitated than the night before, when haste had, in
some degree, superseded thought. She had now passed
a nearly sleepless night, during the long hours of which
a thousand fears and anxieties had visited her pillow, and
on rising, the necessity of quitting her customary dress,

and assuming a disguise, impressed more strongly than ever upon her mind the dangers of her situation.

The only person that seemed fully in her element, was Mrs. Margaret, who though, with the exception of a little selfishness, a most excellent being, could not be expected to have fulfilled for several years the high functions of lady's maid, without having acquired some of the spirit of the office. God knows, in Lady Constance's service, she had possessed small opportunity of exercising, in any way, her talents for even the little intrigue d' ante-chambre; and though, in the case of Sir Osborne, she had done her best to show her tact by retiring à propos, the present was the first occasion on which she could enjoy a real, bustling, energetic adventure; and to do her justice, she enacted the nun to the life. With a vastly consequential air, she hurried about, till the rustling of her black serge and the rattling of her wooden cross and rosary were quite edifying; and finding herself, by dress at least, on an equality with her mistress, she took the bridle off her tongue, and let it run its own course, which it did not fail to do with great vigor and activity.

On the entrance of Dr. Wilbraham, with his face clad in rueful solemnity, and his long strides, at every step spreading out the petticoats with which his legs were environed, like the parachute of a balloon when it begins to descend, Mrs. Margaret laughed outright, and even Lady Constance, while reproving her for her ill-placed gaiety, could hardly forbear a smile.

" My dear Dr. Wilbraham," said Constance, seeing the chagrin that sat upon his countenance, " for how much, how very much have I to thank you! And believe me, I feel deeply all the regard you must have for me, to induce you to assume a disguise that must be so disagreeable to you."

" Well," said Dr. Butts, " you are a sweet creature, and to my mind it would not be difficult to make a man do anything to serve you. However, sit you down, lady;

here is something to break your fast; and as it must serve
for dinner and supper, too, I will have you eat, whether
you are hungry or not; for there must be as little stopping
on the road as possible, and no chattering, Mrs. Margaret; mind you that."

Mrs. Margaret vowed that she was silence itself; and
the meal which the good doctor's foresight had taken
care to provide for them, being ended, he led them forth
by a different door from that which had given them
entrance, not choosing to trust even the servants, whose
discretion he had boasted the night before. Day had now
dawned, and in the court-yard of the inn they found a
large litter, or sort of long box, swung between two
horses, one before and the other behind, and accompanied
by a driver on horseback, who smacking his whip, seemed
tired of waiting for them.

" Come, get in, get in," cried he, " I have been waiting
half an hour. There's room enough for you, sure!" he
proceeded, seeing some little difficulty occur in placing
the travellers: " why, I brought four just like you from
Gloucester in it, three days ago. Here, come over to
this side, Mother Longshanks." This address to Dr.
Wilbraham had again very near overset Mrs. Margaret's
gravity; but at length all being placed, in spite of the
chaplain's long legs, which were rather difficult to pack,
the travellers took leave of the physician, and commenced their journey to the sea-coast.

All passed on tranquilly enough during the forenoon;
and at a little watering-house, where they stopped on
the road, they were enabled quietly to rehearse their
parts, as Sister Wilbraham, Sister Margaret, and Sister
Grey. The good clergyman declared, that his part should
be to keep down his veil and hold his tongue, and Mrs.
Margaret willingly undertook to be the talker of the
whole party, while Constance, not yet at all assured of
safety, listened for every sound with a beating heart, and

trembled at every suspicious look that she beheld, or fancied that she beheld, in the people round her.

As soon as the horses were sufficiently refreshed, they again began their journey, and had proceeded some way, when the galloping of a horse made itself heard behind them, and through the opening of the curtains they could perceive a sergeant-at-arms, with full cognizance, and accompanied by two followers, pass by the side of their vehicle. In a moment after, he stopped on overtaking their driver, who was a little in advance, and seemed to question him in a hasty tone. "Three nuns!" cried he at length. "I must see that!"

Constance, almost fainting, drew back in the corner of the litter. Dr. Wilbraham shrunk himself up to the smallest space possible; and in fact, Mrs. Margaret was the only one who preserved her presence of mind. "If it were the lord cardinal himself," whispered she to her lady, "he would never know you, my lady, in that dress."

In the meantime, the sergeant-at-arms rode up, and drew back the curtain of the litter. "Your pardon, ladies," said he, giving a look round, which seemed quite satisfactory, "I ask your pardon; but as I am sent in pursuit of some runaways, I was obliged to look in."

Here the matter would have terminated, had not Mrs. Margaret, desirous of showing off a total want of fear, replied, "Quite welcome, fair sir, quite welcome. We are travelling the same road." The officer replied; and this brought on a long allegory on the part of Mrs. Margaret, who told him that they were nuns of Richborough, who had been to London for medical advice for poor Sister Mary, there, in the corner (pointing to Dr. Wilbraham), who was troubled with the falling sickness. The sergeant-at-arms recommended woodlice drowned in vinegar, as a sovereign cure, which the pretended nun informed him they had tried; and though it must be owned that the abigail played her part admirably well, yet, nevertheless, she contrived to keep her lady and the chaplain in mortal fear for half an hour longer than was necessary.

At length, however, the officer taking his leave, rode away; and then descended upon the head of Mrs. Margaret, the whole weight of good Doctor Wilbraham's indignation. Not for many years had he preached such an eloquent sermon upon the duty of adhering strictly to truth, as on the present occasion; and he pointed clearly out to the waiting-woman, that she had told at least two-and-thirty lies more than the circumstances required. Mrs. Margaret, however, was obstinate in her error, and would not see the distinction, declaring angrily, that she would either tell no lies at all, and let it be known who they were, or she would tell as many as she thought proper.

" Margaret! " said Lady Constance, in a calm reproachful tone, that had more effect than a more violent reproof, " you forget yourself." The abigail was silent; but nevertheless she determined, in her own mind, to give the good doctor more truth than he might like, on the very first occasion; and such an opportunity was not long in occurring.

With the usual hankering which drivers and postilions always have for bad inns, the master of the litter did not fail to stop for the night at one of the smallest, meanest, and most uncomfortable little alehouses on the road; and on getting out of the vehicle, the three nuns were all shown into one room, containing two beds, one large and one small one. It may easily be supposed that such an arrangement did not very well suit the circumstances of the case; and Constance looked at Dr. Wilbraham, and Dr. Wilbraham at Constance, in some embarrassment. On inquiring whether they could not have another room, they were informed that there was indeed such a thing in the house, but that it was always reserved for guests of quality. The hostess was surprised at nuns giving themselves such airs: the room they had would do very

well for three people—and, in short, that they should have
no other.

During all this time, Mrs. Margaret remained obsti-
nately silent, but at length, seeing the distress of her mistress, she brought up her forces to the charge, and turned
the tide of battle. Attacking the hostess full tilt, she declared that there should be another room found directly,
informing her that the young lady was not a simple nun,
but noble and rich, and just named prioress of, the Lord
knows where; that Sister Mary—i.e., Dr. Wilbraham—
was badly troubled with a night-cough, which would keep
the prioress awake all night; and in short, that Sister
Mary must, and should, have a room to herself, for which,
however, they would willingly pay.

This latter hint overcame the hostess's objections, and
the matter being thus settled, they were allowed to repose
in peace for the night. Fatigue, anxiety, and want of
sleep had now completely exhausted Constance; and
weariness acting the part of peace, closed her eyes in
happy forgetfulness, till the next morning, when they
again set out for Sandwich.

Without any new adventure, they arrived at that town;
and after passing through it, quickly perceived the convent rising on a slight elevation to the left. As soon as
this was in sight, so that he could not miss his way, Dr.
Wilbraham got out of the litter, for the purpose of pulling off his nun's dress under some hedge, in order that, by
following a little later than themselves, he might appear
at the gate of the nunnery in his true character, without
the change being remarked by the driver of the litter, to
whom he said on descending, that he would follow on
foot.

After this, Constance and Mrs. Margaret proceeded
alone, and in a few minutes reached the convent, where,
presenting Dr. Butts's letter to the prioress, they were
received with all kindness and attention, and found themselves comparatively free from danger. Dr. Wilbraham

was not long in arriving, restored to his proper costume; and being admitted to the parlor, entered into immediate consultation with the superior and Constance, as to the best means of concluding their flight as happily as it had commenced.

CHAPTER XX.

" So catchers
And snatchers
Do toile both night **and day,**
Not needie,
But greedie,
Still prolling for their prey."

ALL those who have read the history of that little powerful nook of island earth, called Great Britain, must very
well know, that the imperious minister of Henry the
Eighth was not one to receive contradiction with patient
resignation : what then was his rage on hearing that Lady
Constance de Grey was not to be found at Richmond?
True to what he threatened, Wolsey had not failed, immediately on arriving in London, to send a horse-litter down
to Richmond for his fair ward, notwithstanding the late-
ness of the hour, and the cold he had himself experienced
on the water ; and towards eleven the same night, his
messengers returned, informing him that the lady was not
to be found in the palace ; adding also, that a man belonging to the gate had been employed to carry some luggage
for her down to a two-oared boat, which had received
her at the stairs, and rowed off towards Westminster.

This was the sum of all the news they had obtained,
but it was sufficient to guide Wolsey on the search which
he instantly prepared to institute for the fugitive. Before going to rest, he took every precaution for preventing her leaving the kingdom, ordered messengers to set
out early next morning for every port where she was
likely to embark, and commanded an officer to post to
Richmond that very night, and stationing himself at the
palace-stairs, to await the arrival of the men who rowed
the boat which had conveyed her away, giving him at the
same time an order for their arrest.

22

In regard to the couriers to the various ports, we shall leave them to their fate, not embarrassing ourselves with a search half over the realm, but shall pursue the movements of the other messenger, from whose operations very important results were obtained.

Though heartily wishing the cardinal and Lady Constance at the devil, the one as the proximate, the other as the remote cause of his night-ride, the officer got into his saddle, and accompanied by two followers, set out for Richmond, where they arrived towards two o'clock in the morning.

Nearly opposite to the landing on the left-hand side, stood the hospitable mansion of a beer-retailer, and in his window, even at the hour of two o'clock, was shining a lamp, whereat the officer marvelled, as the neighborhood of the palace enjoined order and sobriety amongst the multitude. Riding up, however, he dismounted; and pushing open the door, perceived that the tap-room was occupied by a single individual of the waterman species, whose sleepy head, nodding backwards and forwards, often approached so near the lamp upon the table, as to threaten his red nose with a conflagration. Without any regard for the rites of Morpheus, the officer shook the sleeper heartily by the shoulder, whereupon he started up, crying, " Well, I'm ready—how long you've been—I've been a-waiting this hour."

" Waiting for whom? " demanded the officer; " not for me, I'm sure, or, with my will, you'd waited long enough."

" Lord bless us, sir! I beg your worship's pardon," said the man, rubbing his eyes; " I thought you were the two yeomen that hired my boat to take the young lady to Lunnun. They promised to be back by one, and so Master Tapster lets me sit up here for 'em. I thought you were them two indeed."

" No, I'm a single man, and never was two in my life," answered the officer. " But about these two yeomen?—

'At one o'clock you say they were to come?—Pray, how came you to let them your boat?"

"Lord! because they asked me, sure," replied the waterman, "that's how."

"But how do you know they will ever bring it back again?" demanded the officer.

"Because they left me ten marks as a pledge," answered the other. "No, no, I wasn't to be outwitted. I saw they wanted the boat very bad, so I let them have it for a mark by the day; but I made them leave me ten others; so if the boat be lost or hurt, I've got double its worth in my own pocket."

"And what did they say they were going to do with it?" demanded the officer.

"Oh, I didn't ask," said the waterman; "but walking about, I saw them lay there at the stairs for near an hour, till presently comes down a young lady, and an old priest, and a waiting-woman, as I judged, and in they get, and away rows the boat toward Lunnun. They were lusty rowers, I warrant you, and good at the trade. But your worship seems mighty curious about them.

"Ay, and so curious," answered the officer, "that they shall both go with me to London, if they come hither to-night; and you too, Master Waterman, so hold yourself ready. Ho, Thomas! come in and stay with this worthy. See that he does not budge. You, Will, put up the horses, and then come down to me at the stairs."

The excellent tipstaff now, after cutting short the remonstrance of the boatman, proceeded to the water side, and crossing his arms, waited, with his eyes fixed upon the bright river, as it flowed on, rippling like waves of silver in the moonshine. In a few minutes he was joined by his follower, and before long a black spot appeared moving up the midst of the stream, while the plashing of distant oars began to make itself heard. As the boat came nearer, two men were plainly to be seen rowing it towards the landing-place, one of whom raising his head, when they were within a few yards distance, exclaimed, "Is that you, Master Perkins?"

"Ay, ay!" answered the officer, imitating, as well as he could, the gruff halloo of a waterman, and walking about with his hands in his breeches' pockets, as if to keep himself warm.

Without more ado, the boat pulled to the shore, and one of the men jumped out, whereupon the officer instantly caught him by the collar, exclaiming, "In the king's name, I charge you go with me."

"Pull off! pull off," cried the man to his companion; "by the Lord he has grabbed me—pull off, boy!"

The other rower, without scruple pushed from the shore before the tipstaff's men could secure the bow of the boat; and seeing his companion caught beyond the power of extrication, he snatched up the other oar, and pulled away down the river, as hard as he could.

"And now, what the devil do you want with me?" cried the man, sturdily, turning to the officer. "Come, off with your hands! Don't be fingering my collar so hard, or I'll crack your nutshell for you." And at the same time he struggled to shake off the other's grasp: but the officer, who seemed accustomed to deal with persons that did not particularly relish his ministry, very soon settled the question with his prisoner, by striking him a blow over the head, with a staff he carried, in such sort as to level him with the ground. It is wonderful how soothing to the prisoner's feelings this mild treatment seemed to be, for without any further effort, he suffered himself to be led away to the ale-house, from whence he was safely removed the next morning to Westminster, the original owner of the boat being carried along with him as a witness.

Carrying his game directly to York House, the worthy and exemplary tipstaff placed his charge in a place of security, and on the cardinal's return from Westminster Hall, informed him of all that he had done to fulfil the mission with which he had honored him. The cardinal praised the tipstaff's zeal, and beginning to suspect that there was some mystery in the business, more than the mere course which Constance had taken, he ordered the prisoner, and the evidence, to be brought instantly before him.

When the man appeared, rather pale with fright, and somewhat nervous with his night's entertainment, he pronounced a most eloquent oration upon the necessity of meeting death with firmness, warning the unhappy man, at the same time, that he had nothing to hope in this world, and bidding him to prepare for the next. Through the whole, however, he suffered to appear, implied, though not expressed, the possibility, that a free confession of all the culprit knew, concerning Lady Constance de Grey, and her evasion, might take the sting out of his offence, and disencumber his windpipe of the pressing familiarity with which it was threatened by a hempen cord.

The poor fellow was desperately frightened, especially as he had upon his conscience more than one hearty crime, which he well knew might at any time prove a sufficient excuse for sending him part of the way to heaven, whether he ever made the whole journey out or not. Therefore, having no great interest in concealing anything he knew, and every interest in the world in telling it, he fell down upon his knees, declaring that he would reveal all, if the cardinal would make a solemn promise that he should have the king's free pardon, and the church's, for every sin, crime, and misdemeanor he had committed up to that day.

It cost him nothing but a bit of parchment, and a little yellow wax, and so the cardinal promised; whereupon the culprit, still upon his knees, began as follows :—

" My master, Sir Payan Wileton—"

" Sir Payan Wileton is your master, then ? " cried Wolsey. " So, so! Go on."

" My master, Sir Payan Wileton, my gracious lord,"

continued the man, "after he had been with your grace
yesterday morning, returned home full speed to his house
by the water's edge, near Tothill, and suddenly despatched
one of our yeomen down to Richmond with a poor foolish priest, saving your grace's presence, who had been
with him some days. After that, he wrote a note, and
giving it to me, bade me take with me Black John, and
gallop down to the court like mad. Whenever we got
there, I was to speak with Hatchel Sivard, whom he had
set to spy all that passed at the palace, and who would
help me to hire a boat for the day. After that was done,
I was to seek the Lady de Grey, and give her the note;
and then, leaving our horses at the bating-house, I and
my fellow were to wait in the boat till the lady came, and
to row her whithersoever she directed; but, above all, to
seem like common watermen, and to take whatever payment she gave us. And if by chance she didn't come, we
were to give up the boat, and return."

As may be supposed, Wolsey was not a little surprised
at the intrigue which this opened to his view. "So!"
said he. "So! Hatchel Sivard, the page of the queen's
antechamber, is a pensioned spy of Sir Payan Wileton.
Good! Very good! Of course you carried the lady to
her relation's house, eh?"

"Not so, may it please your lordship's grace," replied
the man. "At first, she made as if she would have
stopped at Tothill, but then she bade us row on to Westminster, where she landed.

"But you saw where she went," cried Wolsey, his brow
darkening. "Mind, your life depends upon your speaking truth! Let me but see a shade of falsehood, and you
are lost!"

"As I hope for mercy, my lord, I tell you the whole
truth," replied the servant. "When she was landed, I
got out and followed; but, after turning through several
streets, I saw that they marked me watching, so I was
obliged to run down a narrow lane, hoping to catch them

by going round; but they had taken some other way, and
I found them not again."

Wolsey let his hand drop heavily upon the table, disappointed in his expectations. "You say them, fellow!
Who do you mean?" he demanded. "Who was with
her!"

"Her waiting-woman, your grace," answered the man,
"and an old priest, whom Sivard says is her chaplain."

"Ah!" said Wolsey, thoughtfully, "Dr. Wilbraham!
This is very strange! A staid good man—obedient to
my will—coinciding in the expediency of the marriage
I proposed. There must be some deeper plot here of
this Sir Payan Wileton. The poor girl must be deceived,
and perhaps not so much obstinate as misled. I see it—
I see it all. The wily traitor seeks her estates, and would
fain both stop her marriage and bring her within my displeasure. A politic scheme, upon my honor; but it shall
not succeed. Secretary, bid an usher speed to Sir Payan
Wileton, and, greeting him sweetly, request his presence
for a moment here."

It was the latter part of the above speech only that
met the ear of those around, the rest being muttered to
himself in a low and almost inaudible tone. "Pray, pray,
your lordship's grace!" cried the man, clasping his
hands in terror as soon as he heard Wolsey's command,
"do not let Sir Payan have me. I shall not be alive this
time two days, if you do. Indeed I shan't. Your grace
does not know him. There is nothing stops him in his
will; and I shall be found dead in my bed, or drowned
in a pond, or tumbled out of window, or something
like; and then Sir Payan will pretend to make an investigation, and have the crowner, and it will be found all
accident. If it is the same to your lordship's grace, I
would rather be hanged at once, and know what I'm
about, than be given up to Sir Payan, to die no one can
tell how."

"Fear not, fool," said Wolsey; "but tell the whole

truth, and you shall be safe; ay, and rewarded. Conceal anything, and you shall be hanged. Take him away, secretary, and examine him carefully. Make him give an exact account of everything he has seen in the house of Sir Payan Wileton, and after putting it in writing, swear him to it; and then—hark you," and he whispered something to the secretary, adding, " let him be there well used."

The man was now removed from the cardinal's presence; and waiting till the messenger returned from Sir Payan's, Wolsey remained in deep thought, revolving in his keen and scrutinizing mind all the parts of the shrewd plot he had just heard developed, and thinking over the best means of punishing Sir Payan Wileton, in such a manner as to make his fall most bitter. While thus engaged, one of his secretaries entered, and bowing low stood silent, as if waiting for permission to speak.

" What is it? " said Wolsey; " is it matter of consequence? "

The secretary bowed low again, and replied, " It is the herald's opinion my lord, upon the succession of the old Lord Orham of Barneton, the miser, who left the two chests of gold, as well—"

" I know, I know," said Wolsey. " How do they give it? I trust not to that base churl, William Orham, who struck my officer one day."

" Oh, no! your grace," replied the secretary, " there are two nearer than he is. But they say the succession is quite clear. Charles Lord Orham, the great grandfather of the last, had three sons, from one of which descends William Orham; but the eldest son succeeding had two sons and a daughter, all of whom married, and had issue; the eldest son, Thomas Lord Orham, him succeeded, who had only issue the last lord. The daughter had five sons, and the second son, Hugh Orham, had one only daughter, who married Arthur Bulmer, Earl of Willmington, who died, leaving issue one only daughter, Mis-

tress Katrine Bulmer, by courtesy the Lady Katrine Bulmer, whom your grace may remember the queen took
very young, when it was found that Lord Willmington's
estates went in male descent. She is the undoubted heiress."

"Ha!" said Wolsey, "that changes much. Well, well!
go see that it be clearly made out. Now, what says Sir
Payan Wileton?" he continued, turning to the messenger
who had just returned.

"The house is empty, so please your grace," replied
the usher, "all but one old porter, who says that Sir
Payan and his train set out for Chilman yesterday morning, after visiting your reverend lordship. He affirms,
moreover, that the knight never got off his horse, but
only gave orders that the priest should be sent down to
Richmond with all speed, and then rode away himself
for Kent."

"So!" said the cardinal, his lip curling into a scornful
sneer, "he finds his miscreant is caught, and thinks to
deceive me with a tale that would not cloud the eye-
sight of an old woman. But let him stay; he shall lull
himself into a fool's paradise, and then find himself
fallen to nothing. That will do." The usher fell back,
and for a moment Wolsey, as was often his wont, continued muttering to himself—"The Lady Katrine—she
was Darby's fool passion—if it lasts he shall have her—
'tis better than the other—besides, the other girl is away,
and he must have gold to bear out his charges at this
meeting at Ardres—so shall it be—well, well—Send in
whoever waits without," he added, speaking in a louder
voice, and then applied himself to other business.

CHAPTER XXI.

"Sir Knight, if knight thou be,
Abandon this forestalled place as erst,
For fear of farther harm.

                    FAIRY QUEEN.

IT may well be supposed, that under the circumstances
in which we left Sir Osborne, his feelings could not be
of the most tranquil or gratifying nature, when, after
having heard all that passed upon deck, he distinguished
the steps of the officer sent to arrest him, coming down
the ladder. Longpole, for his part, looked very much as
if he would have liked to display cold iron upon the occasion; but the knight made him a sign to forbear, and in a
moment after, a gentleman splendidly dressed, as one
high in military command, entered the cabin, followed
by two or three armed attendants.

"Well, sir," said the knight, not very well distinguishing the stranger's features by the light in which he stood.
"I suppose—" But he had not time to finish his sentence,
for the officer grasped him heartily by the hand, exclaiming, "Now heaven bless us! Lord Darnley, my dear
fellow in arms! how goes it with you these two years?"

"Excellent well, good Sir Henry Talbot," replied the
knight, frankly shaking the hand of his old companion.
"But say, does your business lie with me?"

"No, no! good faith," replied Sir Henry, "I came
upon a very different errand. Since I was with Sir
Thomas Peechy and yourself in Flanders, by my good
Lord Surrey's favor, I have obtained the command of
one of the king's great ships, and as I lay last night off
the mouth of the river, a pursuivant came down from
London, with orders to stop every vessel that I saw, and

search for a traitor who is endeavoring to make his escape to the continent."

The knight's cheek burned, and for a moment he hesitated whether to avow himself at once, and repel the opprobrious epithet thus attached to the name he had assumed, and under which he felt full sure he had never merited aught but honor. A moment's thought, however, showed him the madness of such a proceeding, and he replied, " I believe you will find no greater traitor here, Sir Henry, than myself."

The officer smiled. " If that be the case," replied he, " I may as well row back to the ship. Perhaps he may be in the other vessel that lies to there, about a mile to windward. But come, Darnley, leave this filthy Dutch tub, come with me aboard, and after we have searched the other, I will land you in any port to which you are going, if it be between Middlebourg and Boulogne."

Although the knight did not feel himself bound, even by the most chivalrous principles of honor, to betray his own secret to Sir Henry Talbot, yet he did not consider himself at liberty to take advantage of his offer, and thus make one of the king's own ships the means of conveying him away from pursuit. He therefore replied, that as he was going to Dunkirk in some haste, and the Dutchman was steering thither straight, he thought it would be best to proceed without changing his ship, though he felt extremely obliged by the offer.

The officer received his excuses in good part, and bidding him farewell, with many hearty wishes for his future prosperity, he mounted again to the deck, called his men together, abused the Dutchman vigorously for a few minutes, and getting into the boat, rowed away for his own vessel.

It is hardly necessary here to inform the reader, that the distinction which at present exists between the naval and military services, has not been known above a hundred and fifty years; and that, consequently, Sir Henry

Talbot's having distinguished himself on land, so far from being a disqualification, was one of the highest recommendations to him in the sea service!

Deceiving himself, as we have seen, Sir Henry Talbot left the young knight to meditate over the conduct of Wolsey, who would indeed have committed an egregious piece of folly in sending to arrest him by the name of Sir Osborne Maurice alone, if he had known him to be Lord Darnley, as Sir Osborne thought. Attributing it, however, to one of those accidental omissions, which often disconcert the best arranged proceedings, the knight was congratulating himself on his good fortune, when Master Skippenhausen descended to offer his felicitations also, exclaiming, " My Cot! where did you hide yourself? Under that pile of hammocks, I'll warrant."

" No, you man of salt herrings! No, you cousin german to a tub of butter! " exclaimed Longpole, whose indignation at the captain for having by his delay of the night before, put them in such jeopardy, now broke forth irresistibly. " If it had not been for you, we should never have run any risk, and don't flatter yourself that either you or your dirty hammocks either, had any hand in saving us."

" How did I make you run any risk, pray? " exclaimed the master. " You would have made me and my ship run a risk if you had been found in it; but I made you run none."

" Stockfish, you lie! " cried the custrel. " Did you not lie in the mouth of the river all last night, when, if the blood in your veins had been anything but muddy Dutch puddle, of the heaviest quality, you would have had us over to Dunkirk by this time. Deny it if you dare, Dutchman, and I will prove it upon your body, till I leave you no more shape than one of your own cheeses."

The Dutchman bore the insolence of Longpole with all that calm magnanimity for which his nation is famed. However, Sir Osborne desired his attendant to be silent,

and merely begging Master Skippenhausen to carry them
to their destination as soon as possible, the matter ended.

It was night before they arrived at Dunkirk, and, without troubling the reader with all the details of their dis-
embarkation, we shall merely beg him to look into the
little hall of the Flemish inn, and see the knight and
Longpole seated at the same table, according to the custom of the day, while the host, standing behind the chair
of Sir Osborne, answers the various questions which from
time to time are addressed to him; and that black-eyed,
smooth-faced, dingy serving-boy, who one might swear
was a truly begotten son of Hans Holbein, filches away
the half-finished tankard of raspis from Longpole's elbow,
and supplies its place with an empty one.

"And is Sir Albert of Koenigstein gone to Ratisbon
too?" demanded Sir Osborne, pursuing the inquiries,
which he was engaged in making concerning his old
comrades, amongst whom a sad dispersion had taken
place during his absence.

"Indeed I cannot tell, Sir Knight," replied the landlord; "but very likely he is with the Count of Shoenvelt,
at Cassel."

"What does Shoenvelt at Cassel?" asked the knight
thoughtfully.

"He is collecting adventurers, they say, sir, under a
commission from the emperor," replied the host. "Some
think, to go against the Moors, but most people judge, to
protect the frontier against Robert de la Mark."

"But Koenigstein would not serve under him," said
Sir Osborne, meditating over what he heard. "He is a
better captain a thousand times, and a nobler spirit."

"Well, sir," answered the landlord, "I tell you only
what I heard. Somebody told me so, I am sure. Perhaps they command together. Boy, give his worship
another tankard; don't you see that is out?"

"Odds fish!" cried Longpole, "what, all gone! Your
measures, mine host, are not like that certain knight's

purse, that was no sooner empty than full again, It seems to me they are no sooner full than empty."

"At Cassel, did you say he is?" demanded Sir Osborne.

"Not exactly at Cassel, Sir Knight," replied the host, glad to pass away from the subject of the tankard; "but you know Mount St. Hubert, about a league from Cassel. Your worship will find him there."

Sir Osborne made no reply; and, after a while the host and his legion cleared the table of its encumbrances, and left the knight and his follower to pursue their own thoughts undisturbed.

The report that Albert of Koenigstein, his old friend and companion at arms, had joined the adventurers which the Count of Shoenvelt was collecting at Cassel, led him to imagine, that the cause in which they would be engaged was one that he could himself embrace with honor; although Shoenvelt's name had not been hitherto very famous for the better qualities of chivalry. He doubted not, also, that from the high station which he himself had filled in the armies of Burgundy, he should easily obtain that rank and command which he was entitled to expect, amongst the troops thus assembled.

The history of the various bands of adventurers of that day offers us some of the most curious and interesting particulars of a curious and interesting age. These companies, totally distinct from the regular armies of the time (if regular armies they might be called), were generally levied by some enterprising feudal lord; and commencing, most frequently, amongst his own vassals, afterwards swelled out into very formidable bodies by a junction with other bands, and by the continual accession of brave and veteran soldiers, cast upon the world by the sovereigns they had served, when peace rendered their swords no longer necessary. Of course, the numbers in these companies varied very much according to circumstances, as well as their regulations and deportment.

Sometimes they consisted of thousands, sometimes of simple tens. Sometimes, with the strictest discipline and the most unshrinking valor, they entered into the service of kings, and decided the fate of empires: sometimes they were little better than roving bands of robbers, that lived by rapine, and hardly acknowledged law. Most frequently, however, in the age of which we treat, they volunteered their support to the armies of their own sovereign, or his allies, and often proved more active than the body they came to aid.

But to proceed:—the next morning, by day-break, Sir Osborne and his companion were once more on horseback, and on their way to Mount Cassel; the knight having determined to learn, in the first place, the views of Shoenvelt, and to examine the real state of his troops, before he offered himself as a companion in the adventure. In case he found their object such as he could not himself seek, his mind was hardly made up, whether to offer his services to the emperor, or to Francis, King of France. His old habits, indeed, tended to make him prefer the imperial army; but from all he had heard of the new chief of the German confederacy, there was a sort of cold-blooded, calculating policy in his every action, that little accorded with the warm and chivalrous feelings of the young knight: while, at the same time, there was in the whole conduct of Francis, a noble, candid generosity of heart, a wild enthusiastic spirit of daring and adventure, that wonderfully attracted Sir Osborne towards him.

Journeying on with a quick pace, Mount Cassel soon rose to the travellers' sight, starting out of the vast plains in which it stands, like some high spirit towering above the flat multitude.

Sweeping round its base, the knight turned his horse towards a lesser hill, at about two miles' distance, the top of which was, in that day, crowned by the castle of Shoenvelt.

A broad, fair road offered itself for the travellers'
horses, winding along a narrow rocky ridge, which was
the only part that, slowly descending, joined the hill
gradually to the plain.

Pressing on, Sir Osborne soon arrived at the gate, and
demanded if Sir Albert of Koenigstein was in the castle.

Though in time of peace, no gate was opened, and the
sole response of the soldier to whom he spoke, was, " Who
are you?" uttered through the grille of the barbican.
The knight gave his name, and the man retired without
making any further answer.

" This looks like precaution, Longpole," said the knight.
" Methinks they would run no great danger in letting two
men pass the gate, though they may be armed at all
points."

" I suppose the custom of this castle, is like the custom
of a rat-hole," replied Longpole, " to let but one in at a
time. But I hope you won't stay here, my lord. I have
an invincible hatred at being built up. As much of the
camp and fair field as you like, but Lord deliver me from
stone and mortar. Besides, this place smacks marvellously of a den of free companions. Look at that fellow
with the pike on his shoulder; neither his morion nor his
corset have known sand and the rubbing-stick since his
great ancestor was drowned with Pharaoh; and 'twas
then his harness got so rusty, depend on it."

" In a Red Sea, I am afraid," said Sir Osborne. " But
here comes the janitor."

As he spoke, the guardian of the gate approached, with
a bunch of keys, and soon gave the knight the means of
entrance. Sir Osborne, however, still held his bridle in,
and demanded once more, if Sir Albert of Koenigstein
was in the castle.

" I cannot tell you, sir," replied the soldier. " I know
not the title of all the knights here. All I can say is, that
I gave your name and errand to my lord, who sits at
table in the great hall, and that he greets you heartily,
and invites you in."

At this moment a group of gentlemen appeared, coming through the gate of the inner ballium, and Sir Osborne, not doubting that they had been sent by the count to conduct him to the hall, saw that he could not now avoid entering, whether the officer he sought was there or not. Riding through the gate, then, he dismounted, and giving his horse to Longpole, met the party he had seen advancing, the principal of whom, with much reverence and courtesy, prayed the Sire de Darnley, on the part of Count Shoenvelt, to enter and quaff a cup of wine with him. Sir Osborne expressed his willingness to do so, in the same strain, and then repeated his inquiry for his friend.

"We are unhappy in not having his company," replied the gentleman; "but I believe the count expects him here in a few days."

He was a young man who spoke, and there was a sort of flush came over his cheek, as he announced the probable coming of Koenigstein, which induced Sir Osborne to imagine that his report was not very correct; and fixing his eye upon him, he merely said, "Does he? with a slight degree of emphasis.

"Yes, sir, he does!" cried the youth, coloring still more highly. "Do you mean to say he does not?"

"Not in the least," said Sir Osborne; "as you may see by my seeking him here; and I am sure, that so gallant a squire as yourself, would never swerve from truth."

The young man bent down his eyes, and began playing with his sword-knot, while Sir Osborne, now perfectly convinced that the whole tale was a falsehood, followed on in silence, prepared to act according to this opinion. In a few minutes they passed through the portal of the keep, and entered at once into the great hall, up the midst of which was placed a long table, surrounded by the chief of Shoenvelt's adventurers, with various pages and varlets, serving the meats and pouring out the wine. Round upon the walls hung the arms of the various guests, cum-

23

bering every hook or peg that could be found; and where these had been scanty, they were cast upon the ground behind the owners' seats, together with saddles and bards, and other horse caparisons; while in the corner leaned several score of lances, mingled amongst which were one or two knightly pennons, and many a sheaf of arrows, jostled by the upstart weapons, destined in the end to banish them from the stage, such as hackbuts, hand-guns, and other new invented fire-arms.

At the farther end of the table, digging deeply with his dagger in a chine of wild boar pork, which had been just placed before him, sat the Count of Shoenvelt himself, tall, strong-limbed, and grisly, with a long, drooping, hooked nose, depressed at the point, as if some one had set their thumb on it, at the same time squeezing it down, and rather twisting it on one side. This implement was flanked, if one may use the term, by a pair of small keen hawk's eyes, which expressed more active cunning than vigorous thought; while a couple of immense ears, sticking out on each side of his head, and worn into various irregular calosities by the pressure of his helmet, gave a singular and brute-like appearance to his whole visage, not easy to be described. He was dressed in a hacqueton, or close jacket of buff leather, laced with gold, on which might be seen, especially towards the arms, sundry daubs and stains, to the number of which he had just added another, by dashing all the gravy over his sleeve, in his furious hacking of the large and stubborn piece of meat before him. This accident had called into his face not the most angelic expression, and as he sat he would have made a good picture of an inferior sort of devil; the whole effect being heightened by a strong ray of light passing through a purple pane of the stained-glass window, and falling with a ghastly lustre upon his dark ferocious countenance.

The moment, however, that he perceived Sir Osborne, his brow was smoothed, and rising from his seat, he advanced towards him with great expressions of joy. "My dear Lord of Darnley," cried he, taking him in his arms and pressing him to his bosom with a hug, that the knight would willingly have dispensed with; "welcome! a thousand times welcome to St. Hubert's Castle! Whether you come to stay with us as a companion, or whether you are but a passing guest, your visit is an honor and a delight to all within these walls. Knights and gentlemen," continued he, "pledge me all a cup to the health of the Sire de Darnley."

To the party by whom he was surrounded, such a proposal was, what nobody felt at all inclined to reject, and consequently there was instantly a vast rattling of cups and tankards, and no one complained that their bowl was too full. All pledged Lord Darnley; and he could not refuse to do them justice in a cup of wine. After which, taking the seat that Shoenvelt assigned him by his side, the knight gazed over the various grim and war-worn faces which were gathered round the table, some of which he knew merely by sight, and some, who having exchanged a word or two with him in the various reciprocations of military service, now looked as if they claimed some mark of recognition. Sir Osborne was not the man to reject such appeal, and he gave the expected bow to each, though amongst them all, he saw no one who had greatly distinguished himself for those high feelings and generous virtues that ever mark the true knight.

Many were the questions that were asked him; many the conjectures that were propounded to him for confirmation, respecting the designs of France and England, and of Germany; and it was some time before he could cut them short, by informing his interrogators that he had been for the last three months in his own country, so deeply occupied by his private affairs, that he had given no attention to the passing politics of the day.

As soon as the meal, which was drawing towards its end when Sir Osborne entered, was completely concluded,

Shoenvelt rose, and begged to entertain him for a few minutes in private, which, being agreed to, he led him forth into a small space enclosed with walls, wherein the provident chatelain had contrived to assemble against the hour of need, a very sufficient store of cabbages, turnips, carrots, and other canaille of the vegetable kingdom, which might be very serviceable in case of siege. Here, walking up and down a long path that bordered the beds, with Sir Osborne on his right, and a knight named Wilsten (whom he had invited to the conference) on his left, Shoenvelt addressed Lord Darnley somewhat to the following effect, generally while he did so fixing his eyes upon vacancy, as a man does who recites awkwardly a set speech, but still from time to time giving a quick sharp glance towards the knight's countenance, to see the impression he produced.

"Valiant and worthy knight—a-hem! a-hem!" said Shoenvelt. "Every one, whether in Germany or France, England or Spain, or even here in our poor Duchy of Burgundy—a-hem! a-hem! Every one, I say, has heard of your valorous feats and courageous deeds of arms; wherefore it cannot be matter of astonishment to you, that wherever there is a captain, who having gathered together a few hardy troops—a-hem! a-hem!—is desirous of signalizing himself in the service of his country —a-hem!—wherever there is such a one, I say, you cannot be surprised that he wishes to gain you to his aid." Here Shoenvelt gave a glance to Wilsten to see if he approved his efforts! after which he again proceeded. "Now you must know, worthy knight, that I have here in my poor castle, which is a strong one, as you may perceive—a-hem!—no less than five hundred as good spearmen as ever crossed a horse, which I have gathered together for no mean purpose. A purpose," he continued, mysteriously, "which, if effected, will not only enrich all persons who contribute their aid thereto, but will gain them the eternal thanks of our good and noble emperor— a-hem! a-hem!—I could say more—a-hem!"

" Tonder, man! tell him all," cried Wilsten, who had
served with Sir Osborne, and had the reputation of being
a brave and gallant knight, though somewhat addicted
to plunder; " or let me tell him, for your bedevilled hems
take more time than it would to storm a fort. This is
the case, Sir Knight. A great meeting is to take place
between the King of France and the King of England at
the border, and all the nobility of France are in motion
through Picardy, and the frontier provinces, covered with
more gold than they ever had in their lives before. Even
Francis himself, like a mad fool, is running from castle
to castle, along the frontier, sometimes with not more
than half a dozen followers. Now, then, fancy what a
rich picking may be had amidst these gay French gallants;
and if Francis himself were to fall into our hands, we
might command half the kingdom for his ransom—eh?"

" But I thought that the two countries were at peace,"
said the knight, with a coldness of manner sufficiently
marked, as he thought, to prevent any further communication of the kind.

Wilsten, however, was not to be stopped, and replied,
" Ay, a sort of peace—a peace that is no peace on the
frontiers. Don't let that frighten you—we can prove
that they were the first aggressors? Why, did not they,
less than ten days ago, attack the garrison of St. Omer's,
and kill three men in trying to force the gate? Have
they not ravaged half Hainault? But, however, as I said,
be not startled at that; Shoenvelt saw the emperor about
two months ago, who gave him to understand that we
could not do him a better service than either to take
Francis alive, or give him a stroke with a lance. And
fear not that our plans are well laid; we have already two
hundred men scattered over the frontier; every forest,
every village, has its ten or twelve, ready to join at a
moment's notice, when we sound to the standard: two
hundred more follow to-night, and Shoenvelt and I to-
morrow, in small parties, so as not to be suspected. Al-

ready we have taken a rich burgher of Beauvais, with
velvets and cloths of gold, worth a hundred thousand
florins. But that is nothing; the king is our great object,
and him we shall have, without some cursed accident
prevents it; for we do not hunt him by report only, we
have our gaze-hound upon him, who never loses sight.
What think you of that, Sir Knight? Count William of
Firstenberg, Shoenvelt's cousin, who is constantly with
Francis, ay, and well beloved of him, is our sworn companion, and gives us notice of all his doings. What
think you of that, Sir Knight—eh?"

"I think him a most infernal villain!" cried Sir Osborne, his indignation breaking forth in spite of his better
judgment. "By heaven! before I would colleague with
such a traitor I'd have my hand struck off."

"Ha!" cried Shoenvelt, who had marked the knight's
coldness all along, and now burst into fury. "A traitor!
Sir Knight, you lie—ho! shut the gates there. By heaven,
he will betray us. Wilsten! call Marquard's guard—
down with him to a dungeon;" and laying his hand upon
his sword, he prepared to stop the knight, who now
strode rapidly towards the gate.

"Nay, nay," cried Wilsten, holding his companion's
arm. "Remember, Shoenvelt, 'tis your own hold. He
must not be hurt here—nay, by my faith he shall not—we
will find a more fitting place—hold, I say."

While Shoenvelt, still furious, strove to free himself
from Wilsten, Sir Osborne passed the gate of the garden,
and entered the space of the outer ballium, where Longpole had pertinaciously remained with the two horses, as
close to the barbican, whose gate had been left open when
they entered, as possible, seeming to have had a sort of
presentiment that it might be necessary to secure possession of the bridge.

The moment the knight appeared without any conductors, the shrewd custrel conceived at once that something had gone wrong, sprang upon his own horse, gave

a glance round the court to see that his retreat could not be cut off, and perceiving that almost all the soldiers were near the inner wall, he led forward his lord's charger to meet him.

Sir Osborne had his foot in the stirrup, when Shoenvelt, now broken away from Wilsten, rushed forth from the garden, vociferating to his men to shut the gate, and to raise the draw-bridge, but in a moment the knight was in the saddle; and spurring on, with one buffet of his hand in passing, he felled a soldier, who had started forward to drop the cullis, and darted over the bridge.

"On to the other gate, Longpole," cried he. "Quick. Make sure of it;" and turning his own horse, he faced Shoenvelt, who now seeing him gone beyond his power, stood foaming under the arch. "Count of Shoenvelt!" cried he drawing off his glove, "thou art a liar, a traitor, and a villain, which, when you will, I will prove upon your body. There lies my gage;" and casting down his gauntlet, he galloped after Longpole, who stood with his sword drawn in a small outer gate, which had been thrown forward even beyond the barbican.

"Up, archers, up," cried Shoenvelt, storming with passion; "up, lazy villains—a hundred crowns to him who sends me an arrow through his heart. Draw! draw, slaves! Draw! I say."

In a moment an arrow stuck in Sir Osborne's surcoat, and another lighted on his casque, but, luckily, as we have seen, the more easily to carry his harness, or armor, he rode completely armed, and the missiles from the castle fell in vain.

However, lest his horse should suffer, which not being sufficiently covered by its bard to insure it from a chance arrow, might have been disabled at the very moment he needed it most, the knight spurred on as fast as possible, and having joined Longpole, descended the narrow way by which they had mounted.

Still for some way the arrows continued to fall about

them, though with less assured aim and exhausted force; so that the only danger that remained, might be apprehended, either from the guns of the castle being fired upon them, or from Shoenvelt sending out a body of spearmen in their pursuit. Neither of these, however, took place; the inhabitants of the country round, and the commander of Cassel being too jealous and suspicious of Shoenvelt already, for him to do anything which might more particularly attract their attention; and to this cause, and this cause only, was Sir Osborne indebted for his unpursued escape.

As soon as they were out of reach of immediate annoyance, the knight reined in his horse, and turned to see if Shoenvelt showed any symptoms of an inclination to follow. But all was now quiet: the gates shut, the drawbridge raised, and not even an archer to be seen upon the walls. Sir Osborne's eye, however, ran over tower, and bartizan, and wall, and battlement, with so keen and searching a glance, that if any watched him in his progress, it must have been from the darkest loophole in the castle, to escape the notice of his marking eye.

Satisfied at length with his scrutiny, he again pursued his journey down the steep descent into the vast plain of Flanders, and turned his horse towards Mount Cassel, giving Longpole an account, as he went, of the honorable plans and purposes of the good Count of Shoenvelt.

"Odd's life, my lord," said Longpole, "let us go into that part of the world too. If we could but get a good stout fellow or two to our back, we might disconcert them."

"I fear they are too many for us," replied the knight, "though it seems that Shoenvelt, avaricious of all he can get, and afraid that aught should slip through his hands, has divided his men into tens and twelves, so that a few spears well led, might do a great deal of harm amongst them. At all events, Longpole, we will buy a couple of lances at Cassel, for we may yet chance to meet with some of Shoenvelt's followers on our road."

Conversing over their future proceedings, they now mounted the steep ascent of Mount Cassel, and approached the gate of the town, the iron grate of which, to their surprise, was slowly pushed back in their faces as they rode up. "Ho! soldier, why do you shut the gate?" cried Sir Osborne, "don't you see we are coming in?"

"No, you are not," replied the other, who was a stiff old Hainaulter, looking as rigid and untractable as the iron jack that covered his shoulders; "none of Shoenvelt's plunderers come in here."

"But we are neither friends nor plunders of Shoenvelts," said the knight; "we are his enemies, and have just made our escape from St. Hubert's."

"Ah! a fine tale! a fine tale!" replied the soldier, through the barred gate, which he continued slowly and imperturbably to fasten against them. "We saw you come down the hill, but you don't step in here to-night— so you had better ride away, before the captain sends down to make you. We all know that you can lie as well as rob."

"By my life if I were in, I'd split your morion for you," said the knight, enraged at the cool nonchalance of the Hainaulter.

"Doubtless," replied he, in the same sort of indifferent snuffling tone, "doubtless—you look like it—and that's one reason why I shall keep you out."

Sir Osborne wasted no more words on the immovable old pikeman, but angrily turning his horse, began again to descend the hill. A little way down the steep, there was even then, as now, a small hamlet serving as a sort of suburb to the town above, and towards this the knight took his way, pausing to gaze, every now and then, on the vast interminable plain that lay stretched at his feet, spread over which, he could see a thousand cities and villages, all filled with their own little interests and feelings, wherein he had no part or sympathy, and a thousand roads leading away to them, in every direction, with-

out any one to guide his choice, or to tell him on which
he might expect prosperity or disaster.

"To Aire," said he, after he had thought for some
time. "We will go to Aire; I hear that the Count de
Ligny, whom I fought at Isson, is there, and the Chevalier Bayard, and many other gallant knights and gentlemen, who, perhaps, may welcome me amongst them. Is
not that the smoke of a forge, Longpole? Perhaps we
may find an armorer? Let us see."

As the knight had imagined, so it proved, and on their
demanding two strong lances, the armorer soon brought
them forward a bundle of stiff ash staves, bidding them
choose. After some examination to ascertain the sound-
ness of the wood, their choice was made, and the Fleming proceeded to adjust to the smaller end of each, two
hands'-breadths of pointed iron, which being fastened
and clenched, the knight and his follower paid the charge,
and taking possession of their new weapons rode away,
directing their course towards Hazebrouck, in their way
to Aire.

Their progress now became necessarily slow; for
though both horses were powerful in limb and joint, and
trained to carry great burdens and endure much fatigue,
yet the weight of a heavy iron bard, together with that
of a tall strong man armed at all points, was such that
in a long journey it necessarily made itself felt. Evidently perceiving by the languor of his motions, that the
charger which bore him was becoming greatly wearied,
Sir Osborne ceased to urge him, and proposed to stop
for the evening at the very first village that could boast
of an inn. Nevertheless, it was some time before they
met with such a one, most of the hamlets on the road
being too poor and insignificant to require or possess
anything of the kind. At length, however, a small neat
house with a verdant holly-bush over the door, invited
their steps, and entering, Sir Osborne was saluted heartily by the civil host, who with brandished knife, and

snowy bib, was busily engaged in cooking various savory messes for any guest that Providence might send him. Some specimens of his handiwork were placed before the knight and Longpole, as soon as their horses had been taken care of; and an excellent bottle of old wine, together with some fatigue, induced them to linger a little at the table.

The lattice, which was open, looked out across the road to the little village green, where was to be seen many a school-boy playing in the fine May evening, and mocking, in his childish sports, the sadder doings of the grown up children of the day. Here, horsed upon their fellows' backs, were two that acted the part of knights, tilting at each other with broomsticks; and there, marshalled in fair order by a youthful captain, marched a body of young lansquenets, advancing and retreating, wheeling and charging, with no small precision.

Sir Osborne watched them for a while, in somewhat of a moralizing mood, till his musing was disturbed by the trotting of a horse past the window, and in a moment after he heard the good-humored voice of the host addressing the person who arrived.

"Ah! Master Frederick," he said, "what, back again so soon! I told you you would soon be tired of soldiering."

"Nay, nay, Regnault," answered a voice that Sir Osborne thought he had heard before; "I am not tired of soldiering, and never shall be, but I am tired of consorting with a horde of plunderers, for such is Shoenvelt, and such are all his followers. But while I lead my horse to the stable, get me something to eat, good Regnault, for I do not want to go back to the hall till I have dented my sword at least."

"What, are you going to it again? cried the host; "stay at home, Master Frederick! Stay at home! Take care of the house your father has left you. If you are not so rich as the baron, you have enough, and that is better than riches, if one knew it."

"My father was a soldier," answered the young man, "and distinguished himself; and so will I too, before I sit down in peace."

Here the conversation ceased, and the host entering the room in which sat the knight and follower, began to lay out one of the small tables with which it was furnished. "That is as good a youth," said he addressing Sir Osborne, while he proceeded with his preparations:—"that is as good a youth as ever breathed, if he had not taken this fit of soldiering. His father was a younger brother of old Count Altaman, and after many year's service, came to our village, and bought a piece of ground, where he built a house—your worship may see it from here, over the side of the hill, with the wood behind it. He has been dead now a year, and his wife near three; and so Master Frederick there must needs go soldiering. They say it is all love for the baron's daughter. But here he comes."

As he spoke, the young man entered the room, presenting to Sir Osborne, as he had expected, the face of the youth who had been sent by Shoenvelt to welcome him on his arrival at the castle. An ingenuous blush overspread the young Hainaulter's countenance, when he saw Sir Osborne, and taking his seat at the table prepared for him, he turned away his head, and began his meal in silence.

"Had not you better take off your corslet, Master Frederick?" demanded the host.

"No, no, Regnault," replied the youth; "I do not know that I shall stay here all night. Never mind! give me some wine and leave me."

Thus repulsed, the innkeeper withdrew, and Sir Osborne continued to watch the young soldier, who, whether it was a feeling of shame at meeting the knight, and degradation at having been made, even in a degree, a party to Shoenvelt's attempt to deceive him; or whether it was bitterness of spirit at returning to his native place

unsuccessful, seemed to have his heart quite full; and it
appeared to be with pain that he ate the food which was
placed before him.

Sir Osborne could feel for disappointed hopes, and
after regarding him for a moment or two in silence, he
crossed the room and laid his hand upon his shoulder.

The young man turned round, with a flushed cheek,
hardly knowing whether by anger at the familiarity to
vent the vexed feelings of his heart, or to take it in
good part, and strive to win the esteem of a man whom he
had been taught to admire.

But there was a frankness in the knight's manner, and
a noble kindness of intent in his look, that soon removed
all doubt: " So, young gentleman," said he, " you have
left Count Shoenvelt's company. I thought you were not
made to stay long amongst them; but say, was it with his
will ? "

" I stayed not to ask, my lord," replied the young man;
" I was bound to Shoenvelt in no way, and the moment
the gates were opened after you were gone, I rode out,
and came away."

Sir Osborne shook his head. " When a soldier engages
with a commander," said he, " his own will and pleasure
must not be the term of his service. But of all things,
he ought not to quit his leader's banner, without giving
notice that he intends to do so."

" But, thank God ! " cried the young Hainaulter, " I
had not yet taken service with Shoenvelt. He wanted to
swear me to it, as he does the rest; but I would not do
so, till I saw more of him and of his plans—and so I told
him."

" That makes the matter very different," replied the
knight with a smile, " I am heartily glad to hear it, for
I dare pronounce him a traitorous ruffian and no true
knight. But one more question, young sir, if I urge not
your patience. How came you to seek Shoenvelt at first,
who never bore a high renown, but as a marauder."

The youth hesitated. " It matters not, Sir Knight,"
replied he after a moment's pause, " to you or to any
one, what reasons I might have to seek renown as speedily
as possible, and why the long tedious road to knighthood
and to fame, first as page, and then as squire, and then
as man-at-arms, was such as I could not bear; but so it
was; and as Shoenvelt gave out, that he had high com-
missions from the emperor, and was to do great deeds,
I hoped that with him I might find speedy means of
signalizing myself. After being two days in the castle,
I discovered that his whole design was plunder, which
was not the way to fame; and this morning he made me
deliver you a message, which I knew to be a falsehood,
which was not the road to honor; so I determined to leave
him; and as the spearmen are always dropping out of
the castle by five or six at a time, to go down to the
frontier, I soon found the means of getting away."

" Yours is an error, my good youth," said Sir Osborne, " which I am afraid we are all wont to entertain
in the first heat of our early days; but we soon find that
the road to fame is hard and difficult of access, and that
it requires time, and perseverance, and labor, and strength,
even to make a small progress therein. Even those who,
with a gay imagination, fancy they have made themselves
wings to fly up to the top, soon, like the Cretan of old,
sear their pinions in the sun, or drop into the sea of
oblivion. However, are you willing to follow a poor
knight, who, though he cannot promise either fame or
riches, will lead you, at least, in the path of honor?"

The enthusiastic youth caught the knight's hand, and
kissed it in inexpressible delight. " What, follow you!"
cried he, " follow the Lord Darnley! the knight of Burgundy! whose single arm maintained the bridge at Bo-
vines against the bravest of the Duke of Alençon's horse!
Ay, that I will, follow him through the world. Do you
hear that, Regnault," he cried to the innkeeper, who now
entered, " do you hear that? Instead of the base Shoen-

velt, I am going to follow the noble Lord of Darnley, who was armed a knight by the emperor himself."

The honest innkeeper congratulated Master Frederick heartily upon the exchange; for the knight was now in that part of the country where his name, if not his person, was well known; and in that age, the fame of gallant actions, and of noble bearing, spread rapidly through all ranks, and gained the meed of applause from men whom we might suppose little capable of appreciating it.

All preliminaries were speedily arranged, and the next morning, Sir Osborne set out by dawn for the small town of Hazebrouck, which lay at about two leagues' distance, where he took care to furnish his new follower with a lance, and several pieces of defensive armor that were wanting to his equipment; and then, to ascertain what reliance might be placed on his support in case of emergency, he excited him to practise various military exercises with himself, as they rode along towards Aire. To his no small surprise and pleasure, he found that the young Hainaulter, though somewhat rash and hasty, was far more skilful in the use of his weapons, and the management of his horse, than he could have conceived; and with such an addition to his party, he no longer scrupled to cast himself in the way of some of Shoenvelt's bodies of marauders, to keep his hand in, as Longpole quaintly expressed it, when he heard his lord's determination.

"Come, Frederick," said the knight, "I will not go on to Aire, as I had determined; but, in order to gratify your wish for renown we will lay about on the frontier, like true errant knights of old, at any village or other place where we may find shelter; and if we meet with Shoenvelt, or any of his, mind you do honor to your arms. We shall always have the odds of eight or nine against us."

"No, no, Sir Knight!" cried the young soldier, "do not believe that. It is one of his falsehoods; there are not above ten in any of the bands, and most of them are five or six. I know where most of them lie."

"Hush, hush!" cried Sir Osborne, raising his finger, "you must tell me nothing, that if you should chance to break a lance with him, your hand may not tremble at thinking you have betrayed his counsel. Nay, do not blush, Frederick. A man that aspires to chivalry must guide himself by stricter rules than other men. It was for this I spoke. Here is the fair River Lys, if I remember right?"

"It is so, Sir Knight," replied the other; "there is a bridge about a mile lower down."

"What, for a brook like this?" cried Sir Osborne, spurring his horse in. "Oh, no, we will ford it. Follow."

The young Hainaulter's horse did not like the plunge, and shied away from the brink. "Spur him in, spur him in!" cried Longpole. "If our lord reaches the other bank first, he will never forgive us. He swims like an otter himself, and fancies that his squires ought to be water-rats by their birth-right."

"Down with the left rein!" cried the knight, turning as his horse swam, and seeing the situation of his young follower. "Give him the spur, and bring him to a demivolte, and he must in."

As the knight said, at the second movement of the demivolte, the horse's feet were brought on the very brink of the river, and a slight touch of the mullet made him plunge over; so that, though somewhat embarrassed with his lance in the water, Frederick soon reached the other bank in safety.

To meet with Shoenvelt himself, and if possible, to disappoint his schemes for plunder, was now the knight's castle in the air; and though the numbers of his own party were so scanty, he felt the sort of confident assurance in his own courage, his own strength, and his own skill, which is ever worth a host in moments of danger. Longpole, he was sure also, would be no inefficient aid; and though the young Hainaulter might not be their equal in experience or skill, Sir Osborne did not

fear that, in time of need, his enthusiastic courage and
desire to distinguish himself, would make him more than
a match for one of Shoenvelt's company.

Under these circumstances, the knight would never
have hesitated to attack a body of double, or perhaps
treble his own number; and yet he resolved to proceed
cautiously; endeavoring in the first place to inform himself of the situation of Shoenvelt's various bands, and
to ascertain which he was likely to join himself.

Wilsten having let drop that he himself and the count,
as the two leaders, were to set out the next morning,
Sir Osborne saw that no time was to be lost, in recon-
noitring the ground, to ascertain the real force of the adventurers.

It was also necessary to ascertain where Francis was,
for Shoenvelt might have been deceived, or the king
might have already quitted the frontier, or he might be
accompanied by sufficient escort to place his person in
security; or, in short, a thousand circumstances might
have happened, which would render the enterprise of
the adventurers abortive, and his own interference unnecessary, if not impertinent.

Revolving all these considerations in his mind, sometimes proceeding in silence, sometimes calling upon his
companions for their opinion, Sir Osborne took his way
up one of the deep glades of the forest, still keeping a
watchful ear to every sound that stirred in the wood.

As their horses were now rather fatigued, and the full
sun shining upon the forest, rendered its airless paths
very oppressive, the knight chose a little path before
him, hoping it would lead to some more open space,
where they might repose for a while, and at the same time
keep a watch upon the roads they had just quitted. His
expectations were not deceitful, for after having proceeded about two hundred yards, they came to a little
grassy mound in the wood.

It was the very spot suited to Sir Osborne's purpose;
24

and dismounting, the three travellers leaned their lances against the trees; and letting their horses pick a meal from off the forest grass, prepared to repose themselves under the shadow of the thorns. Previous to casting himself down upon the bank, however, the knight took care to examine the wood around them, and seeing a sort of yellow light shining between the trees beyond, he pursued his way along what seemed a continuation of the little path which had brought them thither. Proceeding in a slanting direction, apparently to avoid the bolls of some enormous beeches, it did not go on for above ten or twelve yards, and then opened out upon a high road, cut through the very wildest part of the forest, at a spot where were an old stone cross and fountain of clear water. Sir Osborne profited by the occasion, and communicated his discovery to his companions, who took advantage of it to satisfy their thirst also. They then lay down in the shade, and, after some brief conversation, the heat of the day so overpowered the young Hainaulter, that he fell asleep. Such an example was never lost upon Longpole, who soon resigned himself to the drowsy god; and Sir Osborne was left the only watcher of the party.

While indulging in waking visions, he thought he heard a distant horn, and listening, the same sound was again borne upon the wind from some far part of the forest. It was, however, no warlike note, but evidently proceeded from the horn of some huntsman, who, as Sir Osborne concluded from the time of year, was chasing the wolf, to whom no season gives repose.

Falling back into the position from which he had risen to listen, Sir Osborne had again given himself up to thought, when he was once more roused by the sound of voices, and the trampling of horses' feet on the road hard by. Rising silently, without disturbing his companions, he glided part of the way down the path leading to the fountain, and paused amidst some oaks and shrubs, through the leaves of which he could observe what passed on the highway, without being seen himself.

Nearly opposite to the cross, already mentioned, appeared two horsemen, one of whom allowed his beast to drink, where the water, gurgling over the basin of the fountain, formed a little streamlet across the road, while the other held in his rein, about a pace behind, as if waiting, with some degree of respect, for his companion. As soon as the horse raised its head, the first cavalier turned round, and presented to Sir Osborne's view a fine and princely countenance, whose every feature, whose every glance, bespoke a generous and noble spirit.

In complexion, the stranger was of a deep tanned brown, with his eyes, his hair, and his moustaches nearly black: his brow was broad and clear, his eyes large and full, though shaded by the dark eyelashes that overhung them; his nose was straight, and perhaps somewhat too long; while his mouth was small, and would have been almost too delicate, had it not been for a certain marked curl of the upper lip, which gave it an expression, not of haughtiness, nor of sternness, but of grave condescending dignity. His dress was a rich hunting suit, which might well become a nobleman of the day, consisting of a green pourpoint, laced with gold, and slashed on the breast; long white hose half-covered with his boots, and a short green cloak not descending to his horse's back. His hat was of velvet, with the broad brims slightly turned up round it, and cut in various places so as somewhat to resemble a mural crown, while from the front, thrown over to the back, fell a splendid plume of ostrich feathers, which almost reached his shoulder. His only arms appeared to be a dagger in his girdle, and a long heavy sword, which hung from his shoulder in a baldrick of cloth of gold. The other stranger was nearly habited like the first, very little difference existing either in the fashion or the richness of their apparel. Both also were tall and vigorous men; and both were in the prime of their days; but the countenance of the second was very different from that of his companion. In complexion he was fair, with small blue eyes, and rather sandy hair, nor would he have been otherwise than handsome, had it not been for a certain narrowness of brow, and wideness of mouth, which gave a gaunt and eager expression to his face, totally opposed to the grand and open countenance of the other.

As we have said when his horse had done drinking, the first traveller turned towards the spot where Sir Osborne stood, and seemed to listen for a moment. At length he said, " Hear you the hunt now, Count William?"

" No, your highness," replied the other, " it has swept away towards Aire."

" Then, sir," rejoined the first, " we are alone;" and drawing his sword from the scabbard, he laid it level before his companion's eyes, continuing abruptly, " what think you of that blade? is it not a good one? At the same time he fixed his eye upon him, with a firm remarking glance, as if he would have read into his very soul. The other turned as pale as death, and faltered something about its being a most excellent weapon.

" Then," continued the first, " I will ask you, Sir Count—should it not be a bold man, who, knowing the goodness of this sword, and the strength of this arm, and the stoutness of this heart, would yet attempt anything against my life? However, Count William of Firstemberg, let me tell you, that should there be such a man in this kingdom, and should he find himself alone with me in a wild forest like this, and fail to make the attempt he meditated, I should look upon him as coward as well as traitor; and fool as well as villain." And his dark eye flashed as if it would have struck him to the ground.

Count William faltered—trembled—and attempted to reply; but his speech failed him; and striking his hand against his forehead, he shook his bridle rein, dug his spurs into his horse's sides, and darted down the road like lightning.

"Slave!" cried the other, as he marked him go, "cowardly slave!" and turning his horse without further comment, he rode slowly on the other way.

CHAPTER XXII.

" Thine is th' adventure, thine the victory,
Well has thy fortune turned the die for thee."
                                        DRYDEN.

SIR OSBORNE immediately turned into the forest, and
rousing his companions, called them to horse; but however, though confessedly the hero of our story, we must
leave him for a little time, and follow the traveller we
have just left upon the road.

For a considerable way, he rode on musing, and if one
might judge from his countenance, his meditations were
somewhat bitter; such as might become the bosom of a
king, on finding the treachery of the world, the hollow-
ness of friendship, the impossibility of securing affection, or any other of the cold lessons which the world
will sometimes teach the children of prosperity.   At
length he paused, and looking to the declining sun, saw
the necessity of hastening his progress; whereupon setting spurs to his horse, he galloped along the road, without much heeding in what direction it led him, till coming to one of those openings, called carrefours by the
French, where a great many roads met, he stopped to consider his farther route.   In the midst, it is true, stood a
tall post, which, doubtless, in days of yore, pointed out to
the inquisitive eye, the exact destination to which each
of the several paths tended; but Time had effaced the
letters, leaving no trace of their purport visible.

The traveller rode round it in vain—then paused,
and listened, as if to catch the sounds of the distant
hunt; but all was now silent.   As a last resource, he raised
his hunting-horn to his lips, and blew a long and repeated
call; but all was hushed and still—even babbling echo,

in pure despite, answered not a word. He blew again, and had the same success

Some road he must choose, and calculating as nearly as he could, by the position of the sun, he made his election, and spurred along it with all speed. A dropping sound amongst the green leaves, however, soon showed that the storm was begun, and once having commenced, it was not slow in following up its first attack: the rain came down in torrents, so as to render the whole scene misty, and the lightning, followed by its instant clap of thunder, flickered on every side with flash after flash, dazzling the traveller's sight, and scaring his horse by gleaming across his path, while the inky clouds overhead almost deprived them of other light. Galloping on then, in despair of finding any sufficient covering, he proceeded for nearly half an hour along the forest road, before it opened into the country; and where it did so, instead of finding any nice village to give him rest, and shelter, and food, and fire, the horseman could distinguish nothing but a wide bare expanse of country, looking dismal and desolate in the midst of the gray deluge that was falling from the sky. About seven or eight miles farther on, he could, indeed, see faintly through the rain, the spire of some little church giving the only sign of human habitation; except where to the left, in the midst of the heath that there bordered the forest, he perceived the miserable little hut of a charcoal burner, with a multitude of black hillocks before the door, and a large shed for piling up what was already prepared.

To this, then, as the nearest place of shelter, the stranger took his way, very different in appearance from what he had been in the morning; his rich dress soaked and soiled, his velvet hat out of all shape or form, his high plume draggled and thin, with all the feather adhering closely to the pen, and, in short, though still bearing the unalienable look of gentleman, yet in as complete disarray of apparel, as the very worst wetting can produce. Without ceremony, he rode up to the door, sprang off his horse, and entered the cabin, wherein appeared a good woman of about forty, busily piling up, with fresh fuel, a fire of dry boughs, over which hung a large pot of soup for the evening meal. The traveller's tale was soon told, and the dame readily promised him shelter and food, in the name of her husband, who was absent, carrying charcoal to the distant village; and seeing that the storm was likely to last all night, he tied his horse under the shed, placed himself by the side of the fire, aided the good woman to raise it into a blaze, and frankly prepared to make himself as comfortable as circumstances would permit. Well pleased with his easy good humor, the good dame soon grew familiar, gave him a spoon to skim the pot, while she fetched more wood, and bade him make himself at home. In a short time the husband himself returned, as dripping as the traveller had been, and willingly confirmed all that his wife had promised. Only casting himself, without ceremony, into the chair where the stranger had been sitting—and which, by-the-way, was the only chair in the place, all the rest being joint stools—he addressed him familiarly, saying, " I take this place, by the fire my good gentleman, because it is the place where I always sit, and this chair, because it is mine; and you know the old proverb,

> " ' By right and by reason whatever betide,
> A man should be master by his own fire-side.' "

" Faith, you are in the right," cried the traveller laughing, " so I will content myself with this settle. But let us have something for supper, for on the word of a— knight, my ride has taught me hunger."

" Give us the soup, dame," cried the charcoal burner. " Well I wot, Sir Traveller, that you might be treated like a prince, here on the edge of the wood, did not those vile forest laws prevent a poor man from spearing a boar as well as a rich one. In good truth, the king is to blame to let such laws last."

" Faith, and that is true," cried the traveller, " and heartily to blame too, if his laws stand between me and a good supper. Now would I give a link of this gold chain, for a good steak of wild boar pork, upon those clear ashes."

The cottager looked at his wife, and the cottager's wife looked at her husband, very like two people undecided what to do. " Fie, now ! " cried the stranger, " fie, good dame ! I will wager a gold piece against a cup of cold water, that if I look in that coffer, I shall find wherewithal to mend our supper."

" Ha, ha, ha ! " roared the charcoal-burner, " thou hast hit it ! Faith, thou hast hit it ! there it is, my buck, sure enough ! Bring it forth, dame, and give us some steaks. But mind," he continued, laying his finger on his lip, with a significant wink, " mind, mum's the word ! never fare well and cry roast beef."

" Oh, I'm as close as a mouse," replied the stranger in the same strain; " never fear me, many a stout stag have I overthrown in the king's forests, without asking, with your leave or by your leave of any man."

" Ha, ha, ha ! " cried the cottager, " thou'rt a brave one ! Come, let us be merry, while the thunder rolls without. It will strike the king's palace sooner than my cottage, though we are eating wild boar therein."

In such sort of fit passed the evening till nightfall and the storm still continuing in its full glory, the traveller was fain to content himself with such lodging as the cottage afforded, for the night. Though his dress bespoke a rank far higher than their own, neither the cottager nor his wife seemed at all awe-struck or abashed, but quietly examined the gold-lacing of his clothes, declared it was very fine, and seemed to look upon him more as a child does upon a gilded toy, than in any other light. When night was come, the good dame strewed out one corner of the hut with a little straw, piled it high with dry leaves, and the stranger, rolling up his cloak for a pillow, laid it under his head, stretched himself on the rude bed thus prepared, and soon fell into a profound sleep.

Taking advantage of his nap, we will now return to Sir Osborne, who with all speed roused his companions from their slumbers, and bade them mount and follow. With military alacrity, Longpole was on his horse in a moment, and ready to set out; but for his part, the young Hainaulter yawned and stretched, and somewhat bewildered, looked as if he would fain have asked whither the knight was going to lead him. A word, however, from Longpole hurried his motions, and they were both soon upon the track of Sir Osborne, who was already some way on the little bridle-path by which they had arrived at the grassy mound where they had been sleeping. When he reached the road they had formerly left, he paused, and waited their coming up.

"Now, Longpole," cried he, "give me your judgment, does this road lead to any crossing, or not? Quick! for we must not waste a moment."

"Most certainly it does, my lord," replied the shield bearer, "most probably to the spot where they all meet in the heart of the wood."

"Perhaps Frederick may tell us with more certainty," said the knight; and changing his language to French, for the ear of the young Hainaulter, he asked the same question.

"Oh yes, certainly," replied Frederick, "it leads to the great carrefour; I have hunted here a hundred times."

"Then are we on French ground, or Flemish?" demanded the knight.

"The French claim it," replied the youth, "but we used to hunt here in their despite."

"Quick then, let us on," cried Sir Osborne, "and keep all your eyes on the road before, to see if any one crosses it."

"He has something in his head, I'll warrant," said

Longpole to their new companion, as they galloped after Sir Osborne. "Oh, our lord knows the trade of war; and will snuff you out an enemy, without ever seeing him, better than a beagle dog with bandy legs and a yellow spot over his eyes."

"Halt!" cried the knight, suddenly reining in his horse as they came within sight of the carrefour we have already mentioned. "Longpole keep close under that tree! Frederick, here by my side—back him into the wood, my good youth—that will do. Let every one keep their eyes upon the crossing, and when you see a horseman pass, mark which road he takes. How dark the sky is growing. Hark! is not that a horse's feet?"

They had not remained many minutes, when the cavalier we have spoken of appeared at the carrefour, examined in vain the finger-post, sounded his horn once or twice, as we have described, and then again took his way to the left.

"Where does that road lead?" demanded the knight, addressing the young Hainaulter.

"It opens out on the great heath, between the forest and Lillers, my lord," answered Frederick.

"Is there any village, or castle, or house near?" asked Sir Osborne quickly.

"None, none!" replied Frederick, "it is as bare as my hand,—perhaps a charbonier's cottage or so," he added, correcting himself.

"Let us on then," replied the knight, "we are going to have a storm, but we must not mind that;" and putting his horse into a quick pace, he led his followers upon the track of the traveller, taking care never to lose sight of him entirely, and yet contriving to conceal himself, whenever any turn of the road might have exposed him to the view of the person he pursued. The rain poured upon his head, the lightning flashed upon his path; but still the knight followed on without a moment's pause, till he had seen the traveller take refuge in the cottage of the charcoal-burner. Then, and not till then, he paused, spurred his horse through some thick bushes on the edge of the wood, and obtained as much shelter as the high beeches of the forest could afford; nor did he pause at the first or the thickest trees he came to, but took particular pains to select a spot, where, though concealed by a high screen of underwood, they could yet distinguish clearly the door of the hut, through the various breaks in the branches. Here, having dismounted with his followers, he stationed Frederick at a small opening, to watch the cottage, while he and Longpole carefully provided for the security and refreshment of their horses, as far as circumstances would admit, although the long forest-grass was the only food that could be procured for them, and the storm still continued pouring through the very thickest parts of the wood. To obviate this, the knight and his shield-bearer piled the underwood behind them with their swords, and soon obtained a sufficient supply of leafy branches, to interweave with the lower boughs of the trees overhead, and thus to secure themselves against the rain.

While thus employed, Frederick gave notice as he had been commanded, that some one approached the cottage, which proved to be the charbonier himself, returning with his mule; and after his arrival, their watch remained undisturbed by the coming of any visitor till nightfall.

As soon as it was dark, Sir Osborne allotted to his followers and to himself, the portion of the night that each was to watch, taking for his own period the first four hours; after which, Longpole's turn succeeded; and lastly, towards morning, came the young Hainaulter.

With his eye fixed upon the light in the cottage, and his ear eager for every sound, Sir Osborne passed the time till the flame gradually died away, and flashing more and more faintly, at last sunk entirely. However, the dark outline of the hut was still to be seen, and the ear had now more power; for the storm had greatly passed away, and the only sounds that it had left, were the thunder rolling faintly round the far limits of the horizon, and the dropping of the water from the leaves and branches of the forest. Towards midnight, Sir Osborne roused Longpole, and recommending him to watch carefully, he threw himself down by the young Hainaulter, and was soon asleep.

Somewhat tired with the fatigues of the day, the knight slept soundly, and did not wake, till Frederick, who had replaced Longpole on the watch, shook him by the arm; and starting up he found that it was day.

" Hist, hist! my lord," cried the youth, " here is Shoenvelt and his party."

Sir Osborne looked through the branches in the direction the young man pointed, and clearly distinguished a party of seven spearmen, slowly moving along the side of the forest, at about five hundred yards' distance from the spot where they lay. " It is Shoenvelt's height and form," said the knight, measuring the leader with his eye, " and that looks like Wilsten by his side—but how are you sure? "

" Because I know the arms of both," replied Frederick. " See, they are going to hide in the wood, close by the high road from Lillers to Aire."

As he spoke, the body of horsemen stopped, and, one after another, disappeared in the wood, convincing Sir Osborne that the young Hainaulter was right.

" Then nerve your arm, and grasp your lance, Frederick," said the knight with a smile, " for if you do well, even this very day you may win your golden spurs. Wake Longpole there! we must be all prepared."

The youth's eyes gleamed with delight, and snatching up his casque, he shook Longpole roughly, and ran to tighten his horse's girths, while Sir Osborne explained to the yeoman that they were upon the eve of an encounter.

" Odds life! " cried Longpole, " I'm glad to hear it,

my lord. I find it vastly cold, sleeping in a steel jacket, and shall be glad of a few backstrokes to warm me. You say there are seven of them. It's an awkward number to divide, but you will take three, my lord—I will do my best for two and a half, and then there will be one and a half for Master Frederick here. We could not leave the poor youth less, in honesty, for I dare say he is as ready for such a breakfast as we are."

The bustle of preparation now succeeded for a moment or two; and when all was ready, and the whole party once more on horseback, the knight led the way to a gap, from whence he could issue out upon the plain, without running the risk of entangling his horse in the underwood. Here, stationing himself behind the bushes to the left, he gave orders to Longpole and Frederick, not to stir an inch whatever they saw, till he set the example; and then grasping his lance, he sat like marble, with his eyes fixed upon the cottage.

In about a quarter of an hour, the door of the hut opened, and the cottager running to the shed, brought up the traveller's horse. By this time, he seemed to have discovered that his guest was of higher rank than he imagined, for when the stranger came forth, he cast himself upon his knees, holding the bridle, and remained in that situation till the other had sprung into the saddle.

Dropping some pieces of gold into his host's hand, the traveller now shook his rein; and putting his horse into an easy pace, took his way over the plain, at about three hundred yards' distance from the forest, proceeding quietly along, totally unconscious of danger. A moment, however, put an end to his security, for he had not passed above a hundred yards beyond the spot where the knight was concealed, when a galloping of horse was heard, and Shoenvelt's party, with levelled lances, and horses in charge, rushed forth from the wood upon him.

In an instant, Sir Osborne's visor was down, his spear

was in the rest, and his horse in full gallop. "Darnley! Darnley!" shouted he, with a voice that made the welkin ring. "Darnley to the rescue! Traitor of Shoenvelt, turn to your death!"

"Darnley! Darnley!" shouted Longpole, following his lord.

"St. George for Darnley! Down with the traitors."

The shout was not lost upon either Shoenvelt or the traveller. The one instantly turned, with several of his men, to attack the knight; the other, seeing unexpected aid at hand, fell back towards Darnley, and with admirable skill and courage, defended himself with nothing but his sword, against the lances of the marauders, who, their object being more to take him living, than to kill him—lost the advantage which they would have otherwise had, by his want of armor.

Like a wild beast, raging with hatred and fury, Shoenvelt charged towards the knight, his lance quivering in his hand with the angry force of his grasp. On, on, bore Sir Osborne at full speed towards him, his bridle in his left hand, his shield upon his breast, his lance firmly fixed in the rest, and levelled in such manner as to avoid its breaking. In a moment they met. Shoenvelt's spear struck Sir Osborne's shield, and aimed firmly and well, partially traversed the iron; but the knight throwing back his left arm with vast force, snapped the head of the lance in twain. In the meanwhile, his own spear, charged at the marauder's throat with unerring exactness, passed clean through the gorget piece and the upper rim of the corslet, and came bloody out at the back. You might have heard the iron plates and bones crunch as the lance rent its way through. Down went Shoenvelt, horse and man, borne over by the force of the knight's course. "Darnley, Darnley!" shouted Sir Osborne, casting from him the spear which he could not disengaged from the marauder's neck, and drawing his sword. "Darnley, Darnley! to the rescue! Now, Wilsten, now!" and turning, he galloped up to where the traveller, with Longpole and Frederick by his side, firmly maintained his ground against the adventurers.

Wilsten's lance had been shivered by Longpole: and now, with his sword drawn, on the other side of the mêlée, he was aiming a desperate blow at the unarmed head of the traveller, who defended himself from a spearman in front; but at that moment the knight charged the adventurer through the midst, overturning all that came in his way, and shouting loud his battle cry, to call his adversary's attention, and divert him from the fatal blow which he was about to strike. The plan succeeded. Wilsten heard the sound; and seeing Shoenvelt dead upon the plain, turned furiously on Darnley. Urging their horses between all the others, they met in the midst, and thus seemed to separate the rest of the combatants, who, for a moment or two, looked on inactive; while the swords of the two champions played about each other's heads, and sought out the weaker parts of their harness. Both were strong, and active, and skilful; and though Sir Osborne was decidedly superior, it was long before the combat appeared to turn in his favor. At length, by a quick movement of his horse, the knight brought himself close to the adventurer's side, and gaining a fair blow, plunged the point of his sword through his corslet into his bosom.

At that moment, the combat having been renewed by the rest, one of the marauders struck the knight from behind so violently on the head, that it shook him in the saddle, and breaking the fastenings of his helmet, the casque came off and rolled upon the plain. But the blow was too late to save Wilsten, who now lay dead under his horse's feet; and Sir Osborne well repaid it by a single back stroke at this new opponent's thigh.

By this time only two of the marauders remained on horseback, so well had Longpole, the traveller, and Frederick done their devoir; and these two were not long in putting spurs to their steeds, and flying with all speed, leaving the knight and his companions masters of the field. Looking round, however, Sir Osborne missed the gallant young Hainaulter, while he saw his horse flying masterless over the plain. "Where is Frederick?" cried the knight, springing to the ground. "By my knighthood, if he be dead, we have paid our victory dear."

"Not dead, monseigneur, but hurt," said a faint voice near; and turning, he beheld the poor youth fallen to the earth, and leaning on one arm, while with the other he was striving to take off his casque, from the bars of which the blood dripped out fast upon the greensward. Darnley hastened to his aid; and having disencumbered him of his helmet, discovered a bad wound in his throat, which, however, did not appear to him to be mortal; and Longpole, with the stranger, having dismounted, and come to his aid, they contrived to staunch the bleeding, which was draining away his life.

When this was done, the noble traveller turned towards Darnley. "Sir Knight," said he, with the calm dignified tone of one seldom used to address an equal, "how you came here, or why, I cannot tell, but it seems as if Heaven had sent you on purpose to save my life. However that may be, I will say of you, that never did a more famous knight wield sword; and, therefore, as the best soldiers in Europe may be proud of such a companion, let me beg you to take this collar, till I can thank you better"—and he cast over the knight's neck the golden chain of the order of St. Michael, with which he was decorated.

"As for you, good squire," he continued, addressing Longpole, "you are worthy of your lord, therefore kneel down."

"Faith, your worship," answered the yeoman, "I never knelt to any man in my life, and never will to any but a king, while I'm in this world!"

"Fie! fie! Heartley," cried Sir Osborne; "bend your

25

knee. It is the king, man! Do you not understand? It is King Francis!"

"Oh, that changes the case," cried Longpole; "I crave your highness's pardon. I did not know your grace "— and he bent his knee to the king.

Francis drew his sword, and laid it on the yeoman's shoulder; then striking him three light blows, he said, "In the name of God, our Lady, and St. Denis, I dub thee knight. Avance, bon chevalier! Noble, or not noble, from this moment I make you such."

Longpole rose, and the king turned to the young Hainaulter, who sitting near, and supporting himself by his sword, had looked on with longing eyes. "No one of my gallant defenders must be forgotten," said Francis. "Knighthood, my good youth, will hardly pay your wound."

"Oh yes, yes!" cried Frederick eagerly, "indeed it will, your highness, more than repay it."

"Then be it so," replied the king, knighting him. "However, remember, fair knights, that Francis of France stints not here his gratitude, or you may think him niggard of his thanks. We will have you all go with us, and we will find better means to repay your timely aid. I know not, sir," he continued, turning to Sir Osborne, and resuming the more familiar first person singular, "whether I heard your battle cry aright, and whether I now see the famous Lord Darnley, the Knight of Burgundy, who in wars, now happily ended, often turned the tide of battle in favor of the emperor."—Sir Osborne bowed his head.—"Then, sir," continued Francis, "I will say, that never did monarch receive so much injury or so much benefit from the hand of one noble adversary."

CHAPTER XXIII.

" We talk in ladies' chambers, love and news."
COWLEY.

ALL was bustle and preparation at the court of England, for the two most magnificent monarchs of the world were about to contend with each other, not with the strife of arms, nor by a competition of great deeds, but in pomp, in pageant, and in show—in empty glitter and unfruitful display. However that may be, the palace and all its precincts became the elysium of tailors, embroiderers, and sempstresses. There might you see many a shady form gliding about from apartment to apartment, with smiling looks and extended shears, or armed with ell-wands more potent than Mercury's rod, driving many a poor soul to perdition, and transforming his goodly acres into velvet suits, with tags of cloth of gold.

The courts of the king's palace of Bridewell rang from morning till night with the neighing of steeds, the clanking of harness, and the sound of the trumpet; and the shops and warehouses of London were nearly emptied of gold, of jewels, and brocade. Men and women were all wild to out-do their French equals in splendor and display; and, in short, the mad dog of extravagance seemed to have bit all the world.

In a small room in the palace, not far from the immediate apartments of the queen, sat a very lovely girl, whom the reader has not spoken to for a long time—no other than Lady Katrine Bulmer—who, with a more pensive air than was usual with her, sat deep in the mysteries of bibs and tuckers, chaperons and fraises, mantuas and hanging sleeves, which last had, for the moment, regained their ascendancy in the public taste, and were now ornamented with more extraordinary trimmings than ever.

By her side sat her two women, Geraldine and Bridget, whose fingers were going with the rapidity of lightning, quickened into excessive haste by the approaching removal of the court to Calais, which was to take place in the short space of one week, while their mistress's dresses were not half-finished, and their own not began.

What it was that occupied Lady Katrine's thoughts, and made her gay face look grave, is nothing to any one. Perhaps she was vexed at not having seen Lord Darby for eight days—the last time having been on the same morning that Sir Osborne Maurice had been driven from the court. Perhaps she was angry with herself for having parted from him with an affection of indifference which she did not feel.

Well aware, that now Wolsey had returned, the pleasure of seeing her lover almost daily, must cease; and that a stiff and formal interview, in presence of the whole court, or a few brief sentences at a mask or pageant, was all they could hope to attain, Lady Katrine did indeed repent that she had suffered her own caprices to mingle any bitter in the few happy hours that fate had sent her.

It may well be supposed that the sudden disappearance of Sir Osborne Maurice, at the same time as that of Lady Constance de Grey, had given rise to many strange rumors, none of which, of course, did Lady Katrine believe: and, to do her justice, although perhaps she was not at all sorry that Constance had judged it right to put an end to any further proceedings regarding her marriage with Lord Darby, by removing herself from the court; yet Lady Katrine suffered no one to hint a doubt in her presence regarding her friend's conduct. But that which was much more in Constance's favor, was the good word of the queen herself, who at once silenced scandal by saying, that she would take upon herself to assert, that Lady

Constance de Grey had never dreamed of flying from the court with Sir Osborne Maurice. It was very natural, she observed, that a young heiress of rank, and wealth, and a proud family, should take refuge anywhere, rather than contract a marriage to which she had always expressed her repugnance; and without meaning offence to the lord cardinal, she could not think but that Constance was right.

Notwithstanding this, many were the tales that were circulated by the liemongers of the court; and it hurt the really generous heart of Lady Katrine to hear them. Meditating then over all these circumstances, nearly in the same desultory way in which they are here written down, she took little notice, when one of the servants of the palace called her maid Geraldine out of the room. After a short while, Geraldine came back, and called out Bridget, and still Lady Katrine continued to work on. After a moment or two she ceased, and leaning her head on her hand, gave herself up to still deeper thought, when suddenly the door opened, and Lord Darby presented himself.

Too much taken by surprise to give herself any airs, Lady Katrine looked up with a smile of unaffected delight, and Darby, reading his welcome in her eyes, advanced, and casting his arm round her, imprinted a warm kiss on the full arching lips, that smiled too temptingly for human philosophy to resist. Luckily did it happen that he did so within the first minute, for, had he waited later, Lady Katrine might not so easily have pardoned his boldness. However, her only remark was, " Well, Darby, you seem to think it so much a matter of course, that I suppose I must let it pass as such too. But don't look so happy, man, lest I should take it into my head to make you look otherwise before you go."

" Nay, nay, Katrine," said Lord Darby, " not so, when I come solely for the purpose of asking you to make me happy."

The earl spoke seriously, tenderly, and there was so much hope and affection and feeling in his glance, that Lady Katrine felt there must be some meaning in his words. "If you love me, Darby," cried she, "tell me what you mean—and make haste, for my maids will be back, and you know you must not stay here."

"Yes, but I may, Katrine," replied he; "no one but you can now send me away. In a word, dear girl, to put an end to suspense, I have the king's and the cardinal's consent to ask your hand, and the queen's to seek you here—will you refuse me?"

Lady Katrine looked at him for a moment, to be sure—quite sure that what she heard was true; then dropping her head upon his shoulder, she burst into a violent flood of tears. So sudden, so delightful was the change in all her feelings, that she was surprised out of all her reserve, all her coquetry, and could only murmur, "Refuse you—no!" But starting up, at length she cried, "I have a great mind that I will too. Don't think that I love you—no, I hate you most bitterly for making me cry—you did it on purpose, beyond doubt, and I won't forgive you easily—so, to begin your punishment, go away and leave me directly."

"Nay, Katrine, I must disobey," replied the earl, "for I have other news to tell you—your relation, Lord Orham, is dead."

"My relation?" cried Lady Katrine, whose tears were ever dried as soon as shed. "Oh, yes! I remember, he was my great grandfather's seventieth cousin by the mother's side. One was descended from Shem, and the other from Japheth, in the time of the flood, or before, for aught I know. Well, what of my antediluvian relative—oh, he is dead, you say—may he rest with Noah!"

"But you must take mourning for him," said Lord Darby, laughing, "indeed you must."

"Certainly," replied Lady Katrine, "a coif and a widow's hood. But I won't be teased, Darby—I will tease everybody, and nobody shall tease me. As to going into mourning for the old miser just now, when all my finery is ready made, to show myself at Guisnes, and captivate all hearts, and make you fight fifty single combats—I won't do it. There, go and ask my singing bird to moult in the month of May, or anything else of the same kind, but don't ask me to leave one single row of lace off my sleeve, for the miser—I disown him."

"Hush, hush, hush!" cried the earl, "Take care he does not come back, and disown you, for otherwise you are his heiress."

"I!" exclaimed Lady Katrine, "am I his heiress? Now, Mistress Fortune, I am your very humble servant. Bless us, what a much more important person Katrine Bulmer will be, with all the heavy coffers of her late dear cousin, than when she was poor Katrine Bulmer, the queen's woman—Darby, I give you notice: I shall not marry you—I could wed a duke now, doubtless—who shall it be? All the dukes have wives, I do believe. However, there is many a peer richer than you are, and though you do count cousinship with kings, gold is my passion now, so I will sell myself to him that has the most."

Though she spoke in jest, still Lord Darby was mortified; for what he could have borne and laughed at in the poor and fortuneless girl that had captivated his heart, his spirit was too proud to endure, where a mercenary motive could be for a moment attributed to him. "Nay, Katrine," said he, "if the fortune that is now yours, gives you any wish of change, your promises to me are null—I render them back to you from this moment."

"Why they were made under very different circumstances, you must allow, Lord Darby," replied she, assuming a most malicious air of gravity, and delighted at having found, for the first time in her life, the means of putting her lover out of humor.

"They were, Lady Katrine," answered the earl, much more deeply hurt than she imagined, "and therefore they are at end—I have nothing farther than but to take my leave."

"Good-bye, my lord, good-bye!" cried she. "Heaven bless and prosper you," and with the utmost tranquillity she watched him approach the door. "Now shall I let him go or not?" said she. "Oh woman! woman! you are a great fool!—Darby—Darby!" she added in a soft voice, "come back to your Katrine."

Lord Darby turned back and caught her in his arms. "Dear teasing girl!" cried he, "why, why will you strive to wring a heart that loves you?"

"Nay, Darby, if things were rightly stated, it is I who have cause to be offended rather than you," answered the lady. "What right had you, sir, to think that the heart of Katrine Bulmer was so base, so mean, as to be changed by the possession of a few paltry counters. Own that you have done me wrong this instant, or I will never forgive you. Down upon your knee—a kneeling confession! or you are condemned beyond hope of grace."

Lord Darby was fain to obey his gay lady's behest, and bending his knee, he freely confessed himself guilty of all the crimes she thought proper to charge him withal; in the midst of which, however, he was interrupted by the entrance of an attendant sent by the queen to call Lady Katrine to her presence.

The lady laughed and blushed, at being found with Lord Darby at her feet; and the earl, not particularly well pleased at the interruption, turned to the usher, saying with the sort of nonchalant air which he often assumed, "Well, sir, before you go, tell the lady, when it was you last found me on my knees, to any of the fair dames of the court?"

"Never, my lord, so please you, that I know of," answered the man, somewhat surprised.

"Well, then," rejoined Darby, "next time, knock at

the door, for fear you should. In which case, you might
chance to be thrown downstairs by the collar."

"Hush, hush, Darby!" cried Lady Katrine, "I must
go to her highness. Doubtless we shall not meet again
for a long while, so fare you well!" and tripping away
after the usher, without other adieu, she left her lover to
console himself in her absence, as best he might.

On entering the queen's apartment, she found her royal
mistress alone with the king, and, according to etiquette,
was drawing back instantly, when Katherine called her
forward: "Come hither, my wild namesake," said the
queen, "his grace the king wishes to speak with you.
Come near, and answer him all his questions."

Lady Katrine advanced, and, kneeling on a velvet
cushion at Henry's feet, prepared to reply to whatever he
might ask, with as much propriety as she could command;
although the glad news of the morning had raised her
spirits to a pitch of uncontrollable joyousness, which even
the presence of the imperious monarch himself could
hardly keep within bounds.

"Well, my merry mistress," said the king, seeing in
her laughing eyes the ebullition of her heart's gladness;
"it seems that you do not pine yourself to death for the
loss of Sir Osborne Maurice?"

"I deeply regret, your grace," said Lady Katrine,
turning grave for a moment, "most deeply, that Sir Osborne Maurice should have incurred your royal displeasure, for he seemed to me as perfect a knight, and as
noble a gentleman, as I ever saw. But in no other respect
do I regret his absence."

"Well, we have tried to supply his place with one you
may like better," said Henry. "Have you seen the Earl
of Darby—eh? What think you of the exchange, pretty
one?"

"I thank your grace's bounty," said the gay girl, "I
have seen his lordship, and looked at him well; and though
he be neither so handsome as Narcissus, nor so wise as

Solon, he may do well enough for such a giddy thing as I am. Saving your grace's presence, one does not look for perfection in a husband: one might as well hope to find a pippin without a spot."

"Thou art a malapert chit, Kate," said the queen, laughing; "sure I am, if your royal lord was not right gentle in his nature, he would be angry with your wild chattering."

"Nay! let her run on," said the king, "a tongue like hers has no guile. If you are contented, sweetheart," he added, addressing Lady Katrine, "that is enough."

"Oh, yes! quite contented, your grace," answered she. "I have not had a new plaything so long, that a husband is quite a treat—I suppose he must be sent to the ménage first, like the jennet your highness gave me, to learn his paces."

"If he was as untamed as you are, mistress," answered the king, "he might need it.—But to another subject, fair one. You were with Sir Osborne Maurice and his party when he encountered the rioters near Rochester. Some sad treasons are but too surely proved against that luckless young man; yet I would fain believe that his misconduct went not to the extent which was at first reported; especially as the accusation was made by that most ruffianly traitor, Sir Payan Wileton, whom the keen eye of my zealous Wolsey has discovered to be stained with many crimes too black for words to paint. Now, amongst other things it was urged, that this Sir Osborne was in league with those Rochester mutineers, the greatest proof of which, was their letting him quietly pass with so small a party, when they boldly attacked the company of Lord Thomas Howard, with ten times the force."

Lady Katrine could hardly wait till the king had ceased. "This shows," cried she at length, "how the keenest wisdom, and the noblest heart, may be abused by a crafty tale. Sir Osborne knew nothing of the rioters, my lord; he took every way to avoid them, because I, unluckily,

having neither father nor brother to protect me, encumbered him by my presence; otherwise, without doubt, he
would have delivered the poor priest they had with them
by his lance, and not by fair words. Never believe a
word of it, your grace. His shieldbearer, indeed, while
the knight drew up his men to defend us, to the best of
his power, recognized the leader of the tumultuaries, as an
old fellow-soldier, and craved leave of his lord to go and
demand a free passage for us, by which means we escaped.
Oh, my lord, as you are famous for your clemency and
justice, examine well the whole tale of that Sir Payan
Wileton, and it will be found false and villanous, as are all
the rest of his actions."

"You are eloquent, lady fair," said the king with a
smile, "we will tell Darby to look to it. But as to Sir
Payan Wileton, his baseness is now known to us, and as
we progress down to Dover, we will send a sergeant-at
arms to bring him with us to Calais, where we will, with
our council, hear and judge the whole. Then if he be
the man we think him, not only shall he restore to the old
Lord Fitzbernard the lordship of Chilham and the stewardship of Dover, but shall stoop his head to the axe
without grace or pardon, as I live. But say, know you
aught of Lady Constance de Grey, in whose secrets you
are supposed to have had a share? Laugh not, pretty
one, for by my life it shall go hard with you if you tell
not the truth."

"Oh, please your grace, don't have my head cut off,"
cried Lady Katrine, seeing, notwithstanding the king's
threat, that he was in one of his happier moods. "I never
told a lie in my life, except one day when I said I did not
love your highness, and that was when you put off the
pageant of the castle dolorous till after Pentecost, and I
wanted it directly. But on my word, as I hope to be
married in a year, and a widow in God's good time, I
know no more of where Constance de Grey is, or where
she went, or when, or how, than the child unborn."

"Did she never speak to you thereof, my saucy mistress?" demanded Henry. "You consorted with her much, 'twere strange if she did not let something fall concerning her purposes, and she a woman too."

"I wish I had a secret," said Lady Katrine, half-apart, half-aloud, "just to show how a woman can keep counsel, if it were but in spite. Good, your grace," she continued, "you do not think that Constance would trust her private thoughts to such a light-headed thing as I am. But, to set your highness's mind at ease, I vow and protest, by the love and duty I bear to you and my royal mistress—by my conscience, which is tender—and by my honor, which is strong—that I know nothing of Lady Constance de Grey, and that even in my very best imaginings, I cannot divine where she is gone."

"Your highness may believe her," said the queen; "wild as she is, she would not stain her lips with the touch of falsehood, I am sure. Get ye gone, Kate, and hasten your sempstresses, for we shall set out a day before it was intended, and mind you plume up your brightest feathers, for we must outdo the Frenchwomen."

"Oh, good, your grace! I shall never be ready in time," replied the young lady. "Besides, they tell me I must put on mourning for my fiftieth cousin by the side of Adam, old Lord Orham the miser. If I do, it shall be gold crape, trimmed with cobwebs, I declare; and so I humbly take my leave of both your graces."

Thus saying, she rose from the cushion, dropped a low curtsey to the king and queen, and tripped away to her own apartments.

No mind, however vast may be its powers of conceiving a bustle, can imagine anything like the court of Westminster for the three days prior to the king's departure for Canterbury.

So continual were the demands upon every kind of artisan, that the impossibility of executing them, threw several into despair. One tailor, who is reported to have undertaken to furnish fifty embroidered suits in three days, on beholding the mountain of gold and velvet that cumbered his shop-board, saw, like Brutus, the impossibility of victory, and, with Roman fortitude, fell on his own shears. Three armorers are said to have been completely melted with the heat of their furnaces; and an unfortunate goldsmith swallowed molten silver to escape the persecutions of the day.

The road from London to Canterbury was covered during one whole week with carts and wagons, mules, horses, and soldiers: and so great was the confusion, that marshals were at length stationed to keep the whole in order, which of course increased the said confusion a hundredfold. So many were the ships passing between Dover and Calais, that the historians affirm, they jostled each other on the road, like a herd of great black porkers; and it is known as a fact, that the number of persons collected in the good town of Calais, was more than it could lodge, so that not only the city itself, but all the villages round about, were full to the overflowing.

At length the king set out, accompanied by an immense train and left London comparatively a desert; while as he went from station to station, he seemed like a shepherd driving all the better classes of the country before him, and leaving not a single straggler behind. His farther progress, however, was stayed for a time at Canterbury, by the news that the Emperor Charles, his wife's nephew, was on the sea before Dover, furnished with the excuse of relationship for visiting the English king, though in reality conducted thither solely by the wish to break the good understanding of the English and French monarchs; or rather to ensure that no treaty contrary to his interest, should be negotiated at the approaching meeting.

With that we have nothing to do; and it is a maxim which a historian should always follow, never to mind anybody's business but his own. We shall therefore only

say, that the king and Wolsey, occupied with the reception
of the emperor, and his entertainment, during the short
time he stayed, entirely forgot Sir Payan Wileton till they
reached Dover, when some one happening to call it a
chilly morning, put Chilham Castle in Wolsey's head (for
on such little pivots turn all the wheels of the world), and
immediately a sergeant-at-arms, with a body of horse-
archers, was sent to arrest the worthy knight, and to
bring him to Calais, for which port the king and the
whole court embarked immediately after ; and, with a fair
wind and a fine sky, arrived in safety towards the evening.

CHAPTER XXIV.

" With clouds and storms
Around thee thrown, tempest on tempest rolled."
THOMSON.

PASSING over all the consultations that took place between the Prioress of Richborough, Dr. Wilbraham, and
Lady Constance de Grey, regarding the means of crossing
the sea to France with greater security; although manifold were the important considerations therein discussed,
we shall merely arrive at the conclusion to which they
came at length, and which was ultimately determined by
the voice of the prioress. This was, that for several days,
Lady Constance and Mrs. Margaret should remain at the
convent as nuns, paying a very respectable sum for their
board and lodging, while Dr. Wilbraham was to take up
his abode at a cottage hard by. By this means, the
superior said, they would avoid any search which the
cardinal might have instituted to discover them, in the
vessels of passage between France and England; and at
the end of a week, they would easily find some foreign
ship, which would carry them over to Boulogne. Such a
one, she undertook to procure, by means of a fisherman
who supplied the convent; and who, as she boasted, knew
every ship that sailed through the Channel, from the
biggest man-of-war to the meanest carvel.

We shall now leave in silence also, the time which Lady
Constance passed in the convent. The days passed
tranquilly enough with her, although, like the timid creatures of the forest, whom the continual tyranny of the
strong over the inoffensive, has taught to start even at a
sound, she would tremble at every little circumstance,
which for a moment interrupted the dull calm of the convent's solitude.

A week passed in this manner, and yet the prioress declared her old fisherman had heard of no vessel that could forward Constance on her journey, though the young lady became uneasy at the delay, and pressed her much to make all necessary inquiries. At length, happening one morning to express her uneasiness to Mrs. Margaret, the shrewd waiting-woman, who, with an instinctive sagacity inherent in chamber-maids, knew a thousand times more of the world than either her mistress or Dr. Wilbraham, at once solved the mystery by saying,—

"Lord love you, lady, there will never be a single ship in the Channel that you will hear of, so long as you pay a gold mark a day to the prioress while we stay."

"I would rather give her a hundred marks to let me go," replied Constance, "than a single mark to keep me. But what is to be done, Margaret?"

"Oh, if you will let me but promise fifty marks, lady," replied the maid, "I will warrant that we are in France in three days."

Lady Constance willingly gave her all manner of leave and licence, and, accordingly, that very night, Mrs Margaret told the chamberer, under the most solemn vows of secrecy, that the lady intended to give the prioress, as a gift to the convent, fifty golden marks, on the day that she took ship. "But," said the abigail, "it costs the poor lady so much, what with paying the chaplain's keep at the cottage, and my wage money, which you know I must have, that her purse is running low, and I fear me, she will not be able to do as much for the house as she intends. But mind, you promised to tell no one."

"As I hope for salvation, it shall never pass my lips!" replied the chamberer; and away she ran to the refectory, where she bound the refectory-woman by a most tremendous vow, not to reveal the tidings she was about to communicate. The refectory-woman vowed with a great deal of facility; and the moment the chamberer was gone, she carried in a jelly to the prioress, where, with a low curtsey, and an important whisper, she communicated to the superior the important news. Thereupon the prioress was instantly smitten with a violent degree of anxiety about Lady Constance's escape, and sending down to the fisherman, she commanded him to find a ship instantly, going to France. To which the fisherman replied, that he knew of no ship going exactly to France, but that there was one lying off the sands, which would doubtless take the lady over for a few broad pieces.

Thus were the preliminaries for Constance's escape brought about, in a very short space of time; and the fisherman having arranged with the captain, that he was to take the lady, the chaplain, and the waiting-maid, to Boulogne for ten George nobles, early the next morning Lady Constance took leave of the prioress, made her the stipulated present, and, accompanied by good Dr. Wilbraham and her woman, followed the fisherman to the sands, where his boat waited to convey them to a vessel that lay about a mile from the shore.

The sea was calm and tranquil, but to Constance, who had little of a heroine in her nature, it seemed very rough; and every time the boat rose over a wave, she fancied that it must inevitably pitch under the one that followed. However, their passage to the ship was soon over, and as she looked at the high black sides of the vessel, the lady found a greater degree of security in its aspect, imagining it better calculated to battle with the wild waves, than the little flimsy bark that had borne her thither.

The ship, the fisherman had informed her, was a foreign merchantman, and as she came alongside, a thousand strange tongues, gabbling all manner of languages, met her ear. It was a floating tower of Babel. In the midst of the confusion, and bustle, which occurred in getting herself and her companions upon the deck, she saw that one of the sailors attempted to spring from the ship into the boat, but was restrained by those about

26

him, who unceremoniously beat him back with marling spikes, and rope's ends; and for the time she beheld no more of him, though she thought she heard some one uttering invectives and complaints in the English language.

For the first few moments after she was on deck, what with the giddiness occasioned by the passage in the boat, and the agitation of getting on board, she could remark nothing that was passing around her; but the moment she had sufficiently recovered to regard the objects by which she was surrounded, a new cause of apprehension presented itself, for close by her side, evidently as commander of the vessel, stood no less distinguished a person than the Portuguese captain, of whom mention is made at the commencement of this history.

It was too late now, however, to recede; and her only resource was to draw down her nun's veil, hoping thus to escape being recognized. For some time, she had reason to believe that the disguise she had assumed would be effectual with the Portuguese, who, as we may remember, had seen her but once; for, occupied in giving orders for weighing anchor, and making sail, he took no notice whatever of his fair passenger, and seemed totally to have forgotten her person. But this was not the case: his attention had been first awakened to Lady Constance herself, by the sight of Dr. Wilbraham, whose face he instantly remembered; and a slight glance convinced him that the young nun was the bright lady he had seen in Sir Payan's halls.

In the present instance, he had several important points to consider: though he felt strongly inclined to carry Lady Constance with him on a voyage which he was about to make to the East Indies, yet there might be danger in the business, if the young lady had really taken the veil, not only danger in case of his vessel being searched by any cruiser he might encounter, but even danger from his own lawless crew, who though tolerably free from prejudices, still retained a certain superstitious respect for the Church of Rome, and for the things it had rendered sacred, which the worthy captain had never been able to do away with. This consideration would have deterred him from any evil attempt upon the fair girl, whom he otherwise seemed to hold completely in his power, had it not been for the additional incentive of the two large leathern bags, which had been committed into his charge at the same time with the young lady; and which, by the relation of their size to their weight, he conceived must contain a prize of some value. Determined by this, he gave orders for making all sail down the Channel, and the ship being fairly under weigh, he could resist no longer the temptation which the opportunity presented, of courting the good graces of his fair passenger. Approaching then with an air of, what he conceived, mingled dignity and sweetness, his head swinging backwards and forwards on the end of his long neck, and his infinite nose protruded like a pointer's when he falls upon the game.—"Ah, ah! my very pretty gal," cried he, "you see you be oblige to have recourse to me at last."

"My good friend," said Dr. Wilbraham, struggling with the demon of sea-sickness, "you had better let the lady alone, for she is so sick she cannot attend to you, though doubtless you mean to be civil in your way."

"You go to the debil, master chaplain," replied the captain, "and preach to hims imps—I say, my very pretty mistress, suppose you were to pull up this dirty black veil, and show your charming face," and he drew aside the young lady's veil, in spite of her effort to hold it down.

At the helm, not far from where the young lady sat, stood a sturdy seaman, who, by his clear blue eye, fresh weather-beaten countenance, and bluff unshrinking look, one might have easily marked out as an English sailor. Leaning on the tiller by which he was steering the vessel on her course, he had marked his worthy captain's con-

'duct with a sort of contemplative frown, but when, stoop-
ing down, the Portuguese tore away Lady Constance's
veil, and amused himself by staring in her face, the
honest sailor stretched out his foot, and touched him on a
protuberant part of his person which presented itself behind. The captain, turning sharply round, eyed him like
a demon, but the Englishman stood his glance with a
look of steady nonchalant resolution, that was not easy
to put down.

"I say, Portuguese," said he, "do you want me to
heave you overboard?"

"You heave me overboard, you mutinous thief!" cried
the captain, "I'll have you strung up to the yard-arm,
you vaggleboned, I will."

"You'll drown a little first, by the nose of the tinker
of Ashford," replied the other; "but hark you, Portuguese, let the young lady nun alone; or, as I said before,
by the nose of the tinker of Ashford, I'll heave you
overboard; and then I'll make the crew a 'ration, and tell
them what a good service I've done 'em; and I'll lay down
the matter in three heads; first, as you were a rascal;
second, as you were a villain; and third as you were a
blackguard: then I will show how, first, you did wrong
to a passenger; second, how you did wrong to a lady; and
third, how you did wrong to a nun; for the first, you
deserve to be flogged; for the second you deserve to be
kicked; and for the third you are likely to be hanged,
with time and God's blessing."

For a moment or two, the Portuguese was somewhat
confounded by the eloquence of the Englishman, who was
in fact no other than Timothy Bradford, the chief of the
Rochester rioters: recovering himself speedily, however,
he retaliated pretty warmly, yet did not dare to come to
extremities with his rebellious steersman, as Bradford,
having taken refuge on board his vessel, with four or
five of his principal associates, commanded too strong
a party on board to permit very strict discipline. It was

a general rule of the amiable captain, never to receive two men that, to his knowledge, had ever seen one another before; but several severe losses in his crew had, in the present instance, driven him into an error, which he now felt bitterly, not being half so much master of his own wickedness as he used to be before. Nevertheless, he did not fail to express his opinion of the helmsman's high qualities, in no very measured terms, threatening a great deal more than he dared perform, of which both parties were well aware.

" Come, come, Portuguese," cried the helmsman, " you know very well what is right as well as another, and I say you shan't molest the lady:—another thing, master, you treat that poor lubberly Jekin like a brute, and I'll not see it done, so look to it. But I'll tell you what, captain, let us mind what we are about. These dark clouds that are gathering there to leeward, and coming up against the wind, mean something. Better take in sail."

The effect of this conversation was to free Constance from the persecution of the captain; and turning her eyes in the direction to which the sailor pointed, she saw, rolling up in the very face of the wind, some heavy leaden clouds, tipped with a lurid reddish hue wherever they were touched by the sun. Above their heads, and to windward, the sky was clear and bright.

By this time the English coast was becoming fainter and more faint; the long line of cliffs and headlands massing together, covered with an airy and indistinct light, while the shores of France seemed growing out of the waters, with heavy piles of clouds towering above them, and seeming to advance with menacing mien, towards the rocks of England.

Still the ship sped on, and the wind being full in her favor, made great way through the water, so that it was likely they would reach Boulogne before the storm began; and the captain, now obliged to abandon any evil purpose he might have conceived towards Lady Constance, steered towards the shore of France to get rid of her as soon as possible. Gradually the hills towards Boulogne, the cliffs, and the sands, with dark lines of tower, and wall, and citadel, and steeple, began to grow more and more distinct, and the Portuguese was making a tack to run into the harbor, when the vane at the mast-head began to quiver, and in a moment after turned suddenly round. Cries and confusion of every sort succeeded; one of the sails was completely rent to pieces, and the ship received such a sudden shock, that Constance was cast from her seat upon the deck, and poor Dr. Wilbraham rolled over, and almost pitched out at the other side. Soon, however, the yards were braced round, the vessel was put upon another tack, and from a few words that passed between the captain and the steersman, Constance gathered, that as they could not get into Boulogne, they were about to run for White-sand haven as the nearest port.

"Go down below, lady, go down below, and tell your beads," cried the bluff steersman, as he saw Constance sitting and holding herself up by the binnacle. "Here, Jekey, help her down."

"Lord 'a mercy, we shall all be drowned, I am sure we shall," cried our old friend Jekin Groby, coming forward transformed into the alleged likeness of a sailor, his new profession sitting upon him with inconceivable awkwardness, and the Kentish clothier shining forth in every movement of his inexpert limbs. "Lord 'a mercy upon us, we shall all be drowned as sure as possible! Mistress Nun, let me help you down below. It's more comfortable to be drowned downstairs, they say. There's a flash of lightning, I declare! Mercy upon us! We shall all go to the bottom. This is the worst storm I've seen, since that Portuguese vagabond kidnapped me, by the help of the devil and Sir Payan Wileton. Let me help you down below, Mrs. Nun. Lord bless you, it's no trouble, I'm going down myself."

Constance, however, preferred staying upon deck, where she could watch the progress of their fate, to remaining below in a state of uncertainty, and consequently resisted the honest persuasions of good Jekin Groby, who, finding her immovable, slipped quietly below unobserved, and hid himself in an empty hammock, courageously making up his mind to be drowned, if he could but be drowned asleep.

In the meantime the storm began to grow more vehement, the wind coming in violent quick gusts, and the clouds spreading far and wide over the face of the sky, with a threatening blackness of hue, and heavy slowness of flight, that menaced their instant descent. Presently, another bright flash blazed through the sky, and seemed to rend it from the horizon to the zenith, while instant upon the red path of its fiery messenger, roared forth the voice of the thunder, as if it would annihilate the globe. Another now succeeded, and another, till the ear and the eye were almost deafened by the din, and blinded by the light; while slow, large drops came dripping from the heaven, like tears wrung by agony from a giant's eyes. Then came a still and death-like pause—the thunder ceased, the wind hushed, and the only sounds that met the ear were the rushing of the waves by the ship's side, and the pattering of each big raindrop as it fell on the deck. Soon again, however, did the storm begin with redoubled fury, and the lightnings flashed more vividly than ever, covering all the sky with broad blue sheets of light, while still in the midst of the whole blaze appeared a narrow zigzag line of fire, so bright that it made the rest look pale.

Still Constance kept upon the deck, and drawing her hood over her head, strove to fix herself amidst the pitching of the vessel, by clinging to the binnacle, which in ships of that day was often supported by a couple of oblique bars. Seeing, in a momentary cessation of the storm, the eye of the steersman fixed upon her with a

look of somewhat like pity, she ventured to ask if they
were in much danger.

"Danger! bless you, no, lady," cried the man; "only
a little thunder and lightning; no danger in life. But
you had better go below,—there's no danger—"

As he spoke, another bright flash caused Constance to
close her eyes, but a tremendous crash, which made itself
audible even through the roar of the thunder, as well as a
heavy roll of the vessel, gave her notice that the lightning
had struck somewhere; and looking up, to her horror,
she beheld the mainmast shivered almost to atoms by the
lightning, and rolled over the ship's side, to which it
was still attached by a mass of cordage.

"Cut! cut! cut!" vociferated the steersman, amidst
the unavailing shouts and bustling inactivity of the crew;
"cut! you Portuguese vagagonds! You'll have the ship
on fire. The idiots are staring, as if they never saw such
a thing before. Here, captain, take the helm. Take the
helm!" And springing forward, with an energy to
which the danger of the moment seemed to lend additional impulse, he scattered the frightened Portuguese
and impassible Dutchmen, who were unclueing ropes and
disentangling knots, and catching up a hatchet, soon cut
sheer through the thicker rigging; and with a roll the
blazing remnants of the mast pitched into the sea, leaving
nothing on fire behind, but some scattered cordage,
which the Englishman and his companions gradually extinguished.

In the meanwhile the mast still flaming in the water
swung round the ship, and the Portuguese whose presence
of mind did not seem of the very first quality, brought the
vessel's head as near the wind as possible, to let it drift
astern, and thus, by this lubberly action, bore right upon
the shore, carried on imperceptibly by a strong current.

At that moment the Englishman raised himself, and
looking out before, vociferated, "A reef, a reef! Breakers ahead! Down with the helm! where the devil are you

going?—Down with the helm, I say!" and rushing aft, he seized the tiller, but too late! Scarcely had he touched it with his hand, when with a tremendous shock the ship struck on the reef, making its very seams open, and its masts stagger. "Ho! down in the hold! down in the hold! heave all the ballast aft," cried Bradford; "lay those cannon here—bring her head to wind, let it take her aback if it will. She may swing off yet."

But just then an immense swelling wave heaved the ship up like a cork, and dashed her down again upon the hidden rocks without hope or resource. Every one caught at what was next them for support; for the jar was so great, that it was hardly possible for even the sailors to keep upon their feet. But the next minute she became more steady, and a harsh grating sound succeeded, as if the hard angles of the rock were tearing the bottom of the ship to pieces. Every one now occupied himself in a different way. Bradford sat quietly down by the tiller, which he abandoned to its own guidance, while the Portuguese ran whispering among his country-men, who as speedily and silently as possible got the boat to the ship's side. In the meanwhile Dr. Wilbraham crept over to Lady Constance, who, turning her meek eyes to heaven, seemed to await her fate with patient resignation.

"I need not ask you, my dear child," said the good man, "if you be prepared to go. Have you anything to say to me, before we part? soon, I hope, to meet again where no storms come."

"But little," answered Constance; and according to the rite of her church, she whispered all the little faults that memory could supply, accusing herself of many things as sins, which few but herself would have held as even errors. When he had heard the lady's confession, the clergyman turned to look for the waiting-woman to join her with her mistress in the consolations of religion; but Mrs. Margaret, who greatly preferred the present to the future, was no longer there; and looking forward,

they beheld that the Portuguese and Dutch had got out
the boats, and were pouring in fast; but that which most
astonished them was to find, that the selfish waiting-
woman had by some means got the very first place in the
long-boat, from which the captain was striving to exclude
two of the Englishmen, pushing off from the ship with
the boat-hook. The lesser boat, however, was still near,
and Dr. Wilbraham looked at Constance with an inquiring glance; but Bradford, who had never stirred from
his position, interposed, saying, "Don't go, lady—don't
go! stick to the ship, she can't sink, for the tide is near
flood, and we are now aground, and it may be a while
before she goes to pieces. Those boats can never live
through that surf. So don't go, lady! take my advice—
and I'll manage to save you yet, if I can save myself."

Even as he spoke, the two Englishmen made a desperate jump to leap into the lesser boat, which was pulling away after the other. One man fell too short, and
sunk instantly; the other got hold of the gunwale, and
strove to clamber in, but the boat was already too full,
and a sea striking it at the moment, his weight put it out
of trim, it shipped a heavy sea, settled for a moment, and
sunk before their eyes.

It was a dreadful sight; and yet so deep, so exciting
was the interest, that even after she had seen the whole
ten persons sink, and some rise again, only to be over-
whelmed by another wave, Constance could not take her
eyes off the other boat, although she expected every
moment to see it share the fate of its companion. Still,
however, it rowed on. The thunder had ceased, the wind
was calmer, and the waves seemed less agitated. There
was hope that it might reach the shore. At that moment
it was hidden for an instant below a wave—rose again—
entered the surf—disappeared amidst the foam and spray
—Constance looked to see it rise again, but it never was
seen more, and in a few minutes she could distinguish a
dark figure scramble out from the sea upon the shore,

rise, fall again, lie for a moment as if exhausted, and then once more gaining its feet, run with all speed out of the way of the coming waves.

"Oh dear, oh dear!" cried a dolorous voice from below. "We shall all be drowned for a sure certainty—the water's a-coming in like mad," and in a moment after, the head, and then the body, of honest Jekin Groby protruded itself from the hold, with strong signs and tokens, in his large thick eyelids, of having just woke from a profound sleep. "Lord 'a mercy!" continued he, seeing the nearly empty deck. "Where are all the folks? Oh, Master Bradford, Master Bradford, we are in a bad way! The water has just woke me out of my sleep. What's the meaning of that thumping? Lord 'a mercy! where's the Portuguese?"

"Drowned!" answered Bradford calmly, "and every one of his crew, except Hinchin, the strong swimmer, who has got to land."

"Lord 'a mercy, only think!" cried Jekin. "Must I be drowned too? Hadn't I better jump over? I can swim a little too. Shall I jump over, Master Bradford? Pray tell me, there's a good creature."

"No, no, stay where you are," replied Bradford. "Help me to lash this young lady to a spar. When the tide turns, which it will at four o'clock, that surf will go down, and the ship will keep together till then. Most likely Hinchin will send a boat before that to take us all off. If not, we can but trust to the water at last. However, let us be all ready."

Bradford now brought forth from the hold some rough planks, to one of which he lashed Lady Constance, who yielded herself to his guidance, only praying that he would do the same good turn to the clergyman, which he promised willingly. He then tied a small piece of wood across, to support her head, and fastened one of the heavy leathern bags, to her feet, to raise her face above the water; after which, as she was totally unable to move, he placed her in as easy a position as he could, and speaking a few frank words of comfort and assurance, he left her to perform the same office in favor of Dr. Wilbraham.

In the meantime, Jekin Groby had not forgotten himself, but willing to put his faith rather in the buoyancy of deal boards, than in his own powers of natation, had contrived to find a stout sort of packing-case, or wooden box, from which he knocked out both the top and bottom, and passing his feet through the rest, he raised it up till it reached his arm pits, where he tied it securely; and thus equipped in his wooden girdle, as he called it, he did not fear to trust himself to the waves.

All being now prepared, an hour or more of anxious expectation succeeded. Little was said by any one, and the tempest had ceased; but the grinding sound of the ship, fretting upon the rock, still continued, and a sad creaking and groaning of the two masts that remained, seemed to announce their speedy fall. The wind had greatly subsided, but the air was heated and close, while the clouds overhead, still agitated by the past storm, every now and then came down in thick small rain. Towards four o'clock the tide turned, and as Bradford had predicted, the surf upon the shore gradually subsided, and the sea became more smooth, though yet agitated by a heavy swell, foaming into breakers along the whole line of reef on which the ship had struck. After looking out long, in the vain hope of seeing some boat coming to their assistance, Bradford approached Lady Constance, and addressing her, as indeed he had done throughout, with far more gentleness and consideration than might have been expected from a man of his rough and turbulent character, " Lady," said he, " there seems to be no chance of a boat; the sea is now nearly smooth; I can't warrant that the ship will hold together all night, and we may have the storm back again. If you like to go now, I will get you safe to land, I am sure. I can't answer for it if you stay."

"I will do as you think right," said Lady Constance, with an involuntary shudder at the thought of trusting herself to the mercy of the waves. "I will do as you think right; but pray take care of Dr. Wilbraham."

"No, no!" said the good chaplain, "make the lady all your care. I shall do well enough."

"Here, good fellow," said Constance, taking a diamond of price from her finger; "perhaps you may reach the shore without either of us; however, whether you do or not, take this jewel, as some recompense for your good service."

The man took the ring, muttering that if he reached the shore, she should reach it too; and then, after giving some directions to Dr. Wilbraham in regard to rowing himself on towards the land, with his arms, which were free, he carried Lady Constance to the side of the vessel, that had now heeled almost to the water's edge. Returning for Dr. Wilbraham, with the assistance of Jekin he brought him also to the side; and then it became the question who should be the first to trust himself to the waves. Constance trembled violently, but said not a word, while Jekin Groby holding back, exclaimed, "Lord 'a mercy! I don't like it—at all like."

It was upon him, however, that Bradford fixed, crying. "Come, jump over, Jekey; there's no use of making mouths at it. I want you to help the clerk to steer—come, jump over!" and he laid his hand upon his shoulder.

"Well, well—I will, Master Bradford," cried Jekin, "don't ye touch me, and I will. Oh dear, oh dear! it's mighty disagreeable—well, well, I will!" and he made as if he would have taken a vigorous leap; but his courage failed him, and he only made a sort of a hop of a few inches on the deck, without approaching any nearer to the water. Out of patience, Bradford caught him by the shoulder, and pushed him at once head-foremost into the water, from which he rose in a moment, all panting, buoyed up by the wooden case under his arms.

"Here, Jekey," cried Bradford, "take the doctor's feet, as your arms are free;" and with the assistance of the worthy clothier, who bore no malice, he let down Dr. Wilbraham into the water, and returned to the lady.

As pale as death, Constance shut her eyes, and held her breath, while the rough sailor took her in his arms, and let her glide slowly into the water, which in a moment after she felt dashing round her uncontrolled. Opening her eyes, and panting for breath, she stretched out her arms, almost deprived of consciousness; but at that moment, Bradford jumped at once into the sea, and catching the board to which she was tied, put it in its right position, so that, though many a domineering wave would rise above its fellows, and dash its salt foam over her head, her mouth was generally elevated above the water sufficiently to allow her full room to breathe.

The distance of the ship from the land was about a quarter of a mile; but between it and the shore lay a variety of broken rocks, raising their rough heads above the waves, that dashed furiously amongst them, making a thousand struggling whirlpools and eddies round their sharp angles, as the retiring sea withdrew his unwilling waters from the strand. Constance, however, did not see all this, for her face being turned towards the sky, nothing met her sight but the changeable face of heaven, with the clouds hurrying over it, or the green billows on either side threatening every moment to overwhelm her. Often, often did her heart sink, and hard was it for the spirit of a timid girl, even supported by her firm trust in God's mercy, to keep the spark of hope alive within her bosom, while looking on the perils that surrounded her, and fancying a thousand that she did not behold.

Still the stout seaman swam beside her, piloting the little sort of raft he had made for her towards the shore, through all the difficulties of the navigation, which were not few or small; for the struggle between the retiring tide, and the impetus given by the wind, rendered almost every passage between the rocks a miniature Scylla and Charybdis.

At length, however, choosing a moment when the waves flowed fully in between two large rough stones, whose heads protruded most perpendicularly, he grasped the plank to which Constance was tied, with his left hand, and striking a few vigorous strokes with his right, soon placed her within the rocky screen, with which the coast was fenced, and within whose boundary the water was comparatively calm. The first object that presented itself to his sight, within this haven, was the long-boat, keel upwards; while, tossed by the waves upon one of the large flat stones that the ebbing tide had left half bare, appeared the corpse of the Portuguese captain, his feet and body on the rock, and his head dropping back, half covered by the water. In a minute after, the sailor's feet could touch the ground; and gladly availing himself of the power to walk upon terra firma, he waded on, drawing the plank on which Constance lay after him, till reaching the dry land, he pulled her to the shore, cut the cord that tied her, and placed her on her feet.

Constance's first impulse was to throw herself on her knees, and to thank God for His great mercy; her next to express her gratitude to the honest sailor, who, weary and out of breath with his exertion, sat on a rock hard by; but bewildered with all that had passed, she could scarcely find words to speak, feeling herself in a world that seemed hardly her own, so far had she been on the brink of another. After a few confused sentences, she looked suddenly round, exclaiming, "Oh, where is Dr. Wilbraham?"

The sailor started up, and getting on the rock, looked out beyond, where about two hundred yards off, he perceived honest Jekin Groby, making his way towards the shore in one direction, while the plank to which the amiable clergyman was attached, was seen approaching

the rocks in another, at a point where the waters were
boiling with tenfold violence.

Constance's eye had already caught his long black
habiliments, mingled with the white foam of the waves,
and seeing that every fresh billow threatened to dash him
to pieces against the stones, she clasped her hands in
agony, and looked imploringly towards the sailor.

"He will have his brains dashed out, sure enough,"
said the man, watching him. "Zounds! he must be mad
to try that—stay here, lady, I will see what can be done;"
and rushing into the water, he waded as far as he could
towards Dr. Wilbraham, and then once more began
swimming.

Constance watched him with agonizing expectation,
but before he reached the point, an angry wave swept
round the good old man, and raising him high upon its
top, dashed him violently against the rock. Constance
shuddered, and clasping her hands over her eyes, strove
to shut out the dreadful sight. In a few minutes she
heard the voice of the sailor shouting to Jekin Groby,
who had reached the shore, "Here, lend a hand!"
and looking up she saw him drawing the clergyman to
land, in the same manner that he had extricated herself.

Jekin Groby waded in to help him, and Constance flew
to the spot which he approached; but the sight that
presented itself made her blood run cold: Dr. Wilbraham
was living indeed, but so dreadfully torn and bruised by
beating against the rocks, that all hopes seemed vain,
and those who best loved him might have regretted that
he had not met with a speedier and more easy death.

Opening his exhausted eyes, he yet looked gladly upon
the sweet girl that he had reared, like a young flower,
from her early days to her full beauty, and who now
hung tenderly over him. "Thank God, my dear child!"
said he, "that you are safe—that is the first thing: for
me, I am badly hurt, very badly hurt—but perhaps I may

yet live—I could wish it to see you happy—but if not God's will be done!"

Constance wept bitterly, and good Jekin Groby, infected with her sorrow, blubbered like a great baby.

"There, leave off snivelling, you great fool," cried Bradford, wiping something like a tear from his own rough cheek, "and help me to carry the good gentleman to some cottage." Thus saying, with the assistance of Jekin, he raised the old man, and followed by Constance, bore him on in search of an asylum.

27

CHAPTER XXV.

"Thou seest me much distempered in my mind."

DRYDEN.

SIR PAYAN WILETON had gone through life with fear-less daring; calculating, but never hesitating; keen-sighted of danger, but never timid. And yet, as we have seen, by one of those strange contradictions of which human nature is full, Sir Payan, though an unbe-liever in the bright truths of religion, was credulous to many of the darkest superstitions of the age in which he lived.

On such a mind, anything that smacked of super-natural presentiment, was likely to take the firmest hold; and, on the morning after Lady Constance had, by his means and by his instigation, effected her flight from Richmond, he rose early from a troubled sleep, overshad-owed by a deep despondency, which had never till then hung upon him. Before he was yet dressed, the news was brought him that one of his men had returned with the boat, and that the other had been arrested in the king's name. He felt that his fortune had passed away—an internal voice seemed to tell him that it was at an end; but yet he omitted no measures of security, quitting the capital without loss of time, and leaving such instructions with the porter as he deemed most likely to blind the eyes of Wolsey; hoping that the servant, whose life was in his power, would not betray him, yet prepared, if he did, boldly to repel the charge, and by producing evidence to invalidate the other's testimony, to cast the accusation back upon his head.

But still, from that moment Sir Payan was an altered being; and though many days passed by, without anything occurring to disturb his repose; though the king's progress towards Dover, without any notice having been taken of his participation in Lady Constance's escape, led him to believe that fear had kept the servant faithful, yet still Sir Payan remained in a state of gloom and lassitude, that raised many a marvel amongst those around him.

Often he questioned himself upon the strange depression of his mind; and the more he did so, the more he became convinced that it was a supernatural warning of approaching fate. Many were the resolutions that he made to shake it off, to struggle still, to seek the court, and urge his claim on the estates of Constance de Grey, as he would have done in former days; but in vain; a leaden power lay heavy upon his heart, and crushed all its usual energies; and the only effort he could make, was to send out servants in every direction, to seek Sir Cesar, the astrologer; weakly hoping to brace up his relaxed confidence by some predictions of success. But the old man was not easily to be found. No one knew his abode, and ever strange and erratic in his motions, he seemed now agitated by some extraordinary impulse, so that even when they had once found his track, the servants of Sir Payan had often to trace him to ten or twelve houses in the course of a day. Sometimes it was in the manor of the peer, sometimes in the cottage of the peasant, that they heard of him; but in none did he seem to sojourn for above an hour, hurrying on wildly to the dwelling of some other, amongst the many that he knew in all classes.

At length they overtook him, in the road near Sandgate, and delivered Sir Payan's message; whereupon, without any reply he turned his horse and rode towards Chilham; where he arrived in the evening. Springing to the ground, without an appearance of fatigue, the old man sought Sir Payan in the park, to which the servants said he had retired; and winding through the various long alleys, found him at length walking backwards and forwards, with his arms crossed on his bosom, and his eyes fixed upon the ground.

It was a strange sight to see his meeting with Sir Cesar; both were pale and haggard; for some cause, only known to himself, had worn the keen features of the astrologer, till the bones and cartilages seemed starting through the skin; and Sir Payan's ashy cheek had lately acquired a still more deadly hue than it usually bore; both too looked wild and fearful; the keen black eyes of the old man showing with a terrific brightness, in his thin and livid face, and the stern features of Sir Payan appearing full of a sort of ferocious light, which his attendants had remarked ever since he had been overthrown in the tilt by the lance of Sir Osborne. Meeting thus, in the full yellow sunshine, while Sir Cesar fixed his usual intense and scrutinizing glance upon the countenance of the other, and Sir Payan strove to receive him with a smile, that but mocked the lips it shone upon; they looked like two beings of another world, met for the first time in upper air, to commune of things long past.

" Well, unhappy man," said Sir Cesar at length, " what seekest thou with me? "

" That I am unhappy," replied Sir Payan, knitting his brow, as he saw that little consolation was to be expected from the astrologer, " I do not deny: and it is to know why I am unhappy, that I have asked you to come hither."

" You are unhappy," answered Sir Cesar, " because you have plundered the widow and the orphan, because you have wronged the friendless and the weak, because you have betrayed the confident and the generous. You are unhappy, because there is not one in the wide world that loves you, and because you even despise, and hate, and reprobate yourself."

" Old man! old man! " cried Sir Payan, half unsheathing his dagger, " beware, beware. Those men," he added, pushing back the weapon into its sheath, " ought only to be unhappy that are unsuccessful—the rest is all a bug-bear, set up by the weak to frighten away the strong. But I have been successful—am successful. Why then am I unhappy?"

"Because your success is at an end," replied the astrologer; "because you tremble on your fall—be-cause your days are numbered, and late remorse is gnaw-ing your heart in spite of your vain boasting. Nay, lay not your hand upon the hilt of your dagger! Over me, murderer! you have no power. That dagger took the life of one that had never wronged you. Remember the rout at Taunton—remember the youth, murdered the night after he surrendered!" Sir Payan trembled like an aspen leaf while the old man spoke.—"Yes, murderer!" continued Sir Cesar, "though you thought the deed hid in the bowels of the earth, I know it all. That hand slew all that was dearest to me on earth!—the child that unhappy fortune forced me to leave upon this cursed shore; and long, long ago should his fate have been avenged in your blood, had not I seen—had not I known, that heaven willed it otherwise. I have waited patiently for the hour that is now come—I have broken your bread, and I have drank of your wine; but while I did so, I have seen you gathering curses on your head, and accu-mulating sins to sink you to perdition, and that has taught me to endure. I would not have saved you one hour of crime—I would not have robbed my revenge of one single sin—no, not for an empire! But I have watched you; go on, gloriously, triumphantly, in evil and in wicked-ness, till heaven can bear no more—till you have eaten up your future, and soon, with all your crimes upon your head, hated, despised, condemned by all mankind, your black soul shall be parted from your body, and my eyes shall see you die."

Sir Payan had listened with varied emotions as the old man spoke. Surprise, remorse, and fear had been the first; but gradually, the more tempestuous feelings of his nature hurried away the rest, and rage gaining mastery of all, he drew his poniard, and sprang upon Sir Cesar. But in the very act, as his arm was raised to strike, he was caught by two powerful men, who threw him back upon the ground, and disarmed him; one of them exclaiming, " Ho, ho! we have just come in time.—Sir Payan Wileton, you are attached in the king's name. Lo, here is the warrant for your apprehension. You must come with us, sir, to Calais."

One would attempt, in vain, to describe the rage that convulsed the form of Sir Payan Wileton, more especially when he beheld Sir Cesar smile upon him with a look of triumphant satisfaction. " Seize him! " exclaimed he, with furious violence, pointing to the astrologer; " seize him! if you love your king and your country. He is a marked and obnoxious traitor. I impeach him, and you do not your duty if you let him escape; or are you his confederates, and come up to prevent my punishing him for the treasons he has just acknowledged? "

" Sir Payan Wileton," replied the sergeant-at-arms, " this passion is all in vain. I am sent here with a warrant from the king's privy council, to attach you for high treason: but I have no authority to arrest any one else."

" But I am a magistrate," cried the baffled knight; " let him not escape, I enjoin you, till I have time to commit him. He is a traitor, I say, and if you seize him not, you are the king's enemies."

" Attached for high treason, sir, you are no longer a magistrate," replied the sergeant. " At all events, I do not hold myself justified in apprehending anybody against whom I have no warrant, especially when I found you raising your hand illegally against the person's life whom you now accuse. I can take no heed of the matter—you must come with me."

" He shall be satisfied," said Sir Cesar. " Venomless serpent! I will follow thee now till thy last hour. But think not that thou canst hurt me, for thy power has gone from thee; and though wicked as a demon, thou art weak as a child. I know that my days are numbered as well as thine. I know that we are doomed to pass the same gate; but not to journey on the same road. Lead on, sergeant, I will journey on with you; and then if this bad man have aught to urge against me, let him do it."

" Go, if you will, sir," replied the officer; " but remember, you act according to your own pleasure—I make no arrest in your case—you are free to come with us or to stay, as you think fit."

Sir Payan was now led back to the house, which was in possession of the king's archers; and as he passed through his own hall, with a burning heart, the hasty glance that he cast around amongst his servants, showed him at once, that though there were none to pity or befriend, there were many full ready to betray: then rushed upon his mind, the many accusations that they might pile upon his head, now that they saw him sinking below the stream. The certainty of death—the dread of something after death—doubts of his own scepticism— the innate, all-powerful conviction of a future state—a state growing dreadfully perceptible to his eye as he approached the brink of that yawning gulf, which his own acts had peopled with strange fears. All that he had scoffed at, all that he had despised, now assumed a new and fearful character—even the world's opinion—the world's contemned opinion, came across his thought— that there was not one heart on all the earth would mourn his end; that hatred and abhorrence would go with him to the grave, and that his memory would only live with infamy in the records of crime and punishment. Burying his face in his hands, he sat in deep, despairing, agonizing silence, while his horse was being prepared, and while the officer put his seal upon the various doors which he thought it necessary to secure.

To the questions of whether he needed any refreshment,

or required anything but the clothes which had been prepared, before he quitted the house, he replied nothing,
but with glaring eyes waved his hand, signifying that he
was ready to proceed.

A few hours brought the whole party to Dover, and
the next day saw their arrival at Calais; but, by that time,
the court had removed to Guisnes, and the sergeant
having no orders to bring his prisoner farther, sent forward a messenger to announce his arrival, and demand
instructions.

CHAPTER XXVI.

"Once more the fleeting soul came back,
  T inspire the mortal frame,
And in the body took a doubtful stand,
  Hovering like expiring flame
That mounts and falls by turns."

DRYDEN.

THE painful situation of Lady Constance de Grey had not lost any portion of its sorrow, or gained any ray of hope on the first of June, three days after we last left her, at which period we again take her story up. She was then sitting in a small, poor cottage between Whitesand Bay and Boulogne, watching the slumber of the excellent old man whose regard for her had brought upon his head so much pain and danger. Ever since he had been removed to the hut where they now were, he had lingered in great agony, except at those times when a state of stupor fell upon him, under which he would remain for many hours, and only wake from it in acute pain. He had, however, that morning, fulfilled the last duties of his religion, with the assistance of a good monk of Boulogne, who now sat with Lady Constance, watching the sweet sleep into which he had fallen, for the first time since their shipwreck.

Across the little window, to keep out the light, Constance had drawn one of her own dresses, which had been saved by the sailor Bradford having tied the leathern case that contained them to the plank which had brought herself to shore; but still through the casement, notwithstanding this sort of extemporaneous curtain, the soft breath of the early morning flowed in; and the murmuring voice of the treacherous ocean was heard softly from afar, filling up every pause in the singing of the birds, and the busy hum of all the light children of the summer.

The calmness of the old man's slumber gave Constance hope: and, with a sweet smile, she sat beside him listening to the mingled voice of creation, and joining mentally in the song of praise, that all things seemed raising towards the great Creator.

In the meanwhile the old monk sat on the other side of his bed, regarding him with more anxiety; for long experience in visiting those who hung upon the brink of another world had taught him, that sleep like that into which the clergyman had fallen as often preceded death as recovery. It had continued thus till towards midday, the cottage being left in solitude and silence, for the sailor, Bradford, had gone to seek remedies from a simpler at Boulogne; and Jekin Groby had stolen away for a visit to Calais, while the people to whom the cottage belonged were absent upon their daily occupations. At length, however, a slight sort of convulsive motion passed over the features of the old man, and opening his eyes, he said in a faint low voice, "Constance, my dear child, where are you? My eyes are dim."

"I am here, my dear sir," replied Constance. "You have been sleeping very sweetly. I hope you feel better."

"It is over, Constance!" replied Dr. Wilbraham, calmly but feebly. "I am dying, my child. Let me see the sunshine." Constance withdrew the curtain, and the fresh air blowing on the sick man's face seemed to give him more strength. "It is bright," cried he, "it is very bright. I feel the sweet summer air, and I hear the glad singing of the birds; but I go fast, dear daughter, where there are things brighter and sweeter,— for surely, surely, God who has clothed this world with such splendor, has reserved far greater for the world to come."

The tears streamed down Constance's cheeks, for there was in the old man's face a look of death not to be mistaken—that look the inevitable precursor of dissolution to man, when it seems as if the avenging angel had come

between him and the sun of being, and cast his dark
shadow over him forever.

"Weep not, Constance," said the old man, with faint
and broken efforts, "for no storms will reach me in my
Redeemer's bosom. In His mercy is my hope, in His
salvation is my reliance. Soon, soon shall I be in the
place of peace where joy reigneth eternally. Could I
have a fear, my dear child, it would be for you, left alone
in a wide and desolate world, with none to protect you.
But no, I have no fear! God is your protector! and never,
never, my child, doubt His goodness, nor think that He
does not as surely watch over the universe, as He created
it at first. Everything is beneath His eye, from the
smallest grain of sand to the great globe itself, and His
will governs all, and guides all, though we neither see the
beginning nor the end. Constance, I am departing," he
continued more faintly—" God's blessing be upon you, my
child! and oh! if He in His wisdom ever permits the
spirit of the dead to watch over those they loved when
living, I will be with you and Darnley—when this frail
body—is dust."

His lips began gradually to lose their power of utterance, and his head fell back upon the pillow. The monk
saw that the good man's end was approaching fast, and
placing the crucifix in his dying hand, he poured the
words of consolation in his ear, but Dr. Wilbraham
slightly motioned with his hand, to signify that he was
quite prepared, and fixing his eyes upon the cross, murmured to himself, "I come, O Lord, I come! Be thou
merciful unto me, O King of mercy! Deliver speedily
from the power of death, O Lord of life!"

The sounds gradually ceased, but yet his lips continued
to move—his lips lost their motion; but still his eyes fixed
full of hope upon the cross—a film came over them—it
passed away, and the light beamed up again—shone
brightly for a moment—waned—vanished—and all was
death. The eyes were still fixed upon the cross, but that

bright thing, life, was there no more. To look at them, no one could say what was gone between that minute and the one before; and yet it was evident that they were now but dust—the light was extinguished, the wine was poured out, and it was but the broken lamp, the empty urn, that remained to go down into the tomb.

Constance closed his eyes, and weeping bitterly, kneeled down with the old monk, and joined in the prayer that he addressed to heaven. She then rose, and seated herself by all that remained of her dead friend, feeling alone in all the world, solitary, friendless, desolate; and straining her sweet eyes upon the cold unresponsive countenance of the dead, she seemed bitterly to drink to the dregs the cup of hopelessness which that sight offered.

No one spake,—the monk too was silent, seeming to think that the prayer he had offered to the Deity was the only fitting language for the presence of the dead, when a sound was heard without, and the door gently opening admitted the form of Jekin Groby. The good clothier thought the old man still slept, as when he had left the cottage, and advanced on tiptoe for fear of waking him; but the lifted hand of the monk, the streaming eyes of Constance, and the cold rigid stiffness of the face before him, warned him of what had happened; and pausing suddenly, he clasped his hands with a look of unaffected sorrow. " Good God! " cried he, " he is dead! Alas the day! "—Constance's tears streamed afresh. " Lady," said the worthy man, in a kindly tone, " take comfort! He is gone to a better place than we have here, poor hapless souls! And surely, if all were as well fitted for that place as he was, we should have little cause to fear our death, and our gossips little cause to weep. Take comfort, sweet lady, take comfort! Our God is too good for us to murmur when He cuts our measure short."

There was something in the homely consolation of the honest Englishman that touched Constance to the heart, and yet she could not refrain from weeping even more than before.

" Nay, nay, dear lady," continued Jekin, affected almost
to tears himself, " you must come away from here; I
cannot bear to see you weep so; and though I am but a
poor clothier, and little fitted to put myself in his place
that is gone, I will never leave you till I see you safe.
Indeed I won't. Come, lady, into the other cottage hard
by, and we will send some one to watch here in your
place. Lord, Lord! to think how soon a fellow-creature
is gone! Sure I thought to find him better when I came
back. Come, lady, come."

" Perhaps I had better," replied Constance, drying her
tears. " My cares for him now are useless; yet, though
I murmur not at God's will, I must e'en weep, for I have
lost as good a friend, and the world has lost as good a
man, as ever it possessed. But I will go, for it is in vain
to stay here and encourage unavailing grief." She then
addressed a few sentences to the monk in French, thanking him for his charitable offices towards her dead friend,
and begging him to remain there till she could send some
one to watch the body, adding that if he would come after
that to the adjoining cottage, she would beg him to
convey to his convent a small gift on her part.

The monk bowed his head, and promised to obey; and
Constance, giving one last look to the inanimate form of
the excellent being she had just lost, followed Jekin Groby
to the cottage hard by, where, begging to be left alone,
she once more burst into tears, and let both her sorrow
and despondency have way, feeling that sort of oppression
at her heart which can but be relieved by weeping.

It is needless to follow farther such sad scenes, to tell
the blunt grief of Bradford, when he returned and found
that his errand had been in vain; or to describe the
funeral of good Dr. Wilbraham, which took place the
next day (for so custom required) in the little cemetery
of Whitesand Bay.

Immediately this was over, Lady Constance prepared
to set out for Boulogne, hoping to find a refuge in the

heart of France, till she had time to consider and execute some plan for her future conduct. We have twice said that the sailor, in tying her to the plank on which she had floated from the shipwrecked vessel, had fastened to the end of the board nearest her feet one of her own leathern cases, for the purpose of keeping her head raised above the water; and in this, as it luckily happened, were all the jewels, and the money which she had brought with her from London.

No difficulty, therefore, seemed likely to present itself in her journey to her own estates, except that which might arise in procuring a litter to convey her on her way, or in meeting with some female attendant, willing to accompany her. The latter of these was soon done away with, for the daughter of the cottagers where she had lodged, a gay, good-humored Picarde, gladly undertook the post of waiting-woman to the sweet lady, whose gentleness had won them all, and Bradford, who, from a soldier, a sailor, a shipwright, and a Rochester rioter, had now become a squire of dames, was despatched to Boulogne, to see if he could buy or hire a litter and horses.

In the midst of all these proceedings, poor Jekin Groby was sadly agitated by many contending feelings. In his first fit of sympathy with Constance, on the death of Dr. Wilbraham, he had, as we have seen, promised to accompany her to the end of her journey, whithersoever it might be; but the thoughts of dear little England, and his own fireside, and his bales of cloth, and his bags of angels, called him vehemently across the Channel, while curiosity, with a certain touch of mercantile calculation, pulled him strongly towards the court of Calais. Notwithstanding, he resolved, above all things, to act handsomely, as he said, towards the lady; and accordingly he accompanied Bradford to Boulogne, to ascertain if he could by any way get off trudging after her the Lord knows where, as he expressed it, though he vowed he was very willing to go, if he could be of any service.

After the sailor and his companion had been absent about six hours, Constance began to be impatient, and proceeded to the door of the cottage to see if she could perceive them coming. Gazing for a few minutes on the road to Boulogne, she beheld, rising above the brow of the hill before her, a knight's pennon, and presently half a dozen spears appeared bristling up behind it. Judging that it was some accidental party proceeding to White-sand Bay, Constance retired into the cottage, and was not a little surprised when she heard the horses halt before the door. In a moment after, a gallant cavalier, in peaceful guise, armed only with his sword and dagger, entered the hut, and, doffing his plumed mortier to the lady, with a low inclination of the head, he advanced towards her, saying in French, " Have I the honor of speaking to the noble Lady de Grey, Countess of Boissy and the Val de Marne?"

"The same, Sir Knight," replied the lady. "To what, may I ask, do I owe the honor of your presence?"

"His highness, Francis King of France, now in the city of Boulogne," replied the knight, "hearing that a lady, and his vassal, though born an English subject, had been shipwrecked on this shore, has chosen me for the pleasing task of inviting, in his name, the Countess de Boissy, to repair to his royal court, not as a sovereign commanding the homage of his vassal, but as a gracious and a noble friend, offering service and good-will. His highness's sister also, the Princess Marguerite of Alençon, has sent her own litter for your convenience, with such escort as may suit your quality."

Constance could only express her thanks. Had she possessed the power of choice, she would of course have preferred a thousand times to have retired to the Val de Marne, without her coming being known to the French king, or his court, till such time, at least, as the meeting between him and the King of England had taken place. However, as it was known, she could not refuse to obey, and she signified her readiness to accompany the French knight, begging him merely to wait till the return of a person she had sent to Boulogne for a litter.

"He will not return, lady," replied the chevalier; " it was through his search for a litter at Boulogne, where none are to be had, all being bought for the court's progress to Ardres, that his highness became acquainted with your arrival within his kingdom."

The knight was proceeding to inform her of the circumstances which had occurred, when the quick sound of horses' feet was heard without, joined to the clanging of arms, the jingling of spurs and trappings, and various rough cries in the English tongue.

" Have her! but I will have her, by the Lord!" cried a voice near the door; and in a moment after, a knight, armed at all points, strode into the cottage. " How now! How now!" cried he; " what is all this? Ah, Monsieur de Bussy," he continued, changing his language to broken abominable French, " what are you doing with this lady?"

"I come, Sir John Hardacre," answered the Frenchman, " to invite her to the court of Francis of France, whose vassal the lady is."

" And I come," replied the Englishman, " to claim her for Henry King of England, whose born subject she is, and ward of the crown; and so I will have her, and carry her to Guisnes, as I am commanded."

" That depends upon circumstances, sir," answered the Frenchman, offended at the tone of the other. " You are governor of Calais, but you do not command here. You are off the English pale, sir; and I say that without the lady goes with you willingly, and by preference, you shall not take her."

" I shall not!" exclaimed the Englishman. " Who the devil shall stop me?"

" That will I," answered the French knight; " and I tell you so to your beard."

The Englishman laid his hand upon his sword, and the

Frenchman was not slack to follow his example; but Constance interposed. "Hold, hold! gentlemen," cried she; "I am not worthy of such contention. Monsieur de Bussy, favor me by offering every expression of my humble duty to his highness, your noble king; and show him that I intended instantly to have obeyed his commands, and followed you to his court, but that I am compelled, against my will, to do otherwise. Sir John Hardacre, I am ready to accompany you."

"If such be your will, fair lady," replied the French knight, "I have nothing but to execute your charge. However, I must repeat, that without your full consent, you shall not be taken from French ground, or I am no true knight."

An angry replication trembled on the lip of the English captain, but Constance stopped its utterance, by once more declaring her willingness to go; and the French officer bowing low, thrust back his sword into the sheath, and left the cottage somewhat out of humor with the result of his expedition.

When he and his followers had ridden away, Sir John Hardacre called up a lady's horse, which one of his men-at-arms led by the bridle; and after permitting Constance to make some change of her apparel, and to pay the good folks of the cottage for her entertainment, he placed her in the saddle, and holding the bridle himself, led her away at a quick pace towards Guisnes. He was a rough old soldier, somewhat hardened by long military service, but the beauty and gentleness of his fair prisoner (for such indeed may we consider poor Constance to have been) somewhat softened his acerbity; and after riding on for near an hour in silence, during which he revolved at least twenty ways of addressing the lady, without pleasing himself with any, he began by a somewhat bungling excuse, both for his errand and his manner of executing it.

"I suppose, sir," replied Constance, coldly, "that you
28

have done your duty. Whither you have done it harshly
or not, is for you to consider."

This quite put a stop to all the knight's intentions of
conversation, and did not particularly soothe his humor;
so that for many miles along the road he failed not every
moment to turn round his head, and vent his spleen upon
his men in various high-seasoned curses, for faults which
they might or might not have committed, as the case
happened; the knight's powers of objurgation not only
extending to the cursing itself, but also to supplying the
cause.

It was nearly seven o'clock when they began to approach the little town of Guisnes, but at that season of
the year the full light of day was still shining upon all
the objects round about; and Constance might perceive,
as they rode up, all the bustle and crowding, and idle
activity caused by the arrival of the court.

Her heart sunk when she saw it, and thought of all she
might then have to endure. Under any other circumstances, however, it would have been a gay and pleasing
sight,—so full of life and activity, glitter and show, was
everything that met the eye.

To the southward of the town of Guisnes, upon the
large open green that extended on the outside of the walls,
was to be seen a multitude of tents, of all kinds and
colors, with a multitude of busy human beings, employed
in raising fresh pavilions on every open space, or in
decorating those already spread, with streamers, pennons,
and banners of all the bright hues under the sun. Long
lines of horses and mules loaded with armor or baggage,
and ornamented with gay ribbons to put them in harmony
with the scene, were winding about all over the plain,
some proceeding towards the town, some seeking the
tents of their several lords, while, mingled amongst them,
appeared various bands of soldiers, on horseback and on
foot, with the rays of the declining sun catching upon the
heads of their bills and lances; and together with the

white cassock and broad red cross, marking them out
from all the other objects. Here and there, too, might be
seen a party of knights and gentlemen cantering over the
plain, and enjoying the bustle of the scene, or standing in
separate groups, issuing their orders for the erection and
garnishing of their tents; while couriers, and pursuivants,
and heralds, in all their gay dresses, mingled with mule
drivers, lacqueys, and peasants, armorers, pages, and tent-
stretchers, made up the living part of the landscape.

Behind, lay the town of Guisnes, with the forest at its
back; and a good deal nearer, the castle, with its protect-
ing guns pointed over the plain: but the most striking
object, and that which instantly caught the eye, was a
building raised immediately in front of the citadel, on
which all that art could devise, or riches could procure,
had been lavished, to render it a palace fit for the luxurious king, who was about to make it his temporary
residence.

From the distance at which they were, when it first
struck her sight, Constance could only perceive that it
was a vast and splendid edifice, apparently square, and
seeming to offer a façade of about four hundred feet on
every side, while the sun, catching on the gilding, with
which it was covered, and the immense quantity of glass
that it contained, rendered it like some great ornament of
gold, enriched with brilliants.

Although her heart was sad, and nothing that she saw
tended to dispel its gloom, she could not refrain from
gazing round with a half-curious, half-anxious glance
upon all the gay objects that surrounded her; almost fearing to be recognized by some one that had known her at
the court, now that she was led along as a kind of prisoner,
—a single woman, amidst a band of rude soldiers. Sir
John Hardacre, however, spurred on towards the bridge,
which was nearly impassable, by the number of beasts
of burden and their drivers by which it was covered; and
standing but on a little ceremony with his fellow-lieges,

he dashed through the midst of them all, cursing one, and striking another, and overturning a third, much to Constance's horror and dismay. Having reached the other side, and created by his haste as much confusion and discomfort as he could in his passage, the surly captain slackened his pace, muttering something about dignity, and turned his rein towards the temporary palace of the king. Proceeding slowly amidst a multitude, many of whom had seen her before, and whose remark she was very willing to escape, Constance's only resource was to fix her eyes upon the palace, and to busy herself in the contemplation of its splendor.

Raised upon a high platform, it was not only visible from every part of the plain, but itself commanded a view of the whole gay scene below, with its tents and its multitudes, standing as a sort of nucleus to all the magnificence around.

Before the gate, to which Sir John Hardacre took his way, and which was itself a massy arch, flanked by two towers raised upon the platform, there stood two objects not unworthy of remark, as exemplifying the tastes of the day: the one was a magnificent fountain, richly wrought with arches and arabesques, painted in fine gold and blue, supporting a figure of Bacchus crowned with vine leaves, over whose head appeared inscribed, in letters of gold, "Faites bonne chère qui voudra" no unmeaning invitation, for the fountain below ceased not to pour forth three streams of various colored wines, supplied by reservoirs in the interior of the palace. On the other side of the gate, was seen four golden lions supporting a pillar of bronze, round the shaft of which twined up various gilt wreaths, interlaced together; while on the summit stood a statue of Venus's " purblind son and heir," pointing his arrows at those who approached the gate.

Nevertheless, it was not on the charmed cup of the one, or the bended bow of the other that the battlemented arch above mentioned, relied for defence; for in the several windows, were placed gigantic figures of men in armor, apparently in the act of hurling down enormous rocks upon the head of whatever venturous stranger should attempt to pass the prescribed bound. At the same time appeared round about, various goodly paintings of the demigods of story; the Herculeses, the Theseuses, the Alexanders, fabulous and historical: while, showing strangely enough in such company, many a fat porter and yeoman of the lodge loitered about in rich liveries, as familiar with the gods and goddesses, as if they had been born upon Olympus, and swaddled in Tempé.

At the flight of steps which led to this gate, Sir John Hardacre dismounted, and lifting Lady Constance from her horse, passed on into the inner court of the palace, which would indeed have been not only splendid but elegant, had it not been for a few instances of the same refined taste, which we have just noticed. The four inner faces of the building were perfectly regular, consisting of two stories, the lower one of which was almost entirely of glass, formed into plain and bow windows alternately, separated from each other by a slight column of gold, and surrounded by a multitude of arabesques and garlands. Exactly opposite to the gate appeared a vestibule, thrown a little forward from the building, and surmounted by four large bow windows, supported on trimmers, the corbels of which represented a thousand strange gilt faces, looking out from a screen of olive branches, cast in lead and painted green; while various tall statues in silver armor, were ranged on each side, as guards to the entrance.

It was towards this sort of hall, that Sir John Hardacre led poor Constance de Grey, to whose heart all the gaiety and splendor of the scene seemed but to communicate a more chilling sensation of friendless loneliness; while the very gaze and whispering of the royal servants, who had all known of her flight, and now witnessed her return,

made the quick blood mount into her beautiful cheek, as
she was hurried along by the brutal soldier, without any
regard to her feelings, or compassion for her fears.

"You must wait here, Mistress Constance," said he,
having led her into the vestibule, which was full of yeomen and grooms, "while I go and tell the right reverend
father lord cardinal, that I have brought you."

"Here!" exclaimed Constance, casting her eyes round,
"surely you do not mean me to wait here, amongst the
servants?"

"Why, where would you go?" demanded he roughly,
"I've no other place to put you. Wait here, wait here,
and mind you don't run away again."

Constance could support no more, and covering her
face with her hands, she burst into a violent flood of tears.
At that moment a voice that she knew, struck her ears.
"This to my cousin, sir!" exclaimed Lord Darby, who
had heard what passed as he descended a flight of stairs
which led away to the left, "this to my cousin, Sir
John Hardacre! You would do better to jump off the
donjon of Rochester Castle, than to leave her with lacqueys and footboys."

"And why should I not?" demanded the soldier, his
eyes flashing fire. "Mind your own affairs, my Lord
Darby, and let me mind mine."

"You are an unfeeling old villain, sir," answered the
earl, passing him and taking Constance by the hand.
"Yes, sir! stare your fill! I say you are an unfeeling
villain, and neither knight nor gentleman."

The soldier laid his hand upon his sword and drew it
half out of his sheath. "Knock him down! knock him
down!" cried a dozen voices. "The precincts of the
court! out with him! Have his hand off!" Sir John
Hardacre thrust his weapon back into the sheath, gazing
however grimly round, as if he would fain have used it
upon some one.

"Your brutal violence, sir," said Lord Darby, "will

bring upon you, if you heed not, a worse punishment than I can inflict; yet you will not find me, in a proper place, unwilling to give you a lesson on what is due to a lady. Come, Constance, I will lead you to her highness, where you will meet, I am sure, a kind reception. You, sir, do your errand to my lord cardinal, who shall be informed by me of your noble and knightly treatment of the Lady de Grey."

Thus saying, he led Constance through a long corridor to an antechamber, wherein stood two of the queen's pages. Here Lord Darby paused, and sent one of the attendants to request an audience, taking the opportunity of the time they waited, to soothe the mind of his fair cousin by informing her of all that had passed in her absence, and assuring her that the queen had ever been her warmest defender.

All the news that he gave her, of course, took a heavy weight from Constance's mind; and drying her eyes, she congratulated him gladly on his approaching marriage, and would fain—very fain, have asked if he could give her any such consolatory information in regard to Darnley, but the earl had never once mentioned his name, and she knew not how to begin the subject herself. While considering, and hesitating whether to ask boldly or not, the queen's page returned and ushered them to her presence. Constance was still much agitated, and even the kind and dignified sweetness, the motherly tenderness, with which Katherine received her, a tenderness which she had not known for so long, overcame her, and she wept as much as if she had been most unhappy.

The queen understood it all, and sending Lord Darby away, she soon won Constance to her usual placid mood, and then questioning her of all the dangers and sorrows she had undergone, she gave her the best of all balms, sympathy; trembling at her account of the shipwreck, and melted even to tears by the death of the good clergyman.

CHAPTER XXVII.

" Men might say
Till this time pomp was single, but now married
To one above itself."

SHAKSPEARE.

MANY were the anxious eyes turned towards the sky
on the morning of the seventh of June, the day appointed
for the meeting of the two kings of France and England.
However, the jolly summer sun came like a cleanly house-
maid, towards eight o'clock, and with his broom of rays,
swept all the dirty clouds from the floor of heaven. By
this time the bustle of preparation had begun at the town
of Guisnes. All was in activity amongst the tents, and
many a lord and gentleman was already on his horse,
arraying his men in order of battle, under the walls of the
castle, from the gates of which presently issued forth the
archer-guard of the King of England, and took the front
of the array. Not long after, Lord Essex, the Earl
Marshal, appeared on the plain, and riding along the line
of foot, gave the strictest orders to the various officers for
maintaining regularity and tranquillity through the day;
well knowing that the excited hilarity of such occasions
often creates more serious evils than infinitely worse feelings. Another cause, however, seemed likely to have interrupted the general good-humor; for, in the midst of
his injunctions to maintain order and propriety of demeanor towards their French allies, an officer was seen
spurring at full speed from the side of Ardres, and as he
rode up, it was very evident, by his countenance, that the
good captain, Richard Gibson, was not the best pleased
man in the world. All eyes were turned upon him, and
a dead silence ensued amidst the archers, while the earl
demanded, " Why, how now, Gibson, what is the matter? "

"So please you, my lord," replied the officer, "the four pennons of white and green, which, by your command, I set up on the edge of the hill, above the valley of Andern, have been vilely thrown down by the French Lord Chatillon, who says, that as the French have none on the other hill, he wills not that we have any either."

A loud murmuring made itself heard at this news amongst the footmen; and one of the young gallants, riding near the earl, put spurs to his horse, as if to ride away to the scene of the dispute.

"Silence!" cried the earl, over whose cheek also an angry flush had passed at first, but who speedily recovered his temper. "Brian, come back, come back, I say, sir, let not a man stir!"

"What, must we stand tamely, and be insulted by the French?" cried the youth, unwillingly reining in his horse.

"They do not insult us, sir," replied Lord Essex, wisely determined not to let any trifling punctilio disturb the harmony of the meeting, yet knowing how difficult it is to rule John Bull from his surly humor. "They do not insult us. The pennons were set up for their convenience, to show them the place of meeting, which is within the English pale. If they choose to be such fools, as to risk missing the way, and go a mile round, why let them; we shall but laugh at them when they come."

The matter thus turned off, he whispered a few words to Gibson, and sending him back to the vale of Andern, proceeded, with the aid of heralds and other officers of arms, to arrange all the ceremonies of the march. However, various were the reports that spread amongst the people, concerning the intentions of the French, some declaring openly, that they believed they intended to surround the field with a great force, and take the King of England prisoner.

While rumor was exercising her hundred tongues, and, as usual, lying with them all, the warning gun was fired

from the castle of Guisnes, giving notice that the King
of England was ready to set out, and all hurried to place
themselves in order. In a few minutes the distant roar
of another large piece of artillery was heard from
Ardres, answering the first; and for the five minutes before the procession was formed, like the five minutes of
tuning before a concert, all was noise, clamor, and confusion. The sounding of the trumpets to horse, the shouts
of the various leaders, the loud cries of the marshals
and heralds, and the roaring of the artillery from the
castle, as the king put his foot in the stirrup, all combined
to make one general outcry rarely equalled.

Gradually the tumult subsided—gradually also the confused assemblage assumed a regular form. Flags, and
pennons, and banderols, embroidered banners, and
scutcheons; silver pillars, and crosses, and crooks, ranged
themselves in long line, and the bright procession, an
interminable stream of living gold, began to wind across
the plain. First came about five hundred of the gayest
and wealthiest gentlemen of England, below the rank
of baron; squires, knights, and bannerets, rivalling each
other in the richness of their apparel, and the beauty of
their horses; while the pennons of the knights fluttered
above their heads, marking the place of the English
cavalry; next appeared the proud barons of the realm,
each with his banner borne before him, and followed by a
custrel with the shield of his arms. To these again succeeded the bishops, not in the simple robes of the Prot-
estant clergy, but in the more gorgeous habits of the
church of Rome; while close upon their steps, rode
the higher nobility, surrounding the immediate person of
the king, and offering the most splendid mass of gold and
jewels that the summer sun ever shone upon.

Slowly the procession moved forward, to allow the line
of those on foot to keep an equal pace. Nor did this
band offer a less gay and pleasing sight than the cavalcade, for here might be seen the athletic forms of the

sturdy English yeomanry, clothed in the various splendid liveries of their several lords, with the family cognizance embroidered on the bosom or the arm, and the banners and banderols of their particular houses carried in the front of each company. Here, also, was to be seen the picked guard of the King of England, magnificently dressed for the occasion, with the royal banner carried in their centre, by the deputy standard bearer, and the banner of their company by their own ancient. In the rear of all, marshalled by officers appointed for the purpose, came the band of those whose rank did not entitle them to take place in the cavalcade, but who had sufficient interest at court to be admitted to the meeting. Though of an inferior class, this company was not the least splendid in the field, for here were all the wealthy tradesmen of the court, habited in many a rich garment, furnished by the extravagance of those that rode before; and many a gold chain hung round their necks, that not long ago had lain in the purse of some prodigal customer.

Thus marched on the procession at a walking pace, with steeds neighing, with trumpets sounding; banners and plumes fluttering in the wind, and gold and jewels sparkling in the sunshine; while loud acclaim, and the waving of hats, and handkerchiefs, from those who stayed behind, ushered it forth from the plain of Guisnes.

They had ridden on some way when a horseman spurred up to the spot where the king rode, and doffing his high plumed hat, bent to his saddle bow, saying, " My king and my sovereign, I have just been with the French party and I hold myself bound, as your liege, to inform you that they are at least twice as numerous as we are. Your grace will act as in your wisdom you judge fit; but as a faithful and loving subject, I could not let such knowledge sleep in my bosom."

An instant halt took place through the whole cavalcade, and the king for a moment consulted with Wolsey, who rode on his left hand; but Lord Shrewsbury, the lord steward, interposed, assuring the king that he had been amongst the French nobles the night before, and that amongst them, the same reports prevailed concerning the English. "Therefore, sir," continued he "if I were worthy to advise, your grace would march forward without hesitation; for sure I am that the French mean no treachery."

"We shall follow your advice, lord steward," replied the king; "let us march on."

"On before! on before!" cried the heralds at the word. The trumpets again sounded, and the procession moving forward, very soon reached the brow of the hill that looks into the vale of Andern. A gentle slope, of not more than three hundred yards, led from the highest part of each of the opposite hills into the centre of the valley, in the midst of which was pitched the most magnificent tent that ever a luxurious imagination devised. The canopy, the walls, the hangings, were all of cloth of gold; the posts, the cones, the cords, the tassels, the furniture, were all of the same rare metal. Wherever the eye turned, nothing but that shining ore met its view, so that it required no very brilliant fancy to name it at once, the Field of the Cloth of Gold.

On reaching the verge of the descent, the cavalcade spread out, lining the side of the hill for some way down, and facing the line of the valley. Each cavalier placed himself unhesitatingly in the spot assigned him by the officers of arms; while the body of foot were drawn up in array to the left, by the captains of the king's guard; so that not the least confusion or tumult took place; and the whole multitude in perfect order, presented a long and glittering front to the opposite hill, before any of the French party appeared, except a few straggling horsemen sent to keep the ground.

As soon as the whole line was formed, and when by the approaching sound of the French trumpets, it was ascertained that the court of France was not far distant,

Henry himself drew out from the ranks, ready to descend
to the meeting; and never did a more splendid, or more
princely, monarch present himself before so noble a host.
Tall, stately, athletic, with a countenance full of imperious dignity, and mounted on a horse that seemed
proudly conscious of the royalty of its rider, Henry rode
forward to a small hillock, about twenty yards in advance
of his subjects; and halting upon the very edge of the
hill, with his attendants grouped behind him, and a clear
background of sunny light, throwing his figure out from
all the other objects, he offered a subject on which Wou-
vermans might well have exercised his pencil. Over his
wide chest and shoulders, he wore a loose vest of cloth of
silver, damasked and ribbed with gold. This was plaited
and bound tightly towards the waist, while it was held
down from the neck, by the golden collars of many a
princely order, and the broad baldrick studded with jewels,
to which was suspended his sword. His jewelled hat was
also of the same cloth, and in the only representation of
this famous meeting that I have met with, which can be
relied upon—having been executed at the time—he appears with a vast plume of feathers, rising from the left
side of his hat, and falling over to his saddle behind.
Nor was the horse less splendidly attired than the
rider. Its housings, its trappers, its headstall, and its
reins were all curiously wrought and embossed with
bullion, while a thousand fanciful ornaments of gold
filagree work, hung about it in every direction.

Behind the king appeared Sir Henry Guilford, master
of the horse, leading a spare charger for the monarch;
not indeed with any likelihood of the king using it, but
more as a piece of state ornament than anything else, in
the same manner as the sword of state was borne by the
Marquis of Dorset. A little behind, appeared nine youths
of noble family, as the king's henchmen, mounted on
beautiful horses trapped with golden scales and sprin-
kled throughout their housings, with loose bunches of

spangles, which twinkling in the sunshine, gave an inconceivable lightness and brilliancy to their whole appearance.

Shortly after this glittering group had taken its station in front of the English line, the first parties of the French nobility began to appear on the opposite hill, and spreading out upon its side, offered a corresponding mass of splendor to that formed by the array of England. Very soon the whole of Francis's court had deployed; and after a pause of a few minutes, during which the two hosts seemed to consider each other with no small admiration, and in profound silence, the trumpets from the French side sounded, and the Constable Duke of Bourbon, bearing a naked sword upright, began to descend the hill. Immediately behind him followed the French monarch, superbly arrayed, and mounted on a magnificent Barbary horse, covered from head to foot with gold. Instantly on beholding this, the English trumpets replied, and the Marquis of Dorset, unsheathing the sword of state, moved slowly forward before the king. Henry, having the lord cardinal on his left, and followed by his immediate suite, now descended the hill, and arrived in the valley exactly at the same moment as Francis. The two swordbearers who preceded them, fell back each to the right of his own sovereign; and the monarchs spurring forward their highly managed horses, met in the midst and embraced each other on horseback. Difficult and strange as such a manœuvre may seem, it was performed with ease and grace, both the kings being counted amongst the most skilful horsemen in Europe; and in truth, as the old historian expresses, it must have been a marvellous sweet and goodly sight to see those two princes, in the flower of their age, in the height of their strength, and in the dignity of their manly beauty, commanding two great nations, that had been so long rivals and enemies, instead of leading hostile armies to desolate and destroy, meet in that peaceful valley, and embrace like brothers in the sight of the choice nobility of either land.

Two grooms and two pages, who had followed on foot, now ran to hold the stirrup and the rein, each of his own monarch; and springing to the ground, the kings embraced again; after which, clasped arm in arm, they passed the barrier, and entered the golden tent, wherein two thrones were raised beneath one canopy.

"Henry of England, my dear brother," said the King of France, as soon as they were seated, "thus far have I travelled to see you, and do you pleasure; willing to hold you to my heart with brotherly love, and to show you that I am your friend: and surely I believe that you esteem me as I am. The realms that I command, and the powers that I possess, are not small; but if they may ever be of aid to my brother, the King of England, I shall esteem them greater than before."

"The greatness of your realms, sir, and the extent of your power," replied Henry, "weigh as nothing in my eyes, compared with your high and princely qualities; and it is to interchange regard with you, and renew in person our promises of love, that I have here passed the seas, and come to the very verge of my dominions."

With such greetings commenced the interview of the two kings, who soon called to them the cardinal, and seating him beside them, with much honor, they commanded him to read the articles which he had drawn up, for the arrangement and ordering of their future interviews. Wolsey complied; and all that he proposed seemed well to please both the monarchs, till he proceeded to stipulate, that when the King of England should go over to the town of Ardres, to revel with the Queen and ladies of France, the King of France should at the same time repair to the town of Guisnes, there to be entertained by the Queen of England. At this Francis mused. "Nay, nay, my good lord cardinal," said he, "faith, I fear not to trust myself with my brother of England, at his good castle of Guisnes; without holding him as a hostage in my court for my safe return; and marry I am sure he would put equal confidence in me, though I stayed not in his city till he was on his journey back."

"This clause is not inserted, most noble sovereign," replied Wolsey, "from any doubt or suspicion that one gracious king has of the other; for surely all trust and amicable confidence exist between ye: but it is for the satisfaction of the minds of your liege subjects, who, not understanding the true nature of princely friendship, might be filled with black apprehensions, were they to see their monarch confide himself, without warrant of safety, in the power of another nation."

"Well, well, my good lord," replied Francis, "let it be, time will show us." And from that moment he seemed to pay little attention to all the precautionary measures by which the cautious Wolsey proposed to secure the future meetings of the two kings, from the least danger to either party. The generous mind of the French monarch revolted at the suspicious policy of the cardinal; and agreeing to anything that the other thought proper, he mentally revolved his own plans for shaming the English monarch and his minister out of their cold and injurious doubts.

The arrangement of these articles was the only displeasing circumstance that cast a shadow upon the meeting: all the rest passed in gaiety and joy. A sumptuous banquet was soon placed before them, and various of the nobles of England and France, were called to mingle in the royal conversation, while the monarchs were at table.

In the meanwhile the two courts and their retainers remained arranged on the opposing sides of the hill; the Englishmen, with characteristic rigidity, standing each man in his place as immovable as a statue, while the livelier Frenchmen, impatient of doing nothing, soon quitted their ranks, and falling into broken masses, amused themselves as best they might; many of them crossing the valley, and with national facility beginning to make acquaintance with their new allies, nothing repulsed by the blunt reception they met with. Not that the English were inhospitable; for having, as usual, taken good care that no provision should be wanting against the calls of hunger or thirst, they communicated willingly to their neighbors of the comforts they had brought with them, sending over many a flagon of wine and hypocras, much to the consolation of the French, who had taken no such wise precautions against the two great internal enemies.

In about an hour, the hangings of the tent were drawn back, and the two kings reappeared ready to separate for the day. The grooms led up the horses; and Francis and Henry embracing with many professions of amity, mounted and turned their steps each to his several dwelling.

The English procession marched back in the same order as it came, and arrived without interruption at the green plain of Guisnes, where Henry, ordering the band of footmen to halt, rode along before them, making them a gay and familiar speech, and bidding them be merry if they loved their king. Shouts and acclamations answered the monarch's speech, and the nobles joining in his intent, showered their largess upon their retainers as they followed along the line. The last band that Henry came to, was that of the privileged tradesmen of the court, most of whom he recognized, possessing, in a high degree, that truly royal quality of never forgetting any one he had once known. To each, he had some frank, bluff sentence to address, while they with heads uncapped and bending low, enjoyed with proud hearts the honor of being spoken to by the king, and thought how they could tell it to all their neighbors and gossips when they got to England. As he rode on, Henry perceived in the second rank, a face that he remembered, which being attached to a very pliable neck, kept bending down with manifold reverences, not unlike the nodding of a mandarin cast in chinaware.

"Ha! my good clothier, Jekin Groby," cried the king, "come forth, man! what, come forth, I say."

Jekin Groby rushed forward from behind, knocking on one side the royal honey merchant, and fairly throwing down the household fishmonger, who stood before him; then casting himself on his knees by the side of the king's horse, he clasped the palms of his hands together, and turned up his eyes piteously to the monarch's countenance, exclaiming, "Justice! justice! your grace's worship! If your royal stomach be full of justice, as folks say, give me justice."

"Justice!" cried Henry, laughing at the sad and deplorable face poor Jekin thought necessary to assume for the purpose of moving his compassion. "Justice on whom, man, eh? Faith, if any man have done thee wrong, he shall repent it, as I am a king—though, good Jekin, I sent for thee a month ago, to furnish cloth for all the household, and thou wert not to be found."

"Lord 'a mercy!" cried Jekin, "and I've missed the job! but it ought all to be put in the bill. Pray, your grace's worship, put it in the bill, against that vile Sir Payan Wileton, who kidnapped me on your own royal highway, robbed me of my bagful of angels, and sent me to sea, where I was so sick, your grace—you can't think how sick! And then they beat me with rope's ends, and made me go up aloft, and damned me for a landlubber, and a great deal more—all on account of that Sir Payan Wileton!"

"Ha!" cried the king, "Sir Payan Wileton again! I had forgot him!—However, good Jekin, I cannot hear you now—come to my chamber to-morrow before I rise, eh, man? then I will hear and do you justice, if it be on the highest man in the land. There is my signet—the page will let you in—at six o'clock, man, fail not!"

"I told you so!" cried Jekin, starting upon his feet, and looking round him with delight as the king rode away; "I told you he would make that black thief give me back my angels. I knew his noble heart—lord 'a mercy, 'tis a gracious prince, surely!"

CHAPTER XXVIII.

"—— Let some o' the guard be ready.
CRAN.—For me?
Must I go like a traitor then?"

SHAKSPEARE.

AND where was Osborne Darnley, all this while?

It was not yet five o'clock in the morning, when the western sally-port of the castle of Ardres was opened by a little page not higher than my thumb, as the old story-book goes, who looked cautiously about, first to the right, and then to the left, to see if any one was abroad and stirring. No sound could he hear, but the light singing of the lark, and the loud snoring of the sentinel on the neighboring bastion, who with head propped on his halberd, kept anything but silent watch, while the vigilant sun, looking over the wall, spied out all the weaknesses of the place; and now having listened as well as looked, the boy withdrew once more within the walls. He left, however, the door open, and in a few minutes two horsemen rode forth, each wrapped up in a large Spanish cloak, with a chaperon, as Fleurange calls it, or in other words, an immense hood, which covered the whole head, and disguised the person completely.

As soon as they were fairly out, the page, who had accompanied them so far, returned, and closed the sally-port; and the two travellers cantered lightly over the green, to a little wood that lay before the castle. When they were fully concealed by the trees, among which they wound along, following the sinuosities of a little sandy road, wherein two, but only two, might ride abreast, they both, as by common consent, threw back their hoods, and letting their cloaks fall upon their horses' cruppers, discovered the two powerful forms of the good knight,

Osborne Lord Darnley, and Francis the first King of
France. Both were dressed with much magnificence, and
both so similarly (for so the king had willed), that though
one was a very dark man, and the other fair, they might
well have been taken for two noble brothers; each bearing the star and collar of St. Michael, with the velvet
mortier and short white plume, the embroidered cloak
of purple velvet, fixed on the right shoulder, and fastened
round to the girdle beneath the left elbow, and the broad
gold baldrick, with the heavy double-edged sword.

"Well, my friend, and my deliverer," said the king, as
they rode on, " 'twill go hard, but I will restore you to
your king's favor; and even should he remain inexorable,
which I will not believe, you must make France your
country. We will try to win your fair Constance for you
from that suspicious cardinal, of which fear not, for I
know a certain way to gain him to anything; and then I
see no cause, why in so fair a land as France, and
favored by her king, you may not be as happy, as in that
little sea-bound spot called England."

By this, it will easily be seen, that Sir Osborne had
confided in the French king some of even his most private
thoughts; and had given him an insight into his hopes
and wishes, as well as into his former expectations and
their disappointment. There was a generous frankness
about Francis, whose contagion was very difficult to
resist, nor would the knight have had any object in re-
sisting it.

Before proceeding farther, however, it may be necessary to say a few words concerning the events which had
occurred since the knight's courage and skill had saved
the king's life from Shoenvelt and his adventurers. One
may well imagine what anxiety had reigned amongst the
monarch's followers, in the forest near Lillers, when they
found that Francis, after having separated from their
party, did not rejoin them on the track appointed for the
·hunt. Such occurrences, however, having several times

happened before, and the king having always returned in safety, they concluded that he, and Count William of Firstenberg, must have taken the other road to Aire, and that they would find him there on their arrival. When they did reach that town, their inquiries immediately announced that the king was missing.

The news spread rapidly to the whole court, and soon reached the ears of his mother, the Duchess of Angoulême, who became almost frantic on hearing it, giving him up for lost from that moment, as she had good reasons to believe that Count William entertained designs against his life. Her active spirit it was, that first discovered the treachery of the Burgundian, which she had instantly communicated to the king; but the generous mind of Francis refused all credit to the news, and he continued his confidence toward Firstenberg, without the slightest alteration, till at length, more certain proofs of his designs were obtained, which induced the monarch to act with that fearless magnanimity which we have seen him display towards his treacherous favorite in the forest of Lillers.

Immediately that the king's absence was known, bands of horsemen were sent out in various directions to obtain news of him, but in vain. Convinced, by the account of the hunters, that he had quitted the wood, and that if he were therein, they could not find him by night, they searched in every other place than that in which they were likely to be successful, so that the whole night that Francis spent sleeping tranquilly in the charbonier's cottage, his guards were out towards Pernes, Fruges, and St. Pol, searching for him without success. When morning came, however, fresh parties were sent off to examine every part of the forest, and it was one of these that came up to the spot not long after the defeat of Shoenvelt and his party.

The joy occasioned by the king's safe return, was not a little heightened by the danger he had undergone, and every one to whom his life was precious, contended who should do most honor to his gallant deliverer. Francis himself knew not what recompense to offer to Sir Osborne for the signal service he had rendered him; and with the delicacy of a truly generous mind, he exacted from him a particular account of his whole life, that he might adapt the gift or honor he wished to confer exactly to the situation of the knight. Darnley understood the motive of the noble-hearted monarch, and told him all without reserve, and Francis, now furnished with the best means of showing his gratitude, resolved not to lose the opportunity.

Thus, for the few days that preceded the meeting between Guisnes and Ardres, the king highly distinguished the knight, made him many magnificent presents, called a chapter of the order of St. Michael, and had him installed in form; but knowing the jealous nature of his own nobles, he offered him no employment in his service; and even when the Constable Bourbon, who knew and appreciated Darnley's military talents, proposed to the king to give him a company of men-at-arms, as a reward for the great service he had rendered to the whole nation, Francis negatived it at once, saying openly, that the Lord Darnley was but a visitor at the court of France.

Having premised thus much, we will now take up the travellers again at the moment of their entering into the wood, near Ardres, through which they passed, conversing over the various circumstances of Sir Osborne's situation.

"It is strange!" said Francis, as the knight repeated the manner of his dismissal from the English court; "I do not comprehend it! It is impossible that your going there under a feigned name, to win King Henry's favor, should be construed as a crime, and made matter of such strong accusation against you." After musing for a moment, he proceeded, "Do not think I would imply, good knight, that you could be really guilty of any higher offence against your king; but be you sure, something has been laid to your charge more than you imagine."

"On my honor as a knight," replied Darnley, "I have accused myself to your highness of the worst crimes upon my conscience, as if your grace were my confessor; though I will own, that it appears to me, also, most strange and inexplicable. I have heard, indeed, that the lord cardinal never suffers any one to be too near the king's regard; and that if he sees any especial favor shown, he is sure to find some accusation against its object; but I can hardly believe that so great a man would debase himself to be a false accuser."

"I know not! I know not!" answered Francis quickly, "there is nothing so jealous as a favorite; and what will not jealousy do? My diadem against a Spanish crown," he continued laughingly, referring to his contention with the Emperor Charles, "Henry of England knows you under no other name than that of Sir Osborne Maurice. However, I will be politic, and know the whole before I speak. Do you put your honor in my hands? and will you abide by what I shall undertake for you?"

"Most willingly, your highness," replied the knight, "whatever you say for me, that will I maintain; on horseback or on foot, with sword or lance, as long as my life do hold."

Thus conversing they rode on, following the windings of the woody lane in which they were till the forest, skirting on the north-west of Ardres, opened out upon the plain of Guisnes. As soon as the castle and town were in sight, the French monarch put his horse into a quick pace, saying with a smile to Sir Osborne—"Your prudent Wolsey, and my good brother Henry, will be much surprised to see me in their castle alone, after all their grave precautions. By heaven! did kingly dignity imply suspicion of all the world like theirs, I would tear away my crown and feed my mother's sheep."

The night after the first meeting of the kings, Henry

had retired to sleep in the fortress, rather than in his palace without the walls; part of which, comprising his private apartments, had been found insecure, from the hurry in which it had been built. Of this circumstance, the King of France had been informed by some of his court, who had passed their evening at Guisnes, and it was therefore to the castle that he turned his rein.

Passing amidst the tents, in most of which Somnus still held undisturbed dominion, Francis and Sir Osborne galloped up to the drawbridge, on which an early party of the guard were sunning themselves in the morning light; some looking idly over into the moat, some gazing with half closed eyes towards the sky; some playing at an antique and classical game with mutton bones, while their captain stood by the portcullis, rubbing his hands and enjoying the sweetness of the morning.

No sooner did Francis perceive them, than drawing his sword he galloped in amongst them, crying—" Rendez vous, messieurs, rendez vous! La place est à moi."

At first, the archers scattered back confused, and some had their hands on their short swords; but several who had seen the king the day before, almost instantly recognized him, and the cry became general of " The King of France! The King of France!" In the meantime, Francis rode up to the captain, and putting his sword's point to the officer's throat, " Yield!" cried he, " rescue or no rescue, or you are a dead man."

" I yield, I yield! my lord!" cried the captain, entering into the king's humor, and bending his knee. " Rescue or no rescue, I yield myself your grace's prisoner."

" A castle soon taken," cried Francis, turning to Sir Osborne. " Now," added he to the officer, " since the place is mine, lead me to the chamber of my good brother the King of England."

" His grace is at present asleep," replied the captain, hesitating. " If your highness will repose yourself in the great hall, he shall be informed instantly of your presence."

"No, no," cried the king, "show me his chamber.
Nothing will serve me, but that I will sound his reveillez
myself. Come, Darnley," and springing from his horse
he followed the officer, who, now forced to obey, led him
into the castle, and up the grand staircase, towards the
king's bed-chamber.

All was silent as they went. Henry and the whole court
had revelled late the night before, so that few even of
the serving men had thought ft to quit their truckle beds
so early in the morning. A single page, however, was to
be seen as they entered a long corridor, which took up
one whole side of the large square tower in the centre of
the castle. He was standing before a door at the farther
extremity; and to him the captain pointed. "The king's
ante-room, your highness, is where you see that page,"
said he, "and let me beg your gracious forgiveness if
I leave you here, for, indeed, I dare conduct you no farther."

"Go, go," cried the king good humoredly. "I will
find it now myself. You, Darnley, stay here. I doubt
not soon to send for you with good news."

With his sword still drawn in his hand, the king now
advanced to the page, who seeing a stranger come forward with so menacing an air, might have entertained
some fears, had he not beheld the captain of the guard
conduct him thither; not at all knowing the person of
Francis, however, as he had not been present at the meeting of the kings, he closed the door of the ante-room,
which had before been open behind him, and, placing himself in the way, prepared to oppose the entrance of any
one.

"Which is the chamber of my brother, the King of
England?" demanded Francis, as he came up; but the
page, not understanding a word of French, only shook
his head; keeping his back, at the same time, firmly
against the door, thinking that it was some wild French
lord, who knew not what was due to royalty.

"It is the King of France," said Sir Osborne, advancing, as he beheld the page's embarrassment. "Let him pass. It is the King of France."

The page stared and hesitated, but Francis, taking him by the shoulder, twisted him round as he had been a child, and opening the door passed in. The page immediately closed it again, putting himself before the knight, whose face he now remembered. "I must not let your worship in," said he, thinking Sir Osborne wished to follow the monarch. "The King of France, of course, I dare not stop, but it is as much as my life is worth to suffer any one else to pass."

"I seek not to enter, good Master Snell," said the knight. " Unless his grace sends for me, I shall not intrude myself on his royal presence." This said, with busy thoughts he began to walk up and down the gallery, and the page, presently after, retiring into the ante-chamber, left him, for the time, to his own contemplations.

Much subject had the knight for thought, though it was of that nature that profiteth not: for little signified it, as it seemed, how-much-soever he took counsel with himself, his fate was in the hands of others, and beyond his power to influence or determine.

Time, ever long to those who wait, seemed doubly long to Sir Osborne, to whom so much was in suspense; and so little bustle and activity did there seem in the castle, that he began to fancy that its denizens must have had their eyes touched with Hermes' wand to make them sleep so sound. He walked up and down the corridor, he gazed out of the window into the court-yard, he listened for every opening door.

Still no one came, though the various noises and the bustle he began to hear in distant parts of the building, announced that the world was more awake than when he arrived. Yet the corridor in which he was, seemed more deserted than ever. The royal servants ceased to pass through, the page showed himself no more, and yet he could distinctly hear steps hurrying along in different directions, and voices, some loud, and some subdued, speaking not far off. Full a hundred times he paced the corridor without a living being passing by; and tired at length, he again placed himself at the window, examining what passed in the court below.

At first it was nearly vacant, a few listless soldiers being its only occupants; but soon there was opened on the other side a door which communicated with a sort of barrack, situated near the chapel in the inner ballium, and from this proceeded a troop of soldiers and officers of arms, with one or two persons mingled amongst them, that Sir Osborne imagined to be prisoners. The height at which he was placed above them prevented his perceiving whether this was certainly the case, or seeing their faces, for all that he could discern, was the foreshortened figures of the soldiers and sergeants-at-arms, distinguished from the others by their official habiliments, and passing along, surrounded by the rest, some persons in darker attire, round whom the guard appeared to keep with vigilant care. An instant brought them to the archway, just beneath the spot where he stood, and they were then lost to his sight.

The castle clock struck seven, but so slowly did the hammer fall upon the bell, he thought it would never have done. He now heard a sound of much speaking not far off, and thought that surely it was Francis taking leave of the King of England; but suddenly it ceased, and all was again silence. Taking patience to his aid, he began again his perambulations; and for another quarter of an hour walked up and down the corridor, hearing still, as he passed the door of the ante-room, a low and indistinct murmuring, which might be either the page speaking in a subdued tone to some other person therein, or some other voices conversing much more loudly in the chamber beyond. The knight's feelings were wound up to the highest pitch of impatience, when suddenly a deep groan, and then a heavy fall, met his ear. He paused—listened, and could plainly distinguish a door within open, and various voices speaking quick and high; some in French, some in English; but among them was to be heard distinctly the tongue of Henry, and that of Francis—though what they said was not sufficiently audible to be comprehended. His curiosity, as may be conceived, was not a little excited; but satisfied of the safety of the two kings, and fearful of being suspected of eavesdropping, if any one came forth, he once more crossed his arms upon his breast, and began pacing backwards and forwards as before.

A few minutes more elapsed in silence, but at length, when he was at the farther extreme of the corridor, he heard the door of the ante-chamber open, and turning round, perceived a sergeant-at-arms, followed by four halberdiers, come forth from within, and advance towards him. Sir Osborne turned and met them, when the guard drew up across the passage, and the officer stepped forward. "Sir Osborne Darnley!" said he, "commonly called Lord Darnley, I arrest you for high treason, in the name of Henry the Eighth King of England and France, and Lord of Ireland, and charge you to surrender to his warrant."

The astonishment of Sir Osborne may more easily be conceived than described. The first appearance of the halberdiers had struck him as strange, and their drawing up across his path might have been some warning, but still he was not at all prepared.

Trusting to the protection of the French king, who had virtually rendered himself responsible for his safety, he had never dreamed of danger; and for a moment or two he stood in silent surprise, till the sergeant demanded, · "Do you surrender, my lord?"

"Of course, of course!" replied the knight, "though I will own that this has fallen upon me unexpectedly. Pr'ythee, good sergeant, if thou knowest, tell me how this has come about, for to me it is inexplicable."

"In truth, my lord, I know nothing," replied the officer, "though I believe that the whole arose from something that happened this morning in his grace's bed-chamber. I was sent for by the back staircase, and received orders to attach you here. It is an unpleasant duty, my lord, but one which we are too often called to perform; I can, therefore, but beg your forgiveness, and say that you must come with me."

Sir Osborne followed in silence, meditating more than ever over his strange fate. His hopes had again been buoyed up, again to be cast down in a more cruel manner than before. There was not now a shade of doubt left: whatever he was accused of was aimed at him under his real name; and it was evident, from the unremitted persecution which he suffered, that Wolsey, or whosoever it was that thus pursued him, was resolved on accomplishing his destruction by all, or any means.

He found some consolation, nevertheless, in reflecting, that he should now have an opportunity of defending his honor and loyalty from any imputation that had been cast upon it, and of proving himself innocent to the conviction of the good and just; although he knew too well that this was no assurance of safety against the enmity of the great and powerful.

That Wolsey was the originator of the whole, he could not doubt; and the virulence of his jealousy was too well known to hope that justice or clemency would be shown, where his enmity had been incurred. "However," thought the knight, "at last, I can but die: I have fronted death a hundred times in the battle-field, and I will not shrink from him now:" but to die as a traitor was bitter, he who had never been aught but loyal and true: but still his conscious innocence, he thought, would rob the block and axe of their worst horror, the proud knowledge that he had acted well in every relationship of life—to his king, to his country, to those he loved. Then came the thought of Constance de Grey, in all her summer beauty, and all her gentle loveliness, and all her sweet smiles: was he never to see them again? To be cut off from all those kind sympathies he had felt—to go down into the cold dark grave where they could reach him never more—it was too much; and Sir Osborne turned away his eyes.

While these thoughts were busy in his bosom the sergeant-at-arms led him down the great staircase, and across the hall, on the ground floor of the castle, then opening a door to the right, he entered into a long narrow passage, but scantily lighted, that terminated in another spiral staircase, down which one of the soldiers, who had procured a lamp in the hall, proceeded first, to light them. Sir Osborne followed in silence, though his heart somewhat burned at the idea of being committed to a dungeon. Arrived at the bottom of the steps, several doors presented themselves; and seeing the sergeant examining a large bunch of keys, with whose various marks he did not seem very well acquainted, the knight could not refrain from demanding, if it were by the king's command that he was about to give him such a lodging.

" No, my lord," replied the sergeant, " the king did not direct me to place you in a dungeon: but I must secure your lordship's person, till such time as the horses are ready to convey you to Calais, and every other place in the castle is full, but that where I am going to put you."

" Well, sir," replied the knight, " only beware of what treatment you do show me, lest you may be sorry for it hereafter."

" Indeed, my lord," answered the man, with a good-humored smile, rarely met with on the faces of his brethren, " I should be very sorry to make your lordship any way uncomfortable, and if you will give me your word of honor, as a knight, neither to escape, nor to make any attempt to escape, while you are there, I will lock you up in the chapel of the new palace, which is empty enough, God knows, and for half an hour, you will be as well there as anywhere else—better than in a dungeon certainly."

The knight readily gave his promise, and the sergeant, after examining the keys again, without better success than before, began to try them, one after another, upon a small iron door in the wall, saying they could get out that way to the chapel. One of them at length fitted the lock, and two enormous bolts, and an iron bar being removed, the door was swung back, giving egress from the body of the fortress, into a long lightsome passage, where the full sun shone through a long row of windows on each side; while the gilded pillars, and the enamelled ornaments round the windows, the rich arras hangings between them, and the fine carpets spread over the floor, formed a strange and magical contrast with the place they had just quitted, with its rough, damp, stone walls, its dark and gloomy passages, and the massy rudeness of all its features.

"This is the passage made for his grace, between the palace and the castle," said the sergeant-at-arms, "let us haste on, my lord, for fear he should chance to come along it."

Proceeding onwards, catching every now and then a glance at the gay scene of tents without, as they passed the different windows, the officer conducted his prisoner to the end of the passage, where they found a door on either hand; and opening that to the left, he ushered the knight into the beautiful little building that had been constructed as a temporary chapel for the court, while inhabiting the palace before Guisnes.

"I know, my lord," said the officer, "that I may trust to your knightly word and promise, not to make any attempt to escape, for I must not even leave a guard at the door, lest his grace the king should pass, and find that I have put you here, which might move his anger. I therefore leave you for a while, reposing full confidence in your honor, and will take care to have the horses pre-

pared, and be back again before the hour of mass." Thus
saying, he ascertained that the other door was fastened,
and left Sir Osborne in the chapel, taking heed, notwithstanding his professions of reliance, to turn the key
upon him as he went out.

As far as splendor went, that chapel might have vied
with anything that ever was devised. In length, it was
about fifty feet, and though built of wood, its architecture
was in that style which we are accustomed to call Gothic.
Nothing, however, of the mere walls appeared, for from
the roof to the ground, it was hung with cloth of gold,
over which fell various festoons of silk, breaking the
straight lines of the hangings. To the right and left,
Sir Osborne remarked two magnificent closets appropriated, as he supposed, to the use of the king and queen,
where the same costly stuff that lined the rest of the
building, was further enriched by a thick embroidery of
precious stones; each also had its particular altar, loaded,
besides the pax, the crucifix, and the candlesticks, with
twelve large images of gold, and a crowd of other ornaments.

The grand altar was still more splendid, the altar-
cloth itself being one mass of gold and jewels, and the
twelve images of gold with which it was decorated, being,
according to Hall, each of the size of a child four years
old. An immense canopy of embroidery of pearls overhung it, while round on all sides appeared basins and
censers, pixes, gospellers, cruets, paxes, and chalices, of
the same glittering materials as the rest of the ornaments.

Sir Osborne advanced, and fixed his eyes upon all the
splendid things that were there called in to give pomp
and majesty to the worship of the Most High, but he
felt more strongly than ever, at that moment, how it was
all in vain; and that the small, calm tabernacle of the
heart, is that wherein man may offer up the fittest prayer
unto his Maker.

Kneeling, however, on the step of the altar, he addressed his petitions to heaven. He would not pray to be delivered from danger, for that he thought cowardly; but he prayed that God would establish his innocence and his honor,—that God would protect and bless those that he loved; and if it were the Almighty's will he should fall before his enemies, that God would be a supporter to his father, and a shield to Constance de Grey. Then rising from his knee, Darnley found that his heart was lightened, and that he could look upon his future fate with far more calmness than before.

At that moment the sound of trumpets and clarions met his ear from a distance: gradually it swelled nearer and more near, with gay and martial tones, and approached close to where he was, while shouts and acclamations, and loud and laughing voices mingled with the music, strangely discording with all that was passing in his heart. Presently it grew fainter, and then ceased; though still he thought he could hear the roar of the distant multitude, and now and then a shout; but in a few minutes these also ceased, and crossing his arms upon his breast, he waited till the sergeant-at-arms should come to convey him to Calais to prison, perhaps ultimately to death.

In a few minutes, some distant steps were heard; they came nearer, nearer still—the key was turned in the lock, and the door opened.

30

CHAPTER XXIX.

"With shame and sorrow fill'd—
Shame for his folly; sorrow out of time
For plotting an unprofitable crime."

DRYDEN.

WE must once more take our readers back, if it be but for the space of a couple of hours, and introduce them into the bed-chamber of a king—a place, we believe, as yet sacred from the sacrilegious foot of any novelist.

In the castle of Guisnes then, and in the sleeping-room of Henry the Eighth, King of England, stood, exactly opposite the window, a large square bed, covered with a rich coverlet of arras, which hanging down on each side swept the floor with its golden fringe. High over head, attached to the wall, was a broad and curiously-wrought canopy, whereon the laborious needle of some British Penelope had traced, with threads of gold, the rare and curious history of that famous knight Alexander the Great, who was there represented with lance in rest, dressed in a suit of Almaine rivet armor, overthrowing King Darius: who for his part being in a mighty fright, was whacking on his clumsy elephant, with his sceptre, while the son of Philip, with more effect, appeared pricking him up under the ribs with the point of his spear.

In one corner of the chamber, ranged in fair and goodly order, were to be seen several golden lavers and ewers, together with fine diapers and other implements for washing, while hard by, was an open closet filled with linen and plate of various kinds, with several Venice glasses, a mirror, and a bottle of scented waters. In addition to these pieces of furniture appeared four wooden settles of carved oak, which, with two large rich chairs of ivory and gold, made up, that day, the furniture of a king's bed-chamber.

The square lattice window was half open, letting in the sweet breath of the summer morning upon Henry himself, who, with his head half covered with a black velvet night-cap, embroidered with gold, still lay in bed, supporting himself on his elbow, and listening to a long detail of grievances poured forth from the rotund mouth of honest Jekin Groby, who by the king's command, encumbered with his weighty bulk one of the ivory chairs by the royal bedside.

Somewhat proud of having had a lord for the companion of his perils, the worthy clothier enlarged mightily upon the seizure of himself and Lord Darnley by Sir Payan Wileton, seasoning his discourse pretty thickly with "My lord did,"—and "My lord said;" but omitting altogether to mention him by the name of Sir Osborne, thinking it would be a degradation to his high companionship so to do, though had he done so but once, it would have saved many of the misfortunes that afterwards befell.

Henry heard him calmly, till he related the threats which Sir Payan held out to his prisoner in that interview, to which Jekin had been an unperceived witness: then starting up, "Mother of God!" cried the king, "what has become of the young gallant? Where is he? eh, man? Now, heaven defend us, the base traitor has not murdered him! eh?"

"Lord 'a mercy, you've kicked all the clothes off your grace's worship," cried Jekin; "let me kiver you up! you'll catch a malplexy! you will!"

"God's life, answer me, man!" cried Henry. "What has become of the young lord, Osborne Darnley? eh?"

"Bless your grace, that's just what I cannot tell you," replied Jekin, "for I never saw him after we got out o' window."

"Send for the traitor! have him brought instantly!"

exclaimed the king. " See who knocks! " Let no one in! Who dares knock so loud at my chamber-door? "

Proceeding round the king's bed, Jekin opened the door, against which some one had been thumping with very little ceremony: but in a moment the valiant clothier started back, exclaiming, " Lord 'a mercy, it's a great man with a drawn sword! "

" A drawn sword! " cried Henry, starting up, and snatching his own weapon, which lay beside him. But at that moment Francis ran in, and holding his blade over the king commanded him to surrender.

" I yield!—I yield! " exclaimed Henry, delighted with the jest. " Now, by my life, my good brother of France, thou hast shown me the best turn ever prince showed another. I yield me your prisoner; and as sign of my faith, I beg you to accept this jewel." So saying, he took from his pillow, where it had been laid the night before, a rich bracelet of emeralds, and clasped it on the French king's arm.

" I receive it willingly," answered Francis; " but for my love and amity, and also as my prisoner, you must wear this chain;" and unclasping a jewelled collar from his neck, he laid it down beside the English monarch.

Many were the civilities and reciprocations of friendly speeches that now ensued; and Henry about to rise, would fain have called an attendant to assist him, but Francis took the office on himself,—" Come, I will be your valet for this morning," said he; " no one but I shall give you your shirt; for I have come over alone to beg some boons of you."

" They are granted from this moment," replied Henry. " But do you say you came alone? Do you mean unattended? "

" With but one faithful friend," answered the French king, " one who not a week ago saved my life by the valor of his arm. 'Tis the best knight that ever charged a lance, and the noblest heart—he is your subject too! "

"Mine!" cried Henry with some surprise. "How is he called? What is his name? Say, France, and we will love him for his service to you."

"First, hear how he did serve me," replied Francis; and while the English monarch threaded the intricate mazes of the toilet, he narrated the whole of his adventure with Shoenvelt, which not a little interested Henry, the knight-errantry of whose disposition took fire at the vivid recital of the French king, and almost made him fancy himself on the spot.

"A gallant knight!" cried he at length, as the King of France detailed the exploits of Sir Osborne; "a most gallant knight, on my life! But say, my brother, what is his name? 'Slife, man, let us hear it. I long to know him."

"His name," replied Francis, with an indifferent tone, but at the same time fixing his eyes on Henry's face, to see what effect his answer would produce,—"his name is Sir Osborne Maurice."

A cloud came over the countenance of the English king. "Ha!" said he thoughtfully, jealous perhaps in some degree that the splendid chivalrous qualities of the young knight should be transferred to the court of France. "It is like him. It is very like him. For courage and for feats of arms, I, who have seen many good knights, have rarely seen his equal. Pity it is that he should be a traitor."

"Nay, nay, my good brother of England," answered Francis; "I will avouch him no traitor, but of unimpeachable loyalty. All I regret is, that his love for your noble person, and for the court of England, should make him wish to quit me. But to the point. My first boon regards him. He seeks not to return to your royal favor with honor stained and faith doubtful, but he claims your gracious permission to defy his enemies, and to prove their falsehood with his arm. If they be men, let them meet him in fair field; if they be women, or churchmen,

lame, or in any way incompetent according to the law
of arms, let them have a champion, the best in France or
England.   To regain your favor and to prove his innocence, he will defy them be they who they may; and here
at your feet, I lay down his gage of battle, so confident in
his faith and worth, that I myself will be his godfather in
the fight.   He waits here in the corridor to know your
royal pleasure."

Henry thought for a moment.   He was not at all
willing that the court of Francis, already renowned for
its chivalry, should possess still another knight of so
much prowess and skill as he could not but admit in
Sir Osborne.   Yet the accusations that had been laid
against him, and which nobody who considers them—the
letter of the Duke of Buckingham, and the evidence of
Wilson the bailiff—can deny were plausible, still rankled
in the king's mind, notwithstanding the partial explanation which Lady Katrine Bulmer had afforded respecting the knight's influence with the Rochester rioters.
Remembering, however, that the whole, or greater part
of the information which Wolsey had laid before him,
had been obtained, either directly or indirectly, from Sir
Payan Wileton, he at length replied, " By my faith, I
know not what to say: it is not wise to take the sword
from the hand of the law, and trust to private valor to
maintain public justice, more than we can avoid.   But
you, my royal brother, shall in the present case decide.
The accusations against this Sir Osborne Maurice, are
many and heavy, but principally resting on the testimonies
produced by a certain wealthy and powerful knight, one
Sir Payan Wileton, who, though in other respects, most
assuredly a base and disloyal villain, can have no enmity
against Sir Osborne, and no interest in seeking his ruin.
Last night, by my order, this Sir Payan was brought
hither from Calais, on the accusations of that good fool,
(pointing to Jekin Groby).   " You comprehend enough
of our hard English tongue to hear him examined your-

self, and thus you shall judge. If you find that there is cause to suspect Sir Payan and his witnesses, though it be but in having given the slightest color of falsehood to their testimony, let Sir Osborne's arm decide his quarrel against the other knight; but if their evidence be clear and indubitable, you shall yield him to be judged by the English law. What say you? Is it not just?"

The King of France at once agreed to the proposal, and Henry turned to Jekin, who had stood by, listening with his mouth open, wonderfully edified at hearing the two kings converse, though he understood not a word of the language in which they spoke. "Fly to the page, man," cried the king; "tell him to bid those who have Sir Payan Wileton in custody bring him hither instantly by the back staircase; but first, send to the reverend lord cardinal, requiring his counsel in the king's chamber. Haste! dally not, I say—I would have them here directly."

Jekin hurried to obey; and after he had delivered the order, returned to the king's chamber, where Henry, while he completed the adjustment of his apparel, related to Francis the nature of the accusation against Sir Osborne, and the proofs that had been adduced of it. The King of France, however, with a mind less susceptible of suspicion, would not believe a word of it, maintaining that the witnesses were suborned, and the letter a forgery; and contended, it would most certainly appear, that Sir Payan had some deep interest in the ruin of the knight.

The sounds of many steps in the antechamber, soon announced that some one had arrived. "Quick," cried Henry to Jekin Groby, " get behind the arras, good Jekin. After we have despatched this first business, I would ask the traitor some questions, before he sees thee. Ensconce thee, man! ensconce thee! quick!"

At the king's command, poor Jekin lifted up the corner of the arras, by the side of the bed, and hid himself behind.

Scarcely was he concealed, when the page threw open

the door, and Cardinal Wolsey entered in haste, somewhat surprised at being called to the king's chamber at so early an hour; but the sight of the French king sufficiently explained the summons, and he advanced, bending low with a proud affectation of humility.

"God bless and shield your graces both!" said he, "I feared some evil, by this early call; but now I find that the occasion was one of joy, I do not regret the haste that apprehension gave me."

"Still, we have business, my good Wolsey," replied Henry, "and of some moment. My brother here of France, espouses much the cause of the Sir Osborne Maurice who lately sojourned at the court, and won the good-will of all, both by his feats of arms and his high-born and noble demeanor; who, on the accusations given against him, to you, lord cardinal, by Sir Payan Wileton, was banished from the court—nay, judged worthy of attachment for treason."

The king, in addressing Wolsey, instead of speaking in French, which had been the language used between him and Francis, had returned to his native tongue; and good Jekin Groby, hearing what passed concerning Sir Osborne Maurice, was seized with an intolerable desire to have his say too. "Lord 'a mercy!" cried he, popping his head from behind the tapestry, "your grace's worship don't know—"

"Silence!" cried Henry, in a voice that made poor Jekin shrink into nothing. "Said I not to stay there, eh?"

The worthy clothier drew back his head behind the arras, like a frightened tortoise retracting its noddle within the shelter of its shell; and Henry proceeded to explain to Wolsey, in French, what had passed between himself and Francis.

The cardinal was, at that moment, striving hard for the King of France's favor, nor was his resentment towards Sir Payan at all abated, though the arrangements of the first meeting between the kings had hitherto delayed its effects. Thus all at first seemed favorable to Sir Osborne, and the minister himself began to soften the evidence against him, when Sir Payan, escorted by a party of archers and a sergeant-at-arms, was conducted into the king's chamber. The guard drew up across the door of the ante-room, and the knight, with a pale but determined countenance, and a firm heavy step, advanced into the centre of the room, and made his obeisance to the kings. Henry, now dressed, drew forward one of the ivory chairs for Francis, and the sergeant hastened to place the other by its side for the British monarch; when, both being seated with Wolsey by their side, the whole group would have formed as strange but powerful a picture as ever employed the pencil of an artist. The two magnificent monarchs in the pride of their youth and greatness, somewhat shadowed by the eastern wall of the room; the grand and dignified form of the cardinal, with his countenance full of thought and mind; the stern, determined aspect of Sir Payan, his whole figure possessing that sort of rigidity, indicative of a violent and continued mental effort, with the full light streaming harshly through the open casement upon his pale cheek and haggard eye, and passing on to the king's bed, and the dressing-robe he had cast off upon it, showing the strange scene in which Henry's impetuosity had caused such a conclave to be held—these objects formed the foreground; while the sergeant-at-arms standing behind the prisoner, and the guard, drawn up across the doorway, completed the picture; till gliding in between the archers, the strange figure of Sir Cesar, the astrologer, with his cheeks sunken and livid, and his eye lighted up by a kind of wild maniacal fire, entered the room, and taking a place close on the right hand of Henry, added a new and curious feature to the already extraordinary scene.

We have before said, that Sir Cesar was known to the whole court, and to Henry amongst the rest, whose

DARNLEY.

opinions concerning him it is unnecessary to investigate here, changing every hour, like his opinions on many other things; sometimes thinking him mad, sometimes inspired, according to the caprice of the moment. However, Sir Cesar was a sort of privileged person, whose eccentricities were tolerated even by royalty; and thus his presence caused no surprise, and the king, without taking any notice, began to address Sir Payan Wileton.

"Sir Payan Wileton," said Henry, "many and grievous are the crimes laid to your charge, and of which your own conscience must accuse you, as loudly as the living voices of your fellow-subjects; at least, so by the evidence brought forward against you, it appears to us, at this moment. Most of these charges we shall leave to be investigated by the common course of law; but there are some points, touching which, as they involve our own personal conduct and direction, we shall question you ourself; to which questions, we charge you, on your allegiance, to answer truly and without concealment."

"To your grace's questions," replied Sir Payan boldly, "I will answer for your pleasure, though I recognize here no established court of law: but first, I will say that the crimes charged against me, ought to be heavier than I, in my innocence, believe them, to justify the rigor with which I have been treated."

An ominous frown gathered on the king's brow. "Ha!" cried he, forgetting the calm dignity with which he had at first addressed the knight. "No established court of law!—thou sayest well—we have not the power to question thee? Ha! who then is the king? Who is the head of all magistrates? Who holds in his hand the power of all the law? By our crown, we have a mind to assemble such a court of law, as within this half-hour shall have thy head struck off upon the green."

Sir Payan was silent, and Wolsey replied to the latter part of what he had said, with somewhat more calmness than Henry had done to the former. "You have been treated, sir," said he, " with not more rigor than you merited; nor with more than is justified by the usual current of the law. It is on affidavit before me, as chancellor of this kingdom, that you both instigated and aided the Lady Constance de Grey, a ward of court, to fly from the protection and government of the law; and, therefore, attachment issued against your person, and you stand committed for contempt. You had better, sir, sue for grace and pardon, than aggravate your offence by such unbecoming demeanor."

" Thou hast said well and wisely, my good Wolsey," joined in the king, whose heat had somewhat subsided. " Standing thus reproved, Sir Payan Wileton, answer touching the charges you have brought against one Sir Osborne Maurice; and if you speak truly, to our satisfaction, you shall have favor and lenity at our hands. Say, sir, do you still hold to that accusation? "

" All I have to reply to your grace," answered the knight, resolved, even if he fell himself, to work out his hatred against Sir Osborne, with that vindictive rancor, that the injurer always feels towards the injured—" all that I have to reply is, that what I said was true; and that if I had stated all that I suspected, as well as what I knew, I should have made his treason look much blacker than it does even now."

" Do you understand, France? " demanded Henry, turning to Francis: " shall I translate his answers, to show you his true meaning? "

The King of France, however, signified that he comprehended perfectly; and Sir Payan after a moment's thought, proceeded.

" I should suppose your grace could have no doubt left upon that traitor's guilt; for the charge against him rests, not on my testimony, but upon the witness of various indifferent persons, and upon papers in the handwriting of his friends and abettors."

" Villain! " muttered Sir Cesar, between his teeth;

" hypocritical, snake-like villain!" Both the king and Sir Payan heard him, but Henry merely raised his hand, as if commanding silence, while the eyes of the traitorous knight flashed a momentary fire as they met the glance of the old man; and he proceeded, " I had no interest, your grace, in disclosing the plot I did; though, had I done wisely, I would have held my peace, for it will make many my enemies, even many more than I dreamed of then. I have since discovered that I then only knew one-half of those that are implicated. I know them all now," he continued, fixing his eye on Sir Cesar; "but as I find the reward that follows honesty, I shall bury the whole within my own breast."

" On those points, sir, we will leave our law to deal with you," replied Henry. " There are punishments for those that conceal treason; and by my halidame, no favor shall you find in us, without you make a free and ful confession—then our grace may touch you, but not else. But to the present question, my bold sir. Did you ever see Sir Osborne Maurice before the day that he was arrested by your order, on the charge of having excited the Cornishmen to revolt? and before God, we enjoin you —say, are you excited against him with feelings of interest, hatred, or revenge?"

" On my life," replied Sir Payan, boldly, " I never saw him but on that one day; and as I hope for salvation in heaven," and here he made a hypocritical grimace of piety, " I have no one reason but pure honesty to accuse him of these crimes."

A low groan burst from behind the tapestry at this reply; and Henry gave an angry glance towards the worthy clothier's place of concealment; but Francis, calling back his attention, begged him to ask the knight in English whether he had ever known Sir Osborne Maurice by any other name, or in any other character.

Sir Cesar's eyes sparkled, and Sir Payan's cheek turned pale, as Henry put the question; but he boldly replied, "Never, so help me heaven! I never saw him, or heard of him, or knew him, by any other name than Osborne Maurice."

"Oh, you villainous great liar! Oh, you hypocritical thief!" shouted Jekin Groby, bolting out from behind the tapestry, unable to contain himself any longer. "I don't care, I don't care a groat for any one; but I won't hear you tell his grace's worship such a string of lies, all as fat and as well tucked together as Christmas sausages. Lord 'a mercy! I'll tell your graces, both of you, how it was, for you don't know, that's clear. This here Sir Osborne Maurice, that you are asking about, is neither more nor less than that Lord Darnley that I was telling your grace of this morning. Lord, now, didn't I hear him tell that sweet young lady, Mistress Constance de Grey, all about it? How he could not bear to live any longer abroad in these foreign parts, and how he had come back under the name of Sir Osborne Maurice, all for to get your grace's love as an adventurous knight. And then didn't that Sir Payan—yes, you great thief, you did, for I heard you!—didn't he come and crow over him, and say that now he had got him in his power? And then didn't he offer to let him go if he would sign some papers? And then, when he would not, didn't he swear a great oath that he would murther him, saying, 'He would make his tenure good, by the extinction of the race of Darnley?' You did, you great rogue! You know you did! And, Lord 'a mercy! to think of your going about to tell his grace such lies—your own king, too, who should never hear anything but the truth. God forgive you, for you're a great sinner, and the devils will never keep company with you when you go to purgatory, but will kick you out into the other place, which is worse still, folks say. And now, I humbly beg your grace's pardon, and will go back again, if you like, behind the hangings; but I couldn't abear to hear him cheat you like that."

The sudden appearance of Jekin Groby, and the light he cast upon the subject, threw the whole party into momentary confusion. Sir Payan's resolution abandoned him; his knees shook, and his very lips grew pale. Sir Cesar gazed upon him with triumphant eyes, exclaiming, " Die, die! what hast thou left but to die?" At the same time, Wolsey questioned Jekin Groby, who told the same straightforward tale; and Henry explained the whole to Francis, whose comprehension of the English tongue did not quite comprise the jargon of the worthy clothier.

Sir Payan Wileton, however, resolved to make one last despairing effort, both to save himself and to ruin his enemies; for the diabolical spirit of revenge was as deeply implanted in his bosom as that of self-preservation. He thought then, for a moment, glanced rapidly over his situation, and cast himself on his knee before the king. " Great and noble monarch," said he, in a slow impressive voice, " I own my fault—I acknowledge my crime; but it is not such as you think it. Here me but out, and you yourself shall judge whether you will grant me mercy, or show me rigor. I confess, then, that I had entered, as deeply as others, into the treasonable plot I have betrayed against your throne and life; nay, more, that I would never have divulged it, had I not found that the Lord Darnley had, under the name of Sir Osborne Maurice, become the Duke of Buckingham's chief agent, and was to be rewarded by the restitution of Chilham Castle, for which some vague indemnity was proposed to me hereafter. On hearing it I dissembled my resentment, and pretending to enter more heartily than ever into the scheme, I found that the ambitious duke reckoned, as his chief hope in case of war, the skill and chivalry of this Lord Darnley, who promised, by his hand, to seat him on the throne. I learnt, moreover, the names of all the conspirators, amongst whom that old man is one," and he pointed to Sir Cesar, who gazed upon him with a smile of contempt and scorn, whose intensity had something of sublime. " Thirsting for revenge," proceeded Sir Payan, " and with my heart full of rage, I commanded four of my servants to stop the private courier of the duke, when I knew he was charged with letters concerning this Sir Osborne Maurice, and thus I obtained those papers I placed in the hands of my lord cardinal——"

" But how shall we know they are not forgeries?" cried Henry. " Your honor, sir, is so gone, and your testimony so suspicious, that we may well suppose those letters cunning imitations of the good duke's hand. We have heard of such things—ay, marry have we."

" Herein, happily, your grace can satisfy yourself, and prove my truth," replied Sir Payan; " send for the servants whose names I will give, examine them, put them to the torture if you will, and if you wring not from them, that on the twenty-ninth of March, they stopped, by my command, the courier of the Duke of Buckingham, and took from him his bag of letters, condemn me to the stake. But mark me, King of England; I kneel before you pleading for life; grant it to me, with but my own hereditary property, and Buckingham with all the many traitors that are now aiming at your life, and striving for your crown, shall fall into your hand and you shall have full evidence against them. I will instantly disclose all their names, and give you such proof against their chief, that to-morrow you can reward his treason with the axe, nor fear to be called unjust. But if you refuse me your royal promise sacredly given, here before your brother king, to yield me life, and liberty, and lands; as soon as I have fulfilled my word, I will go to my death in silence like the wolf, and never will you be able to prove anything against them, for that letter is nothing without my testimony to point it aright."

" You are bold! " said Henry, " you are very bold! But our subjects' good, and the peace of our country, may weigh with us! What think you, Wolsey? " and for a moment or two, he consulted in a low tone with the cardinal and the King of France. "I believe, my liege," said Wolsey, whose hatred towards Buckingham was of the blindest virulence, "I believe that your grace will never be able to prove his treasons on the duke, without this man's help. Perhaps you had better promise."

Francis bit his lip and was silent, but Henry turning to Sir Payan, replied, "The tranquillity of our realm, and the happiness of our people, overcome our hatred to your crimes; and therefore we promise, that if by your evidence, treason worthy of death, be proved upon Edward Duke of Buckingham, you shall be free in life, in person, and in lands."

"Never!" cried the voice of Sir Cesar mounting into a tone of thunder; "never!" and springing forward, he caught Sir Payan by the throat, grappled with him for an instant, with a maniacal vigor, and drawing the small dagger he always carried, plunged it into the heart of the knight, with such force, that one might hear the blow of the hilt against his ribs. The whole was done in a moment, before any one was aware, and the red blood, and the dark spirit, rushing forth together, with a loud groan the traitor fell prone upon the ground: while Sir Cesar, without a moment's pause, turned the dagger against his own bosom, and drove it in up to the very haft.

Wolsey drew back in horror and affright. Francis and Henry started up, laying their hands upon their swords; Jekin Groby crept behind the arras; and the guards rushed in to seize the slayer; but Sir Cesar waved them back with the proud and dignified air of one who feels that earthly power has over him no further sway. "What fear ye?" said he, turning to the kings; and still holding the poniard tight against his bosom, as if to restrain the spirit from breathing forth through the wound. "There is no offence in the dead or in the dying. Hear me, King of England! and hear the truth! which thou wouldst never have heard from that false caitiff. Yet I have little time—the last moments of existence speed with fast wings toward another shore—give me a seat, for I am faint."

They instantly placed for him one of the settles, and after gazing round for a moment, with that sort of distressful vacancy of eye, that speaks how the brain reels; he made an effort, and went on, though less coherently. "All he has said is false. I am on the brink of another world, and I say it is false as the hell to which he is gone. Osborne Darnley, the good, the noble, and the true—the son of my best and oldest friend, knew of no plot, heard of no treason. He was in England but two days, when he fell into that traitor's hands. He never saw Buckingham but once. The Osborne Maurice named in that duke's letter, is not he—one far less worthy."

"Who then is he?" cried the king impatiently. "Give me to know him, if you would have me believe. Never did I hear of such a name, but in years long past, an abettor of Perkyn Warbeck. Who then is this Sir Osborne Maurice eh? Mother of God! name him!"

"I—I—I—King of England!" cried the old man. "I, who had he been guided by me, would have taught Richard, King of England, whom you style Perkyn Warbeck, to wrench the sceptre from the hand of your usurping father—I, whose child was murdered by that dead traitor, in cold blood, after the rout at Taunton. I—I it was who predicted to Edward Bohun, that his head should be highest in the realm of England—I it is that predict it still." As he spoke the last words, the old man suddenly drew forth the blade of the dagger from his breast, upon which a full stream of blood instantly gushed forth and deluged the ground. Still struggling with the departing spirit, he started on his feet—put his hand to his brow—"I come! I come!" cried he—reeled —shuddered, and fell dead beside his enemy.

31

CHAPTER XXX.

"They all as glad as birds of joyous prime
    Thence led her forth, about her dancing round."
                                                SPENCER.

THE bustle, the confusion, the clamor, the questions,
and the explanations that ensued, we shall leave the
reader to imagine, satisfied that his vivid fancy will do
far more justice to such a scene than our worn-out pen.
When the bodies of Sir Payan Wileton and his companion in death, had been removed from the chamber of
the king, and some sand strewed upon the ground to cover
the gory memories that such deeds had left behind, order
and tranquillity began to regain their dominion.

"By my faith, a bloody morning's entertainment have
we had," said Francis. "But you are happy, my good
brother of England, in having traitors that will thus
despatch each other, and cheat the headsman of his due.
However, from what I have gathered, Osborne Darnley,
the knight of Burgundy, can no longer seem a traitor in
the eyes of any one."

"No, truly, my gracious lord," replied Wolsey, willing to pleasure the King of France. "He stands freed
from all spot or blemish, and well deserves the kingly
love of either noble monarch."

"'Slife! my good lord cardinal," cried Henry, "speak
for yourself alone! Now I say, on my soul, he is still a
most deep and egregious traitor. Not only, like that Sir
Payan Wileton, in having planned his treason, but in having executed it."

"Nay, how so?" cried Francis, startled at this new
charge. "In what is he a traitor now?"

"In having aided Francis, King of France," replied
Henry, smiling, "to storm our castle of Guisnes, and take
his liege lord and sovereign prisoner."

"Oh, if that be the case," cried Francis, "I give him

up to your royal indignation; but still we have a boon to ask, which our gracious brother will not refuse."

"Name it! name it!" exclaimed Henry. "By St. Mary, it shall go to pay our ransom, whatever it be."

"You have in your court," replied Francis, "one Lady Constance de Grey, who though your born subject, is no less vassal to the crown of France; owing homage for the counties of Boissy and the Val de Marne, assured to your late subject the Lord de Grey, by Charles the Eighth, when he gave him in marriage Constance Countess of Boissy, as a reward for services rendered in Italy—"

"We see your object, O most Christian king!" cried Henry, laughing. "We see your object! What, what, a messenger of Cupid, are you? Well, have your wish. We give her to your highness, so to dispose of as you may think fit; but at the same time, claim Lord Osborne Darnley at your hands, to punish according to his demerits. What say you? eh!"

"Agreed, agreed!" replied the King of France. "He waits me, as I said even now, in the corridor without, and doubtless thinks I sue for him in vain. Those guards must have passed him in the corridor."

"No, no, they came the other way," said Henry. "Ho! without there! sergeant-at-arms, take four stout halberdiers, and going into the west corridor, attach me for high treason the Lord Osborne Darnley, whom you will there find waiting. Hist! hear me, man. Use him with all gentleness (we do but jest with him), and make some fair excuse to shut him up in one of the chambers of the new palace, the nearer to the great hall the better. Away! make speed, and above all return quick, and let me know where you have put him; but take heed, and let him not see that we mock him—haste!—My good lord cardinal," he continued, turning to Wolsey, "though it be an unmeet task, for one of your grave dignity, to bear a message to a lady, yet on this day of joy, when our good brother France comes here to greet us in

brotherly love, even wise men shall forget their serious-
ness, and be as gay as boys. Hie then, good Wolsey, to
our lady queen. Tell her to call all the fair flowers of
England round about her in our great hall, to welcome
Francis of France, and that we will be there immediately
upon your steps."

The cardinal bowed low, and instantly obeyed; and
Henry proceeded in whispering consultation with Francis,
bid the guard be ready, we will cross the green to the
worthy clothier, who, when he found all the killing and
slaying was over, had come out from behind the arras,
to enjoy the air of royalty, " Come, good Jekin," cried
Henry, " now a task for thee—hark, man;" and he
whispered something to honest Groby, who instantly replied, " Lord 'a mercy, yes, your grace! I know Wilson
Goldsmith well; I'll go to him directly—no trouble in life
—Lord, I guess how it's going to be—well, I'm vastly
glad, I do declare. Lord 'a mercy! I hope your grace's
worship will let me be there!"

" Ay, man, ay!" cried the king, " make speed, and
come with him. Ho, Snell! give me a gown of tissue—
bid the guard be ready we will cross the green to the
palace. Let the marshals be called to clear the way."

In a very few minutes all was prepared, and as the two
kings were descending the grand staircase of the castle,
news was brought that a band of French nobles, anxious
for the safety of their king, had come over from Ardres at
all speed to seek him. Francis sent his commands that
they should dismount in the court; and on issuing out of
the castle, the monarch found a splendid party of the
English and French nobility mingled together, waiting to
give them the good-morrow.

" Ha, Alençon what fear you, man?" cried the King
of France. " We are all safe. Sir Richard Heartley,
look not for Lord Darnley, he is in security: follow, and
you will see him presently."

" Gentlemen all, you are most welcome," said Henry;

" follow us all that love us, to our poor palace, here without; and we will make you better cheer, where ladies'
words shall replace this summer air, and their sweet
looks the sunshine. Sound on before ! "

The trumpets sounded and the ushers and marshals
clearing the way for the two kings, they passed out of
the castle gate, and traversed the green on foot amidst
the shouts and acclamations of the crowd, that the arrival
of the French nobles, together with various rumors of
something extraordinary having happened, had collected
in the neighborhood of the royal lodging.

Arm in arm with Francis, Henry delighting, with
ostentatious magnificence, to show himself to the people,
passed round to the front of the palace; and entering the
court which we have already described, he proceeded at
once to the great hall, called the hall of the cloth of
silver, to which on the announcement of his intentions by
Wolsey, the queen had hastily summoned all the elect of
the court. On the entrance of the kings, with all the train
of noblemen who had followed them, a temporary confusion ensued, while Francis was presented to the Queen
of England, and Henry whispered to her a few brief
hints of what had taken place.

" Room, room, lords and ladies," cried he at length,
" let us have space."

" There would not be space enough for him in the
world, if he had his will," whispered Lady Katrine Bulmer to Constance de Grey, who stood by her side, unwillingly appearing in such a meeting. " On my life, Constance, his eye is fixed upon us. Now, what would I
give to be king, if it were but to outstare him."

" The Lady Constance de Grey ! " said Henry, in a
loud tone, " we would speak with the Lady de Grey."

" Nay, speak gently," said the queen. " Good, my lord,
you will frighten her. Constance, come hither to the
queen, your friend ! "

With a pale cheek, and a beating heart, Constance advanced to the side of the queen, and bending her eyes upon the ground awaited in silence, not daring to look around.

"Fear not, fair one," said Henry, "we are not angry, but only sorry to lose you. Here is our noble brother, Francis of France, claims you as his vassal, at our hands." Constance looked up, and saw the King of France's eye bent on her with a smile that gave her courage. "Now, notwithstanding the great love we bear him," continued Henry, "we might have resisted his demand, inasmuch as you are our born subject, had you not shown some slight perverseness against our repeated commands. We therefore must, and will resign you into his hands, unless you instantly agree to receive such lord to be your husband, as we shall judge fitting for your rank and station."

"Oh, no! no, my lord!" cried Constance, clasping her hands, and forgetting, in her fear of fresh persecution, the crowd by which she was surrounded. "Force me not, I beseech your grace, to wed against my will."

"You see!" said Henry turning to the King of France, with a smile, "you see the lady is headstrong! Take her, my good brother; I give her up to you. There, sweetheart, is your lord and sovereign; see if you can obey him better."

Francis took the fair girl by the hand, and bending down his head, said in a kindly tone,—"Lady, fear not. Lift up your eyes, and tell me if there is one in all this circle you would make your choice."

"No, indeed, my lord," faltered forth Constance, without looking round; "all I ask is to be left in peace."

"If you have ever seen any one to whom you could give your heart, tell me," said Francis. Constance was silent. "Then I am to judge that you have not," continued the king; "so I will choose for you."

Constance raised her eyes with a supplicating look; but Francis's face was turned away towards Henry, who with a laughing glance had taken the queen by the hand, and was leading her towards one of the doors.

"Come, we must follow," cried Francis. "Lord cardinal, we shall need your company."

Constance gazed round with doubt and apprehension, but Francis led her forward immediately after the King and Queen of England, whispering as they went,— "Fear not, sweet lady; you are with a friend that knows all."

The whole court followed along one of the splendid galleries of the palace, preceded by Henry and Katherine, who stopped, however, before a door, from before which a page held back the hangings, and—" Here," said the King of England, putting a key into Francis's hand— "here you take precedence—this is the cage, and here is the fetter-maker," pointing to a respectable-looking merchant in a long furred robe, who stood with Jekin Groby in a niche hard by.

More and more confused, not knowing what to fear or what to believe, the very uncertainty made Constance's heart sink, more than actual danger would have done;— but still the King of France led her forward, even before Queen Katherine, and, putting the key in the lock, threw open the door and drew her gently in: when the first object that met her sight, was Osborne Darnley, with his arms folded on his breast, standing before the high altar of a splendid chapel. Her heart beat—her eyes grew dim—her brain reeled; and she would have fallen fainting to the ground, but Darnley started forward and clasped her to his heart.

"Nay, nay, this is too much!" cried the queen advancing; "see, the poor girl faints. My good lord, indeed this must not be to-day. It has been too much for her already. Some day before the two courts part, we will pray my good lord cardinal to speak a blessing on their love. Bear her into the sacristy, Sir Osborne. Katrine Bulmer, giddy namesake, help your friend, while I pray their graces both to return into the hall."

THE END.

www.ingramcontent.com/pod-product-compliance
Lightning Source LLC
Chambersburg PA
CBHW020917020726
47495CB00002B/227